Barking	8724 8725	Thames View	8270 4164
Fanshawe	8270 4244	Valence	8270 6864
Marks Gate	8270 4165	Wantz	8270 4169
Markyate	8270 4137	Robert Jeyes	8270 4305
Rectory	8270 6233	Castle Green	8270 4166
Rush Green	8270 4304		

THE HEART OF
THE FAMILY

Also by Annie Groves

Ellie Pride
Connie's Courage
Hettie of Hope Street
Goodnight Sweetheart
Some Sunny Day
The Grafton Girls
As Time Goes By
Across the Mersey
Daughters of Liverpool

ANNIE GROVES

The Heart of the Family

HarperCollins*Publishers*

This novel is a work of fiction.
The names, characters and incidents portrayed in it are
the work of the author's imagination. Any resemblance to
actual persons, living or dead, events or localities is
entirely coincidental.

HarperCollins*Publishers*
77–85 Fulham Palace Road,
Hammersmith, London W6 8JB

www.harpercollins.co.uk

Published by HarperCollins*Publishers* 2009

A catalogue record for this book is
available from the British Library

ISBN: 978 0 00 726591 6

Set in Sabon by Palimpsest Book Production Limited,
Grangemouth, Stirlingshire

Printed and bound in Great Britain by Clays Ltd, St Ives plc

Mixed Sources
Product group from well-managed
forests and other controlled sources
www.fsc.org Cert no. SW-COC-1806
© 1996 Forest Stewardship Council
FSC

FSC is a non-profit international organisation established
to promote the responsible management of the world's forests.
Products carrying the FSC label are independently certified
to assure consumers that they come from forests that are managed
to meet the social, economic and ecological needs
of present and future generations.

Find out more about HarperCollins and the environment at
www.harpercollins.co.uk/green

For my readers who have so kindly and generously supported me. I hope you are all enjoying reading about the Campion family as much as I am enjoying telling their story.

Acknowledgements

I would like to thanks the following for their invaluable help:

Teresa Chris, my agent.

Susan Opie, my editor at HarperCollins.

Yvonne Holland, whose expertise enables me 'not to have nightmares' about getting things wrong.

Everyone at HarperCollins who contributed to the publication of this book.

My friends in the RNA, who always have been so generous with their time and help on matters 'writerly'.

Tony, who as always has done wonders researching the facts I needed.

PART ONE

ONE

Wednesday 7 May 1941

It had just gone midnight. Conversation between the occupants of Jean Campion's comfortable and homely kitchen slowed and stuttered, then died.

Jean's twin daughters, Sasha and Lou, Katie, her billetee and her son, Luke's, girlfriend, looked at one another.

Jean's husband, Sam, who had been out working since eight o'clock that morning helping to remove what could be cleared of the devastation left by Hitler's six nights of ferocious bombing, slumped in his chair, looking defeated. All of them were waiting for the dreaded and now familiar sound of the air-raid siren, warning them that Luftwaffe bombers were approaching the city, bringing yet another night's destruction and death.

The tension caused by the heavy bombing of Liverpool had taken hold of them just as it had all those who were now virtually trapped in a city cut off from the rest of the country, its buildings destroyed, its people killed and maimed, a helpless victim now waiting for the deathblow.

Jean looked at the twins. They had been very subdued since Sasha had been rescued on Saturday night after becoming trapped in a bomb site. The young UXB soldier who had taken Sasha's place beneath the bomb so that she could be rescued without the device being disturbed had become a hero to the whole family.

Without his bravery Jean was convinced that there would have been only one of the twins here now. Her heart missed a beat. She mustn't think of what could have been. She must concentrate instead on praying that they would all survive what was happening now. The twins were growing up. Soon they would be sixteen – young women and not merely girls any more. Sixteen and on the brink of woman-hood with their adult lives stretching ahead of them, if they survived Hitler's onslaught on Liverpool.

Just gone midnight. If the bombers were coming then they would know soon. The siren had sounded around midnight for the last three nights.

Jean thought of her two eldest children – Luke in the army and stationed at nearby Seacombe barracks; her daughter Grace in her final year as a trainee nurse and on duty tonight in one of the city's busiest and most vulnerable hospitals – and she prayed as she had done every night since the war had started that those she loved would all be safe.

Surreptitiously Katie looked at her watch. Nearly half-past midnight. Would tonight be yet another spent in the air-raid shelter, trying not to be afraid for Luke, whom she loved so much and whom she knew, as a serving soldier whose unit was on home defence duties, would be in far more danger than they were?

Jean couldn't bear the tension any more. 'I'll put the kettle on—' she started to say, and then stopped as it began: the shrill urgent call to protect themselves, the sound of which gripped a person by the throat and around the heart, a shuddering shocking exhalation of noise that warned of the terrible unbelievable horror that brought death raining down from the night sky.

They exchanged helpless, anguished looks.

'Here we go again,' Sam announced unnecessarily. 'I'll walk you down to the shelter and then I'd better go and report for fire-watching duty.'

'But, Sam, you've worked from morning to night for the last six nights,' Jean protested, as they all picked up the bundles containing the sleeping bags and everything else they would need for yet another night in the air-raid shelter.

'Aye, well, at least I *can* still work, not like some,' Sam replied grimly.

Jean felt her heart bump shakily. On Sunday morning, in the aftermath of Saturday night's heavy bombing, two of his colleagues had been badly injured when a building had collapsed on top of them.

Fortunately, the shelter was only at the end of the road. Ash Grove nestled comfortably between the top end of Edge Hill, with its aspirational working-class inhabitants, and the bottom end of middle-class Wavertree, lying further inland to the east, and was far enough away from the docks and the city centre not to attract the main attention of the Luftwaffe. But not so far that the Canpion family couldn't in happier times walk down to the ferry in under half an hour when they wanted to visit Jean's sister, Vi, and her family who lived across the water in Wallasey. And certainly close enough for Luke to take that same ferry home from the Seacombe barracks, which also lay on the other side of the river from the city.

Once they were outside in the street they were able to see what the blacked-out windows had protected them from.

Below the gentle rise that lifted Edge Hill and Wavertree above the city proper, the probing beams of the anti-aircraft batteries revealed ghoulish images of gutted buildings, still smoking from the fires of earlier bombing raids.

They had reached the shelter now. Sam gave Jean a swift hug and, unusually for such an undemonstrative man, turned to hug both the twins, then placed his hand on Katie's arm and gave it a small squeeze before standing to one side to watch as they all filed into the shelter.

Jean prayed, as she always did, that her husband would return from his work safe and unharmed.

'Not again.'

Grace heard the note of suppressed panic in the voice of the probationer who was new on the ward, and told her calmly, as though she hadn't spoken, 'I think Mr Williams has finished with his bottle now. Go and collect it from him and take it to the sluice room, will you? When you've done that come back and help me get the patients ready to take down to the shelter.'

After pausing to check that her calming words had had the right effect, Grace moved swiftly towards the end of the ward to start securing those patients who had to stay put. Straps hung down at the sides of the beds, ready to fasten over the patients when the siren went off, and the recent spate of attacks now ensured that everyone moved automatically to do what had to be done – even the new probationer, once Grace had calmed her fear.

Grace loved working on men's surgical. The patients were for the most part absolute darlings – although of course there was always the exception, like her own cousin Charlie, who had been brought in on Saturday night suffering from concussion. Charlie was well on the way to recovery now, but not quite well enough to go home, and he was making a thorough nuisance of himself, expecting special treatment because his father was a member of Wallasey's town council, and flirting with the other nurses, despite the fact that he was engaged and due to get married in June.

Now, as she paired up with the probationer so that they could secure the patients, Grace reflected that routine and having a job to do, as she had quickly learned, had a way of calming the nerves and making a person focus on necessities instead of worrying about what might happen – or thinking about the terrible raid three days ago when the hospital had been bombed, and staff and patients killed and injured.

Another bloody air raid. Determinedly Charlie avoided the look he knew his cousin Grace would be sending him. After all, why should he risk his own life pushing ruddy beds around, like those patients who were daft enough to get out of their beds to help the nursing staff? In this world a chap had to put himself first if he wanted to survive.

Whilst he might have been too badly concussed to

be able to remember much of what had happened to him when he had originally been brought into the hospital, once he had started to recover, the memory of what had happened that night had come back to him. Naturally, Charlie had then been quick to edit the truth to show himself in the best possible light. In his version of events, the beating inflicted on him by the ex-soldier-turned-petty criminal who had been blackmailing him had become a tale of him being set upon by some unknown men, no doubt intent on robbing him when he had been on an errand of mercy to see an old comrade.

His mother had been too relieved that he was safe to ask too many questions, and Dougie Richards, the blackmailer, certainly wasn't going to call his bluff, since he had been killed by the bomb that that been dropped on the pub he had made his headquarters.

As for the girl with whom he had spent the night, as an engaged-to-be-married man Charlie wasn't going to tell his mother or anyone else about her, was he? As he joined the exodus of people hurrying down the stairs to the safety of the air-raid shelters, Charlie shrugged dismissively. What a chap did with that kind of girl had nothing to do with the respectable things in life, like getting engaged and married. The girl he'd bedded lived in a different world from the one inhabited by women like his mother and his fiancée, and those two worlds never could and never would meet. That was understood.

Pity he'd left his battledress jacket behind, though. If the discharge he was angling for, so that he could leave the army and return home to Wallasey to work for his father, didn't come soon, he could end up having to fork out for a replacement. He'd got far better things to spend his money on than a piece of army kit he wasn't going to wear.

Everyone who'd heard what had happened to him said how lucky he'd been to have left the pub where he'd gone to meet his ex-comrade, before it had been flattened by a bomb, killing everyone inside, but only he knew just how lucky he was, Charlie acknowledged. With Dougie Richards and his fellow thugs dead, Charlie was now free from the threat of blackmail.

Having assured his mother that his bruises looked worse than they were, Charlie had then told Vi that he didn't want Daphne, so carefully protected from the realities of life by her doting parents, to be unnecessarily upset by the sight of them when she already had the wedding to worry about. The last thing he felt like doing right now was having to comfort Daphne whilst she wept all over him. That reluctance had nothing whatsoever to do with his memories of the passionate warmth in his arms of a girl who was not his fiancée. Of course it didn't. Good Lord, the last thing Charlie wanted in a wife was passion. Daphne was the perfect wife for him.

Yes, he had a lot to congratulate himself about, Charlie decided, with a grin. Poor old Bella, his sister, had had her nose well and truly put out of joint by his sudden ascent to the throne of parental favouritism, and her own removal from it, on account of his upcoming marriage to Daphne.

Daphne's parents not only possessed a double-barrelled surname and titled connections, Daphne's father was a Name at Lloyd's and, in Charlie's father's own words, 'bound to be rolling in money, war or no war'.

9

Edwin was the kind of man who judged other men by one simple criterion – their financial status. Those like his wife's twin sister's husband, who didn't have a hope of ever earning what Edwin did, he despised; those who threatened his supremacy in his own field, he made sure he kept where they belonged – several rungs below him on the ladder, by whatever means, dirty tricks included, if they were called for; those a few steps above him on that ladder he detested and consequently accused in public of using sharp practices, of a type abhorrent to him, of course, otherwise he would have been their equal. But those like Daphne's father, who were members of the 'professional class', and who had family money, were so far above him in his estimation that he could only treat them with reverential awe. To have his son marry the daughter of such a man swelled Edwin's chest with a pride that had had Edwin dismissing Bella's claims on his paternal affections in place of Charlie's. Edwin had decided that Bella was to hand over the keys to the smart house Edwin had bought for her on her own marriage so that they could be given to Charlie and his bride-to-be. What need, after all, did Bella, a widow with no children, have of a detached house, Edwin had asked pointedly. All she had done was fill it with refugees, he had reminded his daughter during the argument that had followed the announcement of his decision.

Remembering that row now, Charlie grinned. Poor old Bella indeed. His sister might be a stunning-looking girl, with her blonde curls and her large blue eyes, and the waist she swore measured only twenty-two inches, but her looks had no effect on their father and nor had her angry reminder that the refugees had been forced on her by the Government, and the council of which he was a member.

In fact, Charlie acknowledged, his future was looking pretty good. Or it would have been if it weren't for this ruddy bombing. He pushed past a group of nurses who had had to adjust their walking pace to the slowness of the patients they were assisting, without stopping to offer to help, his thoughts fixed on his own bright future and securing a decent place in the air-raid shelter.

The night air was thick with the smell of burned wood, the smoke from the fires that had been put out hanging over the city like a November smog. His mother had had forty fits when she had come to visit him, complaining about the fact that it had taken her three hours to get to the hospital because of all the blocked roads.

'They've bombed Lewis's,' she had told Charlie angrily, 'and there were soldiers lolling around in the street, sitting on brand-new furniture that had been removed from some of the shops, and drinking bottles of beer. Disgraceful. I mean who would want that furniture now?'

Charlie could think of any number of people who'd no doubt be only too happy to acquire it, if only to sell it on through the black market, but of course he had known better than to say so to his mother, who wasn't renowned for the acuteness of her sense of humour.

Without anything having to be said, the more senior of the trainee nurses such as Grace had taken it upon themselves to go in turn with those patients who, because of the severity of their wounds, were not

11

only bed bound but also could only be moved very slowly.

Tonight it was Grace's turn. She had seen the brisk nod of approval that Sister had given her when she had come quietly to the bed holding the most seriously injured of all their patients, a young soldier who had been caught in a blast from an unexploded bomb. His face and head were heavily bandaged. It was a miracle, according to the doctors, that he was still alive. Grace, who had been on duty the night he had come out of the morphine he had been given and who had heard him screaming in agony and then begging for death, found it hard to think there was anything miraculous about what he was having to suffer.

He couldn't survive, they all knew that, and for that reason if no other they were all taking extra care to ensure that the fact that he was still alive was respected and that he was treated exactly the same as those patients who would survive.

Hannah, Grace's closest friend from their original training set, had told Grace bluntly that had she been someone who loved him she would have been tempted to place a pillow over the bandaged face to ease his agony for ever.

As Grace and one of the porters slowly pushed his bed towards the exit, a bomb exploded close at hand, causing the patient's body to contort in agonised fear. Automatically Grace reached for his hand to comfort him, holding it in her own.

Just as it had once seemed unbelievable that something like this could happen, now it seemed equally impossible that it would ever cease. The worst of the debris caused from Saturday night's bombing had been cleared away but the scarred seared wall of the courtyard where so many had died, caught in the bomb blast, still stood as a stark reminder of the frailty of life. The patient, who had been trembling convulsively, suddenly went still, the grip of his hand slackening.

They were still several yards from safety and the shelter, but Grace realised she had something far more important to deal with now than her own safety.

Bending towards the bed, she told the porter quietly, 'I think we need the padre, if you can find him for me, please, John.'

They said that you always remembered your first death, but for Grace each one brought her that same sense of loss and pain, and that wish that things could be different and that her patient might live.

What was easier now, though, was to hold tightly to the slackened hand and quietly recite the words of the Lord's Prayer. Sister, in that calm all-seeing way of hers that Grace so admired, seemed to materialise on the opposite side of the bed out of nowhere, her own hands competent and professional as she reached for the dying man's other hand, checking his pulse against her watch, then talking quietly to him once Grace had finished her prayer.

He had gone before the padre managed to reach them, but the formalities of respect had still to be gone through, the blessing said, and a doctor summoned, a space found for the ritual and respect accorded to the newly dead even in the midst of a bombing raid that could take their own lives at any minute. A well-trained nurse did not abandon her patient to protect her own safety.

Grace waited until the doctor gave the brief nod

of his head that signalled that the body was to be taken to the morgue before accepting her own dismissal from Sister and continuing on her way to the shelter.

It was three o'clock. Her eyes felt dry and gritty from smoke, brick dust and uncried tears. When this war was over she would cry an ocean of them, but not now – not when, as their vicar had said from the pulpit on Sunday morning, with every strong heartbeat of hope and courage and the belief that they would prevail they were driving back the enemy, just as with every weak heartbeat of fear they were inviting defeat.

Now instead of thinking about the bombs and worrying about her own danger, she would think instead of Seb and how much she loved him. Like her, Seb was on duty tonight. He was based at Derby House, down near the docks. They tried to time their off-duty hours so that they could be together if at all possible. Nurses weren't allowed to wear engagement rings, so Grace kept hers hidden, wearing it on a fine chain beneath her uniform. When she felt afraid, like she did now, just knowing that it was there and that Seb loved her was enough to calm those fears.

The air-raid shelter was crowded, but a nurse whom she vaguely recognised shuffled along to make room for her, welcoming her with a tired smile.

None of them had taken her full off-duty hours, snatching a few hours of sleep instead and then going back to work, knowing how desperately her skills were needed.

The remorseless throb of aircraft engines overhead made Grace want to cover her ears. They couldn't go on like this much longer, being attacked night after night, everyone said so, talking about the effect the unrelenting attacks were having on people's morale in low hesitant whispers. The unthinkable, the unbearable, had begun to drift into people's minds, obscuring hope in the same way that the smoke-and-dust-filled air was obscuring the sky.

'Lord knows where we're going to put them as gets injured tonight,' the other nurse sighed wearily. 'The whole hospital's already bursting at the seams.'

Grace nodded. It was true, after all. Patients were already having to lie on makeshift beds in corridors. The operating theatres were working at full capacity, with extra surgeons coming in from surrounding towns, including Manchester, and now the staff were facing shortages of supplies, the hospital authorities unable to restock fast enough to cope with the demand. Some patients, like the boy who had died earlier, were so badly injured that there was nothing that could be done for them other than to try to relieve their pain, and even that wasn't always possible. Word had gone round on the grapevine when Grace had been in the dining room earlier that with the city almost cut off from the rest of the country, morphine was to be kept for those patients who could survive and not given as palliative care to those who would not, for fear of the supply running out.

War was such a cruel thing, its horrors thankfully unimaginable to those who had not experienced them. Grace had seen people whose bodies were so badly damaged that if anyone had told her three years ago about such injuries she would have thought they were trying to frighten her.

She closed her eyes, trying to blot out the sound of the continuous waves of incoming bombers and focus instead on the bursts of gunfire from the ack-ack guns. How much longer could Liverpool survive such an onslaught? Not much longer, she suspected. The Germans were bombing the heart out of the city and its people, destroying its buildings, smashing its infrastructure, maiming and killing its people, knowing how much the whole country depended on the vital necessities – raw materials and foodstuffs – that those Merchant Navy convoys whose port was Liverpool struggled to bring in from across the Atlantic.

Cutting off that vital lifeline would be like cutting off the flow of blood to a patient's heart – and only death could follow.

TWO

Down in the protected underground buildings beneath Derby House, Seb couldn't help worrying about Grace. He loved her so much and she was so very brave, as he already had good cause to know, never flinching from putting the safety of her patients first.

Derby House was the Headquarters for Joint Strategic Planning, a combined operation involving both the Navy and the RAF, and Seb had seen the devastating losses the conveys were suffering thanks to the speed and accuracy of Hitler's U-boats.

Churchill had given orders that no effort must be spared in capturing from the Germans one of their Enigma machines. These cipher machines sent signals between the U-boats and their HQ close to Paris, using special codebooks, and if one could somehow be acquired, British codebreakers at Bletchley Park would be able to decipher singals and so warn convoys of the U-boats' whereabouts. But thus far no Enigma machine had been captured and the shipping losses continued to be very heavy.

Seb was part of a secret RAF Y Section, set up to listen in on and speedily record enemy Morse code messages, and he was waiting for the particular sender he was currently monitoring to start transmitting again. It was at times like this, with an air raid going on, the city devastated by what it had already endured, and other men putting their lives at risk to protect what was left of it, that Seb wished that he was playing a more active role in the country's defence himself.

At the beginning of the war when he had been approached to work for SOE, using his radio operator's skills to teach French Resistance cells the skills they would need, Seb had been working in the field in France in conditions of such personal danger that he had truly felt that he was doing his bit. But then with the German invasion of France and the BEF being driven back to Dunkirk, Seb had been recalled to England.

Dunkirk, everything it had been and everything it now represented for the way in which, by some miracle, tens of thousands of soldiers had been rescued from the beaches of northern France, was etched on his soul for ever. He had been lucky, but so many had not.

Back in Liverpool he had expected to be handling Morse code messages sent from France by members of SOE secretly landed there and from the groups of French Resistance he had helped train. Instead he had been put in charge of some newly trained Y Section recruits, dealing with military messages passed between the enemy.

Churchill insisted on seeing every day the transcripts of the messages monitored the previous day, a habit he had begun, so Seb had heard, when he had been First Lord of the Admiralty. The work demanded the highest level of concentration, and the kind of quick mind that could speedily recognise the variations in the ways different operators touched the keys of their machines. As Seb always said when he was lecturing new recruits, a wireless operator's touch on the keys was as individual as a voice.

What they were doing was the other side of war, the hidden side. Where the glory boys of the RAF pursued their targets in full view through the skies, those members of the RAF employed on Y Section duties tracked theirs through countless recordings of Morse code messages. It took concentration, dedication and a special instinct to be able to recognise and follow a specific message sender; to recognise his or her 'way' of tapping out the Morse, to be able to block out the crackles, hisses and jamming devices used by the enemy as though they did not exist and to sense that moment when the sender was about to change frequency and plunge after them to keep track of them.

On a night like this one, though, when your girl was in danger and you weren't, translating Morse code messages didn't really feel much like a proper man's work.

Seb looked at the clock on the wall in front of him. Just gone half-past three. With any luck the raiders would leave before it started to get light. As soon as he went off duty he could go up Edge Hill to Mill Road Hospital where Grace worked to check that she was all right.

Nearly four hours they'd been at it now, Luke thought bitterly, as he lay sleepless on his hard narrow army cot bed listening to the bombers sweeping in.

19

The defiant night fighters of 96 Squadron, based at Cranage, had been screaming overhead but had as yet failed to turn back the incoming waves of the raiders.

Luke and his men would be on duty at first light as they were part of a work party of three thousand soldiers detailed to help in the clear-up operations after the bombers had left, work they'd been engaged in every day since Sunday.

Tonight it sounded as though it was Bootle that was getting the worst of it. Thank heavens his family lived well away from the docks, up at Edge Hill, and Katie with them, although nowhere was safe.

From his vantage point on the roof of a building close to the Automatic Telephone and Electric Company, off Edge Lane, where he was doing his turn on fire-watching duties, Sam Campion could see as well as hear the waves of incoming enemy bombers.

All that was left of St Luke's, the church that had been regarded by many as the most beautiful church in the city, was its tower and a blackened shell. The Town Hall had been hit, as had the New Royal Telephone Exchange in Colquitt Street, and on Duke Street various buildings had been destroyed. The city was at its last gasp. Flames and smoke billowed from newly hit buildings, and it seemed to Sam that there could be only one end to Liverpool's magnificent fight against the Luftwaffe's bombs.

Sam's heart had never felt heavier, nor his emotions more intensely aroused. It was only now, looking down on the burning city, that he realised how much he loved it. Liverpool was being bombed and burned right down to its foundations, and yet not one word of concern had Sam heard spoken on the wireless, nor one word of praise for all that its people were doing to try to save it. Let London be bombed and the whole ruddy country knew about it, but when it came to Liverpool, the powers that be didn't seem to care that the city was in danger of burning end to end.

The acrid smell of the smoke drifting towards him from Brunswick and Harrington Docks, and the Prince's landing stage, stung his eyes, or at least that was what Sam told himself was the cause of his need to knuckle the moisture from them. The overhead railway had been hit and from Gladstone and Alexandra Docks Sam could see ships burning down to the water line.

High above him in the night sky, fighters from RAF Cranage were doing their best to drive back the raiders, and as Sam looked on, an RAF planes pursued one of the bombers, finally catching up with it over the Welsh hills. As he watched the defender bring down the bomber, and then looked down on the burning city, Sam admitted to himself what he had been trying to avoid since the blitz had started.

He might not be able to do anything to prevent his two older children from being exposed to the continuing danger – not with Luke in the army and Grace a nurse – but he could insist that Jean took the twins out of the city for their own safety and hers.

Exhaling on the decision, Sam felt his chest contract with pain. He and Jean had never spent a night apart in the whole of their marriage, she was the best wife any man could have and the only wife he could ever want, but it simply wasn't safe for them to stay in the city any longer.

Lying awake in her comfortable bed in the cottage she was renting in Whitchurch, Emily Bryant too could hear the sound of the bombers on their way to Liverpool, fifty miles away from her new home in the small market town on the Cheshire-Shropshire border and surrounded by farmland. She had definitely done the right thing getting out of the city, and only just in time, judging by what she'd heard on Sunday when she and Tommy had made their first visit to their new church. Everyone had a tale to tell about what they'd heard about the pounding Liverpool had taken and the damage that had been done.

By rights she ought to be asleep. After all, they were safe enough here, with no need to go into some nasty uncomfortable air-raid shelter. She was a fool to have relented and left that worthless husband of hers with a decent sum of money in his bank account – money he'd no doubt spend on those trollops of his. He could, after all, have come with her and Tommy if he'd wanted to, but of course somewhere like Whitchurch would be far too quiet for Con.

It wasn't too quiet for her, though. It fact it suited her down to the ground.

As soon as she'd got everything unpacked and the two of them properly settled in she'd have to see about sorting out a school for young Tommy. It was just him and her now. Mother and son, so to speak. Just thinking those words filled her with so much happiness that she could feel it right down to her toes. And yet for all her happiness, and despite knowing that she had made the right decision in leaving Liverpool – after all, what did she owe the city; what had it ever done for her except give her an unfaithful husband? – the sound of those bombers and their relentless purpose brought a lump to her throat and caused her to say a silent prayer for the city of her birth.

Eight o'clock. She'd better get a move on, Lena decided, otherwise, she'd be late for work and her boss had told her that she wanted her in early because they'd have a lot of women wanting their hair done, since the blitz meant that many no longer had access to proper water in their own homes.

Lena hesitated as she turned the corner and saw a small group of women and children standing on the pavement outside number ten, where the Hodson family lived. Her heart sank. There was no way she could avoid them, not with half the houses down on the other side of the street and no pavement left.

'Ruddy Eyetie,' Annette Hodson said loudly as Lena drew level with them. 'I don't know how she's got the brass neck to show herself here amongst proper English folk when her lot have sided with that Hitler.'

Annette Hodson was blocking the pavement now, her arms folded across her chest as she confronted Lena.

Some of the sparse mousy hair has escaped from her rag curls and was hanging limply over the red scarf that drew unkind attention to her heavily flushed face. The apron she was wearing was grubby, her fingers stained with nicotine. Annette Hodson was a bully whose own children went in fear of her. Somehow, though, she'd set herself up as the street's spokeswoman when it came to who and what was and was not acceptable. She'd had it in for Lena ever since she'd discovered her husband leering at Lena one Saturday afternoon after he'd trapped her in conversation, one hand resting on the house wall as he refused to let her go past.

Initially Lena had been believed when Annette had appeared, quickly making her escape, but then the comments had started, and Lena's aunt had soon backed up her neighbour and friend, warning Lena that no good came to girls who made eyes at married men.

'Course, it's that Italian blood of hers,' Lena had heard her aunt telling Annette.

Lena had never known the Italian side of her family but she did know that the war had turned some of Liverpool's citizens violently against the Italian immigrant community, which had previously lived peacefully in the city.

Italian businesses had been attacked by angry mobs, and Italian people hurt. There had been those who had spoken out against the violence and those too who had helped their Italian neighbours, but there were others who, like Annette Hodson were the kind who seized on any excuse to take against other people.

Then, by order of the Government, all those Italian men who had not taken out British citizenship had been rounded up and sent away to be interned for the duration of the war. That had led to more violence and also to terrible deprivation for those families deprived of their main breadwinners.

Italian families with sons who had British passports and who were in the armed forces found that

24

they were being treated with as much hostility as though they were the enemy, and those with Italian blood had quickly learned to be on their guard.

'I'll bet she was down the shelter last night, though, taking up a space that by rights should have gone to a proper British person,' Annette was jeering. 'If I had my way, it wouldn't just be the Italian men I'd have had rounded up; I'd have rounded up the women and the kids as well and put the whole lot of them behind bars. Aye, and I'd have told Hitler he could come and bomb them any time he liked, and good riddance. 'Oo knows what she gets up to? For all we know she could be a ruddy spy.'

Ignoring Annette's insults, Lena stepped out into the road to walk past her and then gasped as a small piece of broken brick hit her on the arm. Automatically she turned round to see Annette's youngest, four-year-old Larry, grinning triumphantly as he called out in a shrill voice, 'I got her, Mam. Ruddy Eyetie.'

'Good for you, our Larry. Go on, throw another at her, Eyetie spy,' Annette encouraged her son, laughing as he bent down to pick up another piece of broken brick.

She wasn't going to run, Lena told herself fiercely, she wasn't. She would think about *him* instead, her lovely, lovely soldier boy. That way she couldn't feel the pain of the sharp pieces of brick the children gathered round Annette were now hurling at her with shrieks of glee. They didn't mean any harm, not really. It was just a game to them. Lena gasped as someone threw a heavier piece, which caught her between her shoulder blades, almost causing her to stumble.

25

'Eyetie spy, Eyetie spy,' the children were chanting. 'Come on, let's get her . . . Let's kill the spy.'

'What's going on here?'

Lena had never felt more relieved to see the familiar face of the local policeman as he grabbed her arm to steady her.

'Oh, it's nothing, Davey, just the kids having a bit of a joke on Lena on account of her being an Eyetie, isn't that right, Lena?' Annette challenged her.

Lena longed to deny what she was saying, but she knew that if she did Annette would only tell her aunt and then she'd have her aunt going on at her and threatening to tell her uncle to take his belt to her.

Tears of misery and self-pity blurred her eyes. You couldn't miss what you'd never had, not really, and her parents had never been the loving protective sort, too interested in quarrelling with one another to bother much about her, but right now she wished that her dad was here and that he could put Annette Hodson in her place and the fear of God into her just as she was trying to do to Lena.

Davey Shepherd had released her now.

'Aye, well, no throwing stones, you lot,' he told the now silent children. 'Otherwise Hitler will come and get you.'

'Lena's an Eyetie and she should be locked up,' Larry piped up truculently. 'Me mam says so.'

Lena could tell from the way Davey didn't look at her that he didn't want to get any further involved.

'You'd better get on your way,' he told her in a gruff voice.

'Aye, and don't bother coming back,' Annette called after her as Lena made her escape whilst Davey stood watching her.

There was brick dust on her cardigan sleeve. She'd look a fine mess turning up at work all dusty and dirty. Simone would give her a right mouthful and no mistake. The hairdresser might speak to her clients in an artificial and affected posh voice, but when they weren't around and she was in a bad mood, she yelled at the girls who worked for her, using language so ripe it would have made a fishwife blush.

Lena had been working part time for Simone ever since she had left school, fitting the hairdressing work in round the cleaning jobs her Auntie Flo forced her to do, and which really were part of her aunt's own job, but now Simone had offered to take her on full time and Lena had said 'yes' immediately. Other hairdressers might have closed down thinking that the war would be bad for business but Simone had different ideas and she was shrewd. She had told Lena that, with all the rationing and everything else, she reckoned women would want their hair doing more than ever, and that the war could actually be good for business.

She had been proved right. With so many women going into war work and earning their own money, they could afford to treat themselves.

Simone had told Lena right from the start that the main reason she was taking her on was Lena's own hair.

'They'll take one look at you, and come in here expecting to be turned out looking the same. So you just think on to make sure that you tell them wot asks that it's this salon that does your hair.'

Lena knew that her aunt was itching to make her leave the salon and get better-paid work in one of the munitions factories, but luckily for Lena she wasn't old enough – yet. You had to be nineteen at least before they'd take you on, or so she'd heard. She'd heard too about the danger of working in munitions. There was a girl down the road who'd lost an eye and had her hands all burned, and that was nothing compared to the injuries some of the women got. Not that her auntie would care if she was injured.

It wasn't just her that Auntie Flo didn't like, Lena knew; she and Lena's mother had not got on very well either, and her auntie was fond of pointing out that for all that Lena's mother had been so proud of the fact that she was in service with a posh family, that hadn't stopped her from getting herself into trouble with the Italian who had charmed his way into her knickers.

Lena found it hard to imagine that her mother had once loved her father. There had been no evidence of that love during Lena's childhood. Her mother had always been criticising her husband, and Lena's father had spent more time with his Italian family than he did with Lena and her mother. As she had grown up Lena had become used to hearing her every small misdemeanour put down to the 'bad blood' she had inherited from her Italian father. That had been one issue on which her mother and her auntie had been united.

Like many of those who had been in service, Lena's mother had been a bit of a snob in her own way, and uppity too, saying that she wasn't having Lena growing up rag-mannered and not knowing what was what, and how to do things right. Lena's parents had died together in the November bombings of 1940, leaving Lena with no option other than to move in with her mother's sister, whose ideas of what was and what was not acceptable were very different from those of Lena's mother.

Lena could still remember having the back of her hands rapped when she'd hesitated over which piece of cutlery to pick up when her mother had been teaching her what to use.

Witnessing this, her aunt had jeered at her mother and they'd had a rare old argument about it, Auntie Flo claiming that it was plain daft giving Lena airs, and her mother retaliating that she wasn't having her daughter showing herself up by not knowing her manners.

Her mother would certainly have had something to say about the state Liverpool and its people were in now, Lena thought, blinking against the gritty smoky air.

Where the narrow streets opened off the road she was walking along, running down towards the docks she could see new gaps where last night's bombs had hit, and people picking their way carefully through the debris as they searched for their possessions. Fires were still burning in some of the newly bombed-out buildings down by the docks, fire crews playing water hoses on them. Here, though, where the road turned upward away from the docks, the buildings were relatively unscathed, with only the odd collapsed building.

She could see the salon up ahead. Thankfully, at least that was still standing. Lena didn't reckon much to the chances of staying out of munitions if she lost her hairdressing job.

After what had just happened with Annette Hodson she'd have been tempted to pack her things and take herself off. There was plenty of work around now, and she'd heard that the council was rehousing anyone who'd been made homeless. Imagine living somewhere where there was no aunt and cousin, and no Annette Hodson either. But she couldn't leave now, could she, not now that she had met him? She had to be there for when he came looking for her on his next leave.

A small wriggle of pleasure seized her. Hopefully next time there wouldn't be any bombs falling and then they could make proper plans.

He wasn't based at Seacombe barracks, but somewhere down south. She'd found that out from his papers, which she'd found in one of the pockets of his battledress, just as she'd also found out that he was single, his full name and his address in posh Wallasey.

Not that she'd got any need to go looking for him, because she just knew that he would come looking for her when he was next on leave.

Annette Hodson and her woes forgotten, Lena almost skipped the rest of the way to work, her head full of happy plans for the future she was going to share with her Charlie.

Charlie. She hugged the name to her, saying it inside her head and then in a determined whisper, Mrs Charles Firth. Lena gave another wriggle of blissful pleasure. Oh, but she could not wait to stand in front of her aunt with Charlie on her arm and his ring on her finger. That would show Auntie Flo, with all her talk of Lena having bad blood. Her Charlie had loved her dark curls and her dark eyes, and he'd love her curves too. A pink blush warmed Lena's cheeks as she remembered just how much Charlie had loved them and how intimately. Of course, what she had let him do would have been very wrong if he hadn't been a soldier and been at war. She tossed her head. A girl had to do the right thing by her chap when there was a war on. What if her Charlie were to be sent to fight overseas and . . . ? Lena shivered, the joy draining from her. What if he had already gone overseas? She must not think like that. He wouldn't go without coming to find her first. Not her Charlie. After all, he had said that he loved her and that he would marry her, hadn't he?

THREE

Picking her way through the rubble littering the street, Katie stopped when something caught her eye, a bunch of May blossom, the kind that children picked from the hedgerow for their mothers. Its wilting flowers now lay in debris, its stems bruised and the flower petals covered in dust. As she bent down to pick it up tears filled Katie's eyes. What was the matter with her? She hadn't cried when she had seen the broken buildings, had she, and yet here she was crying over a few broken flowers. Where had they come from? Someone's home? One of the houses that had stood in this street of flattened buildings? Katie touched one of the petals. A terrible feeling of help-lessness and loss filled her. How many more nights could the city go on? And then what? Would they walk out of the air-raid shelters one morning to find them surrounded by Germans who had parachuted in during the night? That was the fear in everyone's mind, but people would only voice it in private. Even Luke's father, Sam, had started talking about the city not being able to hold out much longer.

She must not let her imagination run away with her. She must think of Luke and be strong. But she didn't

32

feel very strong, Katie admitted, as she picked her way carefully through the bricks and broken glass covering both the road and the pavement. It was just as well that she could walk from the Campions' house on Edge Hill to the Littlewoods building where she worked as a postal censorship clerk, because there were no buses or trams running.

Everywhere she looked all she could see were damaged buildings, and the people of Liverpool exhausted by six long nights of air raids, each one destroying a bit more of their city and increasing their fear that Hitler was not going to stop until there wasn't a building left standing.

The same people who five days ago had brushed the dust off their clothes and held their heads up high now looked shabby and pitiful. Her own shoes, polished last night by Sam Campion, who polished all his family's shoes every night and included her own, were now covered in the dust that filled the air, coating everything, leaving a gritty taste in the mouth. Her cotton dress – the same one she had worn yesterday because it was simply impossible to wash anything and get it dry without it being covered in dust – looked tired instead of crisp and fresh. As she lifted her hand to push her hair off her face, Katie acknowledged how weak and afraid she felt.

Here she was, going to work, and she had no idea if there would be a building still standing for her to work in, but as she turned the corner, and looked up Edge Hill Road, she saw to her relief that the Littlewoods building was still standing.

As had happened the previous day and the day before that, there were ominous gaps and empty chairs at some of the desks where girls had not turned up for work, but it was the empty chair next to her own that caused Katie's heart to thump with anxiety.

She and Carole had been friends from Katie's first day at the censorship office when Carole had taken her under her wing, and the fact that Carole was dating one of the men in Luke's unit had brought them even closer.

Katie knew that Carole was living with her aunt, whose home was much closer to the docks than the Campions' and, as she looked from the empty chair to her watch and then towards Anne, who was in charge of their table, a terrible thought was filling her mind.

'Carole isn't here yet,' she told Anne unnecessarily, unable to conceal her anxiety.

'I haven't been told anything.' Anne looked tired, dark circles under her eyes, and Katie felt a stab of guilt. Her brother was a merchant seaman, and with one of the convoys, and her fiancé was fighting over-seas. 'Try not to worry. With all the damage that's been done and the trams and buses not running properly she might just have got delayed.'

Katie gave her a wan smile. Anne was right, of course, but it was still hard not to worry.

The disruption to the postal service caused by the blitz meant that the letters they had to check were only arriving sporadically; Katie tried not to look at the empty chair as she started work.

Theirs was important work – vital for the safety of the nation, as they were constantly being told – and it demanded their full concentration, but it was hard to concentrate on the constant flow of written words, checking them for any sign that they might contain an encoded message, when she was so conscious of Carole's empty chair. Katie herself was involved – as part of her work – in correspondence with someone who was thought to be a possible spy.

She wasn't really cut out for that aspect of her work, as she was the first to admit, but as her supervisor had told her more than once, they all had a duty to do whatever had to be done to protect their country from its enemies.

The door to the corridor opened. Katie's head jerked towards it, her breath leaking from her lungs in a sigh of relief as she saw her friend.

'I was getting really worried about you,' she began as Carole sat down, only to break off as she saw the tears fill Carole's eyes and then spill down her face.

'What is it?' Katie asked worriedly.

Carole shook her head, searching in her handbag for an already damp handkerchief before telling her, 'It's our Rachel, my dad's brother's eldest. She bought it over the weekend. Collapsed building. She'd bin up to London to see her hubby back off to camp. He'd bin home on leave. Seven months pregnant, she was, an' all. I were her bridesmaid when she got married the year before last.'

'Oh, Carole . . .' Katie didn't know what to say. It was plain that Carole was very distressed, and with good reason.

Anne looked towards them and said quietly, 'Katie, why don't you take Carole down to the canteen so that she can have a cup of tea? Don't be gone too long, mind. We're short staffed and there's a backlog building up.'

Still crying, Carole allowed Katie to guide her back into the corridor and from there to the canteen where a sympathetic tea lady provided them both with cups of hot tea.

'It will have to be without sugar,' she warned them.

'I can't take much more of this, Katie, I swear that I can't,' Carole wept. 'It's really getting to me, them bombing raids every night, not knowing if I'm still going to be alive in the morning and not getting any sleep, and now this. Our Rachel was only twenty. Her dad, my uncle Ken, thought she was too young to get married but she said that she was going to be a wife to her George whether her dad let her say the words in church or not, just in case anything should happen to him with him being sent overseas, so her dad gave in. But now she's the one that's bin killed and her poor little baby with her. Oh, Katie, what's going to happen to us and to this country? It's all right Churchill saying we've got to stand firm, but it isn't him that's getting bombed every night, is it? I keep thinking that I might never see me mum and dad again, and I've a good mind to get out of Liverpool whilst I still can and go home.'

'London's being bombed as well,' Katie felt obliged to point out.

'Yes, I know, but not like this.'

Katie knew there was nothing she could say, and nothing she could do either, other than put her own hand over Carole's in a small gesture of comfort.

'Come on, lads, tea break's over – back to work,' Luke instructed his men.

They'd been working for over four hours, since six in the morning, helping to clear the debris from one of the main roads out of the city. A few yards away a group of men from the Liverpool Gas Company,

36

aided in their work by men from the Pioneer Corps, had also been having their tea break, the tea supplied by volunteers from the WVS and their mobile canteen.

'You're Sam Campion's lad, aren't you?' one of the older men asked Luke, nodding his head when Luke confirmed that he was, and saying triumphantly, 'Thought you were. You've got a real look of your dad. Working with him the other day, we were, when the Salvage lot were helping us to get what we could out of Duke Street, after it got bombed.'

Now it was Luke's turn to nod. The Gas Company's mains' records and control equipment had been housed in their Duke Street premises and it had been vitally important that they were salvaged.

The city had been lucky in that, despite a large number of electricity substations being damaged, with temporary repairs, the power company was still able to supply everyone with electricity.

'Jerry can't come back much more,' the other man told Luke, handing his cup over to the waiting WVS volunteer. 'There ain't much left to bomb.'

Not much left to bomb and a hell of a lot of clearing up to do, Luke thought grimly, as he turned back to his own men.

They had been detailed to work alongside the men from the city's Debris Clearance and Road Repair Service, shifting the rubble of bombed and collapsed buildings out of the way so that the damage to the roads underneath could be repaired and the roads made passable.

Unlike the previous Sunday when they had been working in the city centre, today they were working closer to Bootle, where the majority of the bombs had been dropped during the night.

37

Whilst one work party cleared the debris into a large mass, another transported the rubble by requisitioned lorries to temporary tips on Netherfield Road and Byrom and Pitt Streets, and a third was responsible for shifting this debris into the lorries.

It was backbreaking work – unless of course you were detailed to drive one of the lorries.

They'd been working for another half an hour when there was noisy commotion in the street behind them. Luke turned and watched grimly as a huge piece of machinery was driven down the road towards them.

He'd already heard all about the fun and games caused by the overenthusiastic help of the newly arrived detachment of American engineers and their heavy excavating and earth-moving equipment, sent to England under the new Lend Lease Act, along with the engineers who were to show the British how to use these monster machines.

In order to speed up clearing the rubble from the bombed buildings, the City Fathers had asked the Americans if they could help. Liverpool's streets, though, were not designed for wide American machinery, and it had turned out that the instructors sent over with them had not actually driven the machines before themselves. There had been one or two unfortunate incidents, including one in which a machine had become stuck down a narrow street. The sight of such a thing lumbering towards them now had Luke's men exchanging knowing looks.

'I guess you guys could use some help,' the gum-chewing sergeant, who had clambered down from the cab of the vehicle along with four GIs told Luke laconically.

One of the tall, broad-shouldered black GIs grinned and commented, 'Hey, Sarge, look at that. They're using shovels. Ain't that something?'

His tone was affable enough but Luke could see that his men were bristling slightly, and he could understand why. He wasn't too keen on the big American's manner himself, although he suspected that rather than being deliberately patronising, the GI simply wasn't aware of the effect his words were likely to have on men who had had little sleep during five continuous nights of heavy bombing, and who had just spent the last four hours trying to deal with some of the aftereffects of those bombs.

'Hey, buddy, we'll have that truck filled for you in ten minutes flat,' the sergeant told Luke.

'Ten minutes. Hey, Sarge, I reckon we could do it in five. In fact I'm ready to bet on it. Ten dollars says we fill the truck in five.'

Luke frowned. He had no ideas of the rules governing the US Army but in the British Army gambling was forbidden. Some of the men might run illegal card schools but they would never have challenged a sergeant to a bet – especially not in public. The Americans were slouching against the cab of their vehicle, laughing and smoking even though they hadn't been given permission to stand easy, and talking to their sergeant as though they were all equals and they had no respect for his rank at all. Luke's frown deepened. He might only be a corporal but he knew how to make sure his men were a credit to their regiment and he would certainly never have tolerated such sloppy, unsoldierly behaviour.

The sergeant, though, far from castigating the soldier,

was unbuttoning the flap on his pocket and removing a wad of notes, peeling some off and slapping them down against the shiny metal of the machinery.

'Ten says you can't and another twenty says you can't do it in four minutes.'

'Hey, boys, come and see the sarge lose his money,' the private called out.

Laughing and whooping, the men crowded round, all of them peeling off notes.

'You'd better have big pockets to match that big mouth of yours, Clancy,' the sergeant derided the GI, ''cos you sure as hell are going to have to dig deep into them.'

The Americans were behaving more as though they were on a bank holiday outing than involved in the serious business of dealing with war-damaged buildings, but then of course this wasn't their home country or their war, Luke thought bitterly, remembering that the American were still neutral and staying out of the war. Given the choice, his pride would have inclined him to turn his back on them and simply pretend that they did not exist. But of course he knew that he couldn't.

'OK, you guys, let's get to work,' the sergeant announced, stepping away from the machine so that the soldier he'd addressed as Clancy could climb up into the cab and set the thing moving.

The sound of it alone, rumbling down the road, was enough to bring down any unstable buildings, Luke thought sourly as he walked alongside it.

Luke took his role as corporal very seriously. His men, their safety and the proper execution of whatever work they were given to do were his responsibility.

Clancy brought the machine to a halt and then

40

activated the large 'shovel' to grab some of the rubble, swinging it over to the waiting truck.

The American soldiers cheered as the claws opened and deposited the rubble into the lorry.

'Hey, buddy, here's twenty bucks says you can't clear the lot in ten minutes,' the sergeant yelled, as a second load was added to the first, and then a third.

'He can't do that,' Luke protested. 'There's a weight limit on those trucks. The axles won't stand up to them being overloaded.'

Strictly speaking the British driver of the truck wasn't under Luke's command and was in any case a civilian. Luke, though, wasn't about to stand to one side whilst the truck driver was placed in danger, and he could see that that was going to happen.

'Hey, buddy,' the sergeant slapped Luke on the shoulder, 'This is the US Army you're dealing with now, and we say there ain't no such thing as can't.'

The American soldier in the cab of the earth-moving vehicle was grinning as he yelled back, 'You're on, Sarge. Watch this.'

Angry now, Luke warned the sergeant, 'Look, you've got to stop this. There's at least two full loads and maybe three there. It's impossible to get it all into one truck.'

Ignoring Luke's warning, the sergeant called up to the driver, 'Go to it, Clancy. Let's show these Brits what being American is all about.'

Luke was in danger of losing his temper. 'Any fool can see that there's too much there to go in one truck, and that it's asking for trouble to try,' he insisted.

41

'Hey, buddy, you're the one who'll be asking for trouble. See these stripes?' the sergeant told Luke. 'They say sergeant in any man's language. Now go watch how we clear the roads in America – and that's an order, soldier.'

Luke could feel his face burning with humiliation and fury. They both knew that the American had no authority over him, but the damage had been done and he had humiliated Luke in front of Luke's own men as well as his own.

Walking away from him Luke went over to where Andy was leaning on his shovel, watching grimly as the lorry was heaped with load after load of rubble.

'Go and find whoever's in charge of the nearest ARP unit for me,' Luke told him. 'Perhaps Mr Know-it-all back there will listen to him—' He broke off as suddenly the lorry buckled and then tilted, calling out a warning to its civilian driver, who had been standing a couple of feet away, smoking. But it was already too late and the man's screams as the lorry fell on top of him were filling the street.

Luke and his men ran towards the scene. The collapsed lorry had disgorged its contents, covering the street in the debris they had spent four hours clearing up, but none of them gave that a second thought as they rushed to the aid of the suddenly silent driver.

Luke had known that there would be nothing they could do – the full weight of the lorry had fallen sideways onto the driver – but he and his men still worked frantically to lift it.

The American sergeant's voice was thin and strained with shock as he muttered, 'How the hell did that happen?'

Luke turned to look at him, saying fiercely, 'You killed him. You know that, don't you, *Sergeant*.'

'It was an accident. We were trying to help.' For such a big man, now he seemed oddly diminished and very afraid, but Luke was in no mood to show him any mercy.

'No, you were trying to win a bet,' said Luke coldly.

Inwardly he was shaking with a mixture of savage fury and despair. Hadn't the city lost enough lives without this? But what did these Americans know? How could they understand? They weren't even in the war.

FOUR

Even though it was now late morning, the small rest centre where Jean worked as a volunteer as part of her WVS duties, handing out cups of tea and offering words of comfort to those who needed them, was packed with people who had been bombed out in other parts of the city, and whose local rest centres had been demolished along with their homes.

Jean had to squeeze her way past them, calming the fraught nerves of people queuing, who thought she was trying to jump in front of them by showing them her WVS badge and explaining that she was on her way to the kitchen to relieve one of her colleagues. The heartfelt apologies that followed her explanation brought her close to tears. People were so frightened and so grateful for even the smallest amount of help.

'Jean, thank goodness you're here.' Noreen Smith, who was in charge of their small group, sighed in relief when Jean finally made it through to the small kitchen. 'We've been rushed off our feet, with last night's bombing. Bootle got hit ever so bad and we've got folk coming in from there with nothing apart from what they're standing up in. I don't know how the city's going to cope, I really don't, what with so many roads blocked, and no proper supplies or outside help able to get in.'

'Well, my Sam and our Luke will be doing their best to get the roads cleared, along with everyone else on clearing-up duties, that I do know,' Jean told her stoutly, a small frown creasing her forehead when she remembered that just before he had left for work this morning Sam had told her that there was something he wanted to discuss with her.

'What is it?' she had asked him but he had shaken his head and told her gruffly, 'There isn't time now. They'll be waiting for me down at the depot.' 'Sam . . .' she had protested, but he had shaken his head, making clear that he wasn't going to be coaxed into saying any more.

'I don't doubt that,' Noreen was saying, dragging Jean's attention back. 'We've all seen the way in which everyone's turned to and got on with things.' She shook her head, her composure suddenly slipping as she added, 'Even my Frank is saying now that we can't hold out much longer.'

The two women exchanged mutually understanding looks as Jean removed her coat and hung it up.

Every rest centre had a store of second-hand clothes and blankets it was able to hand out to those in need to tide them over. The rule was that all blankets had to be returned as soon as Government coupons and fresh papers had been supplied, so that they could be put back in store for the next person in need, but as Noreen had pointed out two nights ago, increasingly people weren't returning the blankets, because they were virtually all they had. The council was doing its best, but the sheer number of people being made homeless meant that supplies were running out.

'At least we had that convoy of Queen's Messengers get in from Manchester before the roads got blocked,' Noreen told Jean.

The Queen's Messengers was the name given to a mobile canteen service provided by the Queen, with convoys based all over the country, staffed by the WVS and ready to rush to any emergency where food was required.

'And it's a mercy that they did. I don't know how they'd have gone on in Bootle if they hadn't, from what my Frank's said.'

Noreen's husband, Frank, worked for the Gas Company, and like Jean's Sam he was spending long hours helping to repair bomb damage.

'From what I've heard they nearly got bombed themselves,' Jean told her.

'Where's that billeting officer?' Noreen continued. 'She's normally here by now.'

On the morning after a bombing raid every rest centre that was operational and not bomb damaged received a visit from one of the City Council's billeting officers, carrying with her lists of available accommodation.

'It's all very well the council saying that no one's ever had to spend a second night at a rest centre on account of them finding them accommodation, but what about all them trekkers?'

In her indignation Noreen's voice lost its careful gentility, her accent becoming stronger.

'And don't tell me that it's not them that's responsible for all our blankets disappearing. After all, blankets don't just walk out by themselves, do they? No. It's not right, that's what I say. No decent folk would want to go roaming around the countryside sleeping in barns and that, like that lot do. Stands to reason, doesn't it, if they choose to do that when the council says it can find them a proper roof over their heads?'

'I wouldn't fancy it myself,' Jean admitted, 'but then I haven't been bombed out, and we've had some in here that have had that happen to them more than once. I dare say there's some folk that are just too plain afraid to stay in the city at night.'

'That's all very well, but in that case they should stay in the country and not come back here expecting to be fed and taking our blankets.'

Noreen was normally a good-natured soul and Jean suspected that her current snappiness could be put down to the strain they were all feeling.

It was also true that there was some hostility to and suspicion of the trekkers, as they were unofficially called, with some people even suggesting that their number included men who were trying to avoid conscription.

From what Jean had seen, though, they seemed decent enough sorts, albeit from the poorer dock area of the city, which had been more heavily bombed, with a lot of them coming in to work during the day before trekking back out to the country at night.

'I've even heard as how the City's putting on special trucks and handing out tickets to them for places on them, to get them out at night.'

If that was true surely it must mean that the city was in an even more desperate situation than anyone was saying, Jean thought worriedly. The only reason the council could have for encouraging them to leave at night had to be because they couldn't provide accommodation for them because so many buildings had been destroyed.

Removing her hat-pin, then taking off her hat and putting it on the shelf above her coat, Jean reached for her apron, ready to relieve the WVS volunteer who was manning the tea urn.

After the first and even the second night of bombing the mood of those who had come to the rest centres had been defiant and determinedly cheerful. Jokes had been cracked and heads had been held high, but now that had all changed, Jean acknowledged as she poured a cup of tea for an exhausted-looking young woman with three small children clinging to her side.

''Ere, get a move on wi' them kids, will yer?' the woman next to her grumbled, impatient for her own cup of tea, and moving up before the young woman could get out of the way properly, accidentally jarring her arm so that her precious cup of tea was spilled.

Tears filled the young woman's eyes.

'Don't worry, love,' Jean tried to comfort her, pouring her a fresh cup of tea. 'The billeting officer will be here soon and get you sorted out.'

The young woman gave a hiccuping sob and shook her head. 'He'll be lucky if he can do that.' She was shaking now.

Catching Noreen's eye, Jean murmured, 'Stand in for me for a few minutes, will you, Noreen love, whilst I see what's to do?'

It was recognised amongst their group that Jean, with her motherly manner, had a way of dealing with situations like this one so Noreen nodded, allowing

48

Jean to leave her post to usher the young woman and her children into the back room, where she offered her a seat on one of its battered hard wooden chairs.

The young woman shook her head again. 'I darsen't 'cos if I sit down I reckon I'll never want to get up again. It's bin three nights now since we had any proper sleep. Me and the kids were living with my hubby's mam, but she got fed up, what wi' the little one crying, and then me and her had words, and she said we had to leave. She's never liked me. Then we went and stayed with my mam but she's got our nan and me sisters there with her, and then when I tried to go back to my Ian's mam's I found out she'd been bombed. Half the street had gone.'

'Our nan got killed by a bomb,' the eldest child announced. 'Served her right, it did, for throwing us out.'

He was too young to understand, of course, but his mother had gone bright red.

'I wouldn't really have wished her any harm, only she didn't half wind me up and sometimes you say things you shouldn't. My Ian will have something to say when he finds out. He's bound to blame me, 'cos she was bad on her legs, you see, and she wouldn't have gone to the shelter.'

Poor girl. How awful to have to carry that kind of burden of guilt, Jean thought sympathetically.

'You mustn't blame yourself,' she told her. 'And as for your husband having something to say, well, I reckon he'll be too relieved to see that you and his kiddies are safe, to do anything but give you a big hug. That's better,' Jean smiled approvingly when the young woman took a deep breath and stopped crying.

'You go and wait for the billeting officer, and no more tears.'

The girl – because she was only a girl really, Jean thought – was, plainly relieved to have got her guilt off her chest. Poor thing, Jean thought sympathetically as she ushered her back to the main hall.

But even though she had been listening to what the girl had had to say, Jean had still been thinking about what Sam had said to her this morning about wanting to have a talk with her.

The small knot of anxiety in her stomach tightened. She was pretty sure she knew what it was Sam wanted to say, but she hoped that she was wrong.

'Charles's release papers arrived this morning,' Vi told Bella in a pleased voice, indicating in the direction of the front-room, where an official-looking buff envelope was propped up on the mantelpiece, against the clock. 'And about time too, with less than a month to go to the wedding. Your poor father hasn't been home for the last four nights and it will be a relief to him once Charles is out of the army and back here in Wallasey working for him. You're going to have to get your skates on, Bella, about getting your things moved back here and the house left nice for Daphne and Charles.'

Bella's mouth compressed. She wasn't at all pleased about being forced to give up her home to her brother and his wife-to-be.

'It isn't as simple as that,' she to her mother. 'I've got refugees billeted on me, remember.'

'Haven't you told them to find somewhere else yet?'

'It isn't up to me to tell them anything. Daddy will

have to tell the council, and they won't be very happy, not with Jan being a bomber pilot and a war hero,' Bella pointed out.

Vi gave her daughter a sharp look. The restrictions of the wartime diet, with its lack of protein and its hunger-appeasing carbohydrates, meant that Vi, like so many of the country's older women, had put on weight around her mid section. As a family the Firths were luckier than most in that Edwin's money and his contacts ensured that they were able to buy goods on the black market that others could not afford, when such goods were available, but everyone was beginning to feel the pinch now. Vi's floral summer dress bought the previous year was straining slightly round her waist. Vi's mouse-brown hair was also beginning to show touches of grey, although she still had it washed and set every week in the sculptured iron-hard waves she favoured. Her nails were painted with clear nail varnish, bought on the black market. The leader of Vi's WVS group disapproved of the volunteers wearing nail polish at a time when the country was in such a dire position, although *Good Housekeeping* magazine was urging its readers to try to look their best to boost everyone's morale.

Carefully checking one of her rigid waves with her fingertips, Vi warned, 'There's no point in you being difficult, Bella. It is your father who owns the house, after all, and I fully agree with him that it makes sense for Charles and Daphne to live there and for you to come home. Your father's got enough to do as it is without having to sort out your refugees, and if I were you I wouldn't risk getting on the wrong side of him. He's been very generous to you, and I do think you might show a bit more gratitude.'

Gratitude for what, Bella wanted to say – taking her home off her? But she had learned some hard lessons these last few weeks, and she knew that she could no longer rely on her mother's support and indulgence.

She looked at her watch. 'I must go. We're having to double up as a rest centre as well as the crèche, and since Laura is still on leave visiting her parents, I'm in charge of everything.'

Laura Wright was in charge of running the government-organised crèche where Bella worked as her deputy.

A note of pride had crept into Bella's voice. Against all the odds, during these last few days she had discovered that she not only had a talent for organisation but that she was also thriving on the need to get things done and make decisions. She had been up this morning at first light, hurrying out to the school, almost in one way actually rather thrilled to see the line of people forming outside – victims of the bombing in Liverpool who had made their way over the water to Wallasey, prepared to sleep rough if it meant a decent night's sleep, and now patiently waiting for a hot drink.

Queuing with them had been ARP workers, and fire watchers, and Bella had dealt with everything and everyone with calm efficiency – until the mothers had started arriving, bringing their little ones to the crèche, and amongst them she had seen *him*, smiling at her as brazen as anything, just as though . . . as though what? Despite what she had told him he actually still expected her to go off for that weekend with him?

'Bella, you aren't listening.' Her mother's protest broke into her angry thoughts.

'I've got to go,' Bella repeated. 'I only came round to ask if you'd managed to get in touch with Auntie Jean to see if everyone's all right. I know it was Bootle that got the worse of it last night but they are in Liverpool.'

Bella could see immediately that her mother wasn't pleased by her remark.

In fact, if she was honest, her concern for her mother's sister's family's safety had surprised Bella herself. She had put it down to the fact that since she was now involved in the war effort herself it was only natural that she should be more aware of what was happening.

'Well, of course they'll be all right. Why shouldn't they be? It's poor Charles you should be worrying about, after what happened to him, being set on like that and left for dead . . . Oh, that will be your father,' Vi announced as they heard the front door being opened. 'Now you'll be able to tell him about those refugees, but I warn you he isn't going to be pleased.'

Her father already didn't look pleased, Bella acknowledged as he came into the kitchen, not even when her mother announced happily, 'Charles's release papers have arrived, Edwin.'

He greeted that news with a mere grunt, before saying that he was going upstairs to get changed and then he was going back to work. 'And don't expect me back tonight if there's another air raid.'

'Hadn't you better open Charles's letter, Edwin? There might be something he needs to sign, and if there is, Bella can go into Liverpool and take it to him. I do wish the hospital would say when he can come home. Poor brave boy. Bella, go and fetch the letter for your father.'

It was easier to comply than to argue, Bella decided, retrieving the envelope and handing it over to her father with an angry swish of the skirt of her cotton dress, thinking to herself: Poor brave boy nothing.

'I'm so glad that Charles will soon be out of the army. He should never have gone in,' Vi told Edwin, as she tried to smooth her dress over the curve of her hip. Thank goodness it was May with the summer ahead of them, during which she could try to lose a few pounds. Presenting a smart appearance to the world was important to Vi. Not that a little extra weight would have mattered if she'd been able to buy herself some new clothes, but with Lewis's bombed there was now a shortage of shops where one could buy smart clothes. Vi certainly didn't intend to go shopping somewhere like Bon Marche, Liverpool's more price-conscious and less stylish department store.

'Well, he did and according to this letter he's going to have to stay in,' Edwin announced, causing Vi to gasp and Bella to look at him.

'But that's not possible,' Vi protested, her face flushing with anger. 'You must have read it wrong, Edwin. He can't possibly stay in the army. He's getting married.'

Edwin shrugged, handing the letter over to Vi, saying curtly, 'Here then, read it for yourself.'

Bella was surprised that her father wasn't making more of a fuss. It wasn't like him to take bad news so calmly.

'You'll have to do something, Edwin,' Vi told him when she had read the letter.

'Like what?' he demanded testily.

'Well, surely there's something you can do,' Vi insisted. 'After all, you can't possibly continue to manage with only that dreadful young woman to help you.'

'Well, it looks like I'm going to have to, doesn't it?' Edwin responded.

'But, Edwin . . .'

'Don't start, Vi,' he warned her sharply. 'I've got more than enough to worry about without you carrying on.'

'But what will Daphne's parents say? And poor Daphne too – she's expecting to move up here with her new husband and how can she do that if the army won't release him?'

'Well, she'll just have to lump it or leave it, won't she?' said Edwin unsympathetically, opening the kitchen door and disappearing into the hall.

Bella looked at her mother as they heard him going up the stairs.

'I really don't know what gets into your father at times,' Vi complained. 'I know he's busy, but you'd think that would make him realise how important it is that he does something about getting Charles out of the army as quickly as possible.'

Vi's pursed lips and flushed face warned Bella that there was likely to be a row when her father came back downstairs. She didn't want to be dragged into it, not when Charlie getting out of the army and coming home with his new bride meant that she had to give up her house.

'Look, Mother,' she told Vi firmly, 'I'd better go. We're going to be inundated with requests to take in more children with all this bombing. I've already requisitioned extra supplies and I want to get back to the school and see if they've arrived.'

'Your father is going to have to do something to get Charles out of the army. He's getting married,' Vi repeated, plainly still too concerned about the bad news in the letter to pay attention to what Bella was saying.

'Being in the army doesn't prevent him getting married,' Bella pointed out, 'and there's nothing to stop Daphne staying where she is with her parents, seeing as Charlie is based closer to them than he is to Wallasey. It's what plenty of newly marrieds are having to do, after all.'

'I might have expected you to say something like that,' said Vi crossly, 'but I wouldn't go counting any chickens if I were you, Bella. I'm sure your father will be able to sort something out. It means so much to him to have Charles home and working with him. He's been looking forward to them working together as father and son ever such a lot. He'll be dreadfully upset.'

Her father hadn't looked particularly upset to her, Bella reflected, as she kissed her mother on the cheek, and then paused to ask her, 'You won't forget to find out if Auntie Jean's all right, will you?'

The look of affronted astonishment her mother gave her was well-deserved, Bella admitted, as she stepped out of the back door and into the May sunshine. After all, she wasn't close to her aunt and uncle and their family – not even to Grace, who was a similar age to herself – and in fact rarely gave them any thought.

A pall of grey across the sky to the south obscured the horizon, and in the air there was a smell that reminded Bella of the scent of the morning after Bonfire Night, only this was much stronger.

She wrinkled her nose. There'd been civil defence workers coming into the newly created rest centre this morning telling tales of bomb blasts that left people covered from head to foot in soot from collapsed chimneys, and Bella had seen for herself the now dispossessed-looking, disgustingly dirty and down at heel. She looked at her own immaculately clean summer frock and gave a small fastidious shudder. She simply didn't know how she could possibly cope without her lovely clean bathroom and her freshly laundered clothes.

Bella's comment about Jean had left Vi feeling thoroughly cross. Since when had Bella had any interest in the welfare of her auntie Jean and her family?

The freedoms that widowhood and having her own roof over her head, not to mention an allowance from her father, had given her were encouraging her daughter to get rather above herself, and all the more so since she'd got involved in this crèche, Vi decided. That was the trouble with this war, it was encouraging young women like Bella to do all manner of things they would not normally have been doing. Vi had heard other mothers of grown-up daughters saying exactly the same thing. The war was giving Bella's generation far more freedom that Vi and her contemporaries had ever enjoyed. Too much freedom, in fact.

It was a great pity that Bella wasn't more biddable and dutiful like dearest Daphne.

Edwin would *have* to do something about getting Charles out of the army.

Vi heard her husband coming down the stairs and went into the hall, but before she could say anything he told her irritably, 'Not now, I haven't got time.'

Vi opened her mouth to protest, but it was too late: Edwin was already opening the front door and on his way out. She certainly couldn't say anything to him now when the neighbours might hear.

She'd have to go into Liverpool and tell Charles the bad news herself. Poor boy, he would be devastated.

Grace's heart sank as the first person she saw when she came back on the ward after her break was her aunt, but it was too late for Grace to avoid her.

'Poor Charles, I hope you're looking after him properly, Grace. He has been through a very bad time, you know. Of course he's been fearfully brave, and I shouldn't be surprised if he wasn't recommended for a medal of some sort. He certainly deserves one.'

He certainly did, Grace thought grimly. She could agree with her aunt on that point, but the medal she would like to pin on her cousin wouldn't be for bravery. Oh, no, it would be for swinging the lead and flirting with any nurse gullible enough to be taken in by him.

'He's just had a terrible shock, you know. I've had to give him some dreadful news, but he's borne it bravely.'

Grace glanced towards the bed where Charlie was lying, his face turned away from them as he watched the new probationer who just happened to have a very good pair of legs.

'I'm sorry to hear that, Aunt.'

'Well, yes, of course. How is your mother?'

'She's fine. I'll tell her that you were asking after her.'

Asking after her but not making any mention of going to visit Mum, Grace thought critically. But then that was her aunt all over.

As he lay watching the probationer with the good legs, whilst his mother stood talking to Grace, Charlie realised that he was by no means as bothered about having failed to convince the Medical Board to discharge him from the army as he had pretended to his mother he was.

Stationed where he was in barracks with easy access to London, and on home duties, might not give him as much money in his pocket as working for his father would have done, but it gave him one heck of a lot more freedom, and besides, there were always ways and means of making a bit of money if you knew how to go about things. There were always spivs hanging about the barracks ready to buy a chap's drink and cigarette allowance – every soldier got either a bottle of Scotch or a bottle of gin a week – and anything else that might be going that could be sold on the black market. A brisk business was conducted selling items that had found their way out of the stores, and then there were the card schools, and one or two other wheezes.

Being here in hospital had given Charlie time to think and what he had been thinking was that he might have been a bit rash in letting his mother persuade him into getting engaged to Daphne. Typically for Charlie, it was always someone else who was responsible for those things in his life for which he did not want to take responsibility. He had conveniently forgotten how pleased with himself he had been when it had first occurred to him that proposing to Daphne would be a good way of getting himself into his parents' good books and getting out of the army.

Now in Charlie's memory of events it was his mother who had urged him to propose to Daphne, and his father who had urged him to leave the army, whilst he had simply and good-naturedly allowed himself to be carried along by their enthusiasm.

Army life was really a bit of a doddle if you knew how to work things in your own favour, which Charlie boasted to himself that he did. He and a few other like-minded lads had scarcely missed a weekend in London the whole time he'd been at the barracks, and even when he had, there had still been some fun to be enjoyed locally, what with the townspeople eager to entertain them and the prettiest girls in the town eager to dance with them.

Marriage was all very well, and something that a chap naturally had to do at some stage, especially with the country being at war, and a chap's parents making a fuss, but lying here in hospital with pretty nurses everywhere made a chap think, it really did, and what it had made Charlie think was that he wasn't sure he was quite ready to get married yet.

The fact of the matter was that he'd actually been thinking about suggesting that he and Daphne put things off for a while. They could stay engaged, of course, but as he'd planned to remind Daphne, her own mother had originally suggested that they should wait. However, when he'd outlined this plan to his mother a few minutes ago, she'd opposed it immediately, getting herself into one of her states, and protesting that it was far too late for him to talk about delaying the wedding now, and reminding him of how lucky he was to have such a sweet girl to marry as Daphne Wrighton-Bude, and how generous his father had been on account of him marrying her.

Listening to his mother had suddenly brought home to Charlie just what his life would be like if he did leave the army and come back to Wallasey to work for his father, which was why right now he was actually feeling rather relieved that his discharge had been refused, and that he was to report back to camp as soon as he had been declared medically fit to leave hospital.

The pretty nurse with the good legs and the knowing smile, with whom he'd already indulged in a bit of harmless verbal flirtation, walked past the end of his bed and, after a quick look to make sure that his mother was still deep in conversation with his cousin Grace, he winked at her and congratulated himself mentally on being one of those people for whom life always had a way of working out well.

'Well, tell your mother that I was asking after her, won't you?' Vi reminded Grace, for all the world, Grace thought indignantly, as though her mother was nothing and her auntie Vi was something very special indeed.

They might be twins but her mother and her auntie Vi were as different as chalk and cheese in nature; you'd never even have thought they were sisters, never mind twins. Privately Grace was glad that her mother's twin lived in Wallasey and not closer at hand, and that they didn't have to see much of her or her family. It might have been through her cousin Bella that she had first met Seb, but she and Bella certainly weren't close and neither were Luke and Charlie, whilst her dad made no secret of the fact that he had no time for Auntie Vi's husband, Edwin.

'Yes, I'll tell her that, Auntie Vi,' Grace agreed politely, proud of the nurses' training that enabled her to keep her composure and not give her real feelings away.

'I dare say your mother wishes she'd listened to me when I warned her to evacuate into the country, especially now. What are those sisters of yours going to do now that Lewis's has been bombed?'

'Lewis's is still going to be doing business, Auntie Vi. They're moving across into a warehouse.' Grace smiled serenely but inwardly she was thoroughly irritated by her auntie's manner.

What she had said about Lewis's was true, but it was also true that the twins had been told that the department store would have much less floor space, and that with the combination of the fire and the lack of goods to sell thanks to rationing, Lewis's wouldn't be keeping on all of the staff.

She had, Grace decided, had enough of her aunt. Perhaps she felt more irritated by her than she should, because not only had she been on nights throughout the bombings, she had also had to come back on duty after only five hours' sleep to fill in for a sick colleague. At least when she finished this shift, since she was starting days again tomorrow she could go straight to bed and get some sleep before the Luftwaffe started dropping their bombs again. She consulted the watch she wore pinned on a chain to the inside of her dress pocket, and then addressed her aunt briskly in her best no-nonsense voice.

'Visiting time's over now, Auntie, and I'm afraid I'm going to have to ask you to leave, otherwise we shall both be in trouble with Sister.'

'What?' Somehow, before Vi could voice her indignation, her niece was walking her down past Charles's bed and through the ward doors, and saying calmly to her, 'I'll tell Mum that you were asking after her.'

Really, the modern generation of young women were most disrespectful to their elders and betters. She would certainly have something to say to Jean about her daughter's behaviour the next time she saw her.

As she left the hospital Vi pressed a handkerchief to her mouth in an effort to keep out the dust. How foolish some people were walking around without their gas masks. Vi never went anywhere without hers. How dreadful Liverpool looked with its bombed-out buildings and its shabby citizens. Thank heavens she did not live here any more. She couldn't wait to get back to Wallasey. She just hoped there wouldn't be any delays with the ferry now that one of them had been sunk by the Germans. Such a nuisance, you'd really have thought that someone would have made sure that the ferry boats were properly protected.

Poor Charles. He had taken his bad news so well, even being gentlemanly enough to suggest putting off the wedding for a year to give Daphne time to grow accustomed to the idea of being married to a serving soldier. How noble he was. Fortunately she had managed to make him see that Daphne would not

63

want him to make such a sacrifice. She would have to make sure that Daphne's mother understood just how noble he had wanted to be, of course, when she telephoned her with the sad news that Charles was not after all going to be discharged from the army.

'So what do you think we should do then?'

Lou and Sasha had just been told that, reluctantly, Lewis's was going to have to let them go – news that wasn't unexpected but that now meant that they would have to find new jobs. Now they were in the cloakroom, changing their shoes and collecting their cardigans.

'Well, we can't join the ATS or anything like that. We're not old enough yet. Dad would have to sign the forms 'cos we aren't twenty-one and you know that he wouldn't.'

Sam was a loving and protective father, and it was true that he would not want to see them enlisting and going into uniform, preferring to keep them close to home. Their mother would support him in that decision as well.

'We could lie about our ages. I heard of someone who did that and—'

'But they probably looked older; we don't even look sixteen properly,' Sasha pointed out to her twin.

It was always Lou who came up with the ideas and Sasha who pointed out the pitfalls in them.

But now it was Sasha who said quietly, 'We could always try to find out if—'

And Lou who stopped her with a quick, 'No, we can't do that. I know we said that we wanted to join ENSA but we can't now, not after what happened. It wouldn't be fair to Mum and Dad.'

'No,' Sasha agreed.

The twins had been mad on music and dancing for as long as they and their family could remember. They had driven their father to distraction with the music they played upstairs in their bedroom on their gramophone player as they practised the dance routines they had seen at the pictures, adapting them and even making up their own routines – and they were good, they both knew that.

With their mum's youngest sister, their auntie Francine, already a singer and a member of ENSA, they had reasoned that if they could just get a bit of stage experience themselves then they could end up famous, and even perhaps go to Hollywood and be in pictures themselves.

But things had gone badly wrong, and five nights ago, on the night that should have been their big moment, they had quarrelled very badly. Whilst Liverpool was being bombed they had come close to losing one another for ever, and they both knew they would never forget how that had felt.

'No more dancing,' Lou had said fiercely, when finally everyone had stopped fussing and they were on their own together in the safety of their shared bedroom.

'And no more . . . boys,' Sasha had said firmly.

'So what are we going to do now?' Lou asked her twin now, straightening her blouse collar in front of the mirror.

'We'll have to find war work of some kind,' Sasha told her as they left Lewis's premises for the last time.

For a moment Lou's eyes lit up with their old enthusiasm, but then she shook her head.

'We've just said that we can't join up or anything,

and Mum's made us promise that we won't go into munitions.'

'Mmm, I know.'

They looked at one another again. It was hard not to feel dispirited, especially when everyone else seemed to be busy doing something.

'Come on,' Lou announced, linking her arm through her twin's. 'Let's go home. Do you think there'll be another air raid tonight?'

'I expect so,' Sasha answered. 'Although it doesn't look like there's much left to bomb really. No, not that way,' she told Lou sharply as her twin made to cross the road in the direction of the Royal Court Theatre.

Sasha's colour was high, and of course Lou knew why. She was afraid that the cause of their quarrel might come walking out of the theatre, and she was afraid because despite what she had told her, really Sasha *was* keen on Kieran Mallory, the good-looking young man who had been making up to them both behind each other's back, and whose uncle worked at the Royal Court Theatre.

A feeling of intense pain gripped Lou. She and Sasha had made up their quarrel and outwardly they were, if anything, even closer than they had been before. They had both sworn that they were never ever going to let anything or anyone come between them again, but despite all the effort they were both putting into pretending that nothing had changed they both knew that something had.

The doctor had finished examining Charlie and now he looked down at him, announcing, 'Well, Private Firth, everything seems to be in order, so I think we can safely discharge you. Go and see the almoner first thing tomorrow morning and she'll sort you out with everything you'll need and let your commanding officer know that you've been discharged as fit to return to duty.'

He wouldn't really mind going back, Charlie admitted. He'd missed his jaunts into London and the fun to be had there.

Charlie had quickly discovered that there was nothing quite like the threat of war to weaken a certain kind of girl's willpower along with her knicker elastic. It was a pity his mother had made such a fuss about his suggestion that he and Daphne should delay getting married. Mind you, marriage didn't have to stop him having a bit of fun. There was a war on, after all, and having a bit of fun didn't mean anything; it was just a bit of fun, with no harm done.

Pity there was no chance of him persuading Daphne to come up to Wallasey to live. She'd be safely out of the way up here, but once she knew he wasn't going to get his discharge she'd insist on staying with her parents. Daphne and her mother were very close. Luckily the Dorset village where they lived was a good two hours' drive away from camp, so he'd have an excuse for not going down if he felt like doing something else instead – like going to London.

Charlie had no illusions about what he could expect from his marriage. Daphne was a 'good' girl. He would have known that even if both she and her parents had not told him so.

But it wasn't because he wanted to take her to bed that Charlie had planned to marry her. What man in his right mind wanted a wife who knew how to lure a man on and excite him? Not him. That kind of wife could cause a man a lot of trouble. No, Charlie had decided to marry Daphne because of who she was, not what she was. Daphne's parents had money and status in the small village where they lived and they thought he was wonderful because they believed he had tried to save their son's life. Initially Charlie had basked in their gratitude but gradually, like Daphne's adoration, it had become something he had taken for granted.

Daphne had said several times recently that she wished they did not have to live so far away from her parents. Whilst his mother was openly delighted at the prospect of having her daughter-in-law living so close, Charlie suspected that Daphne did not share her enthusiasm. Now she would be able to continue to live with her parents, which would please her, just as much as it would suit him. Talk about having your cake and eating it, Charlie thought happily.

Charlie liked fun and excitement, he liked fast cars and pretty girls, he liked the clubs in London that welcomed young men like him, and understood what a chap wanted and supplied it very discreetly, whether it was a drink or a girl.

Now, he told himself confidently, even though he couldn't get out of the army his father was bound to make him a decent allowance. After all, he was going to be a married man and his father couldn't expect a girl like Daphne, whose father was a Name at Lloyd's, to live on a private's wages.

Yes, the more Charlie thought about his future the more pleased with himself he felt.

FIVE

Katie could feel the tension in the Campions' kitchen as soon as she walked in. She was later getting in from work than normal because they had all had to work over to deal with the extra workload caused by the bombs disrupting the delivery service and the girls who had not come into work.

The first thing she'd done was to go upstairs to wash her hands and face, and change out of her office clothes and into an old summer dress, which she could tuck into her siren suit without spoiling it when the air-raid siren went off. Now, coming back down, she glanced round the table and could see how on edge and anxious Jean looked. That alone was enough to cause Katie's own tummy to tense up. Jean was the mainstay of her family, a loving wife and mother, with a practical calm streak that always ensured that her home and especially her kitchen was an oasis of reassurance and loving warmth. Tonight, though, Jean was quite obviously not herself.

Katie's first fear, that there must have been bad news, subsided when she looked at Sam, who was calmly eating his tea. Sam was a good father, who would never have been sitting eating a luncheon meat salad if anything had happened to one of them.

Normally the conversation round the tea table in the Campion household flowed easily, punctuated by the twins' laughter, but tonight only the wireless was producing conversation.

A quick look at Jean's plate confirmed what Katie had already suspected: that she had no appetite for her tea. What was wrong? Jean was normally scrupulous about not wasting food. She might have a husband who worked hard on his allotment to keep them all in fresh home-grown food, but she still had to queue along with everyone else for all those things that were now rationed: meat and eggs, cheese and margarine, to name just a few.

As soon as they had all finished eating, Sam stood up.

'You two can do the washing-up tonight,' he told the twins firmly. 'Me and your mum are going for a bit of a walk down to the allotment.'

Nothing was said, but Katie could tell from the way the twins looked at one another that they were also aware that something was happening, and that it was upsetting Jean.

'You shouldn't have said what you did to the twins, Sam,' Jean told her husband in a troubled voice as he opened the gate at the back of the garden for her. A narrow lane ran along behind the houses, separating their back gardens from the allotments, which ran down to the railway embankment. Sam had been cultivating his allotment ever since they had moved into Ash Grove, and had even been able to take over a spare patch of land, which he shared with several

70

other allotment holders and on which they had planted fruit trees. Because nothing could be cultivated beneath their branches they had let the grass grow and put hen runs there, and in summer this area was a favourite place for families to gather and have picnics. Now the grass was just starting to be shaded with the bluebells that grew wild in the grass, and that would soon form a rich blue carpet.

Jean blinked away painful tears. Funny how it was the little things that it hurt to think about when you realised you wouldn't be able to see them.

'They'll be wondering what's going on, and I don't want them worrying, not after what's happened.'

'Aye, well, it's because I'm worrying myself that I want to talk to you,' Sam told her heavily, guiding her through the gate into his own allotment, and to the rustic seat in its sunny spot close to the tool shed, where he grew a few flowers because Jean loved them so much.

Now she looked down at the Russell lupins, already fat with cream and brown buds thanks to the shelter of their spot. A rose smothered the shed itself but it was too soon for it to flower yet. It seemed incredible that something as fragile as these plants could survive when buildings so close at hand were being destroyed.

Her emotions brought a hard lump to Jean's throat. The evening sunshine slanted across Sam's hands, strong and lean, tanned from his work both on the allotment and with the Salvage Corps.

It wasn't usual for them to touch one another in public, but now something made Jean reach out to put her own hand on top of Sam's as she told him quietly, 'You've always had such good strong hands, Sam.

They were one of the first things I noticed about you when you first asked me out. That's partly why I married you, on account of them hands. With hands like that I knew you'd always keep me and our children safe.'

Sam's expression was sombre as he moved his body to shield her from the bright glare of the dying sun.

'I can't do that any more, Jean. I wish I could, but I can't. Not with what's going on and this war.'

His voice sounded as heavy as her heart felt, Jean realised.

'That's what I want to talk to you about.'

Jean's body shook. She could guess what was coming – had already guessed.

'The thing is about my job that you see things others don't always get to see, and the fact is, Jean, Liverpool can't hold out much longer. I've heard it said by them as should know that another couple of nights like these we've been having, three at the most, and there'll be nothing left to save.'

'But what about the Government? They must be able to do something. Liverpool has to be saved; there's the docks and the convoys coming in.' Jean protested.

Sam shook his head. 'There's nowt to be done, lass. I wish there were. The convoys will have to be diverted, or risk being bombed in the water by the Luftwaffe. The city's a goner, as near as dammit. When the war was first announced I wanted you and the twins to go somewhere where you'd be safe, but you wouldn't hear of it, and to be honest the last thing I wanted was for us to be separated, but it's different now. You've seen what's happening and seen the figures in the papers. Jerry isn't going to stop once he's destroyed the docks; he'll be moving inland and dropping more bombs as he does.' Sam nodded in the direction of the railway embankment. 'We've got the main goods line to Edge Hill right there in front of us. Jerry's already had one go at destroying it, and he'll be back to try again. Another couple of nights of bombing and those of us that are still left alive will be lucky if we don't starve.'

'That's silly talk, Sam, with all that you're growing on your allotment,' Jean protested.

'Veggies are all very well but how do you think meat and fish and that are going to get into the city with the roads and the railway lines unusable? There'll be riots and all sorts.'

Jean wanted to argue that he was wrong but she couldn't. Only this morning whilst she had been in the local butcher's where the family was registered with their coupons, the butcher had told her how he'd heard that the bombing had destroyed so many shops and warehouses that those that were left were beginning to run out of supplies. Because the city was a port, receiving goods in and then distributing them to the rest of the country, it hadn't occurred to Jean before now that they could run out. Feeding her family was the main priority of every housewife in these rationed times, and the thought of her own family going hungry and maybe even starving filled her with fear.

Sam had pulled away from her now and was standing looking towards the embankment, as though he didn't want to have to face her.

Jean's heart thudded with misery. She had known that this was coming. Everyone you talked to was

73

saying how much they wanted those they loved to be safe.

'I want you and the twins to leave Liverpool, Jean. I know the last time we talked about this you persuaded me to change my mind, but I won't change it this time. I need to know that at least some of my family will be safe. I can't do owt about Luke. He's a man now and in the army, and you don't need me to tell you that I'm as proud of him as it's possible for any man to be of his son. And as for our Grace . . .'

He was looking at her now and Jean could see the sheen of his emotions in his eyes.

He shook his head. 'It doesn't seem that long ago that she was following me round the allotment, chattering away to me, sneaking the raspberries when she thought I wasn't looking. And now look at her. She'll soon be a fully qualified nurse. My heart's in me mouth every night worrying about Luke and Grace, but they've got their duty to do, I know that, just as I've got mine.'

'Sam, please, don't make me and the twins go away,' Jean begged him. 'We're safe enough up here, everyone says so. You say you're worrying about us but how do you think it's going to be for me, sitting somewhere safe, not knowing what's going on here with you and Luke and Grace? We can perhaps send the twins somewhere safer, but I want to stay. I've got to stay – there's Katie to think of, and you. Who's going to make sure there's a decent meal on the table for you, and what's our Luke going to think if poor Katie has to find somewhere else? A fine thing that would be.'

'Katie was saying only the other night that she's owed some leave and that she'd like to go and see her parents. And as for me, I can look after meself if I have to. It won't be for long.'

He was lying, thought Jean in despair. It could be for ever if what he was saying was true. It could mean that if she did what he wanted, when she said goodbye to him tomorrow that she might never ever see him again, and he knew that as well as she did. But she also knew what that set determined expression meant. Sam was a good man, a kind, loving man, but he could also be a stubborn, prideful man who was sometimes a bit too set in his ways, traits that Luke had inherited from him.

There was no point in arguing with him. That would only drive him into sticking to his guns, and besides, he did have a point, at least where the twins were concerned.

Jean moved closer to him, pretending not to notice when he moved back, indicating that he wasn't going to let any physical closeness between them change his mind. She put her hand on his arm. There were new lines fanning out from his eyes; he looked tired and determined not to show it, wearied by the nightly bombardment of the city on top of the rigours already imposed on everyone by a war that was ageing them all, including the young. It showed in the stoop of people's shoulders, and in the anxious frowns that everyone seemed to wear when they thought no one else was looking. Jean had seen it in those poor people who came to the rest centre, and who tried to pull themselves up to their full height and wear a smile when they thought they were being observed. She had seen it too in her own dressing table mirror, but this was the first time she had seen it so plainly in Sam.

75

'I agree that the twins should go somewhere safer,' she told him quietly. 'But I want to stay, Sam. Luke and Grace are here, after all, as well as you, and I couldn't bear it if anything was to happen and I couldn't—' She had to bite down on her words as the awful thought she didn't want to voice bubbled inside her head.

'Don't you think I feel the same?' Sam demanded.

'I'll be safe enough, Sam. It only takes a minute to get to the shelter.'

'A minute could be a minute too long and besides, there's been more than one shelter got hit and them inside never got out. You know that. No, Jean, I mean it: you and the children can't stay in Liverpool.'

'Well, we can't just leave. Where will we go?'

'I was thinking of your Vi in Wallasey.'

Jean sucked in her breath. 'You're never expecting me to go cap in hand to our Vi and ask her to take me and the twins in, Sam Campion?'

'I'd rather you were somewhere more out in the country, but Wallasey's a damn sight safer than Liverpool, and your Vi's honour-bound to take you in, seeing as you're family.'

His whole manner said that his mind was made up and that he wasn't going to change it. Sam hated seeing her cry, but Jean just couldn't stop herself.

'I never thought I'd see the day when you expected me to go begging to my sister,' she reproached him. 'Not after everything you've said about her.'

'Can't you see that it's you and the twins I'm thinking of, Jean?' Sam defended himself. 'How do you think I would feel if anything were to happen to any of you? How would you feel if something

76

happened to the twins? It was bad enough that to-do on Saturday.'

Jean shuddered. On Saturday night when the twins had gone missing she had been so afraid for them. Sam was right, she would never forgive herself if they ended up being hurt or worse because she had refused to leave Liverpool.

'If I had my way our Grace would be going with you, an' all,' Sam told her, breaking into her thoughts.

'She can't do that, Sam. It would mean her giving up her nursing and she wouldn't do that, not now she's in her final year.'

She reached into her apron pocket for her handkerchief and felt a surge of fresh tears when Sam pushed his own handkerchief into her hands. The first time he had done that they had been courting and she had started crying over a sad film. How she wished that it was only a sad film she had to cry over now.

'Come on, love,' he begged her gruffly. 'At least I'll be able to sleep a bit easier for knowing that you and the twins are safe.'

Jean sniffed and blew her nose. 'And what about me, Sam Campion? How am I supposed to sleep easy from now on? What's going to happen to us, Sam, if Hitler does bomb Liverpool to bits?'

'I don't know, love. All I know now is that I want you and the twins safe. Come on, we'd better get back.'

So that she could tell them what was going to happen, he meant, Jean knew.

She'd been dreading him saying something like this since Saturday night. She'd seen it in his eyes and she'd prayed that the bombing would stop so that they could stay together as a family just as they always had.

'I suppose Dad's telling Mum that he isn't going to eat any more luncheon meat.'

Lou's weak attempt at a joke barely raised the corners of Sasha's mouth. Neither of them had stopped watching the back door, which they'd opened ostensibly to let in some fresh evening air but in reality to anticipate the return of their parents, and Katie shared their anxiety.

'What do you suppose—' Lou began, only to stop when Sasha gave her a nudge in the ribs with her elbow and warned her, 'Hush, they're just opening the gate.'

It was obvious to Katie the minute she saw Jean that she had been crying. Her own heart lurched into her ribs. Was it possible that she had been wrong and there had been bad news? About Luke? Or Grace? Guiltily Katie recognised how much she hoped if one of them had been hurt that it was not Luke.

Instinctively adopting Jean's own normal manner Katie asked calmly, 'Shall I put the kettle on?' and received a grateful look from Sam.

'Aye, lass, if you wouldn't mind.'

He turned to the twins. 'Your mother's got something to tell you.'

Jean bowed her head, waiting for Sam to announce that he was going back to the allotment, but to her surprise he was obviously intending to stay. To support her or to make sure she did what he wanted?

Behind her Katie was waiting for the kettle to boil. Dear Katie, such a lovely girl and so perfect for Luke. Jean worried about her safety as much as if she were one of her own. Hitler was dropping bombs on London, of course, but Katie had already said that it was much safer where her parents were living. If she went to them she'd be safe, and it would only be for a little while. Until the bombing stopped. Until Liverpool had been destroyed.

Jean took a deep breath to try to steady herself. It wouldn't do to let the girls see how upset she was.

'Me and your dad have been thinking,' she began, 'and we've decided that until all this bombing stops you two and me would be better off finding some- where safer to live outside the city.'

'But what about Katie?'

That was Sasha, looking quickly past Jean to where Katie was standing pouring the now boiling water onto the tea leaves.

'There's no need for anyone to worry about me,' Katie told them all firmly. 'In fact I was already thinking of taking my leave and going home to see my parents.'

She caught another approving nod from Sam and a grateful look from Jean. 'And I think that you and your mum going somewhere safer is exactly the right thing to do,' she told the twins calmly. 'In fact, Luke was only saying the same thing the last time I saw him,' she added, crossing her fingers behind her back. She was sure that Luke would have said that if he had been asked, because he was very much his father's son and Katie knew instinctively that it was Sam who was insisting on them going rather than Jean.

What a terrible decision that must have been for Jean. She had four children, after all, two of whom would have to remain in Liverpool and face the danger from which Sam obviously wanted to protect her and the twins. Katie could imagine how she would have felt in such circumstances.

'But how can we leave Liverpool?' Sasha asked uncertainly. 'Where will we go?'

'I know,' said Lou, as irrepressible as ever. 'We will have to be trekkers. You know, you go and queue up for the trucks in the evening and then they take you out into the country and you have to find a barn or something to sleep in.'

'Don't be silly,' Jean told her. She looked at Sam and then back at the twins. 'We'll be going to Wallasey, of course, to stay with your auntie Vi.'

'What?'

'No!'

The twins spoke together, their words different but their horrified expressions identical.

'Mum, you can't mean that,' Lou protested. 'Auntie Vi doesn't like us and we don't like her. Well, we're not going, are we, Sasha?'

'That's enough of that,' Sam told them sternly. 'You're going and that's an end to the matter.'

Katie could tell that the twins knew he meant what he said. They subsided, still exchanging shocked looks.

'When will we have to go?' That was Sasha, her voice small and wobbling slightly.

'Not until tomorrow,' Jean told them quietly. 'I'll have to go over and see Vi tomorrow and . . . and arrange things with her first.' She was looking at Sam now as though seeking help, but he wasn't looking back at her.

Katie had heard all about the relationship between the two families and she knew that it would be hard for Jean to lower her pride and ask her snobbish sister for help.

Jean looked at Sam's stiff back. The fact that he was prepared to let her go begging Vi for help said how afraid for them he really was. There had never been any love lost between Vi and Sam, and although she had never said so to Sam, in the early days of their courtship Vi had actually tried to persuade her to drop Sam. If she told him that now . . . But no, she must not do that. Sam was doing this for them, and he had been right when he'd said that she would never forgive herself if they stayed in Liverpool and something happened to the twins.

Just as she would never forgive herself if anything happened to Luke or to Grace or to Sam himself, and she couldn't get to them.

It was a situation that thousands of families all over the country were facing, especially those living in the cities that Hitler was targeting. And what about the men fighting abroad – how must their mothers and wives feel?

Jean squared her shoulders. 'It won't be as bad as you think,' she told the twins.

'No, it will be much worse,' Lou muttered gloomily under her breath.

Wallasey and Auntie Vi's.

Lou flung herself down on her bed with a grimace of disbelief. 'I never thought Mum would make us go there.'

'She's going as well,' Sasha reminded her. 'And I'll bet it's Dad who has said we have to go. Did you see how red his ears went when Mum was telling us, and how he wouldn't look at us?'

'Well, what about Katie?' Lou demanded. 'I'll bet

81

she doesn't really want to go and see her parents. She loves our Luke.'

'She was saying the other day that she felt she should go and see them,' Sasha felt bound to point out, adding firmly, 'Look, Lou, we aren't children any more, are we, and after what happened on Saturday, well, I just think that we shouldn't make things hard for Mum, that's all.'

Sasha almost sounded as though she disapproved of what Lou had said. But that was impossible. Hadn't they reassured one another that their closeness, their twinship, was more important than anything else? Once Lou would have known exactly what Sasha was feeling about anything, just as Sasha would have done her, and this feeling that she did not know what her twin was thinking was unfamiliar territory.

'Sash?'

Sasha looked at her twin.

'It's all right with me and you, isn't it? I mean, I know there was . . . Well, I just want you to know that I don't mind if you do still . . . Well, it was you Kieran liked best really, anyway.'

Sasha jumped off her own bed and went to stand next to Lou's, her hands on her hips, her round face flushed with angry colour.

'How dare you say that, Louise Campion? We both said, didn't we, that we were going to stick together from now on?'

'Yes, but—'

'So why are you keeping going on about a certain person who we agreed we'd never talk about again?'

'There's no need to get your hair off with me, Sasha. I was just meaning that if you did think about him, then I'd understand and you can say so.'

Lou didn't know how to say that she was afraid of losing her twin, and afraid too of the way things seemed to be changing, and not just things but they themselves.

'I'd hate it if you and me was to end up like Mum and Auntie Vi,' was all she could manage to say.

The anger died out of Sasha's face. Although traditionally it was always Lou, the younger of the two, who had taken the lead, just lately Sasha had started to feel older than her twin and as though it was up to her to take charge. Somehow, without knowing how, Sasha had started to recognise that for all her bravado Lou was more vulnerable than she was herself.

She sat down next to Lou and told her firmly, 'That will never happen to us, unless of course you keep going on about Kieran.'

'But he liked you.'

'No he didn't, he just pretended he did so that we'd earn money for him with our dancing.'

'But if he did really like you . . .' Lou persisted.

'Oh, stop it, Lou. I just want to forget about the whole thing.' Sasha gave a fierce shudder, reminding Lou of exactly what her twin had been through when she had become trapped and they had both thought that she might die before help arrived.

'I'm sorry.'

'It's all right,' Sasha accepted her apology, before telling her, 'I don't want to go to Auntie Vi's either, you know, but we have to think of Mum, Lou. Just think how awful it must be for her.'

'What, you mean because she and Vi don't get on?'

'No, silly, because Luke and Grace and our dad will still be here.'

*   *   *

Nearly midnight. The rhythmic tick of the kitchen clock made Jean's heart thud with anxiety. When would they come tonight? Sam hadn't been pleased when she had refused to leave for Wallasey this evening. But like she had told him, she and the twins could hardly descend on Vi without any warning.

'Why not?' he had wanted to know. 'I'm sure she'd rather be a bit put out and see you safe than find out summat's happened.'

Not our Vi, Jean had thought. Vi didn't like unplanned visitors, and she certainly wouldn't put the welcome mat out for them. And besides, although she hadn't said so to Sam, Jean wasn't leaving Liverpool without first seeing Grace, even if she might not be able to see Luke. She could give Grace a message for him. And then there was Katie to think of. It was all very well Sam frightening her half to death by warning her about what might happen but arrangements still had to be made.

It was no good, she couldn't sit still any longer.

'Katie, love, I think I'll put the kettle on.'

Jean got up. They were all ready in their shelter clothes, the twins and Katie in siren suits that Jean had made from some material that she and Katie had bought from a shop that sold off-cuts.

Jean was making do with an old pair of Sam's pyjamas that she had cut down.

Kate wondered if she would manage to see Luke before she left. They'd sort of made plans to see one another on Saturday if Luke could snatch a couple of hours of compassionate leave. The CO at the barracks at Seacombe was good like that. Katie felt sorry for those men who did not live close enough for them to get home quickly to check that their

84

families were safe, but Luke had told her that the commander was giving those men with the longest distances to travel twenty-four- and even sometimes forty-eight-hour passes in lieu of the unofficial couple of hours here and there those with families living closer were getting.

'He's a decent chap – all the lads say so – but he knows how to make everyone toe the line as well,' Luke had told her, and Katie had known from his tone of voice that he respected his commanding officer. Luke was someone who saw things in black and white, good and bad, with no shades of grey. Sometime that worried her, especially when he was getting on his high horse about something – or someone he thought had done something wrong. He wasn't always ready to see that there might be extenuating circumstances or to make allowances for other people's vulnerabilities and the fact that they might not be as morally strong as he was himself.

She did love him though – so very much. Katie's expression softened.

Jean looked at the clock. Ten past midnight. It had been gone half-past when they had come last night. They did it deliberately, she was sure, letting people think that they were safe and then coming. Sam was on fire-watch duty, of course. He'd volunteered to stand in for someone else down near the docks. Jean's hands trembled. The docks were the worst place of all to be.

Quarter-past midnight. Luke shifted his weight against the thin hard mattress of his bed. It wasn't comfortable at the best of times, but tonight when, like everyone else, he was straining to catch the first sound of incoming aircraft, and with his muscles aching still from earlier in the day – but no, he mustn't think about that and the horror of removing the debris from the lorry driver's body to find – but he wasn't going to think about that, was he? Those ruddy Americans. Showing off like they had and then three of them puking their guts up when they had seen what was left of poor old Ronnie. Some soldiers they were, for all their fancy uniforms and boastful words.

'I ain't seen no one dead before,' one of them had whimpered.

Luke swallowed the bile gathering in his throat.

He tried to think about Katie. She'd be waiting like they all were for the air-raid warning, ready to go into the shelter with his mother and the twins. Katie didn't always understand how he felt or why he felt the way he did. She didn't understand what being a man meant and how it was up to him to take care of her. That was a responsibility he took very seriously, just as his father did. Luke's first thoughts as he listened to the all clear were the same as they had been every morning since the blitz had begun, and were for the safety of those he loved, his family, and Katie, his girl.

Just thinking about Katie brought him a confusing mix of emotions: fear for her safety, coupled with an fierce male urge to protect her, delight because she loved him, pride in her because of the important war work she was doing, and yet at that same time that pride was shadowed by a certain fear and hostility to that work in case it somehow took her from him.

Did Katie wish he was more like Seb, Grace's fiancé? Seb was an easy-going sort, protective of

Grace, of course, but Grace wasn't the kind who would give a chap any cause to worry about her. Did that mean that Katie was? Luke frowned. He trusted Katie – of course he did, and he knew he could – but she didn't always realise how she might come across to other men; how they might see her smiling at them and think that her smile meant more than it did. He'd tried to tell her about that, but he couldn't seem to make her understand. Luke didn't like it when things weren't straightforward and clear cut. Life had rules and Luke preferred it when people stuck to those rules. Katie was his girl and that meant that he didn't want to lose her to another man. He wasn't keen on that job of hers either. Not really, although he'd tried to pretend that he didn't mind because he'd been able to see that that was what she wanted. And he did want to please her, of course he did, but it made him feel so frustrated when she wouldn't understand the danger she was putting herself in.

If they were to get engaged then maybe he'd be able to have more say in what she did. He'd certainly not have her working doing what she did once they were married.

Come on if you're coming, Lena thought irritably, as she scratched absently at a flea bite on her ankle and waited for the sound of the air-raid siren to start up. She didn't own a watch and there was no clock in the room she shared with Doris. Doris wasn't here tonight, though. She'd gone out to her boyfriend's for tea, and his mother had apparently invited her to stay over in case there was an attack.

Lena laughed to herself. What a lie that was.

Lena knew for a fact that Doris's fella's mother would be spending the evening in the pub where she worked and that she'd use the pub shelter if the siren went off, and Lena knew that because she'd been in the salon in the morning getting her hair done and she'd said so.

No, Lena reckoned, Doris knew perfectly well that she and Brian would have the house to themselves and Lena thought too that Doris wanted to make the most of the opportunity to tie Brian to her. Well, good luck to the pair of them.

When was that siren going to go off? She heard a sound from the room next door – her uncle breaking wind. He didn't half make a noise when he farted and he was a stinker with it, an' all.

Bodily functions and the earthy humour surrounding them were part and parcel of life in the city's slums. How could they not be with several families sharing the same outside lav, and everyone knowing everyone else's business, right down to when a person opened their bowels?

Lena had been shocked at first to see half a dozen lads peering over the half-door of one of the lavvies whilst, she learned soon after, the girl inside delicately removed her knickers and then bent over to show them her bare bum, but then she hadn't been able to help laughing when the girl had insisted that all the boys were to pay her a halfpenny each for the treat.

Of course, Doris denied that *she* had ever done such a thing. Lena knew that she never could have done. Oh, she hid how she felt from everyone because she knew it would make her a target to be tormented and bullied, but she had been brought up better than that, and when her Charlie came for her he'd take her away somewhere decent; somewhere in Wallasey. Her heart began to beat faster. Should she write to him at his barracks and surprise him? She wanted to, but was held back by a memory of her mother telling her that decent girls didn't go running after boys. Anyway, she didn't need to write to him. When she'd put her arms round him and asked him when she'd see him again, he'd said, 'Soon as I can.'

If she closed her eyes she could picture him now. She could always go over to Wallasey, of course, and introduce herself to his family. She'd got their address, after all. She could say something about him leaving his papers with her and her wanting to get them back to him. Her heart jumped a couple of beats. What were they like, his man and dad? Had he got brothers and sisters at home? Well, she'd have to wait and see, wouldn't she, because she wasn't going to go pushing herself in on his family until he was there to introduce her to them proper like, as his girl.

How proud she'd be when he took her home on his arm to meet them. Lena gave a blissful sigh, ignoring the hungry rumble of her stomach. Her auntie had been in one of her bad moods and had hardly spoken to her when Lena had come in for her tea. She'd not given Lena much to eat either, claiming that she couldn't afford to, even though she'd made Lena hand over her ration book – well, not hand it over exactly. She'd taken it from Lena's drawer when Lena was out at work, as well as making her tip up most of the money she earned to go into the family pot.

Lena had managed to keep her tips back for herself, though. She'd even opened a Post Office account to pay them into. Simone had shown her how, and Lena kept the book hidden in her handbag. Twenty pounds ten shillings she'd saved in it now, Lena thought with pride.

One o'clock. Seb frowned. They were normally here by now. He leaned back in his chair and rubbed his eyes. What kind of cat-and-mouse game was Hitler playing with Liverpool now? He'd all but destroyed the city. Another heavy raid, certainly two, would be the fatal blow that would mean that Liverpool was done for. The port would no longer be a safe haven for the Atlantic convoys, bringing in desperately needed food and raw materials, as well as equipment under the recently signed Lend Lease agreement with America, which meant that the neutral Americans, not in the war, could provide much-needed military equipment to the financially hard-pressed Allies, with payment being deferred until a later date. The agreement was very complicated, with many of its terms still kept from the general public in the interests of national security. Its existence, though, had had to be acknowledged to account for the sudden influx to the country of American personnel and equipment to help with the war effort.

Seb stretched again and tried to suppress a yawn.

Grace would be lying in her bed in the nurses' home waiting for the sound of the siren. Seb knew how much nursing meant to her, but increasingly he worried about her safety. The hospital had already been bombed once, and some of the medical staff killed.

He'd sensed her growing fear and desperation when he'd walked her back to the nurses' home on Sunday. When he'd taken advantage of the privacy afforded by a shadowy doorway, she'd clung to him and kissed him, trembling so much in his arms with her passion that he had started to tremble himself.

If they'd been anywhere half decently suitable, he'd have been tempted to answer the need he had seen in her eyes and truly make her his, whilst they were still both alive to share that special loving intimacy.

It had been Grace who had insisted that she wanted to finish her training and that meant that they couldn't marry until she had, but he had respected that decision. These last few days, though, with the knowledge that each bombing raid could take Grace from him, Seb had burned with a fierce urge to make her truly his and to know that they had shared something that could never be taken from them. And Grace had wanted that too – he had sensed it in her even before she had told him so, clinging to him, her eyes wet with her tears as she told him how afraid she was of dying without knowing his love.

Bella couldn't sleep. They'd been promised twenty cot mattresses, and only ten had been delivered. The driver had feigned ignorance but Bella knew she was right to suspect that the other ten would end up on the black market. She moved restlessly beneath her immaculately ironed sheets. Laura had simply shrugged and looked impatient when Bella had complained to her.

'What do you expect with all this rationing?' she had demanded sharply. 'After all, those doing the black market selling aren't the only ones making money from this war, are they?'

Bella had known that Laura was referring to

Bella's own father whose business supplying and fitting pipes to merchant and naval vessels had become so profitable thanks to the war that Edwin had had to treble his work force. Her father liked a gin and tonic, and after the third glass was inclined to start bragging about the fortune he was making. Not that he shared it with his family, Bella thought sourly, or at least not with her. He was showering money on Charlie, buying him a new car, because his small sports car had been stolen, giving him a job, and her house.

She looked at her alarm clock.

Two o'clock. The bombers were normally here by now, dropping their bombs over Liverpool. Bella moved irritably, frowning as she remembered the knowing look Ralph Fleming had given her when he'd come to collect his children from the crèche earlier in the day, her face starting to burn with angry pride. Did he really think that she would be interested in him now that she knew he was married man, and that he'd lied to her?

What kind of girl did he think she was? Her heart started to thump angrily. Well, she wasn't that sort, no matter what he might think. Why were people so horrid and mean to her? Especially men. Bella thought of her father, with his impatience and irritable manner; her husband, who had never loved her as surely she deserved to be loved; Jan Polanski, whose mother and sister were her billetees, and who was getting married in two weeks' time, making out that she had wanted him to kiss her just because he was good-looking, when she hadn't at all; and now Ralph Fleming, pretending he was free to ask her out and then actually having the cheek to laugh at her and look at her as though he knew something about her that meant she didn't care that he was married. Well, she did. She cared a lot. She was tired of other people – other women – treating her the way they did. It wasn't fair that other girls like her cousin Grace ended up with good-looking men and had lots of friends, whilst she, who surely deserved better, was treated so unkindly.

Tears of self-pity welled in Bella's eyes.

It just wasn't fair.

That surely couldn't be dawn, could it, edging slowly and warily up under the darkness, hesitating as though fearing what it might reveal?

Sam rubbed his eyes in case he had got it wrong and he was imagining things. He was tired from being on fire-watch duty. Even though tonight there were no new fires, the acrid smell of smoke still hung in the air and stung the eyes, but no, that was definitely dawn lightening the sky on the horizon.

As he watched, the band of light grew wider, revealing the tired buildings that still remained standing sharply etched against the skyline, black against the dawn sky.

Something – relief, disbelief, gratitude, Sam couldn't pin down exactly what it was – dampened his eyes and made him want to shout his discovery from the rooftops.

The German bombers hadn't come. Incredibly, unbelievably, the final death blow had not been delivered.

On other buildings Sam could see other fire watchers now. Like him they were stretching, and looking around, shedding the burden of the night watch, straightening up and standing tall, and it seemed to Sam that the city itself was doing the same thing, that he could feel in the air its pride in its survival through a night when everyone had thought that all must be lost.

It was a miracle, that's what it was, Harry Fitch, who had shared the watch with Sam, announced, and Sam didn't argue.

SIX

It was a mistake – everyone was agreed on that – a breathing space, that was all. The bombers were bound to return, and yet there was a lightness of heart as people went about their business, a sense of reprieve even if it was generally acknowledged that it wouldn't last.

But it did, and finally, by Sunday morning, after three full nights without a raid, even Sam was cautiously agreeing that maybe there had indeed been a miracle and what was left of the city was safe.

'Mind you, I still think it's a rum business that Hitler didn't send the Luftwaffe in to finish us off,' he told Jean as the family set out for church.

For once the whole family was together, Luke, like the other soldiers who lived locally, having been given compassionate leave, and Grace being off duty.

In with her other prayers this morning there would definitely be one thanking God for saving her from having to go begging Vi for a favour, Jean decided fervently, as she paused to check that her family were looking their best.

The twins must still be growing, she thought, switching her attention from the outer world to her own small family. Their frocks certainly needed letting down. At their age they really shouldn't be showing quite so much leg, Jean decided with maternal concern, even if their legs were very well shaped. Thank goodness she had asked Mrs Nellis, who had run up their red and white gingham frocks on her machine for them, to put on good hems, disguised with white rickrack braid.

'Lou, that isn't a dirty mark on the sleeve of your cardigan, is it?' she demanded, sighing as she saw that it was. 'Just keep your arm by your side, then,' she instructed.

'I don't know if I agree with Mrs Braddock saying that the cinemas should open on a Sunday,' she told Sam.

Bessie Braddock, a local councillor, had been quoted in the papers saying that people needed to be able to celebrate and enjoy themselves, and for that reason the cinemas should be allowed to open on Sundays.

'Well, to be fair, she did say that them as don't approve don't have to go, and there's plenty who will want to have a bit of a fun after what's bin happening,' Sam responded so tolerantly that even if she hadn't already done so Jean would have known how much these three nights without bombs had lifted his spirits. Even so, as a mother of daughters still at an impressionable age, Jean felt it necessary to protest.

'Fun on a Sunday?'

'But remember, Mum,' Luke and Grace chanted together, laughing, 'there's a war on.'

'Oh, give over, you two, as if I didn't know that.'

It was hard to remain stern, though, when the sun

was shining and everyone was in such good spirits and with such good reason.

No wonder it felt as though the whole city, or those who were left in it, were turning out to give thanks for being spared.

Grace hung back from the rest of her family deliberately, slipping her arm through Seb's.

'We are so lucky. I was so afraid, Seb, afraid that something would happen and that you and I would never . . . But here we are, both still safe and well . . .'

'And we still haven't . . .' Seb began teasingly, but Grace blushed and laughed and shook her head at him.

'None of that kind of talk now. You know what we agreed.'

He should have seized his chance whilst he had the opportunity, Seb thought ruefully, but on the other hand Grace was well worth waiting for, even if her passionate response to him earlier in the week had had him lying awake every night since imagining how things might be.

Good girls didn't 'do it' before marriage, supposedly, only of course sometimes they did, and it was such a long time to wait before Grace would have finished her training and they could get married. And now there was that other matter as well.

Seb frowned. He had been taken completely by surprise when his commanding officer had sent for him and told him that he was going to be transferred to a new Y Section that was being set up in Whitchurch.

At first it would just be him and some other trained operatives, but more operatives would join them once they had received their training. The recent news that one of the Enigma machines and its code books had been captured had sent a buzz of elation and excitement through everyone connected with Bletchley Park, where they were working flat out now on the codes.

Seb had been told that his new post would be a promotion but he acknowledged that he would have been feeling much happier about it if it didn't mean that he would be moving away from Liverpool and Grace.

He looked at her. The sunlight caught the curls in her strawberry-blonde hair, and revealed a small dusting of freckles across her nose. She was so pretty, his Grace, with her warm smile and those eyes of hers that reflected the depth of both her emotions and her loyalty. If the months since they had first met at the very beginning of the war, and all that had happened during them had brought a certain gravity and even sometimes sadness to her eyes when she talked of the courage of her patients, then Seb loved her all the more because of it. His Grace was more than a pretty face – much more – and he wouldn't want to change anything about her.

His parents loved her, and he knew that when the war was over and the time came for them to make their lives wherever his work took him, Grace would create a comfortable and a happy home for him and their children, even if that meant she had to move away from her own family to whom she was so close. But for all the maturity she had gained since they had first met, today, in her relief after several nights without any bombing raids, and with her joyous smile, she looked so carefree and happy that he didn't want to spoil that happiness by telling her that he was going to be moved out of Liverpool.

Grace looked at Seb and smiled warmly at him, increasing his guilt at keeping something so important from her, but this wasn't the time to tell her. He wanted to wait until they were on their own.

In front of them, neither Luke nor Katie was smiling.

'Well, I still don't see why you would want to go and see your parents behind my back and without me,' Luke was saying, sticking doggedly to the point he had been trying to make ever since Katie had let slip that she was planning a visit to her family.

'It wasn't like that,' Katie defended herself unhappily. 'I've already told you how it happened. When I thought that your mum and the twins were going to evacuate to Wallasey I decided I'd take some leave that was owing to me and go and see my parents. I couldn't tell you because I haven't seen you, and now that it looks like the bombing raids are over I don't want to let Mum and Dad down by not going.'

'But you don't mind letting me down?' Luke's voice was bitter.

Katie suppressed an unhappy sigh. It upset her so much when Luke was like this, although she was trying hard not to show it. Katie hated scenes. They made her feel physically sick with misery and so anxious to get things 'back to normal' that she was ready to say anything that would appease him. Sometimes, though, no matter what she did say or how much she tried to agree with him, it just seemed to make matters worse.

Today this mood of Luke's when he started accusing her of not loving him because in his eyes she was not putting him first, had caught her off guard, making her feel vulnerable and spoiling things between them on what should have been a happy occasion, with the relief of the blitz having so miraculously ceased.

'If you really loved me you'd wait until I can come with you,' Luke insisted.

He had no idea what drove him to be like this with Katie, whom he loved so very very much, he only knew that somehow the more he tried to make her be open and straight with him, the more she seemed to withdraw from him to a place where he wasn't allowed; and the more he wanted to secure her to him, the more elusive she seemed to become, and that hurt and scared him. Not that he could ever admit to that. He was a man, after all, and men had to be strong and in control of their emotions.

Katie looked away from Luke. She couldn't bear this, she really couldn't. It reminded her of the awful quarrels her parents had had when she had been growing up and brought back her old feelings of fear and misery.

'Very well then,' she gave in, 'I'll write and tell my parents that we'll both go and see them when you've got some leave, if that's what you want.'

Luke frowned. He knew her agreement should have made him feel happy but somehow it didn't. And as for what he wanted – Luke didn't know what it was that he actually wanted, he only knew that whatever it was it would make him feel far happier than he did right now. What he wanted ultimately was for him and Katie to be so close to one another that he didn't have to worry about what she was thinking, or if she really did love him, or was just saying the words because he had pressed her to say them. His mum showed all the time how much she loved his dad. At home his dad's word was law, not that his dad ever had to raise his voice or make demands for anyone to know that. His mother was the one who made sure that everyone knew that Dad was the boss.

Luke admired his father more than any other man he knew, and now that he was a man himself the two of them were every bit as close as a father and son should be. But Luke had grown up seeing his father always being more openly affectionate and loving with Luke's sisters than he had been with him, and somehow that had made him feel left out.

He'd seen how, when all three of his sisters over the years had gone up to their father, put their arms round him, leaned their heads on his shoulder, and sat on his lap when they were small, Sam had always laughed and responded. But when he had gone to his father for the same comfort, say with a cut leg or on those occasions when for one reason or another he was hurting inside in a way that he couldn't explain and had needed his father's reassurance, Sam had always been brusque and offhand with him, pushing him away.

Sam might say that he loved him and that he was proud of him, but sometimes when he felt the way he was doing now, deep down inside Luke couldn't help comparing the difference between the way his father had treated him when he was growing up and the open affection he had shown Luke's sisters.

What did words mean after all? What if the truth was that he just wasn't someone that could be loved? Words were easy enough to say, but how did you

101

know what was really inside someone's heart. How could he give his trust and his own heart to another person when he wasn't sure how she really felt?

Surely if Katie loved him as much as she said she did then she would understand all of this, even though he couldn't understand it or talk about it himself. Women were, after all, the guardians and protectors of their men's emotions, or so it seemed to Luke from witnessing the relationship between his own parents. It was always his mother who did the bending and the coaxing and who was at pains to make sure that her husband and her children were happy. She did that because she loved them, but Katie didn't seem to want to make sure that he was happy.

Luke hated it when these dark moods came down over him. This one had started coming on after the lorry driver had been killed. The sight of the man's crushed body had shocked and nauseated him so much that he had had trouble controlling his re-actions, and had been afraid of showing himself up in front of his own men and the Americans.

That had made him angry with himself. If he was close to crying like a baby because he'd seen one body, what would he be like when the time came for him to go into action? How could he be a proper corporal to his men if deep down inside himself he was worrying that he might be a coward? He had gone through Dunkirk, Luke reminded himself now. But that had been different. They had been running from the enemy then, not fighting them.

How was it possible for him to feel so alone when he was surrounded by his family and when he had Katie at his side?

Luke didn't know. He just knew that he did.

He couldn't explain why quarrelling with Katie gave him that sore scratchy feeling inside, nor could he explain why he found it so hard to trust her and believe her when she told him that she loved him.

'It just doesn't seem right to me that you'd want to go without me in the first place,' he told her now, returning to the argument like a child worrying at a scabbed knee, even though it knew that the end result of its messing was going to be pain. 'Unless there's something you aren't telling me?'

'Oh, Luke,' Katie sighed, pulling her hand from his as the misery inside her grew into despair.

She hated the thought that she and Luke might end up like her own mother and father. What Katie longed for was a marriage like Jean and Sam's; a contented and placid marriage based on trust. She didn't want excitement and drama. She wanted the security of knowing that her husband and her marriage would always be solid, dependable and unchanging. She could never for one minute imagine Sam saying the things to Jean that Luke had just said to her, or provoking a quarrel in the way Luke did between them. She knew that Luke had been treated badly by a previous girlfriend, but he had promised her that he would stop being so unnecessarily jealous, and she had thought he meant it. But now . . .

'Do you want to try for those jobs at the telephone exchange then?' Sasha asked Lou.

Lou dragged her foot, scuffing the side of her shoe, a childhood habit to which she still sometimes reverted, especially when she was feeling on edge.

'I suppose so, only it isn't very exciting, is it?' Lou

answered as they followed their parents towards the modest church they had attended every Sunday for as long as they could remember.

Ahead of them their parents had stopped to talk to other members of the congregation, the adults faces wreathed in smiles if they had been fortunate enough not to have lost anyone in the bombing raid, or shadowed by their pain if they had.

'So what do you want to do?' Sasha demanded impatiently, keeping an eye on their parents as she waited for Lou's response.

Lou didn't know. She only knew that she yearned for something more than working in a telephone exchange. But Sasha didn't. Sasha wasn't like her. Panic filled Lou. That wasn't true. They felt exactly the same; they always had done and they always would do. They had promised one another that nothing would ever come between them now, nothing and no one. The very thought of doing something without Sasha filled Lou with misery and despair.

'I want to do what you want to do,' she told her twin.

'So we'll go tomorrow and see if they'll take us on then,' Sasha told her.

Sasha liked the thought of working at the telephone exchange. It was within walking distance of home, and somehow she knew she'd feel safe there. Feeling safe, both emotionally and physically, was important to Sasha. She been so afraid when she'd been trapped in the bomb site, and afraid too when she and Lou had quarrelled over which of them Kieran had liked the best. She never wanted to feel like that again, about anyone or anything.

*   *   *

Her head held high with pride, her best floral silk frock abloom with bright pinks, yellows, reds and greens, and her Sunday best navy-blue straw hat pushed down firmly on top of her head, Emily beamed with delight in response to the smiles of welcome she and Tommy were receiving from the other church-goers.

Whitchurch was only a small town and already in the few days she had been here she had got to know several people, thanks to her chatty neighbour, Ivy Wilson, whose cousin owned a local farm, and who seemed to know everything about everyone.

'What you want,' she had told Emily when they had surveyed the large uncultivated back garden together over a welcome cup of tea, after she had come round to introduce herself and help Emily to unpack, 'is a man to come and set this to rights for you. I'll have a word with Linda, our Ian's wife. Our Ian farms up at Whiteside Farm and they've got some of them prisoners of war sent to help out with the farm work. I dare say Ian won't mind sparing you one to get you some veggies and that in, especially if you was to offer to feed him. Eatin' her out of house and home, Linda says they are.'

Emily had already registered her and Tommy at the doctor's, and at the local shops with their ration books. She'd had a visit from the vicar to welcome her to his congregation, and a lady from the WVS had been round to invite her to join their local group. Emily had taken Tommy to the library so that they could get tickets, and all in all Emily was extremely pleased with their new home. She certainly hadn't missed Liverpool, nor her husband, Con, not one little bit.

All that fresh air and a summer spent playing out of doors would do wonders for Tommy's thin pale face, especially once he started at school and made some friends.

Emily had no fears now that Tommy might say or do the wrong thing and accidentally let it slip that they weren't related. Tommy never spoke about his life before Emily had found him homeless, alone and living on scraps, too afraid even to speak at all, never mind talk about how he had come to be in such a desperate situation. Emily assumed that he had been orphaned by the war. She had claimed to officialdom and her husband that Tommy's mother had been her own late cousin, and that because of that she was duty bound to take him in. She had organised new papers for him giving him that identity. She loved him as though he was her own child and the only thing that would ever make her give him up to someone else would be Tommy's wish that she do so. Without it having to be said between them, they simply behaved as though they belonged together. They had not discussed the issue, but somehow Emily knew that Tommy understood and wanted them to be looked on as 'family'. What need was there for her to go asking him any questions after all, Emily thought comfortably. Poor little scrap, there was no sense in reminding him of things he'd rather not think about. Who knew what he had been through before she'd found him?

'Hang on a minute.'

Emily turned round to see Ivy, her helpful neighbour, puffing up the slight incline in the road, after them.

Like Emily she was wearing what was obviously

her Sunday best, a navy silk dress with white spots, the fabric stretched tightly across her ample chest.

'Well, you two look smart, I must say,' she said approvingly when she had caught up with them, her face bright pink beneath the brim of her white straw hat. Older than Emily, and widowed, she was obviously determined to take Emily under her wing.

Emily drew herself up proudly to her full height. Tommy did look smart in the grey flannel shorts and shirt and the Bluecoat School blazer she had bought for him in Liverpool from a school uniform supplier who was closing down.

'I was just thinking,' Ivy told Emily, 'I'll have to introduce you to Hilda Jones. She's in charge of the local school and you'll want to get your Tommy registered with her. Teaches them all herself now, Hilda does, since all the men have been called up. A bit of a tartar she is, by all accounts, at least according to our Linda's girls, but some discipline doesn't do young 'uns any harm, especially boys.'

Emily could feel Tommy's hand tightening in her own.

'Tommy's a good boy,' she told Ivy firmly, 'and clever as well.'

'Well, I can see from his blazer that he's bin at one of them posh schools,' Ivy agreed immediately. 'And he speaks lovely, an' all,' she added approvingly.

Tommy did speak well, Emily agreed. He had hardly any trace of a Liverpool accent.

Since the night he had rushed to her defence when she'd been attacked by thieves who had broken into her Liverpool house, hoping to empty her kitchen cupboards to sell her food on the black market, having previously been mute, he had come on by leaps and bounds, and was turning into a regular little chatterbox.

Every afternoon whilst it had been so nice and warm, they'd gone for a walk exploring their new environment, and it had amazed Emily how much Tommy knew and how many questions he asked. Only yesterday she'd had to ask them in the library if they had any books on birds on account of him wanting to know what the birds were they could see in the garden.

'My goodness, you can put a spurt on when you've a mind to it,' Ivy puffed as they reached the church gate.

'Oh, me and Tommy don't like to hang around,' Emily laughed. She felt Tommy's hand tighten in hers again. She looked down at him and saw that he was looking up at her in query.

'We're going to be very happy here,' she told him stoutly. 'You'll like it at school and I bet you'll be the cleverest boy there.'

He had a good sense of humour, with a wide grin that made you want to smile yourself when you saw it. He was smiling now, and Emily smiled back. My, she was going to like it here. It was doing her the world of good to be able to talk with people without looking over her shoulder to see if they were gossiping about her behind her back on account of her galli-vanting unfaithful husband. Poor Con, she almost felt sorry for him remembering how shocked and disbelieving he had been when she had told him that she was leaving. Well, it served him right.

Out of the corner of her eye she caught sight of a column of men being marched towards the church: prisoners of war, under the eye of army guards.

They came to a halt a few feet away from the gathered civilians.

He was certainly a fine well-set-up chap, Emily reflected, her attention caught by the man at the front of the column. He wasn't particularly tall but he was certainly well built with a good pair of shoulders on him and a look about him that said he was a man who knew his own mind. His fair hair was silver grey round his temples and his skin was tanned a nice brown. Emily sighed enviously. She thought tanned skin looked ever so nice but when she got out in the sun all she did was freckle.

The POW turned his head as though he could sense her interest in him. Blushing as hotly as any girl, Emily looked away, lifting her gloved hand to pat her dress self-consciously.

She must find out if there was someone who was good with a needle. What with all this rationing and the worry of the war, she seemed to have lost a bit of weight and last year's dress was now hanging loosely on her.

As they stepped through the gate into the churchyard, Ivy exclaimed, 'Oh, there's Brenda Evans from the post office, with her mother. You wait here and I'll go and bring them over and introduce you.

'Here we are,' Ivy announced, puffing and panting as she reappeared with a small apple dumpling of a woman with rosy cheeks, her iron-grey hair pulled into a bun that looked like a cottage loaf. Everything about her was round, even her sharp blue eyes.

'This here is Emily, Brenda,' Ivy began the introductions.

Emily smiled and shook the post mistress's hand.

'Well, now, and what have we here?' she began

in a singsong Welsh accent, and looking down at Tommy, before turning to her mother to say something to her in their own language.

They were both smiling and Emily had no idea what she had said but the effect on Tommy was electric. The minute he had heard the post mistress's singsong accent he had stiffened, but now with her speaking Welsh Tommy pulled away from Emily, a look of terror on his face as he ignored her anxious 'Tommy!' and bolted for the church gate.

Although she was aware of the confusion and the curious and shocked looks his behaviour was causing, it was Tommy and his safety that concerned Emily the most as she hurried after him, begging him to stop but knowing somehow that he was in such a panic that he probably couldn't even hear her.

And then to her relief, the German prisoner of war she had noticed earlier, moving extraordinarily fast for such a heavily built man, somehow managed to step in front of Tommy, reaching for him at the same time and holding him firmly until Emily arrived.

'Oh, thank you.' She was out of breath now, puffing just as Ivy had been, but although she had thanked the POW her attention was all for Tommy, who was shivering and shaking so much he could hardly stand up.

She might be wearing her Sunday best frock but Tommy was her precious boy. Emily dropped to her knees and took him in her arms, cradling him close.

'Oh, my poor little lad, what's to do?'

Ivy and Brenda Jones had caught up with them now and immediately Tommy tensed again, pulling away from her, but the POW was still there and his hand on Tommy's shoulder managed to stay him.

A small crowd had gathered round them. The postmistress looked anxious and concerned but it was Ivy who unwittingly gave Emily a clue to what might be wrong when she joked, 'It's you speaking Welsh what did it, Brenda. I reckon the poor lad must have thought the Germans had invaded.'

Everyone laughed, and then someone pointed out that they were going to be late for church, and people started to move away.

Emily reached for Tommy's hand and squeezed it, telling him softly, 'It's all right, Tommy. You and me will be all right, I promise you that.'

She could feel him starting to relax. She looked up at the man still holding him.

'Thank you.' She felt self-conscious and awkward, conscious of how she must look in his eyes, a plain fat woman who had nothing about her to appeal to any man, never mind such a well-set-up man as he.

'You are welcome.' His English was stilted, the words carefully spaced.

'He is your boy, *ja*?' he asked.

'Yes, he is my boy,' Emily agreed.

'You are a good boy to your *Mutter*? You take care of her, *ja*?' he asked Tommy, who had calmed down enough now to nod his head.

But Emily was still astonished when Tommy asked the POW politely, 'What is your name?'

'It is Wilhelm,' the man told him promptly. 'What is yours?'

'Tommy.' Emily and Tommy both spoke at the same time.

The soldier guarding the POWs gave a command and the column started to march into the church.

Emily drew Tommy to one side to let them pass.

Wilhelm had ever such a lovely straight back, Emily noticed, as she hurried Tommy into the church ahead of the marching men.

Well, things could not have worked out better for him if he had planned them that way, Charlie decided smugly as he sang lustily along with the rest of the congregation at the parish church of his in-laws-to-be.

The Wrighton-Budes had their own pew right at the front of the small Norman church, with soft kneeling pads embroidered by Daphne's mother and her late grandmother as a gift to the Church, whilst to the left of the pew the stained glass had been another family gift.

On the dark oak commemoration board on the opposite wall, the gilding of Daphne's brother, Eustace's, name was still bright and fresh. His was the last name to appear on the board, and the first so far from the current war.

In a month's time, on the first Saturday in June, Charlie and Daphne would be married here in this church.

His arrival in the village, thanks to a forty-eight-hour pass and the money to replace the sports car he had claimed as 'stolen' but which he had in fact sold to a young officer, had been greeted with tender concern by his loving fiancée, which had quickly turned to tearful delight at the news that she would continue to live with her parents after their marriage.

'To be honest, sir,' Charlie had lied charmingly to his father-in-law-to-be, 'although I know I have a duty to my father to take on the responsibility for his business so that he can retire – and of course there's nothing I want more than to be with Daphne – I felt that my duty to my country had to come first.'

'Quite so, dear boy,' had been Daphne's father's approving response as he clapped him on the back.

The service was over, and the congregation was free to stream out into the sunny warmth of the May morning.

'Charles is such a hero, Daddy,' Daphne enthused, as they walked homewards, tucking her arm through her fiancé's as she smiled happily up at him. 'He put his own life at risk to help that poor soldier by going to see him.'

Charlie was proud of the modest demeanour he managed to conjure up as he dismissed Daphne's praise with a small shrug.

'Of course, Mother is dreadfully disappointed that she won't be able to show you off to all her friends now that you're going to be staying here, Daffers,' Charles told his fiancée cheerfully.

'Oh dear, is she very cross?' Daphne asked him uncertainly.

But her mother was made of sterner stuff and said firmly, 'Don't be silly, Daphne. I am sure that Charles's mother understands that it is far more sensible for you to stay here at home with us. Now, Charles, about the wedding,' she continued briskly. 'I've written to your mother already explaining that in view of our own sad loss and the war, we really feel only close family should attend. I've spoken to the landlord at the Fox and Hounds and I'm sure your parents will be very comfortable there. We'd put them up here, of course, but what with my own sister and her girls – they are to be Daphne's bridesmaids, of course – and the rest of our family there simply wouldn't be room . . .'

'If I could just have a word, Bella . . .'

Bella frowned. She'd just come in from church and the last thing she felt like doing was listening to some complaint from her billetees, and she knew from Bettina's expression that it would be a complaint. Bettina always had plenty to say for herself, unlike her mother.

Bella wasn't in a very good mood. She'd had to walk back from church on her own as Laura had gone to see her family – again. Really, she was spending more time away from Wallasey these days than she was spending here.

To make matters worse Ralph Fleming had been in church with his wife and his children, smirking at her in that horrible way of his. He'd even had the cheek to come across to her when she was standing with her mother, putting his hand on her arm and acting like they were the best of friends. She could imagine what a field day all the nasty old cats of gossips would have been having if she hadn't pulled away from him and pointedly asked after his wife. But even that had only made him give her another of those knowing smiles. He couldn't possibly know about how lonely she felt sometimes at night and how she'd even imagined . . .

Quickly Bella checked her thoughts. What on earth was the matter with her? It must be all this rationing, putting strange thoughts into her head and even stranger urges into her body.

'Oh, very well, what is it?' she asked Bettina.

'Mother and I have found another billet. I'm not sure when we'll be moving out yet, but it shouldn't be very long. We'll be living with some Polish friends. I know you'll be pleased to have your house back to yourself again.'

Bella stared at her. 'But you can't leave now,' she protested, blurting out her panicky denial before she could stop herself. They couldn't leave. Not now. She'd be all on her own. No! That wasn't why she didn't want them to leave. It was because she wanted to keep her house.

Now it was Bettina's turn to frown.

'But you've wanted us to leave from the minute we arrived,' she pointed out.

Bella knew that this was true. But that had been before her father had told her that he was giving her house to Charlie. That would be impossible whilst the Polanskis were living here. They were refugees and not even her father could insist on them leaving, whether he was on the council or not.

'Well, yes,' Bella had to admit, 'but . . . but I've got used to you now,' she told her.

That was true too. She'd also got used to Maria's cooking and the way she ironed Bella's things and kept the house immaculate. She had even got used to the sound of them talking to one another in Polish and had in fact, although she hadn't said so, learned to recognise some of their words and understand a little of what they were saying.

Her panic grew. She couldn't let them leave.

'Are you sure that moving to a new billet is the right thing for your mother? I mean, with that weak chest of hers, some of these billets are very damp, so I've been told.'

'It is Jan who suggested that we move and who found us somewhere.'

Oh, it would be, Bella thought bitterly. Her whole body felt as though it was burning with the heat of her own shame. She hated being reminded of Jan and the way she had shown herself up so badly by letting him think that she wanted him. Of course she had not wanted him, not one little bit. She hated him, in fact.

'As I said, I don't know quite when we will be leaving,' Bettina repeated.

Bella sat down on one of her kitchen chairs. She was supposed to be going round to her mother's for her Sunday lunch but suddenly she didn't feel like doing so. Her mother would go on and on about the wedding and Daphne, and how wonderful Charlie was, Bella thought wrathfully, and she would be expected to smile and agree.

She didn't want to think about how empty the house was going to feel without Bettina and Maria. No more smells of strange Polish dishes cooking when she came in; no more Maria standing in the kitchen doing the ironing, making Bella cups of tea, fussing round her own daughter and, of course, her precious son when he came to visit.

She would be on her own. Completely alone.

What was the matter with her, Bella asked herself. Anyone would think she was afraid that she was going to miss them and that was ridiculous. No! She'd be glad to have her house to herself. Very glad.

SEVEN

'And what, might I ask, is this?'

Lena could feel the blood leaving her face as she stared at the battledress jacket her auntie was holding. How had she found it? Lena had hidden it away in her drawer under all her own clothes.

'Answer me, you little slut.'

Lena winced as the slap from her aunt's hard hand caught her off guard, jerking her head back and leaving her skin stinging. Shocked tears filled her eyes.

'Come on, who is he? And don't you go lying to me 'cos if you do then you uncle will knock the truth out of you,' Auntie Flo threatened.

Lena felt sick. Thank goodness she had thought to hide away Charlie's papers in her handbag, pulling back the lining to put them there along with her Post Office book before sewing the lining back.

'He was just a soldier wot was in the street the night the pub got hit,' she told her aunt. She couldn't risk telling Auntie Flo all about Charlie yet – not until he arrived to claim her and rescue her from the misery of her home life.

'Oh, yes, of course. And this soldier he just

117

happened to give you his jacket, did he? Don't give me that.' Her aunt had raised her hand again but this time Lena managed to dodge out of the way.

She'd been out for a bit of a walk on account of having felt a bit sickly when she'd woken up and she realised now that her aunt must have gone through her things whilst she'd been out.

'You've got bad blood in you – we all know that – aye, and we all know what it leads to as well. Well, I'm telling you now that I'm not having our Doris's chances spoiled by you bringing shame on her by doing what you shouldn't with some soldier. I knew I should never have taken you in. Your mother was bad enough, getting involved with that Eyetie, but you . . .'

Lena had had enough. She had her pride, after all. She lifted her chin. 'I haven't done anything any different than Doris's bin doing.'

'What?' Auntie Flo shrieked. 'My Doris's a decent girl, wot's got an engagement ring on her finger, and wot's getting married. You're nothing but a slut wot's bin rolling around wi' some soldier. What did he do?'

'Nothing,' Lena told her, trying to dodge out of the way when her aunt grabbed a handful of her hair.

'Don't you go telling me that, you lying hussy. I knew you was trouble right from the first. Mrs Hodson is right, you're a bad lot,' her aunt yelled as she banged Lena's head back so hard against the wall that the pain had Lena seeing stars.

Her aunt might have released her but she wasn't finished with her, Lena knew.

'You wait until I tell your uncle Alfred what you've bin doing. He'll have his strap to you and

118

no mistake, and you won't go telling him "nothing", I reckon.'

Now Lena was frightened. She'd been hit with the strap from her uncle's belt before and she knew what the pain was like. Desperate to protect herself she protested defiantly, 'I haven't done anything wrong. My Charlie loves me. He said so, and—'

'Don't give me that,' her auntie Flo interrupted contemptuously. 'No decent man would ever love summat like you. How much did he pay you?'

Lena was too shocked to answer.

Her aunt grabbed hold of her upper arms and shook her violently.

'I said, how much did he pay you? Have you gone deaf as well as being daft?'

Lena wasn't so naïve that she didn't know what her auntie meant. She might have her secret romantic dreams, but she still knew what was what.

'It wasn't like that,' she told her aunt. 'He loves me and I love him, and he's going to come here and take me away, and when he does he'll have something to say to you on account of what you've done to me.' She was crying now, deep gulping sobs of mingled shock and pain, caused by her aunt's cruelty, which shook her whole body as she pushed past Flo, snatching up her handbag from the table, as she ran out through the open back door, desperate to escape from her aunt's taunts and the threat of her uncle's belt.

Her desperation took her down the back alley that ran behind yards to the houses and their outside lavatories, and out into the road intersecting Bessie Street. She had run so fast that she was panting, sweat dampening the underarms of her Sunday best frock that she'd worn for church that morning. Already she could feel the skin over her cheekbone tightening where her face was swelling from her aunt's blow. Her head ached as well. She couldn't go back. She knew her uncle's temper. Her mother had once told her in a rare confidence that her sister's husband had half killed a man way back in a moment of temper, when they had all been young, and had only got away with it because no one had told on him.

She would have to write to Charlie now and ask him to come to take her away. He'd understand, of course, she knew that. After all, he loved her. He had said so. She'd have to stay somewhere, though, until he did come for her. Somewhere where he could find her. Maybe if she went round to Simone's she'd give her a bed for the night. The hairdresser lived only down the street from her salon, but then Lena remembered that Simone had said that she was going to Blackpool for the day with one of her many beaux. Simone had winked when she had announced that she might be staying the night. But then she was one of those women who could get away with that kind of behaviour somehow. Perhaps because she was the best hairdresser in the area and perfectly capable of making sure your hair was ruined for life if it suited her, Lena thought ruefully.

Down at the bottom of the road, beyond the flattened houses and then the warehouses of the dock area, the glint of the sun on the water momentarily caught her attention. Absently she watched the sun-gilded dancing waves, and then it came to her, and she knew exactly what she had to do. Relief poured through her. She would have to tidy herself up a bit

120

mind, but she could do that at the ferry terminal. It was a pity she couldn't change her clothes but at least she was wearing her best frock. Her auntie said that red wasn't a suitable colour to wear for church but Lena knew that red suited her and it was such a lovely colour that wearing it always made her feel happy. Thank heavens she had grabbed her handbag before she'd left.

Oooh, she couldn't wait now that she'd made up her mind. Her tummy was full of butterflies, but that was with excitement at the thought of meeting her Charlie's family. Her family an' all, they would be soon. Then her auntie would see how wrong she'd bin with all that nasty stuff she'd gone and said to her. Her lovely Charlie didn't think she'd got bad blood, not one little bit, he didn't. Tears burned the backs of her eyes.

It would have been different for her perhaps if her mam and dad hadn't taken against one another in the way that they had, both of them going on all the time about how they wished they had never got wed to one another. Her dad, being Italian, had been a bit of a one for raising his voice and waving his arms around when he and her mam were having 'words', and Lena had known from being very young that it was on account of her that they had had to get married and that neither of them had been pleased about that. It was from her father that she'd got her own looks, although he had always said she wasn't properly Italian and his family had refused to have anything to do with her and her mam. They'd wanted to see her dad married to some cousin of his and there'd been a real to-do when he had ended up having to marry her mam. Never forgiven her mam for that, her dad's family hadn't, so her dad had always said.

Fiercely Lena blinked away her threatening tears. She wasn't going to start crying, not for anyone. Her mam and dad were gone and she'd got to get on with her life as best she could. She'd certainly make sure that her Charlie knew how much she loved him and she'd make him proud of her too, that she would.

As she headed for the ferry terminal Lena drifted happily into one of her daydreams – a new one this time in which she was linking arms with her proud new mother-in-law, who was telling her tearfully how grateful she was to Lena for making her son such a wonderful loving wife, and how she couldn't have chosen better for him herself.

Such was the effect of this daydream that by the time she had reached the terminal Lena was well on the way to convincing herself that her auntie finding Charlie's battledress jacket was probably the best thing that could have happened. She was just in the middle of hearing Charlie's mam saying that Lena was better than any daughter could have been when her fantasy was rudely shattered by her seeing her reflection in the mirror in the ladies' washroom at the terminal.

My, but that bruise was a corker, and she'd got blood on the white collar of her frock as well from her cut lip.

Hurriedly Lena set about doing what she could to make herself look decent. Luckily she'd got her comb in her bag and a nice bright red lipstick.

They'd had their Sunday tea with Grace's family and now Seb and Grace were making their way back to the nurses' home, walking slowly hand in hand and savouring the late afternoon sunshine.

'I think that Katie and Luke must have had words again,' Grace told Seb with a small sigh. 'He's my brother and I love him, but I feel ever so sorry for Katie as well. I was talking to Mum about it in the kitchen and she says that Dad was a bit on the jealous side when they were courting.'

'They'll work it out, love,' Seb tried to reassure her, giving her hand a comforting squeeze.

'I hope so, Seb. I can't think of anyone I'd like for a sister-in-law more than Katie.'

Seb smiled but inwardly he couldn't help wondering if it was in part the eagerness of Luke's mother and sisters to make Katie a part of their family that was causing some of the trouble. Katie was the kind of girl who naturally wanted to please others, and Seb hoped that she wasn't being trapped into a relationship with Luke because she knew it was what his family wanted.

It was his and Grace's future in which he was more interested right now, though. He'd have liked to have found somewhere a bit more private and more pleasant to tell Grace his news than the bombed-out streets of her home city, but they would soon be within a couple of minutes of the nurses' home, and if they bumped into any of her friends also returning from a day off the opportunity for them to talk privately would be lost.

Drawing Grace closer to his side, Seb said quietly, 'There's something I need to tell you, some news I was given just before I left Derby House this morning.'

Grace knew immediately that despite his calm, almost casual manner what he had to tell her was important. She stopped walking and turned towards him, a small anxious frown creasing her forehead.

'What kind of news?'

Seb twined his fingers between hers and closed their joined hands into a soft fist.

'There's to be a new Y Section post opening, in Whitchurch, so not too far away, and I'm to be transferred to work there. It will mean a promotion.'

Grace was trying hard to smile and look pleased, but all she could think was that she would no longer have the comfort of knowing that no matter what happened Seb was only a few minutes away from her.

Knowing what she would be thinking, Seb checked that there was no one around to see them and then drew her into his arms, holding her tight.

'It will be all right, I promise,' he said gruffly. 'I know it's a bit of a shock. Took me a bit aback this morning when I was told, I can tell you. Of course it's an honour to be chosen, but all I could think was that you and I were going to be further apart than we've been used to. I'll be honest with you, Grace, if I'd thought I'd be allowed to turn the post down I would have done.'

'Oh, no, you couldn't have done that,' Grace protested just as he had known she would, her voice muffled by the protection of his body. 'Your work is very important, Seb, and like you've said yourself, it's an honour to be chosen for promotion. We are fighting a war, after all. It's just that I can't help feeling a bit upset. I'm going to miss you so much.'

He could feel the dampness of her tears seeping through his shirt.

'I felt the same,' he assured her, 'but it won't be

as bad as you think. There's a good railway service, I've checked already.'

Grace was trying to be brave and to remember that she ought to put her country first, but sometimes an hour was all they had, and she was used to being able to run down to Derby House or have Seb come up to the hospital whenever they could make the time, just to say 'hello' to one another.

Seb wished as he had never wished before that he wasn't sharing his room at his digs with another chap and that Mrs Morris, his landlady, was a bit more obliging. This was definitely one of those times when he felt the best way to reassure Grace would be in his arms and in private.

She really must not be such a baby, Grace warned herself. If she was like this at the news that Seb was moving a handful of miles away, what on earth would she be like if he were ever to be posted abroad? Suddenly she wished desperately that her training was over and that she was free to marry Seb without losing all that she had worked for, but it was only May and it would be well into the autumn before she completed her three-year training period.

As though he had been thinking the same thing, she heard Seb saying huskily to her, 'You know what I reckon we should do? I reckon we should think about setting a date for us to get married, the minute you've finished your training.'

'We did say that we'd wait until the war was over,' Grace felt bound to remind him.

'I know we said that, but I don't want to wait any longer than we have to. I want to make you mine, Gracie. I want that more than I can say.'

'It's what I want as well,' Grace admitted, and for

once she didn't object about someone seeing them when Seb pushed her gently back against the wall of the building they'd been standing next to and wrapped her in his arms to kiss her so passionately, that she ached for him with every single inch of her body.

'That's just a taste of how it's going to be for us,' Seb whispered thickly to her.

'If that's a promise—' Grace began, trying to sound light-hearted.

But Seb stopped her, smiling tenderly at her as he told her softly, 'No, it isn't a promise, Gracie, it's a vow; a vow of my love for you.'

'Oh, Seb,' she protested. 'Now look what you've made me do, and I was trying so hard not to cry.'

Luke's mood had lightened during the afternoon and now as they walked down to Sam's allotment to 'say good night' Katie could feel the weight lifting from her heart, leaving her feeling almost dizzy with grateful relief. She loved him so much, but sometimes he made her feel so dreadfully unhappy.

'I love you, Katie,' he told her, his voice unsteady and thick with love.

'And I love you too,' Katie answered him going into his arms. But even as she responded to his kiss, a small voice was niggling at her, asking her, 'But what if our love isn't enough, what then?'

'Mum?' Sasha began.

Jean looked up from her knitting. The four of them – her and Sam and the twins – were sitting in the back room listening to the wireless whilst they waited for Katie to come back in from saying good

126

night to Luke. Then Jean would make their evening cocoa.

'Me and Lou are going to see if we can get taken on at the telephone exchange.'

Jean looked at Sam, unable properly to conceal either her surprise or her relief.

'You'll be lucky if you get taken on there,' Sam warned.

'You've got to be sixteen,' Sasha agreed.

'And over five foot six inches,' Lou added, 'so that you can reach everything, and me and Sasha are just that, so that's all right.' She was trying desperately to pretend she was as pleased about the thought of becoming a telephonist as her twin, but it wasn't easy, and she hoped that Sasha wouldn't look at her and guess what she was really thinking.

'Well, you'll certainly be tall enough,' Jean acknowledged. At five foot seven each they were a good three inches taller than she was, and taller than Grace, who topped her by an inch. 'And you have good clear voices that people will be able to hear properly,' she conceded.

'All those songs we've practised; people need to hear the words, said Sasha, grinning.

It would be wonderful if they could get taken on at the Edge Lane exchange, Jean thought. If they did she'd have all her children close at hand.

EIGHT

Bella had just been on the point of leaving her parents'
house when they all heard the front doorbell ring.
She'd had enough of listening to her mother going
on and on about how shocked she'd been by Mrs
Wrighton-Bude's embargo on Charles's family
bringing any family members other than themselves
to the wedding, and had even pointed out sharply
to her mother that she didn't know why she was
making such a fuss about Auntie Jean and her family
not being invited when she'd said herself previously
that she was glad she wouldn't be able to go.

Bella had only come round because she'd hoped
to catch her father in a good mood, under the influence of his Sunday G and Ts. However, despite the
fact that he'd already downed four large ones instead
of his normal three, and had poured himself a fifth,
his mood if anything was even more sour than usual.
Bella had been hoping that with Charlie now definitely staying in the army and Daphne continuing to
live with her parents after the wedding, not only
would she get to keep her house but also she'd get
an increase in her allowance out of him.

Vi frowned as the doorbell pealed a second time.

No one came visiting on a Sunday evening. It simply wasn't done, at least not without an invitation and certainly not in Wallasey. She just hoped that that sewing woman who had been recommended to her did a good job of adding those new bunches of flowers to the hat she'd had for Bella's wedding. She hadn't intended to wear it again but seeing as no one she knew would be at Charles and Daphne's wedding it seemed a shame not to wear the lovely outfit she'd had for Bella's big day. And if it outshone Daphne's mother's outfit then that was just too bad, Vi thought grumpily as she opened the door.

'You're my Charlie's mam, aren't you? I'm Lena wot he's going to marry and I'm sorry to land up on you like this, but I'm in ever such a fix. I dare say he'll have told you all about me, and how I saved him when Bessie Street was bombed and how him and me are courtin' now.' As the words tumbled out one on top of another without her stopping to draw breath, Lena acknowledged that she hadn't intended things to be like this. All the way up here from the ferry – she'd walked because she'd been told it would only take her half an hour but it had been more like three-quarters, and her nice red shoes were all dusty now, and she was all hot and sweaty, as much with nerves as anything else – she'd been practising what she was going to say, only to have it all come out wrong and in a muddle on account of her being so nervous.

She'd known that Wallasey would be posh but she hadn't expected that her Charlie would live in a house as big as this one – with a car in the drive, an' all. Wallasey was nothing like the streets that Lena was used to with the houses in long rows and the pavements right outside the front door. All the houses she'd passed on the way up here had big front gardens and gates, there had been cars in the drives, and plenty of space around the houses even when there were two of them standing together.

She'd got that nervous that she'd walked up and down outside Charlie's mam and dad's house ten times and more whilst she tried to pluck up the courage to go and knock, telling herself that she was being plain daft to worry, since Charlie had told her that he loved her and she'd as good as saved his life, an' all.

For once in her life Vi was lost for words. She stared in horrified disbelief at the creature standing on her front doorstep. She was on the point of slamming the door in her face when she suddenly realised that the neighbours might see the dreadful common-looking girl, so instead she stepped back into the hall, allowing Lena to come inside, and then quickly closed the door.

'I'm reely sorry to dump meself on you like this, but I knew you'd understand, you being my Charlie's mam, and me and him being the way we are with one another,' Lena beamed in relief.

Hearing the unfamiliar voice and the strong Liverpool accent, Bella followed her mother out into the hallway, her eyes widening as she took in Lena's appearance.

Bright red lipstick, a too-tight red dress and red shoes said quite plainly exactly what Lena was, and yet for some reason the sight of the bruise on her face and the anxiety in her eyes caused Bella to feel an unexpected pang of sympathy.

'I don't know who you are or what you think you are doing here,' Vi began in a freezing voice as soon as she had got over her initial shock, 'but if you know my son – which I very much doubt—'

'Want do you mean?' Lena interrupted uncertainly. 'You are Charlie's mam, aren't you?'

Bella stepped forward. 'Yes she is, and I am his sister.'

'Bella . . .' Vi began angrily.

'Since Charlie's friend has come to see us, Mummy, the least we can do is offer her a cup of tea,' Bella told her mother, ignoring Vi's furious expression and earning herself a grateful look from Lena.

'Ooooh ta, yes, please. I'm fair parched. I haven't had so much as a bite since me auntie threw me out this afternoon.'

'Why don't you come through to the kitchen?'

'Bella,' Vi warned again, but Bella ignored her, merely wrinkling her nose discreetly as Lena advanced towards her, preceded by the strong smell of cheap scent. She had lovely hair though, Bella acknowledged.

'So you and Charlie are friends, are you?' she asked Lena as she took her into the kitchen and set about filling the kettle, a domestic task that Bella would normally have disdained, but she was irritated enough with both her parents to relish the prospect of listening to this artless young woman describing her exact relationship with her brother. Charlie's elevation to favourite child still rankled, as did the fact that he had stolen her jewellery.

'We're going to be married,' Lena confided happily. She'd been a bit worried when she'd first seen Charlie's mam, but his sister was friendly enough and a good-looker too.

'Of course, it's all happened a bit sudden like, but then that's what it's like when two people fall in love. I read that in *Fatal Passion* that was one of the library books I got for old Mrs Watson, who me auntie goes cleaning for. Well, she's supposed to do her cleaning, only more often than not she makes me do it.'

'So you and Charlie are engaged then?' Bella encouraged Lena as she poured the now boiled water on the tea leaves, then opened the cupboard to remove the tin that held her mother's black market Garibaldi biscuits.

Lena's eyes gleamed when she was offered the biscuits. This was a bit more like it. But she hadn't forgotten her mother's training and she nibbled daintily on her biscuit and then crooked her little finger when she lifted the china cup to her lips.

Bella was struggling not to laugh out aloud. This girl really was priceless.

'Oh, yes,' Lena confirmed. 'We plighted our troth the night Bessie Street got bombed and I rescued Charlie. Lying in the street, he was, where Dougie Richards's men had left him after they'd beaten him up. It's lucky for my Charlie that Dougie and his men got killed when the pub was bombed. A real nasty lot, they were, and no mistake. Told me he owed them some money, Charlie did.

'Anyway I managed to get him into me auntie's – they'd all gone down to the shelter, but I hadn't bothered. Meant to be, it was, you see – me and your Charlie,' she informed Vi before biting into a second biscuit, then saying, 'Oh, pardon me,' when her stomach suddenly rumbled loudly. 'At least it's not as loud as me uncle's farts.'

Bella didn't dare look at her mother, in case she

did burst out laughing. The passing of wind was something that did not exist in the Firth household. Edwin and Charlie were under permanent instructions to go to the back door if the need arose, and, of course, well-brought-up women did not have 'wind'.

Sitting in her Charlie's mam's lovely warm kitchen, and with the sympathetic audience of his sister, Lena's confidence was returning and with it her normal exuberant happiness.

'Of course, I would have stayed at me auntie's and waited for Charlie to bring me to meet you himself, like, but then me auntie found his battledress jacket, and she fired up, wanting to know what was going on and saying all sorts about me and him that just wasn't true. She's never liked me on account of me dad being an Eyetie. Said she'd get me uncle to take his belt to me, and she meant it an' all.'

Now Bella frowned. Having had a physically violent husband herself she couldn't help but understand how afraid Lena must have been, for all her insouciant air of confidence now.

Bella wasn't as a general rule interested in or concerned about the way other members of her sex lived. If she made friends with another woman it was because it suited her to do so and she had some particular purpose in forming the friendship so it came as a shock to her to recognise that the unfamiliar emotions she was experiencing were sympathy for this young girl.

Listening to Lena it had suddenly come to Bella that there were two distinctly different kinds of women and that the line that divided them had nothing whatsoever to do with family background, or even good looks. Girls and young women like her cousin Grace, like Daphne, and like the loathsome Trixie Mayhew whom her own husband had loved when he should have loved her, all belonged on one side of that line, the safe, respectable side, which meant that men married them. But she – and Lena, with her common-looking, too-tight dress and too-bright lipstick – were on the opposite side of that line, which meant that men cheated on them and used them. It was a sobering thought.

Bella wasn't used to having such deep and uncomfortable thoughts, but then she recognised she was thinking a lot of things these days that had simply never occurred to her before. And thinking itself was new to her.

'Well, really,' Vi cut across Lena's confidence, 'I've heard quite enough of this nonsense. It's disgraceful what some people will do. Bella, call your father, will you? It's obvious that this . . . this person is making the whole thing up. There's no way Charles would ever become involved with someone like her, even if he wasn't already engaged to darling Daphne.'

On the contrary, Bella thought to herself, Lena was exactly the type of girl that would appeal to Charlie – for a bit of fun, though, and not marriage.

Whatever her mother might choose to think, Bella did not believe for one moment that Lena was a hardened little tart who had come round intending to threaten Charlie's family into paying her some money, nor to make trouble. No, Bella thought almost protectively, the poor girl genuinely loved him, just as she herself might have loved Ralph Fleming if she hadn't found out the truth about him in time. It was worse for Lena, of course, because she obviously

134

believed that Charlie had promised to marry her. Bella could guess what Lena had given Charlie in return for that promise.

Lena was oblivious to Bella's sympathy. Her stomach was a mass of churning, furious indignation. She knew what Charlie's mam was up to.

She stood up, her anger heating her face, as she challenged Vi fiercely, 'You're my Charlie's mam, and I don't like to be disrespectful but don't think I don't know what you're after doing, lying to me like you have and saying that my Charlie is engaged to someone else when I know that he isn't. I'm not that daft,' she told Vi scornfully. 'He told me himself that he loved me and that it's me he wants to wed, and he wouldn't have said that if he was already engaged to someone else. And he wouldn't have done what he did neither. As good as married already, we are,' she told Vi proudly, lifting her chin. 'And you should be ashamed of yourself, making out that your own son is a liar.'

Vi was outraged. How dare this . . . this creature, in her common-looking clothes virtually push her way into Vi's home, and then start accusing her of lying. It was only because she was the decent person she was that she wasn't already telling Bella to telephone the police, Vi decided, ignoring the fact that the unpalatable ring of truth about the girl's description of how she had come to meet Charlie, and her own knowledge of her son's nature, made it more than likely that he had somehow got himself involved with this dreadful girl. No matter what he had told this Lena, Vi refused to believe that he had actually wanted to marry her. However, it was just as well that he wasn't here. Dealing with the wretched girl was better left to her and Edwin. Vi shuddered to think of how dreadful it would be if Daphne or, even worse, her parents were to somehow get wind of this common creature, especially before the wedding. How on earth would she be able to face her neighbours and her colleagues in the WVS? No, the girl had to be got rid of.

'Bella,' she instructed her daughter, 'go and bring that photograph Daddy had framed of Daphne and Charles when they got engaged.'

Lena had been confident that nothing could make her believe that her Charlie was engaged to someone else, but the photograph his sister was holding out to her made the blood drain from her face and her heart drop like a stone.

'Well, now?' Vi demanded triumphantly. 'What have you to say to that?'

'There's no need to rub it in, Mummy,' Bella protested quietly.

Vi gave her an angry look. Really, Bella was so difficult these days, always setting herself against everything that Vi said or did. Vi didn't know what she had done to deserve such an ungrateful daughter. When she thought of the money she and Edwin had lavished on Bella, and the chances she had had . . .

Even though she could see the evidence of Charlie's engagement to someone else with her own eyes, Lena still shook her head, protesting shakily, 'No! He can't be engaged to someone else. It's me he's going to marry and me he loves. He said so, and he's not the sort as would say summat like that if he didn't mean it.'

Poor Lena, Bella thought wryly, Charlie was exactly the sort that would do exactly that. She obviously didn't know him very well.

Vi had had enough time now to recover from her initial shock. She might put on airs and graces now and act as though she'd never lived anywhere but Wallasey, but Vi had grown up not a million miles away from Bessie Street and in a very similar, if much cleaner and more loving home to Lena's and she knew instinctively that what the dreadful girl had said about the way she had met Charlie was the truth.

Not that she was going to let her know that. There was no way Vi was going to let anything stand in the way of Charles's marriage to Daphne.

'Bella, get your father, will you?' she instructed. 'He's the one to sort this out.'

Edwin Firth wasn't in the mood for dealing with one of his wife's outbursts. He'd got more than enough on his plate as it was. One look at the girl in the kitchen, though, as he listened to Vi's angry explanation of what she was doing there, told him that he had to do something. If he didn't, and the ruddy Wrighton-Budes cancelled the wedding and refused to let Daphne marry Charles, then he'd have his son coming back home when he was on leave, and then Vi would be nagging him to take Charles down to the office with him, and then . . . Edwin glowered as he looked at Lena. A bloody fool, that was what Charles was – always had been and always would be.

'Now you listen to me, you little tart,' he told Lena angrily. 'We all know what you've come here for and you aren't going to get it. I don't care how many times my son took you to bed, he isn't going to marry you, and if you think I'm going to pay you to take yourself off then you can think again.

137

One word from you about my son, and I'll have you up before the magistrates for soliciting, and that's a promise.'

Lena couldn't speak or move. Her heart was thudding so heavily that she could hear the sound of the beats. She felt frightened and angry too.

'You don't understand,' she told Edwin. 'I love Charlie and . . .'

Against her will, and against her own best interests as well, Bella discovered that she felt pity – and it had to be pity and not a sense of fellow feeling, of course – for Lena. So much so that uncharacteristically she reached out and touched Lena's arm warning her, 'I'm sorry but it's true. Like my mother said, my brother is engaged to someone else and in fact they are getting married very soon. When he told you he loved you and wanted to marry you, he lied to you.'

'No!' Lena protested. 'No, he wouldn't do that. He said he loved me and he meant it.' Her head was pounding and she felt sick. It couldn't be true and yet when she looked at Charlie's sister, something in her face told Lena that it *was* true and that Charlie had lied to her and that he was going to marry someone else. The pain was like no other pain she had ever known. Lena didn't have the words to describe it but she knew that when she read in Mrs Watson's library books that the heroine's heart was breaking she now knew exactly what that felt like.

She was trembling, sick with shock and anguish and disbelief.

Vi was opening the kitchen door with a dramatic flourish, insisting, 'Now I'll thank you to leave and take yourself off to wherever it was you came from.'

'Aye, and don't go spreading any rumours about my son, because if you do it will be the worse for you, I promise you that,' Edwin added brutally.

'You'd better go,' Bella told her quietly.

Distraught, Lena admitted, 'I haven't got anywhere to go to. Me auntie won't have me back.' She scarcely knew what she was saying, she was in such a state of shock.

'You could try one of the rest centres,' Bella suggested practically. 'They'll give you a hot drink and somewhere to sleep for the night, perhaps sort out some proper accommodation for you.'

'For goodness' sake, Bella, stop encouraging her,' said Vi sharply. 'It's plain what she is. The cheek of it, coming here and telling her lies about Charles. Thank heavens poor Daphne wasn't here to have to listen to them. Not that she would ever have doubted Chrles for one moment. He adores her and she knows that.'

Now Lena's spirit was breaking along with her heart. She had been taken for a fool, just like her mother had always warned her not to be. She stumbled towards the door. Watching her, Bella reached for her handbag, and removed her purse.

Immediately Lena stiffened, her pride returning. She shook her head, her face bright red.

'No!' she told Bella fiercely. 'I don't want your money. I don't want anything from any of you. You make out that you're better than me but at least I'm not a liar. I feel sorry for her, I really do,' she told Vi, nodding in the direction of the engagement photograph. ''Cos if he's been sweet-talking me behind her back before they're married then what's he going to be like afterwards?'

139

'I've warned you about speaking out of turn about my son,' Edwin reminded Lena threateningly.

She paused in the doorway. Now that she looked at him properly she could see that he wasn't very different from her uncle, and that he had the same mean nasty look in his eyes, for all his smart clothes and his posh way of speaking.

She was glad to be getting away from them, Lena told herself as she walked shakily towards the front gate and then opened it. The tears she wasn't going to let herself cry made the scene in front of her shimmer. She was in a real mess now and no mistake. Even if her auntie let her back in the house she'd never stop going on at her, and once the likes of Mrs Hodson got to know what she'd done with Charlie it wouldn't just be Eyetie that everyone would be calling her, Lena acknowledged as she set off on foot on her return journey to the ferry and Liverpool.

'Well, really, Edwin, I'm surprised you didn't call the police and have her taken in to custody,' Vi announced sharply as soon as Lena had gone.

'For what?' Bella challenged her mother. 'Being lied to by Charlie?'

'We've only got her word for what happened,' Vi insisted. 'It was obvious that she was making the whole thing up. Disgraceful that a woman of that type would dare to come knocking on our door.'

'She wasn't a woman, Mummy, she was just a girl,' Bella felt bound to point out.

'I don't understand you, Bella, or why you are choosing to sympathise with her, never mind trying to offer her money. A very odd sort of way for a daughter and sister to behave.'

'I felt sorry for her, that's all,' Bella defended herself.

'It's your poor brother you should feel sorry for,' Vi told her tartly. 'Edwin—'

'Oh, leave it alone, will you, Vi?' Edwin stopped her angrily. 'Nag nag nag, that's all you ever do.'

'Well, really!' Vi objected.

'I've got work to do. I'm going down to the office,' Edwin announced.

'On a Sunday? You never go to the office on a Sunday.'

'Well, I am now,' Edwin told her, ignoring Vi's angry protest.

Lena had stopped crying by the time she had reached the ferry terminal, or rather she had no more tears left to cry. It couldn't be true what she had been told but she knew that it was. Charlie, her Charlie, was marrying someone else. He'd never loved her at all.

NINE

The ferry had been full, and Lena let the crowd of people getting off it carry her with them. Where was there for her to go, after all? Her stomach ached but not with hunger; it was a different sort of pain that gnawed away inside her. In front of her in the crowd she could see a young couple, the lad holding his girl protectively close so that she didn't get pushed and shoved by the crowd, warning off another lad who came too close to her, whilst she clung to her lad's arm. To one side of Lena was a small family, a young girl with her parents, each of them holding one of her hands. Why was it that other people were loved and she was not, Lena wondered miserably.

She was different from other girls, Lena knew that. She was looked down on, despised by her mother's family and her aunt's neighbours because she didn't look like their daughters, with their thin mousy hair and their pale skin. But she was also shunned by the Italian community whose daughters were always carefully chaperoned, their marriages arranged for them by their families. Lena had seen the looks she was given by Italian men and women when they saw her. The men eyed her boldly and said things to her in

Italian that she didn't understand whilst the women glared angrily at her.

'See, even your own sort don't want to know you 'cos they can see that you're a little tart, and fit for only one thing,' Doris had taunted her during one of their quarrels. 'Bad blood, that's what you've got. You want to take yourself off down the dock road. That's the right place for your kind, my mam says. An' I'm telling you now, it won't be a ring and marriage lines that you'll be offered. Your sort never are.'

She hadn't paid much attention then because she hadn't really cared what Doris thought about her, but tonight in Charlie's mother's eyes she had seen the same contempt, and felt the same awareness that she wasn't 'acceptable' or 'right', and she had cared.

A man pushing past her paused to look again, staring deliberately at her chest.

Lena turned quickly away from him, a sudden spurt of indignation overriding her wretchedness. She was wearing her best frock, after all. That had been a nice frock his sister had been wearing, even though the colour had been a bit dull for Lena's taste. She hadn't reckoned much to that twinset Charlie's girl had had on in that photograph, though. Proper plain, it had looked, and her too. Lena had seen women dressed like that on Bold Street and in Lewis's. Ladies, her mother had called them, before saying warningly to Lena, 'And a lady's something you'll never be, not with that bad blood of yours and them Eyetie looks.' Her mother would have said that Charlie's girl was a 'lady', Lena knew that instinctively. That knowledge brought fresh pain stabbing into her.

The sun was setting. Caught up in her own

thoughts she had let the crowd of people leaving the ferry carry her along with it, but now it was thinning out, as people headed for their homes and their families. Soon she would be alone. Panic and despair swamped her with bleak misery. A tear rolled down her face, which she rubbed away. She couldn't go back, not now, knowing that Charlie had just been making a fool of her. Her aunt would love knowing that, and it wouldn't be long before the whole street knew as well.

She was in the centre of the city now, the empty spaces where there had been buildings making everywhere seem alien. People were leaving the cinemas, having taken advantage of the city's decision to allow them to open despite the fact that it was Sunday. Pity she hadn't thought to go to see a film herself; if she had she'd still be thinking that Charlie loved her.

Lena frowned, remembering what Charlie's sister had said to her about spending the night in a rest centre. She didn't want to but she didn't have any choice really, did she? There was an ARP post at the end of the street. Reluctantly she walked towards it, tensing when the ARP warden standing outside it drinking a mug of tea looked her up and down and then asked, 'And what can I do for you, my lovely?'

'I was wondering where the nearest rest centre is,' Lena answered him. The way he was looking at her made her want to tug up her dress neckline and pull down the hem of her skirt.

'Well, if it's a bed you was wanting for the night—' he began, and then stopped as an older man emerged from the ARP post, and asked, 'What's going on, Reg?' then grimaced when he saw Lena.

Lena could feel her face burning.

'I was just asking where the nearest rest centre is,' she repeated before the first man could say anything, deliberately lifting her chin and confronting them both.

'Straight up here, love, then turn right and it's on your left,' the older man told her in a more friendly manner. 'But you'll be lucky if they've got room for you, seeing as how many they've had to take in.'

Thanking him, Lena set off in the direction he'd told her.

It didn't take her long to reach the centre but her heart sank when she saw how many people were queuing up outside to get in.

Within a few seconds of her joining the queue an elderly woman arrived to stand behind her. Lena tried not to stare as the woman gave her a beaming smile but it was hard not to do so, because the woman was wearing what looked like a blanket in which she had cut a hole for her head, over what looked like a man's shirt. On her legs she was wearing a pair of red, yellow and green striped knitted socks, one of which had fallen down to wrinkle round her ankle, whilst on her feet she had a pair of white court shoes. Although the woman's body was heavy-looking and round, her legs looked thin and spindly, which no doubt was why her sock has fallen down, Lena guessed, as she tried not to stare at the incongruous pairing of the striped socks and the white shoes. On her head was what looked to Lena rather like a tea cosy, but which she assumed must be a knitted hat – in pink with yellow knitted flowers stitched to it.

'On your own, are you, duck?' she asked Lena,

puffing a bit as she put down the large wicker basket she had been carrying.

Lena nodded. Three up from her in the queue two young boys had seen the elderly woman and were nudging one another and giggling. Lena was torn between feeling sorry for the old lady and wanting to protect her from their laughter, and wanting to distance herself from her in case anyone thought they were together. The woman, though, seemed oblivious to the odd sight she made.

'Bombed out, I dare say?' she asked Lena sympathetically, confiding without waiting for Lena's reply, 'Three times it's happened to me now. Our Gavin says I've more lives than a ruddy cat.' She gave a deep belly laugh, causing her plump jowls to wobble. 'He should talk. You want to get yourself one of these blankets,' she advised Lena in a confidential whisper. 'Come in ever so handy, mine has. Of course, you're supposed to hand them in in the morning but seeing as I were blown out of me bed in me nothings, I ain't going to be parting with mine any time soon.'

Poor woman, she was obviously having to wear whatever she had been given to replace her own clothes.

'Luckily, though, I had me bedsocks on.' Lena's new companion looked down admiringly at her striped legs. 'Knitted these meself, I did. I like a bit of colour. Cheers a person up, it does, and no mistake. Hoping to spend the night here, was you?'

Lena nodded.

'Well, you'll be lucky if you can get a bed here, love. Turning folk away every night, they've bin.'

Lena tried not to show how desperate she was beginning to feel.

'I've heard that some people are sleeping in the air-raid shelters,' she ventured.

'Aye, but all the beds are gone there as well, and I've heard there's bin some nasty fights broken out over folk trying to take over other folks' beds. If you really haven't got anywhere to go, you can always come with me.' She offered with a wide smile. 'I'm only queuing here 'cos I want a blanket, and a decent cup of tea. Give you ever such a nice cup of tea here, they do, and two biscuits, an' all. Our Gavin laughs at me. But like I told him, he doesn't have to come wi' me if he doesn't want. And it's his loss, an' all. I hope they get a move on, only our Gavin will go mad it if I'm late for the buses they put on for us. He's gone up already to save us a seat. Found us ever such a nice place, our Gavin has, in a lovely warm barn. Of course, you've got to be a bit careful, like. Most of the other trekkers are decent sorts, but then there's some as aren't.'

'Trekkers?' Lena asked her, confused.

The woman laughed. 'That's what they've started calling us on account of us trekking out into the country to sleep at night. Sleeping rough, some folk call it, but it's all right for them as can afford to turn up their noses; some of us don't have any other choice.'

Sleep rough in the country! Lena shivered. She was a townie and from what she'd heard about the country she didn't think it was somewhere she'd like.

'Looks like we're getting in at last. Stick wi' me, love. I'll mek sure they give you a decent blanket. Know me here now, they do. Allus give me a nice cup of tea, and let me tek the weight off me legs. I've got a bit of rheumatism in them and they don't

147

half give me some gyp at times. Here we are,' she announced as they reached the desks where the WVS volunteers were seated. 'We'll get your blanket and then you and me—'

Lena was getting desperate. The last thing she wanted to do was spend the night in the country, but neither did she want to offend the old lady who was, after all, only trying to be kind, despite her comical appearance.

'You're very kind,' she managed to interrupt her. 'Only, I've sort of been promised a bed here.' It was a lie, of course.

'Oh, well, suit yourself,' the old lady told her good-naturedly, turning away from Lena to be swallowed up by the crowd of people inside the rest centre.

Rest centre – there would be precious little rest for anyone in here with so many people and so much noise, Lena thought tiredly. At least talking to the old lady had taken her mind off her own problems for a few minutes. Poor thing.

Lena felt dazed with a mixture of misery and tiredness. Was it really true that people were going out to the country every night simply to sleep? She just hoped that the WVS would be able to find her a bed. She'd sleep anywhere. She could feel threatening tears burning the backs of her eyes. Everything should have been so different. When she had left her auntie's she had pictured herself being welcomed by Charlie's family, and being fussed over by his grateful mother once she knew that Lena had saved his life. She had thought that she would be spending the night tucked up in a comfy bed in a posh house in Wallasey, knowing that Charlie's family were going to look after her until Charlie came home to claim her and put a ring on her finger.

Lena caught back a small hiccuped sob. Well, Charlie would be putting a ring on someone's finger but it wouldn't be hers, and his parents had made it plain that they would never welcome her into their home nor into Charlie's life.

'It's your turn next, dearie.'

Lena gave the woman behind her who had nudged her a wan smile as she hurried over to where the WVS volunteer was seated behind a table, waiting.

The woman dealing with her looked harassed, her tired professional smile quickly replaced by a frown as she listened to Lena explaining that she had nowhere to spend the night.

'So you're homeless, are you?' she queried.

'Yes, yes, that's right.' Lena confirmed.

It was the truth, after all, although she knew her face was firing up with guilty colour when the woman asked, 'Bombed out?'

Lena nodded as though that was the truth.

'And on your own without any papers or your ration book?'

Again Lena nodded.

The WVS volunteer sighed. 'We've got strict orders to give priority to mothers and young children, and we're struggling to make room for them. I'm really sorry, dear, but we just haven't got room for you here.'

'I don't mind sleeping on the floor,' Lena told her, beginning to panic. If she couldn't stay here then what on earth was she going to do? Even if she could bring herself to go back to her auntie's she suspected that she wouldn't be allowed back in.

'I wish I could help you, dear, but really I can't, and it's the same with all the other city rest centres.' The woman paused and then offered, 'The only thing I can suggest is that you join the trekkers.' She looked at her watch. 'Officially it's not allowed but with so many people homeless the corporation's not only turning a blind eye, it's also laying on transport to take people out of the city and into the country. You can come back here in the morning and get all your paperwork sorted out and a temporary ration book issued. In the meantime the best I can do is give you a blanket.'

'This trekking,' Lena stopped her anxiously, 'is it safe? Only I've never been to the country.'

The WVS woman's expression softened. 'It's perfectly safe,' she assured Lena, 'as long as you stick with everyone else. If I were you I'd look for a decent family to keep company with. Here's your blanket,' she added more briskly, reaching behind her and handing Lena a washed-out blanket so thin it felt more like a sheet, before warning her, 'You'd better cut along pretty sharpish now, dear, otherwise you'll miss the transport and end up having to walk.'

'Well, look who it isn't.'

Lena's heart jerked with a mixture of guilt and dismay when she recognised her companion from earlier in the evening. With so many people milling around the area where trucks and buses had been laid on to take the homeless out of the city, it seemed unfair that she should have been spotted so swiftly by someone she would have preferred to avoid, and for a second she was tempted to turn away and pretend that she hadn't seen or heard the other

150

woman, but it was already too late and she was bearing down on her, beaming from ear to ear.

'So you decided to tek me advice after all, did you, lass? Give you a decent blanket, did they?' She reached out, rubbing the thin fabric between her thumb and her finger, and then snorting with derision. 'Call that a blanket? It's no more than a bit of bare-arsed rag. Just as well it's a warm evening.'

She put her hand on Lena's arm, holding on to her as she turned away to shout into the crowd, ''Ere, our Gavin, I've found that lass I was telling you about. She's decided to come along wi' us after all. You stick with me and our Gavin – we'll see you right,' she told Lena.

It was mean of her to feel so uncomfortably conscious of the picture the poor woman made, especially when she was trying to be so kind. She was in fact the only person, apart from Charlie's sister, who had shown her any kindness, Lena reminded herself.

'What's your name then, lass? Mine's Dolly. Daft Dolly, some call me.' She laughed, her whole body shaking with amusement. 'But it's them what's daft, not me.'

'Lena,' Lena told her automatically, and then wished that she had thought to make up a different name for herself. Not that it was likely that anyone was going to come searching for her, especially not here. She gazed round at the stream of people filling up the transport, both relieved and slightly shocked to realise how ordinary they looked. Somehow she had expected them all to be as colourful as Dolly, and even slightly disreputable-looking, but instead they appeared just like anyone she might have seen in the city going about their ordinary business.

There were families huddling together, and then larger groups of people who all seemed to know one another and who were laughing and joking together.

Nudging her, Dolly said, 'See that lot over there just getting in that truck? The Hinford lot, they call themselves 'cos they allus head out for Hinford. That's how it's got now for all of us: we've all got our own villages what we go to. Our Gavin's found us ever such a nice one. Proper pretty, it is, wi' a farmer who lets us sleep in one of his barns.'

'Come on, Gran, otherwise we'll be going without you.' The male voice was teasing.

'Giveover, our Gavin. You'd never go off and leave me behind.'

So the Gavin to whom Dolly had been referring wasn't her husband but her grandson. Disinterestedly Lena looked at him. Just over medium height and solidly built, he had a shock of thick wavy brownish-fair hair that needed cutting and fell down over his forehead into his eyes.

Lena frowned. A well-set-up lad like him ought to have been in uniform.

'Lena here is coming wi' us, Gavin,' Dolly informed her grandson determinedly. 'Homeless, she is, and on her own.'

'I dunno, Gran. You're a one for picking up waifs and strays, you are, and no mistake. Well, I dare say we can make room for her.' The grin that accompanied his words might have been intended to take the sting from them but Lena wasn't in any mood to be placated after everything she had already been through.

Instead she bridled and told him coldly, 'There's no need to go putting yourself out on my account.'

'Tek no notice of our Gavin, Lena,' Dolly laughed. 'He's just pulling your leg. Allus liked a joke, he has. I hope you've saved me a comfortable seat on one of them buses, Gavin, 'cos I'm not travelling in one of them lorries again. Bruised me old arse black and blue, it did.'

'What, with all that padding you've got? Where's your stuff?' he asked Lena, bending down to pick up the basket his grandmother had been carrying.

'Lost everything, she has, poor little soul,' Dolly answered for Lena.

'Still got her temper, though, Gran. Now come on.'

Somehow, without having any intention of going with them, Lena found that she was being bundled onto one of the buses, Dolly's basket thrust unceremoniously into her arms whilst Gavin helped his grandmother onto the bus. There was no seat for Lena and she was almost jerked off her feet when the bus pulled off, making her fall heavily against Dolly's grandson.

'Ooh, looks like Lena's falling for you, Gavin,' Dolly cackled. 'You'd better tell her about that girl of yours wot your mam's allus going on about.'

'Go on with you, you're just jealous 'cos I said that her mum was a good cook.' There was genuine love for his grandmother in Gavin's voice as well as laughter.

'Tek no notice of him, Lena,' Dolly warned. 'Allus trying to wind me up, he is.'

She turned round and looked down the bus, calling out, 'Come on, we're on a chara so let's have a singsong!'

Vi lay in bed unable to sleep. She'd gone to bed far too early but she'd been bored sitting downstairs all on her own. She put her hand on her chest to try to ease the uncomfortable feeling that her heart was beating too fast and unsteadily, which she got so often these days. The other side of the bed was empty. Edwin still hadn't returned from his office. It was shameful the way the Government was making him work so hard and such long hours. Vi blamed that useless young woman he'd been forced to take on.

Her heart was jerking all over the place. It was entirely that dreadful creature's fault, of course. And if females of her type weren't something that no respectable woman would ever refer to she'd have had something to say to Charles the next time she saw him. Of course, it was obvious that the girl had been the one to instigate things, taking advantage of Charles in the way that her kind did. She'd taken one look at Charles and known she was on to a good thing. The gall of her, coming up here in the way that she had. They could have been entertaining one of Edwin's fellow councillors, or she could have had some of her WVS friends round. She just hoped that Muriel from next door hadn't seen her. She was a dreadful gossip and Vi wouldn't have put up with her if it wasn't for the fact that she had such good contacts for getting 'things'.

It was a relief really that she wouldn't be able to invite Jean and her family to the wedding. They'd have stuck out like sore thumbs and shown her up. She was going to have to talk to Bella as well, and point out to her that this could be a chance for her to meet someone and find herself a much better second husband than her first one had been. After all, Edwin couldn't be expected to support her for ever.

It was well gone ten o'clock. Edwin wouldn't come back in now. At least he had a decent bed in his office so that he could snatch a bit of sleep in between doing all this paperwork the War Office kept on demanding. He should take on a proper clerk and get rid of that young woman. She was giving herself far too many airs and graces. Vi hadn't liked the way she'd looked at her when she'd seen her the other day, not one little bit. Smirking like a cat that had got the cream, she'd been, and well she might with Edwin paying her what he was. There now, her heart was jumping all over the place again . . .

Seb was being transferred to Whitchurch. Of course she mustn't be silly and make a fuss about it, but even so, she couldn't help wishing that he was staying here in Liverpool, Grace admitted. It wouldn't change things between them, of course – how could it? – and she was pleased for him getting his promotion. But even so . . .

Lou lay in bed wide awake, staring up at the ceiling. She knew that Sasha was asleep; she could tell from the sound of her breathing. She wanted to reach out and wake her twin so that she could beg her to reassure her that things weren't changing, that *they* themselves weren't changing, but she knew that they were.

She didn't want to become a telephonist. She wanted to do something exciting. She wanted . . . She didn't know what she wanted, Lou admitted, only that what was happening was something she did not want. She couldn't tell Sasha that, though. She would be upset. How had it happened that she was keeping secrets from her twin when they had

155

always shared everything, always known everything there was to know about one another?

Did Sash keep secrets from her? Like really being sweet on Kieran Mallory? A sharp pang of pain pierced her. It was only because of her and Sash, that was all. Nothing more. It was not because of Kieran. Not one little bit.

Lena stared around in disbelief.

'You mean we've got to sleep here?' she demanded, waving her hand in the direction of the gloomy interior of the vast and, to her, alien and even slightly intimidating barn, with its dark corners and its hayloft and its country smells that struck so sharply against her town nose. Several bales of straw were laid out on the stone-flagged floor of the barn itself, obviously intended to be used as 'beds'.

'Well, you can always sleep out in one of the fields if you want to,' Gavin told her cheerfully. 'Although you'll have to watch out for the cows. Not too keen on townies, they aren't.'

Cows! Lena shuddered. She had seen some of the huge strange-looking creatures as the bus had driven them into the first village where most of the trekkers had got off, leaving only a third or so of the bus full for the second stop in the village they'd just left to walk up a track that that been alternately muddy or so sharp-stoned that Lena had worried that the stones would cut right through the soles of her shoes, in the growing dusk. How on earth Dolly, in her white high heels, had managed the walk Lena did not know, although of course Dolly had had her grandson to help her. Lena would never have come with them if she'd know what they were coming to, or that it would just be the three of them.

'Nothing quite like sleeping out under a hedge, especially when you've had a bit of nice fat roasted hedgehog for your supper,' Dolly announced, smacking her lips. 'Allus said there was nowt like an hedgehog, my granddad did.'

'Gran's grandparents were Romany folk,' Gavin explained calmly to Lena.

'Aye, they were, and I'm not ashamed to say so neither – not like that mother of yours,' Dolly told her grandson roundly.

Lena's eyes had rounded as she listened to their exchange. She'd seen the Romany women coming round selling heather and pegs, and now as she looked at Dolly she realised that she did bear a passing resemblance to them. Thieves and worse, her mum and her auntie had called them, but they'd been scared of them as well on account of their curses and their ability to read folk's futures in the tea leaves.

'If my mam hadn't married me dad then I'd have grown up a Romany meself,' Dolly was saying sorrowfully. 'I were lucky that her mam and dad had owt to do wi' us 'cos there's many a Romany family turn their backs on them of their own that marries out.'

Whilst Dolly was speaking, her grandson was busying himself lighting several lanterns and hanging them on nails, obviously put there for that purpose, in the wooden beams.

'There's no smoking allowed in here,' he warned Lena. 'We don't want to set the place on fire, do we, Gran, otherwise we'd be the ones that would end up roasted.'

Whilst Lena shuddered again, Dolly laughed.

'You'll have to make sure that you cover the straw with your blanket,' Gavin told Lena, 'otherwise, you'll be scratched to death.'

When Lena looked fearfully at the nearest bale as though it was alive with vermin, Dolly grinned and told her, 'He means that the straw will chaff you, love. Gavin, go up the farmhouse and use them good looks of yours to some purpose and get us all a mug of tea from the farmer's daughter.'

As he turned to leave she called after him, 'And don't spend half the night there wi' her neither. We don't want to come back tomorrow and have her dad coming after you with his gun.'

As soon as he had gone Dolly turned to Lena and said proudly, 'Not that I'd blame her if she did take a fancy to him 'cos he's a fine-looking lad and good with his head as well as with his hands.'

'I'm surprised he isn't in uniform,' Lena told her, unable to stop herself from making the comment. There was something about the way Dolly's grandson looked at her that made her bristle defensively. It wasn't so much that his face said she wasn't good enough for him, it was more as though somehow he felt sorry for her. Well, Lena didn't want anyone's pity.

'Course he's in uniform. He's training to be a pilot on one of them boats that bring in the convoys,' Dolly told her proudly. 'My Janet might like to give herself airs and graces, but she's certainly done well by her kids. Her hubby worked down the docks before he got killed in an accident, and with her insurance money she got Gavin apprenticed, like, on one of the pilot boats, and her two girls have both joined up. Hilda's in the ATS and Veronica's joined the Land Army.'

The door to the barn opened and Gavin came in carrying a tray with three steaming mugs on it.

'Got you a bit of bread and cheese, an' all,' he told Dolly, 'although I dare say you'll be complaining that it's given you indigestion.'

'I dare say I will,' she agreed, but Lena saw that she was tucking into it eagerly enough as she sat down on the straw bale where Gavin had spread his own blanket.

''Ere, you'll never guess what, our Gavin. Lena has just asked me why you aren't in uniform.'

Lena's face flamed as she saw the comprehension in his gaze when he turned to look at her.

'Thought I was skiving off doing me bit, did you?' He was smiling as though it was a joke, but Lena suspected that he didn't really think it was a joke at all.

'Course she didn't. She probably thought you'd got flat feet or summat,' Dolly told him. She was obviously enjoying herself hugely, having Lena as a captive audience and taking the opportunity to boast about her family, Lena guessed. 'Anyway, I've put her straight and told her as how you're training to pilot one of them boats wot brings in the convoys. You know what, Lena? I've really taken to you,' Dolly announced. 'And I reckon it's on account of you having a bit of a look of me when I was a young 'un. I had them same dark curls. You've got a bit of a Romany look about you.'

'My dad was Italian,' Lena felt obliged to tell her.

'Dead, is he?'

'Yes, both my parents were killed when a bomb hit the house.'

'And now you're all on your own. I'm surprised a pretty girl like you hasn't got a chap in tow.'

Lena shook her head and then sipped her tea. She had thought she'd got a chap in tow. She'd thought she'd got Charlie. Well, she'd never make that kind of mistake again, would she? She might have been daft enough to be taken in by him, but she was a quick learner and she'd know better next time. She'd be better off taking a leaf out of Simone's book and getting herself a nice little business going instead of reading library books and thinking daft stuff about falling in love.

Dolly took a swig of her tea and smacked her lips appreciatively before wiping the back of her hand over them and announcing, 'You know what I reckon, I reckon it's a crying shame that you're going out with that dull schoolteacher of yours, our Gavin, when here's a lovely girl like Lena who'd suit you much better.'

Lena had never felt more embarrassed. She couldn't bring herself to look at Dolly's grandson. Thank heavens that he did have a girlfriend.

'There's nothing wrong with being a teacher, Gran,' Gavin was saying.

'Well, I know your mother thinks the world shines out of her backside. How I ever came to produce someone like my Janet I'll never know. Takes after her dad, she does, and no mistake.'

'She's done a lot for those little 'uns she teaches,' Gavin defended his girl.

'Oh, aye, she likes everyone knowing how good she is for going "slumming",' Dolly agreed. 'Well, let me warn you, our Gavin, the trouble with them butter-doesn't-melt-in-their-mouths wimmin is that the reason it don't melt is on account of them being so cold. What you need is the opposite of someone like her, with them dull schoolteacher looks of hers. What you want is a lively warm-hearted girl like Lena here. I'll bet she isn't the prim and proper type, and knows how to—'

'That's enough, Gran.'

Gavin's voice was calm and pleasant but obviously its firm tone meant something to Dolly because immediately she heaved a heavy theatrical sigh and swigged what was left of her tea, turning her shoulder towards him as she did so, but still refraining from continuing to criticise his girl.

When Gavin went to take the empty mugs back to the farmhouse, Lena made good use of his absence to place her blanket on top of a bale to one side of the one Dolly had selected, and spread it out as Gavin had already done his grandmother's.

'That's it,' Dolly approved. 'Then you lies in the middle and wraps the sides round you. Snug as a bug in a rug, like.'

By the time Gavin had returned Dolly was fast asleep and snoring her head off, but Lena was finding it harder to relax enough to go to sleep. The straw felt all scratchy, despite her blanket, and she suspected although she had tried to wrap it round herself carefully it must have slipped because one piece of straw was sticking into her leg as sharp as any needle.

It was no use, she was going to have to do something. She'd never sleep with that straw irritating her skin like it was.

Lena sat up.

'What's wrong?' Dolly's grandson asked her in the kind of voice that said that he didn't really want know and in fact that he didn't want anything to do with her at all.

'I can't get me blanket right,' she admitted, pushing it away and then attempting to stand up on the bare straw, only realising too late how slippery it was when she lost her footing and started to fall.

Gavin caught her before she hit the floor, swinging her up against his chest in a powerful hold, his hands biting into the soft flesh of her arms. Her senses reacted immediately to his alien male scent, her body stiffening in rejection of his closeness, her 'Thank you' stilted and quiet.

'Give me a shout when you've got settled, then I'll put the lamp out.' His voice was curt, almost as though he disliked her, Lena recognised. Then, to her shock, as she looked at him she realised that he thought she had deliberately engineered her fall so that she would end up in his arms. Indignation and shame burned hotly inside her.

'I can see what you're thinking,' she told him, 'but I didn't do it on purpose.'

She looked and sounded more like a child than a wanton little piece who'd been trying to flaunt herself in front of him and get a reaction from him, Gavin acknowledged. Dressed the way she was, though, it was hard not to think what he had thought. This war had brought out something in some girls that he didn't like or approve of. He wasn't one for free and easy ways, and he wasn't inclined that way himself. His mother had seen to that.

'I never said that you did,' he answered.

'No, but you looked like it was what you was thinking,' Lena defended herself. 'I'll have you know that I'm not the sort wot goes throwing herself at lads. As good as engaged, I . . .'

Mortified tears stung her eyes. She had forgotten for the moment how Charlie had deceived her.

Gavin saw the tears and frowned. She was only a bit of a kid really, too young to be on her own with no one to look out for her.

'How old are you?' he asked her brusquely. When Lena told him he exhaled heavily. 'That's too young to be as good as engaged, and if you was my sister—'

'Well, I'm not. And anyway, it's all over now.'

There was a note in her voice that told Gavin that she felt she'd had her heart broken, and despite himself he discovered that he felt sorry for her. She was only a bit of a kid. His mother would never allow either of his sisters to go out dressed the way she was, even now at their ages, never mind when they'd been as young as she.

His inbuilt sense of male responsibility made him want to do something to protect her but all he could think of to say was a grim, 'It doesn't do for a girl to go acting like she's summat she isn't, 'cos it will make other folk think she's a bad lot.'

Lena was mortified and afraid. After all, wasn't the truth that she *was* a bad lot now that she knew that Charlie wasn't going to marry her?

TEN

'See you here tonight then, Lena love,' Dolly beamed at Lena as both she and Gavin helped the elderly woman off the bus.

'They told me at the rest centre to go back today so that they can sort out me papers and get me a proper billet,' Lena told her. She didn't want to say outright that the last thing she wanted was to spend another night with Dolly and her grandson, especially after what had happened last night, and her making a fool of herself the way she had. She had seen from Gavin's expression that he thought she'd flung herself into his arms like that on purpose and not because she'd been struggling with her blanket. Lena could feel her face starting to burn whilst the same angry humiliated tears that she had wanted to cry so many times since she found out how Charlie had deceived her threatened to spill over and betray her. Well, she wasn't going to let them. She'd got more backbone than that, and she wasn't going to let them that wanted to look down on her have the satisfaction of doing so. She certainly wasn't. She'd survived the bombing, hadn't she, and she would survive this as well.

Gavin frowned as he watched her. His heart had sunk when he'd first seen her. For all that she liked to pretend she knew what the world was about, his gran was, in reality, easily taken in. He'd taken one look at that short skirt and that hair and those liquid eyes and that soft pouting mouth, and he'd decided that whatever Lena had attached herself to his gran for, it wasn't for his gran's benefit. But last night reluctantly he had come to realise that Lena, for all her outward air of confidence, was in fact very naïve. She might look like she knew every trick in the book of how to attract man, but when it came to it she didn't have a clue and it had been innocence and self-conscious anger he'd seen in her eyes when she'd fallen into his arms and not a come-on at all.

Poor kid. She wasn't fit to be let out on her own. With those looks of hers she'd have every Jack-the-lad in Liverpool trying to take advantage of her. Not that it was any of his business.

'Well, if you change your mind you know where to find us – same place as last night,' Dolly repeated.

Lena nodded. She had grown unexpectedly fond of the old lady in the short space of time she had known her. At least Dolly accepted her, and not just that, but actually approved of her, although Lena could well imagine what Charlie's mother and even her own auntie would have to say about Dolly. She'd better go and see Simone first, she decided after she had said her goodbyes to Dolly and Gavin. Then she could go back to the rest centre and sort out her replacement ration card and everything. And as for Charlie and her broken heart, she wasn't going to think about them. There was no point in crying over spilled milk. She'd just got to get on with things, hadn't she?

Sasha and Lou had only gone to the telephone exchange to ask for application forms for jobs, but when these had been handed over to them they had been told to wait and had then been taken to a small room where they had had to fill in the applications under the eagle eye of a stern-looking grey-haired woman, who had introduced herself as Mrs Withers.

They had then been sent to the canteen for a cup of tea and told to wait, and they had been there for over half an hour. Lou had been on the point of suggesting to Sasha that they left when they had been summoned for a full interview.

That interview seemed to be taking for ever, Lou thought miserably.

There had been questions about their family – with Mrs Withers nodding her head over the fact that Grace was training as a nurse and Luke was in the army.

Then they'd been measured, a process during which Lou had held her breath, half hoping that they might turn out to be under the five foot six height requirement, and then hating herself when she had seen Sasha's beam of relief when they had both turned out to be just over five foot seven. Because the switch-boards were very high, even with a metal trim at the base of their seats for the telephonists to stand on, anyone under five foot six would not have been able to reach up to get the plugs in the necessary holes fast enough.

If their application was successful, they would be trained on dummy switchboards, Mrs Withers told

166

them, after she had given them both individual mental arithmetic and verbal tests, and they had read out a series of numbers and then a paragraph from a sheet of paper for her.

It had been warm outside when they had arrived, but now, shut in this bleak, windowless room, Lou was beginning to feel trapped and cold and desperate to escape. Sasha, though, was nodding her head and listening intently whilst Mrs Withers explained to them what their training would involve. Her twin had turned her chair slightly to one side so that Lou couldn't even catch her eye in that special way they had always had. Lou felt as though a heavy weight had settled inside her.

'Thank you. We'll be in touch,' Mrs Withers told them both briskly, indicating that the interview was over.

'Oh, Lou,' Sasha announced breathlessly once they were back outside, 'I do hope they take us on. It would be just perfect. We're only ten minutes or so away from home, and the canteen looked ever so nice and clean.'

Lou forced herself to agree as she tried to pretend to share Sasha's excitement, but the truth was that she was already dreading the thought of working at the exchange.

Well, he'd done it, and there was no going back now, Kieran thought doggedly, torn between pride and the recognition that he'd get an earful from his mother when she found out what he'd done. But he hadn't had any choice really, had he? He'd had a taste of his uncle Con's life and for a while he'd thought that he could take to it, but then he'd seen the way that other lads – lads in uniform – looked at him, and the way the prettiest girls looked at them and he'd begun to think that maybe working with his uncle wasn't such a good idea after all.

It was that business with the twins that had made up his mind, though – not that he would ever let on to anyone about that. They'd think he'd gone soft in the head if he did. It hadn't been his fault that they'd gone running off the way they had and one of them had nearly got herself killed. But somehow the whole thing had stuck inside his head and had made him feel uncomfortable. Anyway, it was too late to start worrying about why he'd done what he'd done now. He'd done it. He looked back at the RAF recruiting office he'd just left, and his chest started to swell with a mixture of pride and apprehension. Another twenty-four hours and he'd be reporting for duty as Aircraftman Mallory.

'So what time do you call this then?' Simone demanded as soon as Lena walked into the salon, standing with her hands on her hips and an angry frown on her face.

'I'm sorry,' Lena tried to apologise, 'only—'

Ignoring her, Simone reached out to pluck a piece of straw from Lena's sleeve.

'And what's this? If you're late coming in to work because you've been rolling around in some field with a lad—'

'No I haven't—' Lena began to defend herself.

But before she could say any more the shop door crashed open and Lena heard her auntie saying angrily, 'So you are here, then? I'm surprised at you, Simone. I'd have thought you'd want to be rid of her in case she gives your business a bad name. Or hasn't she told you what she's bin up to yet?'

Fortunately there were no customers in the salon, nor any due as it was only Monday morning. Even so, Simone jerked her head in Lena's direction and told her sharply, 'You'd better put the lock on the door.'

Whilst Lena was doing as she had told her, she could hear Simone asking her auntie, 'So what's this all about then?'

'It's about her doing what she shouldn't with some army lad – aye, and boasting about it, an' all, claiming that he's going to marry her. As if anyone would believe that. I allus knew she'd turn out like this. Her own mother used to say she'd got bad blood in her. Well, she's not going to be carrying on under my roof any longer, so you needn't come crawling back just like you've done nowt wrong, if that's what you were thinking of doing,' her auntie Flo told Lena nastily. 'I've got my Doris to think of. She's a decent respectable girl, who's about to get a decent respectable chap's ring on her finger and I'm not having her shamed in front of her in-laws-to-be on account of having you as her cousin. You can take yourself back off to wherever it was you spent the night last night and you can stay there. And if you've any sense you'll give her her cards, an' all,' Lena's aunt told Simone, ''cos I'm telling you now you're going to lose a lot of customers if they come in and find her working here when they hear what she's bin up to. As for you,' she added turning back to Lena, 'it won't just be my Alfred's belt you'll be feeling if you try to come back.'

'But what about my things? My clothes and my ration book,' Lena protested.

'What ration book? I ain't got no ration book of yours. See?' She turned to Simone. 'See what a liar she is, trying to mek out I've got her ration book. You want to think yourself lucky I don't report you to someone in authority – trying to mek out that a respectable woman who's done nowt but put herself out to give you a good home is trying to thieve off you. And as for your clothes, I've sent the lot of them off to one of them places that takes stuff like that. Best place for them.'

She'd gone before Lena could say a word, slamming the door so hard that the whole frame shook.

'It isn't true what she said about me ration book. She has got it,' Lena told Simone.

'And this soldier lad – what about him? Is that true?'

Lena hung her head. 'He said he loved me and that we was going to be married.'

'And you believed him?' Simone shook her head in disbelief. 'I thought you'd have known better than that. Not left you wi' owt you wouldn't want to be left with, has he?'

'Just his jacket,' Lena told her, missing the point of what Simone was trying to say.

Simone gave her an exasperated look. 'I thought you'd have had more about you than to fall for some lad spinning you a yarn just so that he could get into your knickers. Well, I hope you know where you can find him, just in case. That's all I can say.'

'He's getting married to someone else.' Lena bit down hard on her bottom lip. 'I went to see his mam last night and she told me.' She couldn't bring herself to admit to Simone exactly what had happened.

'Well then, I dare say you'll know better the next

time, won't you. Lads will tell you owt when they're after a bit of how's your father, you daft head, especially lads in uniform. I won't be able to keep you on here now, you know that, don't you?'

Lena made a strangled sound of protest, the blood draining from her face.

'But I've got to have a job. I can't join up or go into munitions. I'm too young, and I haven't got me papers. They've told me to go back to the rest centre later and they'll sort me out with some new ones.'

'Then you'll have to tell them they need to sort you out with a new job as well, won't you? It's no use you looking at me like that, Lena. You're a good worker and that hair of yours brings in the customers but there's no getting away from the fact that them looks of yours turn them away.'

'Because I look Italian?'

'That, and on account of you being as good-looking as a film star. Some of them don't like that, see. They see their men hanging around eyeing you up and it's you they blame and not them. That's human nature, Lena, and the sooner you recognise that the better. They see their chaps eyeing you up and they blame you 'cos you're young and pretty and they aren't, but they won't admit to that so they say that it's because you look a bit Eyetie and that Eyeties should be locked up on account of that Mussolini of theirs.'

'You could cut my hair and I—'

'It's no use you trying to soft-soap me, Lena. If it was left up to me I'd keep you on but I've worked hard to build up this business, and a nice little earner it is now, an' all, but if I get me clients dropping off because of you then I'd have to sack you anyway

171

'cos there wouldn't be any work for either of us, would there, so it makes no sense me keeping you on. You must see that.'

Lena could.

'Look, I'll tell you what,' Simone offered, relenting. 'I'll give you the name of a friend of mine wot runs a salon near the Royal Court Theatre. She gets a load of them girls from there going in to her, and some of the stars as well. I'll write you a note to give to her, saying that you'll do her nicely as a junior, but I'm not making any promises that she'll tek you on, mind,' she warned as Lena's face broke into a smile of grateful relief.

As she checked through the unfinished paperwork Laura had left behind when she had taken off for another visit to her family – without so much as a by-your-leave either – Bella tried not to let Lena's image from last night come between her and her work, but the young girl with her common-looking clothes emphasising her curves in a way that had been so much at odds with her pitifully naked pain when she had learned the truth about Charlie, insisted on intruding. So much so that in the end Bella gave an exasperated sigh and pushed to one side the paper containing the growing list of mothers wanting to enrol their children at the nursery, and stood up.

It was another warm day – she had been able to walk to the school earlier wearing a thin pink cardigan over her floral silk dress with its patterns of rich pinks and blues.

As she picked up her handbag, her sunglasses and her gloves she called out to the nearest of the nursery staff, 'Aggie, I've got to go out. I won't be very long.'

She really had no idea at all why she had felt such an out-of-character and very odd sense of fellow feeling towards Lena last night, Bella told herself as she stepped out into the sunshine. She was nothing like the younger girl, with her dreadful cheap clothes and her stupidity in believing whatever line Charlie had spun her. She certainly wasn't going to allow her parents, and especially her father, to bully her the way he had bullied Lena, and to prove it she was going to go down to her father's office right now and tell him in no uncertain terms that now that Charlie was staying in the army and Daphne was staying with her parents, there was no reason at all for her to move out of her lovely house.

It was a pity that Laura was away, otherwise Bella could have suggested to Laura that she move in with her. She knew that Laura was looking for a new billet and having her staying with her would back up Bella's own claim on the house.

Edwin's office was on the opposite side of Wallasey village to his and Bella's homes, and close to the sea, as befitted a business dealing with the refitting of the internal pipe work of ships. When Bella walked into the smart office her father maintained, a short walk away from the yard where the pipes were made ready for fitting, there was no sign of him. Instead, Pauline Green, her father's assistant, greeted her, flicking a coolly arrogant look in Bella's direction.

Bella didn't know Pauline very well, but something about her manner immediately got Bella's back up. Like Bella, Pauline was widowed, although she was older than Bella, closer to thirty-five than twenty-five. She had a son from her marriage, who had been evacuated to live with a cousin of Pauline's in Shropshire.

Pauline certainly dressed well for a widow who had been left badly off enough to need to go out to work, Bella decided grudgingly. She couldn't imagine her father paying anyone who worked for him over-generously. The collar of Pauline's striped blouse was turned up at the back, its deep V front subtly empha-sising the shadowy area between her breasts. Her plain royal-blue linen skirt matched the colour of the stripe in her blouse and when she stood up to walk over to a filing cabinet to remove some papers, Bella saw that her legs below the hem of her straight skirt were encased in what looked very much like silk stockings.

Bella's frown deepened. She certainly couldn't afford silk stockings, or indeed any kind of stock-ings for everyday wear.

Pauline's dark hair was dressed in a smart chignon at the back with soft curls artfully framing her face. Bella's eyes narrowed. That was the kind of hairstyle that took a great deal of time and patience – or the skill of an expensive hairdresser.

When Pauline turned round to return to her desk, catching Bella studying her, she gave her a mocking smile that left her pale blue eyes every bit as hard and shrewd-looking as they had been when she had been assessing Bella's own appearance earlier.

It was not often that Bella found herself being outclassed in any way by a member of her own sex, but on this occasion she was forced to admit that Pauline had the upper hand and that the other woman knew it.

174

Being made to feel small and insecure by another woman was a new experience for Bella and one that had her face burning with anger.

'Where is my father?' she demanded sharply, determined to wrest control of the situation away from Pauline and back into her own hands.

'Excuse me.' Turning her back on her, Pauline tapped the scarlet painted nails of one hand on the desk whilst she ran a pencil down the list in front of her, writing something into the margin of whatever it was she was studying, before putting down the pencil and turning back to Bella with an exaggerated sigh.

'I'm sorry about that but I do so hate being interrupted when I'm in the middle of something, don't you? Now what was it you wanted, Bella?'

Her smile now was patient and indulgent, the kind of smile a confident adult might give a fractious child, Bella recognised with growing anger.

'I asked you where my father is.'

'I'm sorry, Edwin left instructions that because of the confidential nature of his current business talks no one was to be told where he is. You can leave a message for him with me, of course. I promise I'll make sure he gets it. What is it, another advance on your allowance?'

Now Pauline's smile was warmly encouraging and almost kind, but Bella wasn't in the least bit deceived.

Just wait until she saw her father: She'd certainly have something to say to him about Pauline rooting through his private papers. There was no other way she could know about Bella's own financial affairs. Her father was always reluctant to discuss money with his own family, never mind with a mere assistant,

175

probably because he didn't like anyone knowing too much about the way he did business. But thanks to her late husband, Alan, and his habit of saying things he should not have said when he had been drunk, Bella knew a very great deal about her father's business methods. She knew, for instance, that he was able to make a very handsome profit indeed on the work he did for the Navy, thanks to the fact that he had seen off his only two competitors in the area by very dubious means.

Perhaps she ought to remind her father of just how he had become the sole contractor working for the War Office, Bella thought grimly. Then they'd see just how smug Pauline felt like being over Bella's allowance.

'I am sorry, Bella. I know the situation must have been urgent for you to come all the way down here instead of waiting for your father to be at home, but I know you'll understand my position. Confidentiality and loyalty are so important in the kind of relationship I have with your father.'

Something about the smug words and the smile that accompanied them sent a small *frisson* of alarm feathering through Bella's mind, but before she could question exactly what it was that was causing her that alarm the telephone had started to ring.

'Please do excuse me.' As she reached for the receiver, Pauline looked meaningfully towards the door, making it clear that she expected Bella to leave. The sunlight coming in through the window glittered on the facets of the large diamond engagement ring Pauline was wearing, distracting Bella and causing her further displeasure. Pauline's late husband had certainly provided her with a far better ring than Bella had had.

For a mere assistant in the office of small businessman like her father, Pauline certainly had expensive and very stylish tastes. She had made her feel positively down at heel, Bella admitted, as she set off back to the school.

She would be on her own in the house this coming weekend as Saturday was the day when Jan Polanski, her billetees' son and brother, was getting married to the Polish girl whose parents had been friends of his parents.

Bella stopped dead in her tracks. What on earth was she doing thinking about Jan Polanski, when she hated him so much? He had humiliated her and mocked her, and his stupid Polish fiancée was welcome to him. She, Bella, certainly never wanted to see him again. Bella resumed walking, faster this time, her head down as she blinked away the tears threatening to obscure her vision.

'Dad said as how you wanted some help with your garden so he's sent down Wilhelm here.'

Emily had gone automatically to open the back door when she had heard someone knock and now she was all of a flummox. She certainly hadn't been expecting to see the red-faced farm boy who was twisting his cap in his hands as he stood on her step, his ears going redder by the minute, whilst the German POW who had been so kind to Tommy on Sunday stood quietly behind him.

'Oh. That's very good of your father, but is it all right, I mean with . . . Wilhelm being . . . well, I mean, aren't there certain rules?' She was floundering, Emily knew, and it certainly wasn't that she expected to see the POWs handcuffed and dragging chains – that would be wicked and unthinkable – but she didn't want either to be responsible for getting anyone into trouble, just because the garden of her rented house was a bit overgrown.

'Dad's had a word with him wot's in charge of the camp, and he says it's all right seeing as Dad says that he can spare Wilhelm. We've got some of them there land girls come now, see.' The boy blushed ever harder, the knuckles standing out on his hands as he twisted his cap frantically, half falling over his words as he explained proudly, 'Dad's set me on to showing them how to do the milking. He reckons that girls are better wi' the cows than men, so he can easily spare Wilhelm. Oh, and me mam says to tell you that she's got a spare coop and some good layers if you was wanting half a dozen hens.'

Fresh eggs! Emily's face lit up. She'd heard that it was possible to eat better in the country if you knew the right people and you were prepared to do a bit of bartering, although Emily did not know what she could possibly offer the farmer's wife in return for her kindness.

'You'll have to feed Wilhelm, Mam said to tell you,' the boy added, offering Emily a possible explanation. She knew that farmers were given an allowance for feeding the POWs and that sometimes their rations were better than those of the farmer and his family. Well, she certainly wasn't going to object.

She could hear Tommy clambering down from the stool at the kitchen table where she had been listening to him read from Charles Dickens's *A Tale of Two Cities* when they had been interrupted. Ever such a good little reader, he was an' all, only faltering every

178

now and again over the longest and hardest words. Emily was determined that, come the new school year in September, Tommy would be ready to join the local children at the small village school where the schoolmistress taught all the children in the same large room, no matter what age they were.

She wouldn't exactly call Tommy a chatterbox but now that he had found his voice he was quite a happy to talk to her a lot when they were on their own. It was just when they were with others that he tended to clam up. Mind, she never asked him about his past. Things were better that way, Emily reckoned. After all, if he wanted to talk to her about it he would do, wouldn't he?

'I'd better be getting back.'

The farmer's son was obviously eager to get back to the land girls.

'Dad said to tell you that he's seen to it that the POWs' transport stops here for Wilhelm after they've picked up the others and that they'll drop him off again in the morning.'

The farmer's son might look clumsy and awkward, but he could move fast enough when he wanted to, Emily decided as he disappeared at speed, leaving her and Wilhelm facing one another, and Emily feeling a bit uncomfortable.

It was Tommy who broke the ice, wriggling into the open doorway next to her and saying to Wilhelm, 'You're the German, aren't you?'

'That is correct,' Wilhelm agreed in that stiff way he had of speaking English. 'We met one another first outside the church on Sunday, did we not?'

'Yes,' Tommy agreed.

'Tommy, Wilhelm here is going to be getting the

179

vegetable patch sorted out for us, so why don't you take him and show him where the tool shed is whilst I put the kettle on? Here's the key.' She reached the key from its peg on the wall to one side of the sink.

'There are some tools in there but I don't know if they'll be any use,' Emily told Wilhelm. 'I'm city born and bred, you see, and I haven't had much to do with gardens.'

'That is not a problem. I grow up in the town but my uncle, he have a farm and I go there in the summer to work.'

'Well, when you've shown Wilhelm where the shed is, Tommy, you can both come back here and have a cup of tea.'

It was only when they had disappeared out of her view, swallowed up by the blossom-covered branches of what her neighbour had told her were apple trees in the small orchard that separated the back garden proper from the vegetable plot, that Emily realised that Wilhelm might have thought she had sent Tommy with him because she was afraid that he might try to escape. Poor chap, it couldn't be much fun being a POW in a foreign country. He seemed ever such a decent sort as well. She only had to remember how he had stepped in on Sunday with Tommy. Emily knew that there were those who would not approve of her sympathising with a German POW but she didn't care, she decided with a small uncharacteristic toss of her head. She didn't want to fall out with anyone, but from now on she was going to make her own decisions about things instead of letting other people tell her what she should think, like Con had always tried to do.

* * *

'Seeing as we're both off on Saturday I thought we could go out to Whitchurch, perhaps even make a bit of a weekened of it and stay somewhere overnight,' Seb suggested, as he and Grace walked towards the hospital via Edge Hill Road, having managed to snatch an hour together to meet at Joe Lyons in the centre of town for a cup of tea.

Grace's hand trembled slightly in Seb's as he made this suggestion, causing his own to squeeze it protectively.

Katie and Luke had spent a whole bank holiday weekend exploring Cheshire together and had stayed in various boarding houses and pubs, but that had been different. They had not been an acknowledged couple then and they weren't engaged like she and Seb. For her and Seb, staying some-where together overnight had a whole different meaning and one that was already setting her heart pounding heavily with longing.

'Yes, I'd like that,' she agreed, trying to sound calm.

'Whitchurch is right out in the country,' Seb continued as though nothing of any import had occurred and as though they hadn't just both taken a tentative step towards taking their relationship to a much intimate level. 'And I thought you'd be glad of an opportunity to see where I'm going to be working before there's anyone official around. After all, it won't be long now, only a couple of months or so.' Seb gripped Grace's hand tightly. He had just been told that the date for his transfer was likely to be brought forward, and he wanted to prepare Grace for this as gently as he could. He was dreading their coming parting every bit as much as he knew she

181

was, but it was up to him to be strong for both of them.

Seb's words were like a shock of cold water. Grace's longing for the intimacy that spending the night away together could offer them was immediately pushed to one side by her awareness of how much she was dreading Seb leaving Liverpool. She thought about that and felt miserable about it every spare minute she had, and she wished desperately that Seb was not going to be transferred. Grace knew that she wasn't being entirely fair or making things easy for Seb, and she felt guilty for feeling the way she did, but she just couldn't help it. She was surprised herself at the way she was reacting but they were in the middle of a war and everyone knew that that did things to your feelings that just wouldn't happen in peacetime. She didn't want to bring the date for his move any closer or to make it a proper reality. She'd much rather leave it where it was in some distant nebulous future, where she didn't have to think about it and could pretend that if she ignored it somehow it might not actually happen.

'Anyone would think you want to go,' she accused Seb almost sharply and then bit her lip guiltily. 'Oh, Seb, I'm sorry. I shouldn't have said that or be acting so nasty with you. It's just that I'm going to miss you so much.'

Seb had opened his arms whilst she'd been speaking and now Grace went into them, giving way to her tears as he held her tight.

'I'm being proper daft and I know that Mum and Dad would give me a real old telling-off. There's girls who've got fiancés in uniform that have been sent abroad, and here's me making a fuss because you're going to be twenty miles or so away.'

'I'm glad that you are making a fuss,' Seb told her, and meant it.

'You are?' Grace was so relieved that she pulled away from him to look up into his face, searching his expression uncertainly. She was so lucky to have met Seb. She only had to see the problems poor Katie was having with Luke to see how difficult life could be when a girl fell in love with a man who wasn't as easy-going or understanding as her wonderful Seb.

'Of course I am. It shows that you love me, doesn't it? Not that I had a moment's doubt.' The smile in his eyes darkened to tenderness and concern. He pulled her back into his arms, cradling her there with her head leaning on his chest so that he could rest his chin on the soft thickness of her hair.

'And you mustn't doubt me either, Gracie,' he told her gently. 'Because you don't have to, you know, and I wouldn't want to think that I'd ever said or done anything to give you the impression that you did.'

Was there a quiet warning in those loving words, Grace wondered guiltily. If so, then it was one she deserved, because Seb was right. He had never ever given her any cause to doubt him in any way at all.

'Look at it this way,' Seb continued. 'If you were to be transferred to a hospital in the country – one of those where they send women who are about to give birth, for instance – how would you feel if you knew that your doing your duty was hurting me, especially when you were wishing we didn't have to be apart yourself?'

'Oh, Seb!' Now Grace felt more guilty than ever. 'We've been lucky, I know, working and doing our bit for the war effort so close to one another for so long.'

'I'm glad *you* think I'm doing my bit,' Seb told her ruefully. 'Sometimes I wonder if I really am. My work isn't like your Luke's – a serving soldier who everyone can see it pulling his weight.'

'Seb, of course you are doing your bit,' Grace defended him immediately. 'And I don't want to hear you saying that you aren't.'

Grace knew a little of Seb's work, although of course a little was all that he could tell her. Her obvious championing of him and belief in him flooded his heart with a fresh surge of love for her, though.

'Everything will be all right, you just wait and see,' he comforted her as they managed to snatch a quick kiss before releasing one another.

Tommy and the German POW had been down in the shed for ever such a long time and Emily was beginning to felt a bit panicky. What if the POW had taken the opportunity to run off and poor Tommy was too scared to come back and tell her? Or what if something worse had happened? The thought of any harm befalling her beloved adopted son had Emily tugging off her apron and hurrying out of the kitchen, leaving the back door open as she almost ran to the shed.

When she got there, the door was open. Tommy and the German were inside, Tommy leaning on the old bench, propping up his face with his hands as he watched the POW sharpening a scythe.

Once what she could see had laid Emily's maternal anxiety to rest, she couldn't help noticing how the long careful stroke of the sharpening block against the scythe tightened the POW's shirt across his muscular back. He had a strong back and muscular arms, arms that could hold a woman safe against the dangers of life. A painful feeling of anger and contempt burned inside Emily. She was forty years old, plain and overweight, and she had no right to be noticing things like that about any man. Hadn't she learned anything from her marriage and the way that Con, her husband, had treated her? The only reason he had married her in the first place had been for her father's money, as he had made cruelly plain very early on in their marriage. But her feeling of angry contempt for herself didn't just come from what she knew Con thought about her, it came from herself as well. She had her Tommy to think of now, filling the empty ache in her heart she had never allowed herself to admit to until she had found him. What would he think, innocent trusting little lad that he was, if she were to humiliate him and show him up by making a laughing stock of herself? And she *would* make a laughing stock of herself if anyone ever guessed what she had just thought.

'This is how you must do this, in one way only and away from you. You do not want to cut yourself with the sharpness you will make with the stone.' The German's words were slow and precise, as though he had to search carefully for them, reminding Emily that English was not his first language. It was only then that she realised that the inappropriate thoughts that had angered her so much had been for a man who was an enemy. Somehow it was hard to think of someone as an enemy, who was displaying so much patience and care as he instructed Tommy in what he was doing, Emily admitted.

Tommy. She looked at her adopted son. He was

nodding his head as he listened to Wilhelm. Neither of them had seen her yet, but then Wilhelm looked up and carefully put the scythe and the stone to one side as he got to his feet.

'Wilhelm says that the tools are rusty and that he can't use them until he's cleaned them up and sharpened them,' Tommy explained quickly to Emily.

'This will take time,' Wilhelm joined in. 'If you do not care for that I could ask the farmer if he will lend what I need.'

Emily shook her head, subduing her guilt at the thought of extending the amount of time Wilhelm would have to spend with them. Tools were precious and not easily replaced now that there was a war on, she reminded herself, and so it made sense to allow Wilhelm the extra time to get the tools in the shed back into working order.

These were the darkest days of the war so far and for her home city in particular, and yet at that moment Emily's heart lifted at the prospect of her new life in the country. Some might call her courageous for moving away from the place that had always been her home, others might call her foolish for taking in a stray child, but what Emily thought was quite simply that she had been blessed as though by her own personal miracle, and that for Tommy's sake she would have found the courage to do far more than move to Whitchurch.

ELEVEN

Lena was familiar with the streets around the Royal Court Theatre and what had been the centre of the city before the Luftwaffe had blasted the heart out of it.

Now the big Lewis's store, which had dominated Ranelagh Street, was an empty shell, with the store's business being carried out from a much smaller warehouse nearby, and the shops that only a month ago had been filled with goods on sale were now able to offer only 'bomb-damaged stock'. The warm May sunshine had brought out the city's shoppers, determined at least to look as though they were carrying on as normal. Women with shopping baskets over their arms, and dressed in brightly coloured summer frocks, who obviously still had homes that were intact, were tripping lightly along streets only just cleared of rubble, their heads held high. Lena looked enviously at them, conscious now of her own grubby and untidy appearance. It had been proper mean of her auntie to give away her clothes, but then why had she expected any different? At least she'd got her precious Post Office savings book, and once she got her replacement papers and a new ration book from the rest centre, along with a proper billet, she'd be able to set about smartening herself up a bit. She'd buy a couple of lengths of fabric off one of those market stalls that had a notice saying the fabric was end pieces or second-hand, although she'd heard that it was no such thing and some of the prices stall holders were asking were twice what anyone in their right mind would normally pay for top-quality stuff.

Still, she had to have something to wear. She could run herself up a couple of frocks and maybe a nice skirt. Lena was good with her needle, a skill her mother had always said darkly she must have come by 'from your dad's lot, 'cos you'll never catch me mekin' me own clothes, like I've just come out of the poorhouse.'

One thing she had to say for her mother was that she had always dressed well, but then she'd got most of her clothes from her employers, snatching them up when those rich women had thrown them out. Some proper lovely stuff, her mam had had, but it had all disappeared when the house had been bombed. By the time Lena had got there with her auntie, everything that was worth having had been picked over and taken.

She paused on the corner of one of the streets watching people going into a Lyons Corner House, tempted to follow them. She was thirsty and hungry too, but she was reluctant to go in looking like she did now. She frowned slightly. The cessation of the blitz and the warmth of the sun had brought the women around her out of their coats and winter skirts and jumpers and into their summer clothes. She couldn't help noticing that the summer frocks worn by the other girls she could see didn't fit

188

anything like as tightly as hers, and their lipstick was a soft pink, not a bright red. Charlie's sister had been like that, dressed in something soft and sort of draped on her body like instead of clinging to it, and it had been obvious to Lena that she was smart and a definite cut above her cousin Doris and her friends. It was Doris's lead Lena had followed in choosing her own clothes, and in fact most of her clothes were rejects from Doris's wardrobe, things she had grown tired of and which had been passed on to Lena. She'd had to alter them a fair bit to make them fit her as snugly as they had fitted Doris, of course, but now, watching the young women going into Lyons, Lena found herself wishing that she had one of those soft-fitting pretty frocks that made them look so ladylike. Would Charlie have thought better of her if she'd been dressed like that and not treated her like he had? Was that how this other girl that he was marrying dressed?

There was a lump in Lena's throat. Determinedly she swallowed past it, and made herself a promise that she would spend some of her first wages from her new job on a second-hand frock like those she had seen girls wearing today.

'If I could have a word, please, Bella?'

'Yes of course, Mr Benson,' Bella agreed in her most businesslike voice, as she pushed the laundry list she had been checking to one side and stood up. Gerald Benson, the senior civil servant and government official who had overall responsibility was implementing the Government's scheme to provide crèche facilities for working mothers with young children, so that they could aid the war effort, didn't normally pay a visit without his secretary telephoning in advance, and although she wasn't going to let him see it, Bella could feel surge of anxiety invading her stomach. Although her own father was a local councillor, he was nowhere near as important as Gerald Benson, who had been sent from London to take charge of the scheme and others related to it.

Bella's anxiety increased when, instead of saying whatever it was he wanted to say to her immediately, Gerald Benson ushered her towards the small room that had been the headmaster's private office when the school had had a headmaster and not just one very harassed teacher.

When he held open the door for her to precede him into the office, instead of immediately taking a seat as she would normally have done, Bella hesitated, waiting for him to invite her to sit down. She had no idea what it was he wanted to say to her but she did know that she wanted to keep her job. It still amazed her, whenever she had time to think about being amazed, how much she loved her work and how determined she was to do everything she had to do to keep her job, even if that meant conforming to rules about working hours, and discipline that normally would have had her tossing her head in the air and flatly refusing to countenance.

'How are you finding your work here, Bella?'

'I like it very much,' Bella answered him cautiously.

Laura had warned her that she was only being taken on on a probationary basis, and that the situation would have to be reviewed. Had Laura been complaining about her behind her back? She certainly had no cause to do so, Bella thought angrily. After all, she was the one who was forever having to stand in for Laura when she had time off, and she'd covered up for her a couple of times as well when she'd found a mistake that Laura had made.

There was a file on the desk, Bella realised now, and Mr Benson was opening it and studying it.

'You were originally taken on as an assistant to Miss Wright, so I understand,' Mr Benson asked Bella.

'Yes.'

'Miss Wright tells me that although you were her assistant, there were occasions on which you took sole responsibility for certain duties that were more properly hers.'

Bella's heart knocked against her ribs. Now what should she do? Was she going to be in trouble for stepping into Laura's shoes? She had only done so because at the time it had seemed the sensible thing to do and the best way to get things done. Since Laura had started seeing an army captain stationed close to her parents' home she had taken so much time off that Bella had felt obliged to act on her own initiative. Not that she had minded for one single minute. In fact, she had loved the responsibility and being in charge. There was nothing she enjoyed more than making lists and then ticking off things as they got done.

'We had so many extra little ones coming in because of the blitz that sometimes I've had to take matters into my own hands and make decisions,' she answered him as calmly as she could.

To her relief a faint smile warned the sternness of his face.

'I received a telephone call from Laura this morning. It appears that due to personal circumstances she no

191

longer feels able to continue in her position here as manageress of the crèche.'

Laura was leaving?

'That being the case, Bella, I am empowered to offer you the vacancy that now arises.'

Mr Benson was offering her Laura's job? Bella felt positively giddy with excitement and delight. Of course, she wasn't going to let Mr Benson see that. It wouldn't do at all for the newly promoted crèche manageress to act in a manner that was not completely professional. She had a position to maintain now, after all.

Bella folded her hands firmly in her lap, and sat up a little bit straighter, as she said as calmly as she could, 'Thank you, Mr Benson. I accept.'

Bella could hardly believe it, even now, an hour after Mr Benson had gone. She had been promoted. She was now manageress. Just wait until she got home and told those refugee Poles. Abruptly her delight faded when she remembered that Maria and Bettina wouldn't be there. Well, that didn't matter. She could go and tell her mother instead. But somehow that wasn't the same. She could just imagine the fuss that Maria would have made if it had been one of her own offspring who had won such an important promotion. She'd have set to, cooking a celebratory meal, praising her children and hugging them, and behaving altogether in a thoroughly foreign and overdramatic manner, Bella told herself scornfully, determinedly refusing to acknowledge the sharp stab of aloneness she had just felt.

Justine, who was the owner of the Coiffeuse de Paris salon, or to give her her real name, Judith Walker,

192

nodded her own expertly coiffured blonde head with its shoulder-length and waved hair, the front of which was caught up in a large roll just like the really big film stars had, as she listened to her client complaining about the drop in standards amongst the modern chorus girls.

'Couldn't kick in time if they had a trombone up their arses, that lot couldn't,' Awesome Audrey, the Glaswegian songbird, announced in a decidedly unsongbirdlike voice as she sniffed and then picked at her nose with her finger, whilst Justine worked swiftly on her thin grey hair.

Aud was eighty if she was a day, Judith was sure of it. She'd been doing a show at the Royal for as long as Judith's ma could remember, never mind Judith herself. The smell of slightly stale sweat, Judith's special made-to-a-secret-recipe shampoo (a bit of soap boiled down and added to a jug of water, which was then perfumed with whatever scent Judith could get her hands on) which Judith never ever let anywhere near her own immaculate locks, and the heat from the fancy American beauty salon hair dryers that one of Judith's admirers had been persuaded to bring back from New York, and which regularly needed the attentions of Judith's handy father, filled the private room of the 'salon' where Judith attended to her most privileged and famous clients without hoi polloi being able to see them.

Poor Aud, she'd be bald in a bit, Judith reckoned, lifting one hand from the pin curls she was carefully making to glance in the mirror behind Audrey and smile admiringly at her own reflection. Just as well that Aud wore a wig when she was on stage. Mind you . . . Judith looked at the yellowing false head of hair on the wig stand resting on the 'vanity unit', another American innovation she had 'imported' – or nagged her dad into copying from a picture she had seen in an American magazine.

'Pity you let that ruddy cat of yours pee on your wig, Aud. I don't reckon I'm going to be able to get the stain out, you know.'

'Well, you'll have to try harder then, won't you?' Audrey sniffed. ''Cos it's the only one I've got. I was wearing that when I was touring in American and Fred Astaire asked me to dance. Have I ever told you about that?'

Only every time you come in, Judith thought grimly.

'Mad for me, he was. Wanted me to be his full-time partner, and I don't just mean on the dance floor neither.'

In your dreams. Justine thought as she tugged hard enough on the thin grey hair to cause Audrey to object and forget to boast any more about her imaginary affair with Fred Astaire.

Lena was so nervous that she'd stood apprehensively on the pavement outside the salon for several minutes before she was able to pluck up the courage to go in.

The salon looked ever so smart and Lena's eyes nearly popped out of her head when she saw the three fancy dryers along one wall, each with a client underneath it.

All three young women were made up to the nines, the looks they gave Lena laced with varying degrees of hostility and female assessment.

'I've come to see the salon owner,' Lena told the girl behind the reception desk in a whisper.

'If it's about a job, she's not taking anyone on,' the girl told her without lifting her gaze from the copy of *Picture Post* she was reading.

'A friend of hers, Simone, said to tell her specially that she had sent me and she's written me a note for her,' Lena persisted. There was a smell of singing hair in the air, and when one of the young women under the dryers yelped and screeched out, 'Get this ruddy thing off of me! It's burning me to death!' Lena automatically leaped into action, removing the dryer and reassuring the client in her best professional manner.

'Gawd, if this has frizzed me hair, I'll have Justine's guts for garters. I've bin understudying the lead role for months and now tonight she's gone orf sick and it's me big chance.'

Lena felt dreadfully sorry for her. A quick look at the rag-rolled hair suggested to Lena that it had indeed been singed, but it wasn't her place to pass on this bad news, thank goodness.

Justine, alerted to the impending crisis both by the smell of burning hair and the squawk from her client, emerged from the 'private room' in a jangle of 'gold' bracelets, pink lipstick, blonde hair and lilac 'robe', to direct a 'just you wait until later' look at the now wary-looking receptionist, who had been told to keep an eye on the ruddy dryers, before sweeping towards the shrilly accusatory understudy.

'I don't know, Jacetta, anyone would think you'd never smelled perm lotion before,' she announced briskly. 'And you were the one who insisted that you wanted them front waves reperming. I said to you, I know, that I thought you was taking a bit of a risk with your hair being so fine an' all.

'Did you hear that, Audrey? she called back over her shoulder. 'I wanted her to leave well alone, but of course Miss Know-it-all only has to see some actress in a film with her hair overcurled to think that she wants the same.'

As she spoke Justine was deftly removing the curling rags and even more deftly blocking everyone's view of the understudy, apart from Lena's, as she quickly produced a pair of scissors from the pocket of her lilac robe and proceeded ruthlessly to shingle off the frizzled hair. Without pausing, she jerked her head at Lena and then nodded silently in the direction of a box on the shelf above Lena's head. When Lena reached for it, Justine quickly dropped both the burned hair and then the rag curlers into it, whilst the understudy continued to bewail the fate of her coiffure.

Only once did Lena betray what she was thinking, her eyes widening slightly when Justine looked at her own hair and then leaned towards her, removing the precious Kirbigrips Lena had pushed into it in an effort to keep it tidy. Within seconds, by some sleight of hand, the grips were holding down the inch or so of shingled hair so that it looked for all the world as though it had been 'rolled'.

''Ere, I felt that and it 'urt. What's going on? What are you doing?' the understudy demanded suspiciously.

'I'm doing your hair, that's what I'm doing, just like you're paying me to do,' Justine answered her, reaching up to the shelf for a hand mirror, which she held strategically for the understudy to look at the back of her hair – the top now a mass of 'rolls' above the longer length of the hair that had mercifully escaped being burned.

The understudy's face was picture, Lena admitted, as she watched grudging approval replace the suspicion in the hard blue eyes.

'Well, it looks all right, I suppose,' she admitted reluctantly, 'although it's no thanks to you that me scalp isn't burned red raw. I don't know why we come here, really I don't. It's not as though you're the only hairdresser in Liverpool, after all.'

'I might not be the only one, but I am the best,' Judith retorted.

Now that the crisis was over Judith finally had time to recognise the fact that the far too pretty girl in the far too tight and grubby frock who had rescued her client and her salon's reputation from being scorched was a complete stranger to her.

'And who might you be?' she demanded as she reached into her pocket and removed her cigarettes, lighting one for herself without bothering to offer Lena or anyone else one, and then leaning back against the basin, her free arm crossed over her body.

'Simone, from Clarendon Street, sent me and she's given me a . . . a letter of recommendation for you. She said she thought that you might have a job for me.'

'Well, she thought wrong because I haven't.'

Justine never took on trainee or junior hairdressers, running the salon by herself with the help of a receptionist, who was sometimes called upon to help out with a shampoo or removing a client from beneath a hair dryer. Would-be hairdressers were either a complete waste of time and upset the clients so much that they lost you business, or they were so good that they got ideas above their station and stole them away to start up on their own. And as for this girl – she'd have the women's backs up in no time at all with them looks of hers.

Lena felt sick with disappointment. She'd been counting on getting this job. Now what was she going to do?

Judith watched her. The reality was that right now, despite the fact that it went against her belief that juniors were an expensive nuisance, with all the new acts coming into town to entertain the workers and the troops, she did need some trained help if she wasn't going to have to turn business away. Her receptionist was useless as a hairdresser, as she'd already proved.

'I'll have a think about it,' she told Lena. 'Come back at five o'clock and I'll see if I've made up me mind.'

Lena agreed. It wasn't what she'd hoped for but at least she still had a chance of getting taken on.

As she left the salon she decided that she might as well use the time she now had on her hands to go down to the rest centre and get her papers and a billet sorted out. With a bit of luck it wouldn't be as busy today.

'A billet, you say. Well I'm sorry, my dear, but the billeting officer has already been and gone and he won't be back again now until tomorrow, but I should warn you that it's extremely unlikely that he'll be able to find you anywhere. We've still got families that need to be rehoused. Are you sure there isn't anyone – a relative you might not have thought of, perhaps?'

Lena wished that she could conjure up a long-lost relative who would be willing to take her in, but of course she couldn't and she had to say 'no' as apologetically as though she was in some way responsible or the fact that she was both homeless and without any family. She didn't dare tell the WVS volunteer about her auntie. She suspected that if she did the Rest Centre would insist that she must go back. But what was the point when she knew that the auntie would not have her back?

'And you've lost your papers and your ration book, you say?'

Lena nodded.

'Mmm . . . You do know, I hope, that it's an offence to try to claim a new ration book when you've already got one.'

Lena's face burned with indignation. 'I haven't got one,' she insisted truthfully.

'That's all right, dear. I can see that you're an honest truthful girl, but there's some that aren't, you know, and we have to be careful. Now, name, please, and date of birth . . . ?'

It was well over an hour before all the paperwork had been done and Lena had been issued with a new ration book and everything else.

'I'll hand you over to Mrs Cutler now,' the WVS volunteer told her, 'and she'll take you to our clothes store and kit you out with enough to tide you over. We can only provide the basics, of course, but she'll tell you where you can go to buy some decent second-hand clothes.'

'But what about a billet for me?' Lena asked anxiously.

The volunteer sighed and looked at Lena over the top of her spectacles. She was thin with a pointed nose and greying too tightly permed hair, her skin crepey and faintly yellowing. When she pursed her lips as she was doing now Lena could see all the lines fanning out from them. When she turned her head to look purposefully towards the queue of people still waiting to be dealt with, the light caught her chin, revealing several hairs.

'I've already told you, dear, as a single girl you aren't priority. The billeting officers can't find enough rooms for those people who are priority, never mind finding one for you. The best I can do is advise you to keep coming in. Where did you sleep last night?'

'I went with the trekkers,' Lena told her.

'Then that is what I recommend you continue to do until the billeting officers can find you somewhere.'

She looked down the line of tables, some of which had volunteers seated at them and some of which did not, calling out, 'Mrs Cutler, dear, will you come and take this young lady to get some clothing?'

The woman who came bustling up was the same age as the volunteer who had been dealing with Lena, but plumper and with a kinder smile.

'Let's get you a cup of tea first, shall we, love?' she suggested, guiding Lena towards the tea urn, pouring her a cup of tea and giving her two biscuits.

Lena hadn't realised how hungry she was until her mouth started watering at the sight of them. They were only thin plain things, not custard creams or fig rolls, but Lena nibbled slowly on them, relishing every morsel, refusing to give in to the temptation of gobbling them up so quickly that they'd be gone before she'd even tasted them properly.

'Well, now, I can see that someone's taught you some very pretty manners,' Mrs Cutler approved.

'Me mum. She was in service,' Lena told her. For no reason at all her eyes were suddenly stinging with tears. Her mother had been hard on her at times, but she had still been her mother. She'd often said that she only went on at her because she wanted Lena to better herself, and not make the mistakes she had made. The WVS volunteer's praise had suddenly brought home to Lena just how alone she was without anyone to call her own, and how much, deep down inside, she did miss her parents.

'There now, I've gone and upset you. I'm sorry, love. Finished your tea, have you? Very well then, we'd better go and sort you out with some clothes. This way.'

Putting down her now empty tea cup, Lena followed the other woman through a door and into a narrow corridor, past an office in which women were busy working on typewriting machines, and then into a large room that was crammed with racks and shelves of second-hand clothes of every description, including footwear.

'Right, we'll start with underthings first, shall we? Now what size brassiere would you say you were, love?' Mrs Cutler asked her.

'A 34.' Lena told her, suddenly feeling slightly self-conscious as she saw Mrs Cutler looking from her chest to her narrow waist. Lena was aware of the fact that she was, as her mother had often complained, 'all out of proportion' with narrow shoulders and a narrow waist, but a full bosom for her just over five foot one inch height.

She was wearing her one and only brassiere, washed on a Monday, when she had to wear an old liberty bodice instead, and then worn all week until the next washday came along.

'Here we are,' Mrs Cutler told her, reaching for a cardboard box that had the figure '34' written on the side, and removing the lid. 'You can have a look through for yourself, but you can only have one, remember.'

Lena hadn't known what she was expecting but the ugly blancmange-pink brassieres inside the box were not in any way appealing.

'They're what they give the ATS girls as part of their uniform,' Mrs Cutler explained.

No wonder they'd been given away, Lena thought as she touched the stiff fabric. Still, beggars couldn't be choosers, could they?

She picked one up and Mrs Cutler nodded her head in approval, putting the lid back on the box and saying, 'Now knickers.'

If the bra was ugly and unappealing that was nothing compared with the knickers she was expected to choose from, Lena decided a few seconds later, looking into a box full of bottle-green school knickers so voluminous they would have done for two and still had room to spare.

'We were given them by a school outfitter that was closing down. Ever such good quality, they are.'

Lena smiled wanly.

Thank goodness it was summer and it wasn't going to be necessary for her to wear stockings all the time. As luck would have it, she had been wearing her garter belt when she walked out, and so she was able to assure Mrs Cutler that she didn't need another one.

From the underwear section they moved on to

blouses and Lena ended up with a plain grey short-sleeved blouse with its collar edged in red. It wasn't really to her taste at all.

'You'll be able to buy yourself something a bit prettier at one of the second-hand clothes shops. These are only to tide you over, and we do ask that you return everything once you've got yourself sorted out. Now let's see if we can find you a skirt.'

Eventually they did, although Lena was horrified when she realised that Mrs Cutler expected her to wear a heavy black linen gathered skirt with a pattern round the bottom in red and white, contrasting it with the pretty floral softly cut frocks she had seen earlier and thought so smart, and admitting that she felt bitterly disappointed.

She hadn't expected to get something as nice as them, of course, but she had hoped she would get something a bit more to her own taste.

'Go ever so well with that grey blouse, this skirt will,' Mrs Cutler announced happily, holding it up for Lena's inspection, and then before Lena could refuse it, Mrs Cutler was telling her, 'All you need now is a towel and a piece of soap, and then we'll find you a bag to put this lot in and you'll be all set. Got a nice billet, have you?' she asked chattily, as she guided Lena back towards the exit.

'No, there aren't any unless you're a priority, and me being on my own I'm not, so I've having to join them trekkers.'

'Well, at least summer's coming, and I dare say they'll find you somewhere soon. Now what about one of these big straw baskets? Hold ever such a lot, they do.'

Lena's heart dropped. She had a mental image of

Dolly and her straw bag. A wave of self-pity washed over her. Only the thought of having to go cap in hand to her auntie and then being turned away kept her from bursting into tears.

'We give you a bit of cash as well. Have you got a purse?'

Lena had. As she opened her bag she could feel the sharp edge of her Post Office savings book inside its lining. The knowledge that she had her savings steadied and comforted her.

Once she was back outside, she looked at the cheap second-hand watch she had bought for herself when she had first started work. It was too soon for her to go back to the salon. Instinctively Lena knew that it wouldn't do anything to improve her chances of getting a job if she turned up at the wrong time.

She'd been given two pounds ten shillings by the WVS to tide her over. She might as well go and have a look round one of the second-hand places the WVS woman had mentioned to her. She certainly wasn't going to wear the clothes she had been given if she could help it.

An hour later, as she emerged into the sunshine from the darkness of the second-hand clothes shop, Lena felt if anything, even more depressed. There had certainly been plenty to choose from but in styles more suited to someone of her auntie's age and proportions, and those dresses that would have fitted her looked like they'd come off school girls. She wouldn't be wasting her money on anything like that.

It was still only four o'clock. She had another hour to go yet before she could go back to the salon and her feet were beginning to hurt. She had a pair of plimsolls in her straw bag and it was only female pride that stopped her from putting them on.

The women she had seen earlier in their summer dresses had all disappeared, gone back to their homes, Lena thought enviously. they obviously hadn't been bombed. They probably lived somewhere posh and safe, like Charlie's mum and dad. The now familiar feeling of bleak misery started to invade her insides again. Why hadn't Charlie meant what he had said to her? Why had he lied to her? It would all have been so different if he had loved her. Lena sniffed back her emotions. She wasn't going to show herself up by crying in the street. She didn't have a hand-kerchief so she had to use a corner of the sleeve of her cardigan to pat her face dry, stopping at the entrance to a narrow street as she did so, so that no one could see her. After she had recovered her compos-ure she decided that she might as well use some of the money she had been given to treat herself to a slap-up tea at Joe Lyons.

And then she saw it. The frock! Exactly as she had pictured it inside her head. It was in the window of a smart-looking shop – the kind she would normally never have dreamed of going into, but there was a war on, she reminded herself determinedly, and the shop had a sign across the window, saying, 'Second-hand "models" on sale here.'

She'd got her hand on the door handle before she knew it, hesitating only for a second and then taking a deep breath before opening the door and going in.

The woman inside the shop was elderly but upright, her white hair smoothed into an immaculate chignon, the diamond rings on her fingers glittering despite the dimness of the shop's interior. She was wearing a plain fawn skirt with a matching cardigan over a cream silk blouse, and instinctively Lena knew that her clothes were somehow a cut above even the clothes that Charlie's mother and sister had been wearing. They set the woman in the shop apart, marking her out as someone to be respected and treated with caution.

The shop itself had seen better days, Lena decided as she took in the faded blue carpet and the little gilt chairs with the gilt paint worn off in places and their blue satin seat covers as faded as the carpet.

The woman would have got on well with her own mother, Lena recognised as she withstood the steely, openly dismissive visual inspection to which she was being subjected.

'The trade entrance is at the back of the shop,' the woman announced eventually in a crisp cold voice.

Perhaps if she hadn't said that, or if she hadn't looked at her the way she had, reminding her of everything that Charlie's mother have made her feel. Lena might just have given in and scuttled off, but now, with her obvious contempt, the woman had aroused in Lena a stubborn pride she had not previously known she possessed.

Unconsciously mimicking the woman's own stance, Lena stood tall, refusing to be cowed as she said firmly, 'I was wondering about the frock you've got in the window.'

'The silk tea dress?'

Was that what it was called? It had to be since it was the only thing in the window. Well, Lena certainly wasn't going to let on that she hadn't known what it was called.

'Yes. What size is it, please?'

'It's two guineas,' the woman told her sharply, without answering her question.

Two guineas! Normally Lena would have shown her reaction by letting her jaw drop and then speaking her mind, scoffing at the impossibility of a bit of cloth costing so much, but somehow a new Lena was starting to grow inside her, a Lena whose roots came from the pain and humiliation Charlie's parents had heaped on her, and her desire to prove that no matter what they or anyone else thought, she was as good as any girl and she could prove it.

She pursed her lips. 'It would have to be in very good condition for me to pay that much. After all, it is second-hand.'

Something changed in the other woman's expression, a something so faint that Lena wasn't even sure she had really seen it.

'It is in perfect condition. It's an ex-model gown. Do you know what that means?' she demanded as she went to unfasten the door to the window.

Lena was tempted to say that she did, but as though she already knew that she did not the woman told her, 'It means that the dress has been worn only for private showings in an exclusive shop from which specially selected customers could then order their own tea dresses to be made up for them. It's French, from before the war.'

The woman backed out of the window, the frock over her arm. Lena's heart lurched sideways inside her chest. What was she doing in here? She was way out of her depth and her price range, but the woman was holding up the dress and Lena's panic melted in a surge of female longing. She reached out to touch the fabric. It slid softly against her fingers.

'I'll have to try it on,' she told the woman determinedly.

Again she was subjected to an assessingly critical look. She half expected to be told that she couldn't, but instead the woman stepped back further into the shop pulling back a thin curtain to reveal a small changing cubicle.

'In there, and you can leave your things out here. I'm not having you putting it into your bag and then trying to make off with it.'

Lena's face burned. The woman was making it plain what she really thought of her. She felt a sharp resurgence of her earlier pride.

It look her longer than she had expected to get into the dress, mainly because she was so nervous, all fingers and thumbs as she fastened hooks and eyes, but finally it was on and she was ready to step out of the cubicle and look at herself in the long mirror she had seen in the main area of the shop.

Although she herself wasn't aware of it Lena was a natural observer, storing away what she had seen inside her head, and now as she walked out into the shop she adopted unconsciously the way she had seen Charlie's sister walk, her head held high, her steps deliberate and full of pride in herself. And yet when she saw herself in the mirror her first reaction was one of disappointment. To Lena, who was used to skirts and frocks cinched in at the waist, the silk dress seemed to turn her from someone with the kind of curves that Charlie had so admired into someone of a very different shape. Inside her own head Lena thought that the reflection looking back at her from the mirror was dull and not at all eye-catching, a look that was emphasised by the fact that she had forgotten to renew her lipstick after her cup of tea and biscuits at the rest centre, so that even her face looked plainer than usual.

However, when she looked towards the older woman, expecting to see her own feelings reflected in her eyes, instead what she saw was unexpected approval.

'Well, it's certainly an improvement on those dreadful clothes you came in here wearing. You're Italian, aren't you?'

'My father was,' Lena answered warily.

The older woman nodded. 'Take some advice from me, and in future when you buy clothes remember that with your looks you do not need to emphasise them with what you wear. A simple well-cut skirt and blouse, and a dress like the one you're wearing now would look far better on you. Tight clothes make a young woman your age look cheap and easy. If you hadn't come in here and asked to try on the tea dress I would have assumed from looking at you that you wanted to look that way, but since you obviously don't my advice to you is that in future you should look for plain understated clothes in creams and browns, good-quality wool in winter, linen in summer and silk all the year round.'

Lena was so astonished to receive this advice that her mouth fell open. Her pride was urging her to object to the older woman's assessment of her and to defend her own taste, but then she remembered how the minute she walked into the shop she had been struck by her elegance, and how she had felt that she had looked so much smarter than even

Charlie's mother. Someone who looked like her would always command respect. Slowly and a little bit painfully Lena's mind assimilated those facts. She touched one of the elbow-length slightly puffed sleeves on the silk dress. It was true that the way the dress skimmed her breasts and only hinted at her waist before falling softly to a couple of inches below her knees did make her look different, but what if it *was* a difference that meant others would treat her with respect?

She looked at the older woman. 'I'll give you one pound and ten shillings for it,' she told her bravely.

The woman laughed. 'I'm practically giving it away at two guineas, and if it wasn't such a small size it would have sold months ago.'

'And it could be here for a lot more months if someone small enough doesn't come in,' Lena pointed out firmly.

The woman studied her with narrowed eyes.

'Two pounds,' she announced, 'and I wouldn't be letting it go at that if it wasn't for the fact that my son is insisting that I close down the business and move to the country to live with him and his wife.'

Two pounds! If she bought the dress that would only leave her with ten shillings, and if the rest centre found her a billet, she'd have to pay for that, and if she didn't get that job she'd be without any money until she found one. But she had her savings, Lena reminded herself. She took a deep breath and then nodded her head vigorously.

'All right then, and I'll keep it on.'

Ten minutes later she was strolling along the street feeling as though she were walking on air, pausing to look at herself in every shop window she passed, her old clothes bundled up in the straw basket along with everything else.

It was time for her to go back to the salon. Lena's tummy was twisting into nervous knots. The sulky receptionist-cum-junior had gone and the only person in the salon was its owner, whose eyebrows rose when she saw what Lena was wearing.

'Well, there's a change and no mistake. I dunno know why you've come looking for work here if you can afford to buy a frock like that, because I'm telling you straight, the most I'd be paying you is two pounds a week – that is, if I was willing to offer you a job and I dunno know that I am.'

Lena caught her breath. She'd heard that women working in munitions were earning over double that, but she was too young for that kind of work and besides, it didn't really appeal to her. Two pounds, though – it was less than Simone had paid her.

'Simone's a good friend,' Judith continued, 'but the thing is, I've already got a receptionist and I don't want the bother of training up a junior.'

'I'm not a junior,' Lena protested. 'I've bin learning to do perms and cuts. And Simone was training me up to be a proper stylist.'

Judith had been doing some more thinking in Lena's absence. Much as she hated paying out good money to someone else, as today's events had just proved, the influx of new acts to the theatre meant that if she wasn't careful she was going to start having to turn business away, and that would be even worse than paying someone to work for her. But was Lena the right person?

'Hmm, so why are you here looking for a job then? Ruined someone's hair, have you?'

'No!' Lena gasped indignantly at the unfairness of the comment when she had been the one to save the salon's client from exactly that fate only a matter of hours ago. Something, though, warned her that it would not be a good idea to remind Judith of that fact.

'What then?'

'I've had words with my auntie,' Lena admitted reluctantly, 'and she's thrown me out and told Simone that it will be the worse for her if she keeps me on.'

'Thrown you out? What for? Mekin' eyes at her hubby?'

'No.' This time Lena's denial contained shocked revulsion.

'Mmm . . . Well, as it happens you're in luck on account of a new show being booked for the theatre and a fresh cast arriving. They'll be starting rehearsals next week and I dare say they'll be in here wanting their hair done, as well as all the wigs for the show, so I'm prepared to take you on on trial.'

Lena felt almost light-headed with relief, but before she could say anything Judith was warning her, 'And I do mean on trial. Any mistakes and you'll be out. I can't afford to have the reputation of my salon damaged. Like I said, I'll pay you two pounds a week, and when it comes to tips, you're to hand them over to me and then they'll get shared out between the three of us at the end of the week – half to me and the other half shared between you and Jill, the other girl.'

Lena frowned. Simone had always allowed her to keep the pennies she was sometimes given by way of a tip, but she knew instinctively that to say so wouldn't go down well with her new employer.

'You're to wear one of me special overalls whilst you're here working, but if you take it home with you then the cost of it will be deducted from your wages. And same goes if I find out that the shampoo is going down too fast. Oh, and no doing your own hair in my time neither. You can start tomorrow. Where are you billeted?'

'I haven't got anywhere yet,' Lena was forced to admit. 'Although the rest centre has told me to come back tomorrow.'

Now it was Judith's turn to frown. She was a shrewd judge of character and she guessed that Lena would be hard worker, on to whom she could load extra work without Lena complaining. She had the right way of dealing with the clients too, as she'd already proved and, like Simone before her, Judith could already see the potential of an assistant stylist whose hair could be put in any style at all and still look good. Now that she had made up her mind to take her on Judith didn't want to risk losing her simply because she ended up being given a billet too far away for her to travel to work. And besides, always keen to make one penny do the work of two, Judith could see an opportunity to kill two birds with one stone, as it were.

'I might be able to help you out there. Me nan died a couple of weeks ago and so me mam and dad have a spare room. They was going to get in touch with the billeting lot, but I dare say I could have a word with them on your behalf. You'll be expected to muck in, though, and help me mam out around the house, and that.'

Lena nodded vigorously. She could hardly believe her good luck. Here she was with a new job and the hope of somewhere to stay.

'I'm not promising anything, mind,' Judith warned. 'Me mam might have found herself someone for the room already, or she might not take to you. A bit funny like that, she is, so don't go getting your hopes up too high.'

TWELVE

'There's not been any more letters from that spy of yours then?' Carole asked Katie chattily as they left the Littlewoods building from where the censorship service operated, at the end of their day's work.

Katie gave a quick worried look over her shoulder. Unlike her, Carole seemed not to worry about the secrecy rules they had been warned they must never break, but then Carole seemed to take everything much more lightly than Katie ever could.

'No, thank goodness,' she confirmed once she had assured herself that no one was within earshot.

'That will make your Luke happy then. Do you think you and Luke will be going to the Graffie on Saturday? Only if you are, then the four of us could pair up if you like, 'cos me and Andy are going.'

'I don't know if Luke will be off duty or not. Can I let you know later in the week?' Katie hadn't seen or heard from Luke since Sunday. Was he still cross with her about her plans to go to see her parents? She hoped not. She hated it when there was an atmosphere between them, and in fact it made her reluctant to be with him. She did love him, of course, but she just wished he was more relaxed about things, like

Grace's Seb. It felt so disloyal just thinking that kind of thing that Katie hastily pushed the thought into that shadowy place inside her heart where she put all those things that made her feel worried and upset.

'Of course you can,' Carole agreed.

'. . . and Seb's going to take me to show me where he'll be working on Saturday since we've both got the day off. He's borrowing a motorcycle from someone he knows so that we won't have to worry about getting the train.'

'Well, I'm very pleased for you both love.' Jean assured her daughter. 'With Seb being made up that will give you a good start when you get married.'

'Don't forget he'll need to find himself a job once this war is over,' Sam warned. He was sitting at the kitchen table reading the *Liverpool Post* whilst Jean bustled about the kitchen preparing tea. He'd already done his bit towards their evening meal. On the draining board were some freshly washed new potatoes, along with a lettuce, and some radish from his allotment, whilst the last of the rhubarb had been stewed for a pudding, which would be sweetened with a spoonful of their precious condensed milk.

'There's going to be a lot of men needing to find themselves work once the war's over, just like there was last time.'

'Seb will be able to find work, Dad,' Grace defended her fiancé loyally. 'Don't forget he's got his training to back him up. Seb was saying, Mum,' Grace continued turning back to her mother, 'that we should think about staying over in this Whitchurch on Saturday night, so that we can have a proper look round.'

'Oh, no, Grace, you can't do that.' The words were out before Jean could stop herself. She was glad that she was removing some scones from the oven so that Grace couldn't see her face, which would give away what she was really thinking. She knew that Grace was a sensible girl, but Jean could see in Seb's eyes how much he loved her daughter, and young people being what they were and having the feelings they did meant that it wasn't a good idea for them to be alone together too much, when they were in the position that Seb and Grace were and couldn't marry until Grace had finished her training. Staying away from home together overnight was in Jean's maternal opinion too much of a risk. Not, of course, that she could say so to Grace. Her daughter would be mortified and embarrassed, and would no doubt accuse her mother of not trusting her. Jean felt embarrassed herself when she remembered the number of time she and Sam had nearly given in to temptation during their engagement.

'Why ever not?' Grace was asking her now, surprise and just a hint of wariness in her voice that warned Jean that if her daughter were to suspect her real fears, she'd get on her high horse and then things might end up being said that both of them would regret. Grace was a good girl and a wonderful daughter, but she also had her own mind and a great deal of spirit, and Jean knew that she would not like what her mother was thinking.

Quickly she told Grace, 'Because I was counting on your help on Sunday for this picnic we're having on the allotment. A sort of celebration because the bombing is over.'

'You never said.'

217

'Well, that's the first I've heard of any picnic on my allotment.'

Grace and Sam both spoke at the same time, leaving Jean even more grateful for the excuse of the heat of the oven to cover her guiltily red face.

'Well, I'm sure I did,' she fibbed. 'But never mind that now. Do you remember how much fun we used to have with those picnics we had on the allotment when the kiddies were little, Sam?'

'I remember when Grace here went and took a bite out of every single one of me ripening strawberries, taking the covers off them so that she could do it and then leaving them all fit for nothing.'

'Oh, Dad, don't remind me,' Grace protested, looking mortified, and then laughing.

'She was only four, Sam,' Jean defended their daughter, even though Sam was grinning as well, showing that he had only resurrected the memory in order to tease their daughter. 'Grace had seen that the strawberries had started to go red and, bless her, she didn't know that they hadn't ripened all through so she kept on tasting them, not realising what she was doing.'

Sam shook his head. 'And then there was that time the twins dug up all the young lettuce so that they could stick the leaves on their mud pies to make patterns.'

Jean laughed herself now, and pointed out, 'Well, they won't be doing that this time.'

'When will they hear from the Exchange, Mum, about those interviews they went for?' Grace asked.

'Not for a day or two yet. Sasha's really keen to go there, but I'm not so sure about Lou.' A small frown wrinkled Jean's forehead. She was worried about the twins, and not for the reasons she usually worried about them. Something had changed between them that night when Sasha had nearly lost her life. The last thing Jean wanted was for her daughters to end up like her and her own twin – estranged and only able to make polite conversation with one another. On the other hand, neither did Jean want them to be so close that when the time came they weren't able to go off and have lives of their own with families of their own. They had very different personalities from her and Vi's, had Lou and Sasha, and they were very different from one another in that way as well, for all that on the outside they were as alike as two peas in a pod, as the saying went. Sasha, the elder, was quieter and shyer, whilst Lou was the one who instigated the mischief in which Sasha had always enthusiastically joined her. Now, though, Lou seemed to have lost the exuberance that had so often made Jean shake her head in despair whilst Sasha seemed to be putting herself forward a bit more and taking the lead in their relationship. Jean admitted to herself that she had never thought she'd see the day when she was actually worried about Lou becoming quieter. Perhaps it was the shock of almost losing her twin that had brought about the change, she decided.

'Well, if you're dead set on this picnic then, Mum, I suppose I'll have to tell Seb that we'll need to get back.' Grace knew that Seb would be as disappointed as she was, but what else could she do? It would only make her mother suspicious if she told her that they couldn't change their plans, and the last thing Grace wanted was her mother treating her as though she was still the same age as the twins and giving her a warning lecture about the dangers of allowing Seb too much intimacy. The relationship she and Seb shared was a proper grown-up one, not some girl-and-boy thing. They were engaged, after all, but Grace knew her mother, so she stifled her disappointment and tried to put a brave face on the need for her and Seb to change their plans. At least she knew that Seb would understand and that he wouldn't kick up a fuss. And that, of course, was because he truly loved her and wanted her to be happy. She was lucky, Grace acknowledged, her heart overflowing with love for her fiancé.

'Knowing your mother, she's probably invited half the next street as well as our own,' said Sam, 'so you'd better get here bright and early otherwise no one will get anything to eat. In fact, it might be a good idea if Seb dropped you off here on Saturday so that you can stay the night – I dare say Katie won't mind sharing with you. That way you'll be ready for an early start.'

Jean gave her husband a surprised look behind Grace's back and then went pink when Sam winked at her. He *knew* she had made it up about the picnic, and she suspected he knew why she had done it as well. Jean felt guilty all over again, but relieved at the same time that Sam understood and approved of what she had done.

'I thought that Katie was going to see her parents next weekend?' Grace said.

'She was, but she's decided to wait until Luke can go with her. Oh, here's Katie now,' Jean announced, as the sound of the back door opening had her turning towards it with a warm smile to welcome Katie home from work.

The Campion kitchen had a lovely feeling to it, Katie thought as she and Grace exchanged affectionate hugs. She knew too that the warmth it possessed was down to Jean and her love for her family. The Campion family was the kind that secretly Katie had always longed to be part of when she had been growing up. Now that Katie was Luke's girl, Jean, with her motherly generosity and love, had made her feel as though she was part of the family. That acceptance and sense of belonging was very important to Katie. She didn't think she could marry a man whose family did not accept her, and nor, if she was honest, would she really want to marry a man who came from a background like her own. It wasn't just Luke whom she loved, it was his family as well, and if the two of them were to fall out and go their separate ways it wouldn't just be a future husband she would lose, it would be the family as well, and Katie didn't think she could bear that. But she wasn't going to have to bear it, was she? Luke loved her, she knew that, and she loved him.

'You run upstairs and get washed up, Katie,' Jean instructed. 'I'm just about to get tea served.'

'Where are the twins?' Grace asked, dipping her finger into the cooling bowl of stewed rhubarb behind her mother's back and then grimacing at its tart taste, because of the sugar rationing.

'Playing tennis.'

When Grace's eyebrows rose, Jean told her, 'They've joined the Tennis Club. It was Sasha's idea.'

'The next thing we know they'll be off to Wallasey to invite Cousin Bella to play with them then, will

221

they?' Grace joked, adding, 'Have you heard anything from Auntie Vi yet about the wedding?'

'I had a letter this morning. Seemingly Daphne's parents want to keep things quiet on account of losing their lad, so there's not going to be a big do, only immediate family.'

'So we won't be invited then?' Grace guessed.

'No. Mind you, Vi did say that they'd take our wedding presents with them to save us the cost and the trouble of taking them to the post office.'

Grace looked outraged. 'Does she really expect us to buy them something when we haven't even been invited to the wedding?'

'Now, Grace love,' Jean calmed her daughter, 'to be honest with you neither me nor your dad fancied going all that long way in the first place, and if Daphne's family are as full of themselves as our Vi is making out, then I wouldn't fancy mixing with them anyway. To read Vi's letters you'd think their Charlie was marrying a member of the Royal Family.'

'She was just as bad when Bella was getting married,' Grace reminded Jean. 'Going on and on about Bella's in-laws-to-be being so important, and look what happened there? In the end in turned out that Bella's husband and his father had been stealing from the council.'

Jean sighed. 'Vi always was one for being impressed by anyone who put on a bit of a show, and going on and on about them. I remember how she went on about her Edwin when she first me him. To hear her talk you'd have thought he was Rudolph Valentino. I could hardly keep my face straight the first time I met him. I remember our mum saying that Vi must be smitten to go on about him being so good-looking when he was anything but. Now, about my picnic, Grace . . .' Jean went on briskly, changing the subject.

THIRTEEN

She had got a job, and with a bit of luck, come tomorrow she could even have a billet as well. For the first time since she had realised that Charlie didn't love her Lena felt a slight easing of the tight band of pain that had locked round her heart.

She was, though, going to have to join the trekkers again tonight, after all she'd said about not doing so. It was only for one more night, Lena comforted herself, and if Dolly's grandson wanted to poke fun at her and have a laugh at her expense because of that then let him. It would be no skin off her nose what he said or how he looked at her, would it? Why should she care what he thought? She didn't. She could always try to avoid Dolly and her grandson, but if she were honest Lena knew that she would feel safer with them than she would on her own.

With the relief of knowing that she had a job, the cramping tension had left her stomach and she was, she discovered, very hungry. Since the trekkers' transport wouldn't leave until later in the evening she had several hours to fill. She could always go to see a film – she'd have a nice comfy seat that way – but with what she'd spent on her new frock – her *tea dress*, she corrected herself mentally, automatically mimicking inside her own head the manner and intonation of the woman in the shop – she hadn't got very much money left, so instead she decided to find a chip shop and buy herself a nice bit of fish and some chips, and then she could start walking slowly back to the rest centre to collect a blanket and check that there wasn't after all somewhere better for her to spend the night.

By the time Lena had found a chip shop that was open and undamaged by the previous week's bombing the shop itself was full and there was a queue outside it. By now her stomach was gnawing at her with hunger so she joined the queue, waiting patiently with the others in it to be served whilst her stomach was tormented with the smell of fish and chips.

When Lena did reach the front of the queue there was another delay whilst a fresh batch of chips finished cooking, but eventually she was served by one of the two women working flat out behind the counter, both of them as dark-haired and Italian-looking as Lena was herself. There was a tradition amongst Liverpool's immigrant Italian families of owning fish and chip and ice-cream businesses, although the men who had once run those businesses had now disappeared – either shipped off out of the country as aliens or because as younger generation grandsons and sons of immigrants they had taken English nationality and were now in uniform.

As soon as she was outside Lena reached hungrily into her pennyworth of chips, so hot and freshly cooked that they almost burned her fingers and her mouth.

A couple of young boys, seeing her with them, gave voice to the familiar boyish chant of, 'Go on, give us a chip,' but Lena shook her head. She was far too hungry to share them with anyone. She headed for the rest centre, eating her chips as she walked, her basket now an increasingly heavy weight on her arm.

'No, I'm sorry, mothers with young children take priority.'

Lena nodded as she listened to the now familiar chant, letting the queue take her towards the tea urn as she accepted the blanket she was handed.

At least she'd be able to use the facilities here to have a wash and a brush-up, before she left to join the trekkers, and then tomorrow she would have a proper room again, Lena comforted herself, as she gulped thirstily at the tea she had been given.

The rest centre had a shower block and lockers but the lockers were all taken so Lena had to put her basket on one of the slatted wooden seats outside the showers, where she could keep it within view whilst she stood beneath a trickle of water that was barely warm, before wrapping herself in the clean, dry but very thin and old towel she had been able to 'buy to use' for one penny.

Once she was dry and dressed in her own clothes, the silk tea dress carefully and lovingly folded and then wrapped up in the horrid skirt to protect it before being put in her basket, Lena plaited her still wet hair, to keep it tidy.

She had been on her feet virtually all day and now they were beginning to ache so she put on her second-hand pumps.

226

It was time for her to leave if she didn't want to miss the trekker transport. She just hoped that her new employer would keep her word and that her parents would agree to take her in.

She didn't want to have to show herself up by looking for Dolly and her grandson, but the proximity of a group of rough-looking men, one of whom kept on looking at her, was making her feel uncomfortable. Her discomfort increased when he said something to the others and they all burst out laughing. The crowd of waiting trekkers was growing, and Lena tried to wriggle deeper into it, but the woman she was trying to squeeze past rounded on her and told her, 'Here, watch what you're doing with them elbows, will yer?' turning back to the man she was with to say so loudly that Lena knew she was intended to hear, 'The cheek of it, her elbowing an adult out of the way when she's only a bit of a kid. Time was when kids her age knew how to treat their elders and betters.'

A bit of a kid? She certainly wasn't that, Lena thought indignantly, her attention distracted when a fight broke out amongst the group of men she had wanted to avoid. Very quickly a crowd gathered round them, jeering and cheering as they egged them on.

Lena shrank back as far as she could into the crowd and looked away. She didn't like seeing physical violence; it made her feel sick and all trembly inside. Her mum and her auntie had laughed at her for it, but she'd always been that way. Her mother had reckoned her reaction had come from watching her dad taking part in a boxing match when she'd been very young.

'Cried your eyes, you did, when your dad was knocked out in the first round,' her mother had told her.

Street fighting was a fact of life in the poorer areas of the city, and there was a proud history of the Italian boxing clubs producing some world-famous boxers, but Lena just couldn't bear the thought of men beating one another up with their fists, never mind the sight of them doing it.

The transport was arriving. She tried frantically to remember exactly where it was she had seen Dolly the previous evening. They had gone on one of the coaches, she knew that, so it made sense to go and stand by them.

'On your own, are you, sweetheart? Why don't you come along with us? I might even let you sit on me knee.'

The man who had been watching her earlier had managed to sneak up on her without her realising it.

Lena tried to walk past him and then froze as he curled his hand round the handles of her basket, and told her with a leer, 'Why don't you let me carry that for you?'

'Thank you but I'm meeting some friends,' Lena told him firmly.

'You and me could be good friends. How old are you, sweetheart, thirteen? You've got a nice pair of tits for your age – but then I bet all the men tell you that, don't they? Let anyone have a feel of them yet, have you? I bet you've all them boys at school chasing after you like you was a little film star.'

He was pulling on her basket now, trying to force her to go with him. Panic flooded through her.

'Let go of the basket.'

The male voice was icy cold – and familiar. Lena obeyed it automatically, reacting to its command before her brain was able to assimilate what was happening rationally, and it was only when the command was repeated that she realised that it wasn't meant for her but for the man who had grabbed hold of it, and who now was glowering at her as he too let go of it, spilling the contents as he himself disappeared into the crowd.

'My golly, Lena, it was lucky that my Gavin saw what was going on.'

Dolly and her grandson. Lena's face burned as she kneeled down to pick up her things and push them back into the basket. Grateful as she was to have been rescued, she couldn't help wishing that it had been anyone but Gavin who had driven off the man and his unwanted attentions.

Now her things were all over everywhere, and Gavin had hunkered down besides her, helping her to pick them up. Her face went an even brighter red as she saw that the hideous pink brassiere was lying right by his feet. She tried to snatch it up before he could see it but she was too late and she was left having to stammer her thanks as he picked it up and gravely handed it to her.

'You didn't get a billet then?' Dolly asked cheerfully once everything had been put back in the basket and Lena was standing up.

She shook her head but then added proudly, 'But I have got a job and a promise of somewhere to sleep from tomorrow.'

'Come on, let's get the pair of you on the bus.' For some reason the thought of her and Dolly being referred to as a pair made Lena want to giggle, and she found that once she had started to do so, she couldn't stop, so that by the time Gavin had found her and Dolly seats, she was out of breath from laughing.

'Oh, now I've gone and given myself a stitch,' she complained.

Gavin didn't comment. He was not surprised she was a bit hysterical. The chap he'd seen off had plainly meant business, and she had just as plainly been shocked and frightened by him. He had seen that in her face when he'd first caught sight of her and she hadn't realised he and Dolly were there. He wouldn't have known her if it hadn't been for her dress, not with those pumps on and her hair in that plait. Last night she'd looked like a regular vamp but now she looked more like a kid. His mouth hardened with angry disgust as he remembered the way the other man had been leering at her.

'Yes, you had a lucky escape and no mistake, thanks to my Gavin,' Dolly continued proudly as the bus lurched into movement. ''Oo was he, anyway – someone you know?'

'No. I've never seen him before.' And then still a little in shock from what had happened she added shakily, 'He thought I was thirteen.'

'Well, you do look a lot younger with your hair in that plait,' Dolly agreed, plainly as naïvely unaware of the loathsomeness of the man's comment as Lena was herself, Gavin recognised.

He flexed the muscles in his back. He'd be glad to return to the comfort of his bed, in his billet with the pilot and his wife, but he couldn't let his gran go off on her own without someone to keep an eye on her. His gran and the girl both needed someone to keep an eye on them – although for different reasons, Gavin decided grimly as he listened with half an ear to Dolly telling Lena all about her childhood and her Romany grandparents. Gran didn't half like egging the bread when she told her tales, and with Lena she'd got a captive audience. The words 'Lena' and 'captive' passing through his head at virtually the same time aroused both his anger and his protective instinct.

'So what's this job you've got then?' he asked her.

Lena was tempted to tell him that it was none of his business. She was still mortified over what had happened and the horrible pink brassiere. On the other hand, he had rescued her from that dreadful man, she acknowledged fair-mindedly.

'Coiffeuse,' she told him, and then when he looked mystified relented enough to explain, 'Hairdresser. It was a hairdresser I was working for before me auntie . . .' she stopped and then continued firmly, 'before. But I wanted to better meself a bit, so I've got a new job now at a better salon where they do all the stars that are on at the Royal Court Theatre. I'm to start there tomorrow and the owner says she thinks that she can find me a billet with her mum and dad.'

Gavin frowned. 'It's the billeting officer that says where folk are to go,' he reminded Lena. It wasn't really any of his business if she got taken advantage of but somehow he still couldn't help worrying about her, envisaging the 'parents' as another man in the mould of the one from whom he had just rescued her.

Unaware of what Gavin was thinking, Lena tossed her head and told him triumphantly, 'I know that, but this room's only come free on account of my new boss's nan having died and her mum hasn't had time yet to tell the council. Judith says that with me working for her and not having anywhere to sleep that makes me a priority case, 'cos she can't have someone who looks like she's spent the night in a haystack working in her salon. I have to wear a special overall – lilac, it is, with the name of the salon embroidered on it in grey. Judith has them specially brought over from New York by a friend of hers who is in the Merchant Navy,' Lena told them importantly.

Listening to her, Gavin grimaced a little to himself. Perhaps it was unfair of him, given the danger they endured, but he didn't entirely approve of the fact that some merchant seamen brought back goods with them from America, and not just for their own families. Some of them earned themselves a very nice extra income supplying the black marketeers with rationed goods.

Suddenly feeling self-conscious when she realised that whilst he was listening intently to her, Gavin had not contributed anything further to the conversation, Lena stopped talking. The motion of the bus was making her feel slightly queasy and before too long she had to smother first one and then another yawn, placing her hand in front of her mouth just as her mother had taught her.

Watching her, Dolly gave a belly laugh and nudged Lena in the ribs, telling her admiringly, 'Well, I never. You've got ever such fancy manners, haven't you? Proper posh.'

'My mum was in service,' Lena told her, 'and she was always going on about the right way to do things.'

Dolly nodded approvingly. 'Took me for ever such

a nice meal tonight, our Gavin did, in a proper hotel. Treats his gran like a queen, he does.'

Lena smiled tiredly. She couldn't wait for tomorrow night and the comfort of a proper bed.

They had reached the village and the bus lurched to a halt. Once again Gavin ushered both Lena and Dolly towards the farm and settled them both in the barn before going up to the farmhouse to get them a hot drink.

'Sweet on him, the farmer's wife is,' Dolly told Lena as soon as Gavin had gone, rubbing the side of her nose knowingly with her finger as she added, 'He thinks I'm wrong but I know I'm not. I must say that I never thought that a grandson of mine would go and start courting a dull stick like he's got himself involved with. Mind you, I blame our Janet. Always had fancy ideas, she has, and there'll be no getting that head of hers through the door if she does end up with a teacher for a daughter-in-law, it will be that swelled.'

Dolly was beginning to grow on her, Lena admitted as she laughed at her description of her daughter. She was so tired that she was virtually falling asleep sitting up, listening to Dolly's apparently endless stories about her Romany grandparents when Gavin arrived back with mugs of cocoa for them.

Neither the scents of the barn nor its shadowy corners felt as alien to her as they had done last night, and the cocoa was warming and relaxing. Her mother had always made bedtime cocoa. Tears suddenly stung Lena's eyes. She always told herself that she didn't miss her mother, but right now for some reason she did.

Dolly was starting another story.

'That's enough now, Gran,' Gavin announced, getting up and coming over to pick up the empty mug Lena had just put down. 'Lena here's falling asleep, and I certainly need to get some kip.'

They'd got a full convoy due in tomorrow night, and he'd be working. Most of the convoys arrived in the early hours – it was safer that way but it meant that he often had to work nights.

This was the second time she was having to feel grateful to Gavin this evening, Lena acknowledged sleepily. Not that she wanted to feel grateful to him. She didn't want to have to feel anything for him. She had, after all, seen the way he had looked at her when Dolly had first introduced them. Well, let him prefer his teacher girlfriend and think that she wasn't good enough for someone like him. She certainly didn't care.

Something made Lena wake up abruptly and give a sharp cry of protest that immediately woke both Dolly and Gavin.

'Wassar matter?' Dolly demanded gummily, having removed her teeth before she went to sleep, whilst Gavin was already sitting up, and lighting one of the paraffin lamps the farmer had left for them.

'Something ran over my legs. I could feel it,' Lena told them shakily.

'Probably be a rat. Barn is bound to be full of them,' Dolly told her dismissively before settling down to go back to sleep.

A rat? Lena looked wildly round the small dimly lit area, drawing up her knees and wrapping her arms protectively around them.

'More like you moved in your sleep and a bit of straw prickled you,' Gavin offered soothingly, but Lena wasn't reassured. Dolly, with her talk of the barn being full of rats, had scared the wits out of her and Lena knew she couldn't possibly go back to sleep now.

Seeing her expression, Gavin sighed. Trust Gran to say what she thought without thinking about the consequences. Lena was now plainly horrified and would, he suspected, refuse even to think of going back to sleep. He looked at his watch. Half-past two.

'If it was anything, like as not it would have been a cat,' he told Lena. 'There are several of them about.'

The farmer kept them to kill the mice and rats, but he didn't want to risk giving Lena that piece of information. Any country-bred child would have known and accepted that a barn would be home to vermin, but Lena was not country bred.

Lena was still trembling, stiffening at every small sound as she looked fearfully into the shadows.

'You're starting your new job tomorrow so you need to get some sleep,' Gavin reminded her, wanting to calm her down so that they could all go back to sleep. Unlike his gran, who was now snoring away happily, Gavin's conscience wouldn't let him go back to sleep himself whilst Lena was huddled up like she was and plainly terrified, little as he approved of her. She wasn't his sort at all. Gavin's mother had raised her children to work hard and have ambitions. When Gavin settled down it would be with a no-nonsense sensible sort of girl who would be a loyal wife and a good mother, not someone like Lena who would have other men looking at her all the time with that figure of hers and that almost too pretty face. It stood to reason that a girl like her would attract male attention. Even he wasn't able totally to control his instinctive male reaction to her. She was that sort, Gavin thought disapprovingly, and trust his gran to take up with her.

'I daren't lie down in case it comes back again,' Lena admitted in a small voice.

No matter what he might think of her Gavin knew that she wasn't making up her fear and that it was very real for her. Another thing his mother had taught him was to always look out for the weaker sex and to mind his manners. Struggling to conceal his impatience he swung his feet onto the stone floor and then pushed his straw bale over to Lena's, telling her brusquely, 'Shove up then,' as he sat down on his bale next to her.

The warmth of his body against her side was immediately and unexpectedly comforting. So much so that Lena could feel her face starting to burn bright red. Not that he would be able to see that, thank goodness.

'If it does come back again it can run over my legs and not yours, so why don't you try and go back to sleep?' Gavin told Lena firmly.

'I can't. I'm too scared,' she admitted reluctantly.

Gavin needed his sleep and was beginning to regret giving in to his Sir Galahad impulse. Determinedly he leaned down and extinguished the lamps, ignoring Lena's small gasp of protest. The pool of light from the lamps had been comforting and had made her feel safer.

'We can't waste them,' Gavin pointed out 'and anyway it wouldn't be safe to leave them on. Now why don't you lie down and go to sleep?'

236

'I *can't*. I'm too scared.' Lena insisted, adding pleadingly, 'I'll be all right if you just keep talking to me. I won't be able to think about the rat coming back then.'

The last thing Gavin wanted to do was talk to anyone, least of all a girl like Lena. Girls like her were dangerous, even when they weren't your type. That was something he knew instinctively, and he knew that his mother would agree with him, but he was too well brought up and naturally compassionate towards others to turn his back on her.

'Only if you lie down,' he told her firmly.

Reluctantly, Lena slid back down into her blanket.

'So how long have you been on your own?' Gavin asked her, once his own eyes had adjusted to the dark and he could see that she was lying still.

'My mum and dad were killed in the November bombings. I'm not really on my own,' Lena admitted. Then when he didn't make any comment she said, 'I've got an auntie.' Now what on earth had made her admit that? Lena didn't know. She only knew that something about Gavin, despite his disapproval of her, made her want to be truthful with him.

'I was living with her but she's thrown me out and told me that her hubby will take his belt to me if I try to go back, because . . . because of summat I did that she didn't like.' She couldn't bring herself to tell him about Charlie. Suddenly what she had done with Charlie, instead of being something loving and special, felt more like something wrong and shameful. She knew instinctively that Gavin would think that it was and that he would think the worse of her for it. Good girls like his schoolteacher didn't go around letting men share intimacies with them

237

without the benefit of a wedding ring. She had been a fool and she wished now that she had had more sense.

Gavin could guess all too easily what that 'summat' had been. What did surprise him, though, was that Lena should admit to it. That made her either very brazen or very naïve. Naïve? A girl like her? He was the one who was naïve if he thought that.

'It's all on account of my dad being Italian, and me having bad blood.' Lena's voice was defensive now.

Gavin frowned in the darkness. The last thing he wanted was to feel sympathetic towards her, but there'd been a fair bit of talk in his own family about his gran's Romany blood, and Gavin knew that his mother preferred not to talk about it and was ashamed of it, even if his gran was fiercely proud of her grandparents.

Lena yawned. Her eyes felt heavy but she didn't want to go to sleep. Not with that rat around. Besides, there was something reassuring and comforting about lying here talking to Gavin and knowing that he was listening to her.

'I've told you about me, it's your turn now. Tell me something about you,' Lena demanded.

Gavin tensed. Was she trying some kind of come-on? If so she was wasting her time.

'There isn't anything to tell excepting that I'll be glad when my mother gets here from Shropshire to take Gran back there with her. Not that I've told Gran that yet, and you're not to either,' he warned Lena firmly, 'otherwise we'll have her taking off again. Part of the trouble is that she's never liked staying in the same place for too long. She likes to tell everyone it's on account of her Romany blood but my mother says it's because when she was a kid her mum and dad were forever moving around to dodge the debt collectors. He was one of them who preferred shirking to working, was my granddad, by all accounts,' Gavin admitted ruefully. 'I can't say that I'm not looking forward to seeing my own bed again either.'

'You've got a billet then?' Lena asked him enviously.

'Yes. I've been lodging with Chris Stone, the pilot of the tug boat, and his wife ever since Mum decided to evacuate. Mum wanted Gran to go with her, but she insisted on staying put in the house she was renting, and of course when that got bombed she'd nowhere to go. Mrs Stone is doing her best to find somewhere close to them for Gran until Mum can get up here to collect her, but I daren't let her out of my sight. She likes to make out she can take care of herself and that she's as tough as old boots, but I don't like to see her living rough like this, especially not at her age.'

This was safe enough ground, talking about his grandmother.

'I dare say your school teacher girl wouldn't approve either,' Lena felt daring enough to say with the darkness to act as a barrier between them.

'Alison is a terrific person, and Gran would be able to see that for herself if she only gave her a chance. She's done wonders for those kids she teaches, and it can't have been easy for a girl like her to come up here and have to deal with slum kids.'

'How did you meet her?' Lena couldn't help but

be curious, and besides, asking questions helped to subdue that funny painful hurting feeling she got inside when she heard his admiration for his Alison in his voice.

'At night school. She teaches there a couple of nights a week. I want to get my pilot's exams as fast as I can so that I'm properly qualified. It isn't enough any more just to know the Mersey and the tides; you've got to be able to read charts and project tides, and show that you're up to the work. It's like Alison says, once you've got proper qualifications you can work anywhere. Course, then I was daft enough to tell Mum that I'd met Alison and now she's putting two and two together and hearing wedding bells.'

Gavin sounded more amused by his mother's hopes that annoyed. Lena could hear his love for his mother in his voice, and a small hard lump of loneliness clogged her throat as she wondered what it must be like to be part of a family like Gavin's. Well, she'd never find out, would she, because from the sound of her, Gavin's mother would no more countenance someone like her as a prospective daughter-in-law than Charlie's had.

Lena gave a tired yawn and snuggled deeper into her blanket, her breathing slowing and then deepening into sleep.

Gavin, however, remained awake, watching over her until he was sure that she was asleep, even though he told himself that he had no cause to concern himself over her in any kind of way and that he'd warn his grandmother in the morning not to go getting involved with Lena. She was the sort that his mother would have described as 'common'. Easy on the eye and probably easy in other ways as well, if he had guessed right about the reason her auntie had thrown her out.

FOURTEEN

'They've come. Look.' Sasha danced excitedly round the kitchen as she waved the two official-looking envelopes in front of Lou and Jean, the expression on her face one of both hope and apprehension.

Lou said nothing, but there was a tight uncomfortable feeling in her stomach.

'Here's yours.' Sasha handed Lou one of the envelopes and then started to open her own, only to stop and shake her head.

'I can't. You open yours first, Lou.'

Now it was Lou's turn to shake her head.

'Oh, give them here,' Jean demanded, her own nerves on edge on the twins' behalf, but whilst Lou passed their mother hers, Sasha opened her envelope, pulled out the letter and read it quickly before looking at her twin and her mother, her face alight with relief.

'They've accepted me,' she told them unnecessarily. 'Hurry up and open yours, Lou.'

'You do it, Mum.'

Jean told herself that it was Lou's anxiety in case she hadn't been accepted that was making her look so glum, but even when Jean had opened the letter and given her the good news that she too had got a job as a trainee telephonist, Lou's smile wasn't anywhere near as wide as Sasha's.

'We've got to celebrate,' Sasha announced. 'I know, let's go to the Grafton tonight.' When Jean frowned Sasha told her quickly, 'We're old enough now, Mum, and besides, Katie and Luke are going. Katie said so.'

'Very well then,' Jean agreed, giving them each a fierce hug. 'I'm ever so pleased for you both and ever so proud of you as well. Just wait until your dad hears.'

'It will only take us ten minutes to walk to the exchange, and once we've done our training and we're not probationers any more then we'll be in reserved occupations so we can stay here in Liverpool, *and* we'll be doing our bit for the war effort,' Sasha announced happily.

With every word that Sasha said, Lou's heart grew heavier. She felt both guilty and scared because she couldn't share her twin's enthusiasm. What was happening to them?

The Naafi was filled with the low buzz of urgent conversation, as more men came in, wanting to talk about the 'Orders' that had been made known to the troops just over an hour ago.

'We all knew it had to happen and that we wouldn't get to sit the whole war out here,' Luke heard one of the other corporals saying.

Out of the blue they had been told that they were being sent into combat, and that within a week they would be on troop ships on their way to an unnamed destination.

They were all pretty sure that that destination

must be the desert, and Luke was filled with conflicting emotions and thoughts. As a soldier he itched to do his bit in a proper arena of war, instead of being on home defence duties. It was what he had trained for, after all. But then he was also worried that he wouldn't be up to the demands that going into action would place on him when it came to his responsibility towards his men. Then as a son he felt anxious for his parents, knowing how worried his news would make them, especially his mother. And then lastly, and perhaps most important of all, he thought of Katie and what his news and his posting would mean to their relationship.

He would be seeing her later on – they were going dancing at the Grafton – and he'd arranged to call round at his parents to collect her.

When they'd first declared their love for one another, Luke had told Katie that if he should get sent into action, he would want to put his engagement ring on her finger before he did so.

'Are you going to tell Katie tonight then?' Andy, one of his men, asked him. Andy was seeing one of the girls who worked with Katie and the four of them would be meeting up later at the Grafton.

'I'll probably tell her this afternoon,' Luke answered him. 'What about you?'

'Seeing as Carole's auntie has invited me round for me tea, I'll probably tell her then. What do you think, Corp? I don't fancy the desert and all that sand. It's worse than Southport, so I've heard,' he joked.

'It might be, but seeing as we don't know where we'll be going I wouldn't go out buying a bucket and spade yet if I was you.'

Ribbing one another was their way of dealing with the situation and all those things that could not be said, like their apprehension about what lay ahead. And anyway, Luke had more important things to think about than where they were going right now, like getting to the post office to draw out enough money to buy that engagement ring he'd promised Katie so that he could claim her as his future wife before he had to leave her.

If he were honest, Luke felt relieved that he would be putting a ring on Katie's finger. That way there could be no confusion and no chance of other men thinking that she was fancy-free. Given his own way he'd have had Katie wearing his ring already. She had been the one who had said that they should wait. But she had agreed that it would be different if he were to be sent overseas. He'd never been entirely comfortable with the fact that she wasn't already wearing his ring, even though they'd both agreed that they wouldn't marry until the war was over.

Emily shook her head with fond indulgence, watching Wilhelm talking to Tommy as the POW worked on the vegetable patch and Tommy helped him. She'd been a bit put out at first when Tommy had shown such a liking for the German, but then sensibly she had told herself that it was a good thing for Tommy to spend time with an adult member of his own sex, and one who was far kinder to him than Con had ever been. She'd never known anyone have as much patience as Wilhelm, or be as careful about muddy boots on her kitchen floor, or be as well mannered.

'I've brought you each a cup of tea,' she told them unnecessarily.

'Wilhelm says we're going to need some string.'

Emily sighed. 'Well, when you've had your elevenses, you can get on your bike and cycle down to the ironmonger's, Tommy, but I doubt that you'll be able to buy any.'

String was one of those things that people hoarded and used sparingly, knowing that it was almost impossible to replace.

Tommy had come on ever such a lot and had taken to living in Whitchurch like a duck to water, apart from that funny incident that first Sunday.

'You have a good boy,' Wilhelm told her in his careful English as they both watched Tommy run down the path.

'Have you got any children?' Emily felt obliged to ask him. She had heard that some people didn't think it was right to talk to the German POWs but she felt obliged to ask, seeing as he had praised Tommy.

'*Nein.* I have no wife either. I have to work on my father's farm and there is no time to find a wife. Then my father is gone and so is the farm, and I have to join the army and fight, and that is bad.'

Emily felt very sorry for him.

'But now I am here and that is good,' he told her.

She shouldn't be staying out here – she had no reason to do so, after all – and yet Emily discovered that she was reluctant to leave and go back into the house. There was something about being here in the warm sunshine, sharing a companionable silence with Wilhelm whilst he worked, which made her want to linger.

So this was Whitchurch. They had arrived just over ten minutes ago, and Seb had been granted permission to leave the borrowed motorcycle safe and secure in the small shed belonging to the owner of the café where they had gone for a cup of tea.

'Come here visiting someone, have you?' the teashop owner asked with friendly curiosity after she had brought a pot of tea to their table.

'We're just enjoying the good weather,' Seb answered her easily, 'and we thought we'd see where the road took us.'

The woman laughed good-naturedly and left them to their tea, much to Grace's relief. She didn't like not being honest, but Seb had stressed to her the importance of not saying anything.

Grace was still feeling guilty about having to tell Seb that they'd have to get back instead of finding somewhere to stay. He hadn't said anything, only given her a bit of a look.

'It isn't my fault,' she had protested. 'And if I'd made a fuss it would only have set Mum off asking awkward questions.'

Looking at Seb now, she reached across the table to cover his hand with her own and whispered, 'I am truly ever so sorry about tonight, Seb. I know you must be disappointed.'

'Yes. Very,' he agreed almost tersely, increasing Grace's feelings of guilt. She'd been aware of the increased passion and need in his kisses these last few weeks.

'I'm disappointed too,' she told him, 'but you know what Mum's like, and if she'd started getting suspicious . . .'

'It isn't your fault,' Seb assured her, but Grace felt that his heart wasn't entirely in reassuring her, and that hurt, especially when she herself was also feeling

247

disappointed and guilty, caught between her mother's expectations and Seb's passion, and wanting to please them both. Right now more than anything else what she wanted from Seb wasn't passion but tenderness and the comfort of his arms holding her tight whilst he whispered to her that he loved her. Seb, though, instead of reassuring her, seemed somehow to be slightly distant from her. Because he was disappointed and because he was a man, and men felt these things differently from women, Grace tried to comfort herself.

'Come on,' said Seb. 'If you've finished your tea we'd better go and have a look round.'

As it was a Saturday the town was busy, and there was even a small market, although the stall holders didn't appear to have very much to sell, thanks to rationing, and several of them were closing up already, even though it was only late morning.

'Whereabouts is this place you're being posted to?' Grace asked Seb.

'It's a quarter of a mile or so outside the town. Not that far.'

'Will there be accommodation on site for you?'

'I don't think so. I think we'll be billeted on people instead.'

The sleepy little agricultural town was a world away from Liverpool, Grace reflected, discreetly studying a group of Land Army girls standing outside one of the shops in their dungarees and Wellington boots. A bit further down the road was a cinema. Was there a dance hall, Grace wondered. There must be. Would Seb be going to dances there without her?

As though he had read her mind, Seb's hand tightened on hers.

'I'm going to miss you so much.'

'I'm going to miss you too,' she agreed huskily, not far from tears. She turned to him and said impulsively, 'I wish we *could* have spent the full weekend together, Seb, just you and me.'

Suddenly Grace wanted very much for them to make that final physical commitment to one another that would surely tie them even more firmly together.

'Perhaps it's for the best that we can't,' Seb told her gently. He knew how much her nursing meant to her and if out of his love for her he ended up not being as careful as he should be, and if because of that they had to get married quickly, then Grace would be dismissed from her training programme, and he knew that she would hate that.

'We've only got to wait a few more months,' he reminded her. 'As soon as you're qualified we'll be getting married.'

Grace nodded. They had originally said that they would wait until after the war had ended before they married, but now when Churchill himself had said that they were in it for the long haul, she and Seb had talked things over with their parents and had decided that they would marry as soon as Grace was qualified.

When they had made that decision Grace had assumed that Seb would remain based in Liverpool and that they could live with her parents until the war was over. Now, though, with Seb getting transferred down here, that wouldn't be possible.

Guessing what she was thinking, Seb told her lovingly, 'Once you're qualified you could apply for a transfer down here, Grace. I could apply to live out and we could find somewhere to rent.'

Grace entwined her fingers with his. She was being silly feeling all upset like this, she knew, but she had got used to taking it for granted that he was close at hand.

They had drawn level with a newsagent's and Seb disengaged his hand from hers, telling her, 'Hang on here a minute, will you? I need some cigarettes.'

It was pleasant standing in the sunshine, or at least it would have been if she hadn't been feeling that this alien country town was going to take Seb away from her, Grace decided.

A boy came cycling towards her, stopping his bike outside the ironmonger's. Grace watched him idly, and then stiffened.

'Grace, what is it? What's wrong?' Seb demanded anxiously as he came out of the tobacconist's and saw her face. 'You look as though you've seen a ghost.'

'I feel like I have,' Grace told him feelingly. 'You won't believe it, Seb, but there's a boy just gone in that ironmonger's that is the image of Jack. You know,' she reminded him when he frowned, 'Auntie Vi's youngest, that was sent to Wales when the war began and then got killed when a bomb was dropped on the farmhouse where he was staying. It can't be him, of course – I know that – but seeing him gave me ever such a turn.'

Seb had taken her arm and was leading her firmly away from the ironmonger's. Grace pulled back and turned to look over her shoulder but the bicycle had gone and so, she assumed, had the boy.

She didn't think she liked Whitchurch very much, Grace decided, and she knew that she wished that Seb hadn't been posted here.

*   *   *

250

'Hurry up with them curlers, will you, Lena? Oh, and don't forget them clean towels as well.'

Lena was rushed off her feet. The town centre salon, with its proximity to the Royal Court Theatre and its theatrical clientele, was far busier than Simone's had ever been, and its clients far more demanding. But not, Lena acknowledged tiredly, as demanding as her new employer, who always seemed to be yelling at her for something or other. Lena could understand why, as the sulky receptionist had confided to her, Judith's assistants never stayed very long. The hours were long and the pay was small, and with Judith taking so much from the tips for herself, Lena barely had enough to cover the rent she had to pay to Judith's mother, who claimed that she was not charging her as much as she might have done as a favour to her daughter, but that she expected Lena to help out with the household chores in recognition of her generosity.

Still, on the other hand, she did have a job and a roof over her head, and just listening to the clients kept Lena open-mouthed and wide-eyed. She had even struck up a bit of a friendship with the sulky receptionist who had turned out to be nowhere near as bad as Lena had first imagined, and they were talking about going out dancing together if ever Judith let them finish early enough to do so.

Unlike Simone, Judith operated a business that was open well into the evening, with chorus girls and sometimes even the big stars coming in without an appointment, all in a state and wanting their hair doing.

Sometimes, Judith had told Lena, when it was a really big star, they got asked to go over to her dressing room to do her hair there.

Lena was determined not to think about Charlie, and most of the time she didn't. She was so exhausted when she finally went to bed that she fell asleep the minute her head touched the pillow. She did occasionally think about Gavin, though, and wondered if he had sorted out his gran and if Dolly had given in and allowed her daughter to take her back with her into the country.

FIFTEEN

Although Jean had insisted that her younger sister, Francine, would not mind one bit if Katie wore the beautiful clothes she had left behind when she had joined ENSA and gone abroad, now that she was settled in Liverpool Katie still felt a bit guilty about doing so, so tonight she was wearing one of her own summer dresses, in cornflower blue with white daisies appliquéd round the hem.

'Here's Luke, and he's early,' Jean called out to Katie as she saw her son walking through the garden to the back door.

Luke was a very good-looking young man, tall and broad-shouldered, with thick dark hair, strong features and blue eyes, but it always made Katie's heart give an extra bump of mixed love and fear when she saw him wearing his uniform.

She wasn't the kind of girl who could bring herself to run to her young man and openly embrace him, especially in front of others, so she hung back a little whilst Jean hugged her son and told him about the twins' successful job applications.

'I've agreed that the twins can go to the Graffie tonight, but you and Katie will have to keep an eye out for them, Luke,' Jean warned her son. 'You know what they're like. Oh, and we're having a bit of a picnic at the allotment tomorrow after church, if you can manage to get time off.'

'Dad around?' Luke asked the minute Jean had released him and with such an air of studied nonchalance that Katie knew immediately that something had happened. Her stomach muscles tensed and she looked at Jean, but for once Luke's mother didn't seem to have picked up on what Katie herself had sensed, so Katie tried to calm herself, thinking that she must have made a mistake. She and Luke were still so newly in love and she was still got so easily upset and on edge when they had a falling-out that Katie acknowledged to herself that she was never totally relaxed in the first few seconds when they saw one another again after an absence, no matter how brief that absence had been.

'He's here now,' Jean answered.

'Thought you'd be here about now,' Sam greeted his son.

Katie knew from Jean how much Sam loved his son, even though he didn't often show that love in the same easy affectionate way he did with his daughters.

'We've had orders,' Luke announced abruptly in a soldierly manner and with a mixture of bravado and pride.

It took several seconds for his words to sink in, and it was Sam who spoke first, demanding curtly, 'Have they said where you'll be going?'

Jean placed her hand over her mouth as she protested shakily, 'Oh, Luke, no,' and Katie moved closer to Luke's side, all the colour leaving her face.

'Not yet,' Luke answered Sam, 'but we're all taking a guess that it will be the desert.'

He turned towards Katie and reached for her left hand. 'Remember what I said to you about if I got posted overseas?'

She was still in too much of a shock to think properly, so she simply nodded in assent.

Luke was still holding her hand and she could feel the slight tremble in their fingers, although she didn't know if it was just from her own or if Luke's fingers were trembling as well.

Luke had produced a small jewellers' box from his pocket, and now he was holding it in his free hand.

'I've spoken to your dad to ask his permission to do this,' he told Katie gruffly, as he kneeled down in front of her. 'Will you wait for me, Katie? Will you wear my ring whilst I'm gone and marry me when I come back?'

A huge wave of love and fear for him swamped her. All their petty little quarrels and all her own equally silly doubts were forgotten.

'Yes,' she told him, her voice choked with emotion. 'Yes, Luke. I'll be proud to do all of those things.'

Tears glistened in her eyes, making the pretty diamond ring he was removing from the box and sliding onto the ring finger of her left hand sparkle and shine in her sight. It fitted perfectly, and then Luke lifted her hand to his lips and kissed her fingers. A huge sob was wrenched from Katie's throat, her tears falling on Luke's down-bent head as she leaned towards him.

It was Sam's cough that broke the intensity of the moment, his stern, 'Come on now, you two, that's enough of that,' bringing Luke to his feet, and having Katie reach into her pocket for her handkerchief. However, when she'd dried her eyes and looked at both Luke's parents, she could see that their eyes were wet with tears too, and she knew they shared her own love and pride in Luke – and her fear for him.

'Don't you go forgetting that you're mine now,' Luke warned. He was still holding her hand tightly. Was he afraid too of what this posting could mean? The thought of Luke being vulnerable and even possibly wounded and far away almost broke Katie's heart with protective love.

'As if she would,' Jean scolded him, adding, 'And you can be sure that we'll look after her for you, Luke. I couldn't think of anyone I'd rather have as a daughter-in-law than Katie.'

Katie tugged her hand free of Luke's to go into Jean's open arms, and then they were hugging one another tightly, both of them crying and laughing at the same time, whilst to one side of them Sam started to ask Luke when exactly he would be leaving.

'Don't know yet, Dad, but it's going to be soon, I reckon, seeing as they're giving everyone extra leave this weekend.'

When the twins – who had been upstairs finishing getting ready for their Saturday night at the dance hall, which was so popular with Liverpool's young people – came into the kitchen, Luke's news had to be told all over again. The way Lou and Sasha went automatically each to one side of him, and the way he hugged them both, made Katie smile lovingly. The Campions were such a close family and she was so very happy that she was going to be a part of it.

Her own parents, much as she loved them, were more like a responsibility and a worry to her than a source of comfort and protective love, and a part of her had always craved the mothering that Jean gave to her children. She would be so very happy being part of this family and knowing always that she could turn to Jean for help, support and advice. Fresh tears stung her eyes. She would never forget this day or the fact that it was Luke who had made it possible for her to become a part of his family. She could have loved him for that alone. But of course she didn't – she loved him for himself.

'Grace will have a shock when she gets in, Luke, and she learns that you're going overseas,' Sasha told her brother, adding as she turned to Katie, 'The picnic tomorrow will have to be your engagement party, Katie.'

'That's a very good idea,' Jean approved, but as she and Sam exchanged looks, Jean knew that, delighted though she was about the engagement, it was Luke and his imminent departure that would be foremost in their minds, and that she and Sam would not feel very much like celebrating. Not, of course, that she would say as much to the young ones and spoil their happiness. Poor Katie had looked as white as sheet when Luke had told them he had been posted overseas. War was so hard on everyone.

It must be because of the warmth of the May evening that she was feeling so restless and so aware of the emptiness of her house, Bella decided, as she got up from the deck chair in her garden, where she had been sitting since finishing some paperwork. It was now official that she was the manageress of the crèche

– not that her mother had been as impressed as Bella had expected her to be. She had been more interested in complaining about how hard Bella's father was having to work and how little she saw of him.

Bella was in the garden because the house had felt so empty. It was today that Jan had been getting married, and naturally Bettina and Marie had gone to Cookham, where the bride and her father lived, for the wedding.

She bent down, tugging at one of the weeds growing in the lawn, wrenching at it to tug out its roots and then sitting back, scarlet-faced with effort, when all that came away were leaves. With the root still embedded in the lawn, the wretched thing would grow back, just like her own anger and self-contempt over that stupid, stupid incident when she had tried to seduce Jan. How could she have humiliated herself like that? Would he tell his new wife?

Everything was so quiet after the bustle of the crèche and people coming and going. What was the matter with her? She didn't have to be on her own, after all. She had turned down an invitation on Friday to attend the Tennis Club's Saturday evening dance with a young army officer, who was home on leave and to whom she had been introduced by the vicar. The young man had made it plain enough that he thought her attractive but, conscious of her new status and the importance of maintaining a professional attitude, Bella had decided to refuse. She was tired of men who thought they could deceive her and make a fool of her, and an unfamiliar lack of confidence had made her feel that she no longer knew which men were serious and which were not. And besides, she wasn't really interested in dating anyone. She had more important things on her mind now that she was manageress.

There was something so very bittersweet about dancing with Luke tonight, Katie thought, knowing that this might be the last time they would dance together for a long time, and knowing too that this was the first time she had worn his ring.

Carole and Andy had met up with them inside the Grafton, and Katie had seen immediately that Carole had been crying.

They had been planning to get engaged on her birthday in July, Carole had confided to Katie, and today Andy had tied a piece of cotton round her ring finger in lieu of the ring he hadn't got as yet.

'He says he'll bring me one back when he comes home,' she had told Katie whilst the boys had been at the bar getting their drinks, her face crumpling as she had added tearfully, 'All I want is for him to bring himself home, Katie.'

Katie knew exactly what she meant. After all, that was the way she felt about Luke.

'Would you like to dance?'

Sasha's face went pink, and she looked from the self-conscious cleanly scrubbed face of the young man standing at their table to that of her twin, her expression one of uncertainty.

'Course she does, just as long as you haven't got two left feet,' Lou answered for her twin, giving Sasha a nudge as she told her, 'It's him that took your place the night you fell under that bomb.'

'I know,' Sasha retorted, her face a deeper shade

of pink now, whilst the young bomb disposal sapper had gone crimson.

The twins had been sitting on their own at the table they were sharing with Luke and Katie, Carole and Andy, and very much under Luke's stern elder brotherly eye. However, Luke and Katie were dancing now, and from the looks of them they weren't in any state to pay too much attention to anyone other than one another, Lou decided.

She looked away from her brother and his new fiancée to study her twin instead. The bomb disposal lad was a good dancer, and whatever he was saying to Sasha was making her laugh.

The tiny little tear in Lou's heart, made by the fact that she and Sasha seemed to be changing and growing apart, deepened. One day Sasha would dance away from her for ever in some lad's arms and then nothing would ever be the same again. Lou shivered. She'd never really thought before about them growing up and getting married, and what that would mean . . .

She glanced idly round the dance floor and then froze. Kieran! And in RAF uniform. Her heart banged into her ribs. It couldn't be him. He'd never join up, at least not willingly. She looked again. It *was* him, and the girl he was dancing with looked as though she thoroughly approved of both her dance partner and his uniform. Well, she didn't know him like Lou did, and what was more she was welcome to him. All he'd ever done to her was lie to her and lead her on, pretending he liked her best, and then going and saying exactly the same thing to Sasha. A girl would have to be a total fool to waste any time thinking about Kieran Mallory.

The music had stopped. He was looking towards the table. Had he seen her? Would he come over? Even as she shrank back into the shadows, Lou's heart was banging like a drum.

Sitting together on the bench in her father's allotment in the fading light that was not yet dusk, Grace leaned her head on Seb's shoulder. They had got back too late to go to the Grafton to catch up with the others, and besides, Grace wasn't sure that she wanted to be there. It was all very well for the newly engaged like Katie and Luke, and girls like the twins, but right now more than anything else what she wanted was to be with Seb and only Seb.

It was a warm evening, but she still snuggled closer to him, her hand resting against his chest and his heartbeat, whilst his arm held her close.

'I'm going to miss you so much, Seb.'

He kissed the tip of her nose and automatically she lifted her face towards his, yearning for the sweetness of those kisses that increasingly lately had taken them deeper into dangerous waters. Tonight, though, she didn't care about the dangers. All she cared about was showing Seb how much she loved him.

It had been a shock to get home and learn that Luke was being sent overseas, and one that had snapped her out of her own misery, to think instead how lucky she was that Seb would be remaining in England where it was so much safer. She had let her own feelings blind her to the fact that there were others far worse off than she was herself, Grace acknowledged, and now she was feeling a bit ashamed of herself.

Seb stroked her hair off her face, his hand tenderly

cupping her jaw. As he kissed her Grace moved closer, exhaling in a soft sigh when his hand moved down to her breast, her, 'Oh, Seb' quickening with longing, as their petting grew steadily more urgent until eventually Seb very gently pushed her away, his voice thick with longing and that amusement that she so loved about him as he told her, 'I don't think your dad would be very pleased if he were to come out now for a last smoke.'

Grace gave a small giggle. 'He'd probably insist that you marry me immediately.' All her longing that they were actually in a position to do that was in her voice.

'Don't tempt me,' Seb warned her, hearing that longing and sharing it. 'You know you'd never forgive me if you had to give up your nursing.'

Grace did know it, but she also knew how much she loved him and wanted them to be together as husband and wife.

'I'm so lucky,' she told him tenderly. 'When I think of poor Katie, newly engaged and with Luke on the point of going overseas, I'm sorry I've been so unhappy about you going to Whitchurch.'

'I like it that you're unhappy that we're going to be apart,' Seb assured her gently, bending his head to kiss her again.

A warning cough alerted them to the fact that, just as Seb had suggested, Sam was on his way down the garden for his last cigarette of the evening.

SIXTEEN

'Well, yes, the weather is lovely now but Daphne has always wanted to be married in June, just like her father and I were.'

Charlie tried to move out of earshot of Daphne's mother's voice but with so many people emerging from church after the service and congregating outside, it just wasn't possible.

Even so, his small bid for freedom had been noticed and now Daphne herself was tugging on his sleeve and whispering reproachfully, her face pink, 'Charles, Mummy's speaking, and it looks so ill mannered when you start looking round like that instead of listening.'

Just for a second Charlie contemplated the blissful luxury of pointing out that since he had already heard more times than he wanted to remember that Daphne wanted to get married in June just like her parents, he was entitled to feel bored, but only for a second. As he had learned rather painfully since his return to his unit and his CO's suggestion that he might want to recuperate fully from his injuries via some compassionate leave with his bride-to-be and her family, Daphne did not take kindly to plain speaking. Charlie had never known a girl cry as much or as easily. And as for Mrs Wrighton-Bude, she had a way of looking at him that made it plain that she considered him solely responsible for Daphne's happiness and her tears.

If he had thought for one minute that he could get away with doing so, Charlie would have broken off his engagement with a glad heart. There was no chance of his being allowed to do that, though. Charlie felt quite sure that even if his CO turned up and announced that Charlie was leaving with him to go overseas with his unit immediately, Daphne's mother would insist that he and Daphne were to be married first. The only bright side of things was that at least once they were married and he was declared fit he would be able to return to duty at the barracks, and once he did he was certainly going to make up for all the fun and freedom that had been lost to him.

He really resented having to hang about here, playing the doting fiancé whilst Daphne's mother watched him like a hawk, and all because that silly little cousin of Daphne's had gone running to Daphne's mother to complain that Charlie had tried to kiss her. As though that was some kind of crime. They were going to be related, weren't they, and it had only been a bit of a peck, just a bit of fun. Mrs Wrighton-Bude had not seen it that way, though, and there had been an uncomfortable and mutually embarrassing and resented lecture from Daphne's father to Charlie to the effect that people of their social standing did not behave as they obviously did in Wallasey, and that Daphne was not to be embarrassed by a fiancé who did not know the correct way to conduct himself.

Oh, yes, Charlie would have backed out of marrying Daphne if he could, especially now that he had heard from the silly little cousin that Daphne's parents had had high hopes of Daphne marrying the son of a well-to-do local landowner, only he had gone and joined the RAF and then married some dreadful common girl he had met and broken his parents and poor Daphne's heart.

Charlie, the silly little cousin had implied nastily, had come along at just the right moment to prevent Daphne from looking as though she and her parents and their plans had virtually been jilted at the altar.

Daphne's father was talking to the retired major who was their neighbour, about 'gof', as he and all his neighbours pronounced golf. He'd taken Charlie for a round earlier in the week and Charlie had lost count of the number of times his lack of officer status had been met with looks of surprise.

Soon it would be time for them to return to the house for lunch – overcooked meat and watery cabbage because 'Cook' had left to go and do her bit. His own mother could be a pain in the backside, and often was, but at least she could cook. Charlie's belly growled at the thought of her Sunday roasts with all the trimmings. He'd eaten better in the Naafi than he was doing at Daphne's parents'.

His boredom increasing, he moved his weight from one foot to the other, the movement causing the letter in his pocket to crackle.

He had been surprised when Bella had written to him. They weren't exactly close, and he supposed he should thank her for taking the trouble to tell him that a girl from the slums had been round to their parents' looking for him, claiming that he had promised to marry her. Not that she had written to him for his own benefit. Oh, no. Her letter had been more of a criticism of his behaviour to 'a poor young girl to whom you lied in the cruelest way'.

He had laughed out aloud at first until he remembered that there had been a girl like the one Bella had described to him, although he was damn sure he had never promised her anything other than payment for a bit of fun. To read Bella's letter you'd think he actually owed the girl something. Charlie didn't know what was happening to his sister. Since she had started working at that crèche she had become far too much of a do-gooder, extraordinary though it was to think of someone as selfish as his sister changing to such an extent. Still, at least, according to Bella, his parents had seen the girl off. Though now that Bella had reminded him about her, Charlie felt even less enthusiastic about his marriage and Daphne, and even more impatient to start having fun again.

The small area next to the shed on Sam's allotment was filled with people. Sam's own family and their neighbours who had come round to celebrate Katie and Luke's engagement and to wish Luke good luck, although officially, of course, no one was supposed to know that he was leaving.

As Jean looked around herself, she decided that what she had promoted out of protective maternal instinct was turning out to be an event for which she was now reaping what she felt in reality was un-deserved neighbourly praise, with everyone saying what a good idea her picnic was and how much they were enjoying it.

266

The still-bare stems of the wisteria climbing against the shed were just beginning to show the soft greyish buds that would be the long racemes of lilac-blue flowers in another couple of weeks' time, while the bluebells beneath it were in full flower. Sam had planted that wisteria when Luke had been a year old, and they'd grown to maturity together, Jean thought as she touched one soft feathery bud with tender fingers, knowing that she couldn't touch her son with that same tenderness now that he was all grown up, and certainly not in public.

The fruit trees were emerging into blossom, and thanks to Sam's careful husbandry and use of protective cloches there was plenty of early lettuce to join the first of the new potatoes, normally such a treat but not quite the same without a generous helping of butter, Jean admitted.

At least Grace seemed happier, Jean noticed with relief, and much more her normal self as she bustled about handing out sandwiches and cups of tea.

Everyone who could had helped out with donations of food so that the fictional party Jean had fibbed about to keep Grace at home overnight had become a reality.

'And what's this about you having an admirer, Sasha? A certain young man was very keen and attentive last night, so I've heard,' Grace teased her younger sister. She felt so very different about Seb's move now in the knowledge that Luke was being sent overseas, and she was determined to make the picnic a happy occasion, especially for Katie and Luke, newly engaged and so soon to be parted.

'He was just being polite,' Sasha denied Grace's teasing, but then blushed so hard that everyone laughed. Everyone, that was, except Lou, who bent her head and scuffed the side of her sandal-clad foot against the ground. A horrible tight angry feeling had filled her chest, and humiliatingly she felt as though she might actually start to cry.

Sasha had not mentioned the bomb disposal lad at all to her last night when they had got back home and they were on their own in their room; she had not said one single word about him, or about the number of times he had danced with her, or how he had hung around their table for so long that Luke had eventually been obliged to ask him to join them – nothing, and yet the moment Grace mentioned him Sasha had gone all silly, laughing and blushing and acting like there was something between the two of them.

'What about you, Lou?' Seb asked in a kind voice. 'Who did you dance with?'

'Lots of boys asked her to dance, but she wouldn't,' Sasha answered for her twin.

'I danced with you,' Lou told her sharply, unable to resist adding the pointed reminder, 'We said that we would before we went out.'

There was a small silence, awkward and prickly and just like the way she felt inside, Lou acknowledged miserably. She hadn't said anything to Sasha about having seen Kieran in uniform. Had her twin seen him and was she too not saying anything? The misery inside her was making her feel sick and close to tears.

The afternoon slipped into evening, neighbours with young families gathering their children together and saying their good nights to one another and their goodbyes to Luke, whilst Jean watched with a huge lump in her throat. It didn't seem all that long ago that Luke had been the age and the size of the little ones now held in paternal or maternal arms as their tiredness caught up with them. Now Luke was a man, a fine upstanding son that anyone could be proud of, and Jean was fiercely proud of him. But a part of her also wished that he was still a little boy who could be held safe from all harm in her arms.

PART TWO

SEVENTEEN

November 1941

'You're carrying, aren't you?' Judith demanded in a voice hard with bad temper and recognition.

When Lena didn't answer her immediately, she gave an angry shake of her head and demanded again, 'You're pregnant, aren't you, you stupid little tart? And don't bother denying it, 'cos if me mum says you are, and she does, then you are. And there was me thinking you was just putting on a bit of weight. Well, you can't carry on working here now, and that's a fact, not in that condition and you without a ring on your finger. The woman wot I rent this place from has some funny ideas about things like that, and she'll have me out as well as you if she gets to hear. Besides, the clients all know you aren't married and I don't want me salon getting a reputation on account of you not having any marriage lines and a belly that will soon be as bit as a barrage balloon.'

Still Lena said nothing and the reason for that was that until Judith's mother, Mrs Walker, had confronted her in her bedroom this morning, coming in without knocking just when Lena was getting dressed, and

273

informing her caustically that she had had her suspicious for a while, Lena herself had had no idea that the reason for her expanding waistline could have something to do with the time she had spent in Charlie's arms.

'How far gone are you?'

Lena counted back mentally and told Judith shakily, 'Six months.'

'Oh, so you know who he is then, the chap wot give it to you?'

Lena nodded.

'And there's no chance of him doing the right thing by you, I don't suppose?' Judith's voice was sarcastic.

Now Lena shook her head.

'Well, I dunno what's to be done with you and I dunno why I should worry either, seeing as you ain't my responsibility, thank heavens. You know that my mum won't have you back in the house, don't you?'

Again Lena nodded. It had been Judith's mother who had marched her downstairs and then announced to Judith that Lena was pregnant, and that she wanted her out of her house immediately.

'It's bad enough you carrying on the way you do, our Judith, coming in at all hours and setting tongues wagging. I'm not having the likes of her making things even worse.'

Under Judith's mother's eagle eye Lena had been forced to pack all her belongings into the straw basket she had arrived with all those months ago when she had first got her job with Judith, and an old battered holdall that Judith had found for her, and now they and Judith and Lena were down at the salon, and Lena was being told that she had lost her job as well as her room.

She couldn't take it all in. She had known that she was getting plumper but she had not thought anything much of it. Naïvely she realised now it had never occurred to her that she might be going to have a baby. But now that she knew, an unexpected feeling of protective love was growing inside her that was as much of a surprise to her as the baby itself, and it was a feeling that overrode her shock and the sick feeling of panic that had engulfed her when Judith's mother had confronted and accused her and then announced that she was throwing her out.

'You'll have to tell the authorities,' Judith warned. 'I dare say they'll send you to one of those mother and baby homes out in the country whilst you have it, and they'll give it to the nuns or summat like that to find a good home for it.'

Although she didn't say anything Lena immediately tensed her body and placed her right hand protectively over her belly. No one was going to take her baby away from her, no one.

'And don't you go thinking that you can come back here afterwards and expect me to give you your job back because I can't. Me mum will be down on me like a ton of bricks if I do. If you ask me it's a pity you've not got a bit of a family to help you out, take you in and that. Anyway, here's your wages and a bit extra,' Judith told her, pushing some money into Lena's hand, 'although I'm a fool to myself for being so daft and generous, I dare say. If you was to take my advice you'd try one of the churches first. Catholic, are you?'

Lena denied it. That had been another bone of contention between her parents: her mother was Church of England and had refused to convert to

275

Catholicism when she had married Lena's Italian father.

'Well, I dare say they're both used to dealing with girls that have got themselves into trouble.'

Lena could feel the fluttering sensation that had invaded her belly increase as she realised that now that Judith had had her say she was waiting for her to leave.

She had liked working in the salon, despite Judith's bad temper and the poor wages. She reached down to pick up her cumbersome bags. She was wearing most of her winter clothes. It was easier to carry them that way, and it had been a cold morning with a white frost on the bedroom window.

Judith opened the door for her. Feeling sick with dread Lena walked through it.

Bella rarely came into Liverpool city centre any more – even those shops that had not suffered bomb damage hardly had anything to sell – but this morning she'd been invited to attend a City Council meeting about crèche places, so that she could tell the committee members what she had learned from her own crèche. To Bella's delight, her crèche had recently been singled out as one of outstanding excellence, both in administration and from the point of view of the mothers who used it for their children.

Bella had even been given a larger budget so that they could increase the number of children they took in. That, though, meant finding extra staff, and with so many women now doing war work Bella knew that wasn't going to be easy.

She didn't want to linger in the city. It was cold and she had work to do.

*   *   *

276

If she had been shocked and frightened when Judith's mother had told her that she was pregnant, that was nothing to what she was feeling now, Lena admitted shakily.

She'd gone to a church as Judith had suggested, but the clergyman to whom she'd poured out her anxieties and her desire to keep her baby had sent her to see a council official, who had told Lena firmly that it was out of the question for her to keep her baby and that she would make arrangements for her to be found a room at a special home for girls like her who had got themselves into trouble. Lena had left her office feeling as though she was about to be sent to some kind of prison. She hadn't eaten all day, and her arms ached so much from carrying her bags that she had to put them down. She had just done so when a couple of rough-looking boys ran towards her, weaving their way through the people on the street, to grab hold of her handbag. Lena reacted immediately and instinctively, determinedly holding on to it and refusing to let go. When the stronger and older of the boys pushed her to the ground she called out for help.

Bella heard the commotion as she was on the point of crossing the road, and turned automatically to see what was going on. She recognised Lena immediately and with an unwanted jolt of shock. She could and should ignore her, Bella told herself. After all, the girl was nothing to her. She turned away and continued to cross the road, but something made her stop and look back and then reluctantly retrace her steps.

Lena put her hand on her handbag. Thank goodness they hadn't managed to steal it. She would have lost everything if she'd lost that. The wages Judith had paid her earlier were in it, along with her ration book and her Post Office savings book.

She struggled to sit up.

'Are you all right?'

Lena looked up, her eyes widening when she saw Bella leaning towards her, and she recognised her immediately.

'Yes,' Lena began and then to her own shame, she suddenly started to cry, blurting out, 'No, I'm not all right. I'm having your Charlie's baby, and I've lost me job and me room, and now I'm to go to some home for fallen women until I have the baby and then they'll take it away from me and give it to someone else.' She was sobbing uncontrollably now, causing a small crowd to gather round them.

'What's to do with her?' asked an older stout woman with a disapproving expression.

'Looks like she's homeless, to me, and in the family way. I know her sort. Someone wants to find someone in authority and let them deal with her.'

'She isn't homeless,' Bella heard herself saying.

'Oh, and how would you know that? It looks like she's homeless to me, and not married neither.'

The stout woman had folded her arms now and was confronting Bella as though it would give her some kind of personal satisfaction to have Lena dragged off by the authorities. The poor little thing looked terrified, Bella recognised, and that baby she was carrying was her niece or nephew.

'She works for me,' Bella lied to the stout woman,

'Works for you? Doing what, I'd like to know.'

'I'm the manageress of a crèche in Wallasey and I've just taken on Lena here to work there as a trainee nursemaid. Come along, Lena,' Bella demanded, turning her back on her aggressor and putting a hand under Lena's elbow to help her to her feet. 'I did warn you to keep up with me. Now get your things together and give me one of those bags.'

Lena gawped at Charlie's sister.

'Come along, Lena, we haven't got all day,' Bella urged her. She didn't want to hang around in case the stout woman decided to go and summon someone in real authority, and then she suspected they would both be in trouble.

Charlie's sister really wanted her to go with her?

Lena struggled to her feet, determined not to let on how sick and dizzy she felt in case Bella changed her mind and went off without her. How different they looked, Bella in her smart winter coat with its fur collar and her matching fur hat, her hands covered by leather gloves and little button boots on her feet, whilst Lena was wearing a heavy multicoloured long cardigan she had knitted herself from rewound wool, over one of the two elasticated-waist thin winter skirts she had made for herself, and a second-hand jumper. She did not have any gloves or a hat, and her shoes were stuffed with newspaper because the soles were nearly through.

What on earth was she doing, Bella asked herself as she marched off, gingerly carrying Lena's grubby wicker basket with Lena herself trailing behind her. Had she gone mad? This girl meant nothing to her and nor did her child. She had a position to maintain, a reputation now as crèche manageress; she couldn't possibly involve herself with someone like Lena, and especially not an unmarried and pregnant someone like Lena. She'd wait until they were out of sight of the stout woman and then she'd give her a couple of pounds and leave her to it, Bella decided.

It was November already and Luke had been gone for over five months. Katie had received a letter from him earlier in the week. His letters were arriving regularly now, not like at first when they hadn't heard anything for weeks, and they'd all sat round the Campions' table at night looking at an old atlas Katie had begged from her parents when she had gone to visit them, trying to work out just how far Luke's transport ship would have travelled if he and his men were going to fight in the desert. Then they'd received his first letters home, heavily censored and sent from South Africa, where the troop ships had put in on their long journey. They'd all had several letters within a matter of days of the first, and then nothing until Luke had reached Alexandria.

Katie missed him dreadfully and worried for him even more, but she knew she had to be brave for Jean and Sam's sake. Sometimes, though, she and Carole went out together and had a little cry for their brave boys, and tried to reassure one another that all would be well.

She bent her head over her work, reminding herself that she had to do her bit.

Grace had had to hang around outside the nurses' home during her lunch break, instead of having her lunch, in order to catch the postman and receive her precious daily letter from Seb, the receipt of it all the sweeter because it had not arrived with the early morning post, but now, as she read it quickly, Grace's spirits rose. This would be her last shift before she and Seb had two precious shared days off together. They'd got it all planned. She was going to go to Whitchurch by train, and Seb had managed to get her a room. He and the men he worked with were all billeted with local families and Grace knew that there would be very little opportunity for them to be alone together, but at least they would be together. This would be the first time she had gone down to Whitchurch since Seb started work there. On previous days off Seb had come to Liverpool, sleeping in Katie's room whilst Katie generously shared with the twins. Grace was in her final month of training now, and soon she and Seb would be able to start making proper plans to get married.

'From your fiancé, is it, your letter?' The voice of the new ward sister, who had replaced the previous ward sister, who was pregnant, interrupted Grace's concentration on Seb's letter, good manners forcing her to refold it and put it back in its envelope as she said politely, 'Yes,' even whilst her heart sank. Maureen Westland, who had caught up with her on her way back into the hospital, was pleasant enough but she had a poor opinion of the male sex and always seemed to be offering dire warnings of the heartache in store for girls who were, as she put it, 'soft enough to let men twist them round their little finger'.

'Well, I hope for your sake he's not one of those men who pretend to be faithful to a girl but who secretly plays around behind her back.'

'Seb would never do anything like that,' Grace defended her fiancé.

'I've lost count of the number of girls I've known who've thought that, only to get a nasty shock.

Personally I wouldn't trust any man, but there you are, that's me, and I know that there's a lot of girls around who get taken in and don't realise what's going on until it's too late. At the hospital where I was before, in Manchester, there was one poor nurse engaged to this army sergeant. Thought the sun shone out of him, she did, until she found out that he was as good as engaged to another girl as well. It's this war that's to blame, I reckon. Put a man in uniform and he thinks he can behave how he likes.'

'Some men might behave like that but my Seb isn't one of them, and just as soon as I've finished my training we're getting married.'

Grace was longing to escape from Maureen and her cynical comments. She was beginning to suspect that the other girl actually liked causing upset and uncertainty to members of her own sex with her warnings about men not being trustworthy. As she'd said to Katie when she'd gone home to see her family earlier in the week, even though she knew she had nothing to worry about with Seb, Maureen's comments were really beginning to get her down.

'Marriage doesn't stop them playing the field,' Maureen was saying now. 'I've heard of any number of married men acting like they was single just because they're in uniform, but of course there's always girls who will believe what they want to believe because they want to get married, and they'd rather hang on to a fiancé even if he is messing around with other girls. Of course, then you get that type of girl who sets her cap at a chap even if he is engaged to someone else. I've met a fair few of those in my time as well. There was a nurse I knew that used to boast about how many couples she'd broken up.'

'Well, I don't believe that what you're talking about goes on anything like as much as you seem to think,' Grace told Maureen spiritedly.

'You'd be surprised,' Maureen came back darkly, adding, 'Work with any girls, does he, your fiancé? Only I've heard that you wouldn't believe what goes on at some of these places where they've got men and women in uniform working together. I know that if I was engaged I'd certainly not want my fiancé working with other women.'

Although Grace wasn't going to acknowledge it, Maureen had touched a bit of a sore spot. It had been only just over a week ago that Seb had mentioned in one of his letters that a contingent of young women operatives had now arrived on a training course to work under the guidance of the more senior operatives like himself, and that he was responsible for overseeing the ongoing training of four of these girls. He had described them to Grace as a jolly bunch, eager to learn and all showing promise, and then added that their desire to engage in out-of-hours larks was giving him a taste of what it would eventually feel like to be the father of spirited daughters. That comment had made Grace smile but she admitted that she had felt a small stab of jealousy of the four young women who were now spending more time with her Seb than she was. Sensibly, though, she had reminded herself that she spent more time with the male patients on her ward than she did with Seb, but that did not mean for one single second that she preferred their company to his or that she was about to transfer her affections to any of them. Even so, she did wish that Maureen wouldn't go on so much in the way that she did.

*   *   *

'So what happened then?'

Lena looked warily at Bella, who was sitting in front of her on one of the two chairs she had pulled out from the table in her immaculate and, to Lena's eyes, very fancy kitchen.

'I was working for a hairdresser and I'd got a room at her mother's, only her mother threw me out this morning because . . .'

'Because you're pregnant?' Bella supplied for her.

'Yes. I thought I was just putting on a bit of weight. It was that much of a shock when she said.'

Bella tried to imagine being six months pregnant herself and being so naïve and ignorant that she hadn't known until her landlady had pointed the reality out to her. To her own astonishment a tug of something that was close to sympathy closed its fingers round her heart. Sympathy for the baby, poor little thing, not for Lena, Bella told herself firmly.

'And I've lost me job, an' all, and then her that I was working for said that I'd have to go and see someone at the church and that they'd sort me out, only when I did, they said as how I'd have to go to this special place and that I'd have to give up my baby.' Lena bent her head, her thin shoulders heaving as tears ran down her face and dripped onto the clasped hands she was moving so apprehensively on her lap.

'I take it that the baby is Charlie's, is it?'

For some reason Bella's blunt question had Lena folding her hands protectively over her body.

Still dazed from the speed with which her life had so abruptly and uncomfortably changed in the space of less than a day, Lena still wasn't sure what she was doing allowing Charlie's sister to take charge of her in the way she had, and she certainly had no idea why Bella had wanted to, but she had retained enough backbone to stand up for herself, at least where Charlie was concerned.

'Yes it is,' she answered, adding defensively, 'And before you say anything, I'm not going to give it up, no matter what anyone says.'

Lena's voice developed a note of defiant panic as she made this claim, and once again Bella was caught off guard by her own sympathy for the younger girl. She still didn't know what on earth had motivated her to step in and protect Lena from the woman who had been attempting to bully her, never mind bringing her home with her.

'Well, if you're planning to keep it you're going to have to invent a husband for yourself and a father for your baby,' Bella told her frankly. 'I suppose we could always pretend that you got taken in by some man who turned out to already have a wife when he married you. Yes, that's what we'll do.'

Bella stopped speaking abruptly. What on earth was she doing? She had only brought the girl back with her out of curiosity and because she had wanted to know if the child she was carrying was Charlie's. She hadn't forgotten that Charlie had stolen her jewellery, and had got away with doing so, so the opportunity to have the upper hand over him in any way wasn't one she was going to miss out on, was it?

Discussing how Lena and her pregnancy could be given a decent veil of respectability wasn't necessary for her to make use of that opportunity.

'What, lie, you mean and pretend that I thought I was married?'

'Yes,' Bella confirmed, 'and it will be even better if you met this chap somewhere else – Birmingham or somewhere – and he and his real wife are now dead. Not, of course, that it makes any difference to me what you do about the fact that you aren't married. After all, it's not as though I'm responsible for you or that,' she told Lena, nodding her head in the direction of Lena's belly.

'Maybe not, but your Charlie is,' Lena pointed out, surprising herself as much as she obviously had done Bella.

'I wouldn't say too much about that if I were you,' Bella warned her. 'It won't do you any good and it could get you into a lot of trouble. My father is a very influential man in Wallasey. He's on the local council, and besides,' she relented slightly when she saw how alarmed Lena looked, 'it will be much better for you and the baby if you do as I suggested and pretend that you thought you and the baby's father were properly married. You'll get a lot more sympathy that way.'

'And no one will try and take my baby away from me?'

'I shouldn't think so,' Bella answered. Privately she thought that the authorities had more than enough orphans to find homes for as it was, without taking on Lena's as well.

'Now look,' she told Lena briskly, 'you can stay here for tonight and then in the morning you can go back to Liverpool, and you can go and see the author-ities and tell them what I've just suggested: that you thought you were married to this chap but now you've found out that he was already married to someone else and that he and his real wife are both dead.'

286

'But what if they ask me for his name?'

'Make one up – if he had been married already he'd probably have lied to you about his name anyway. Oh, and you'll need a wedding ring. I've got one upstairs you can have.' Her late mother-in-law's thin gold band would be perfect. If it was too big then Lena could tell the authorities some sob story about her supposed husband telling her it had belonged to his mother.

'They'll give you a new ration book with coupons for the baby and sort you out with everything, including somewhere to stay. When the baby comes you can put it in a crèche and get yourself a job.'

'But I've only just had new papers.'

'Then tell them that you were so upset and ashamed about what had happened that you didn't say anything until you realised that you were pregnant.'

Bella made everything sound so easy, but then things probably were easy for her, Lena thought enviously.

'Haven't you got something better to wear than what you've got on?' Bella asked abruptly. 'Only you'll find that you'll get much better attention from the authorities if you dress nicely.'

'I've got me tea dress,' Lena told her proudly, 'but it's too tight across me middle now.'

Bella thought of the maternity smocks folded away neatly upstairs in the chest of drawers on the landing. She'd bought them in a fit of defiance against her late husband when she'd first decided she was going to make sure that she fell pregnant. They'd never been worn. After all, there'd been no need, had there? She'd lost the new life she'd been carrying before there'd been any real need. The thought of giving this scruffy

287

little girl from the slums even one of her beautiful smocks filled Bella with a surge of angry hostility. They were far too good for her and would be totally wasted on her. On the other hand, the girl was here in her kitchen and if by some mischance someone should call round and see her here, Bella didn't want her appalling appearance reflecting on her.

'Like I said, you can stay the night, but first thing in the morning you're going to have to leave. I'll take you upstairs so that you can have a bath and clean yourself up properly. I can probably find you something better to wear as well,' she added casually, telling herself that it was, after all, in her own interests to make sure that when Lena left she would be able to sort herself out. After all, Bella didn't want her coming back, did she?

'Go on. It's you they're yelling for out there.'

The comedian standing in the wings of the Shaftesbury Avenue theatre with Francine gave her a small shove as he urged her to go back on stage and take another bow.

They had had a good audience tonight, Fran acknowledged. The theatre had been packed, the result, she had heard, of a growing influx of American military into the capital, even though officially America was not at war.

Briefings and meetings were the reason for this influx, so it was being said, to discuss the number of young Americans who had volunteered to join the British war effort.

Francine knew nothing about that but she did know that men in American uniforms were an increasingly familiar sight in London.

She had arrived back in the country in late September and had quickly been invited to join one of the many shows in the city as its lead singer.

As she left the stage and headed for her dressing room her mind was on the speed with which she would have to get changed if she wasn't going to be late to join a semi-official welcoming party at the Savoy for yet another batch of Americans, to which she had been invited as a member of ENSA. It was becoming quite common for members of the Entertainments National Service Association to be asked to attend official functions to provide a bit of 'light relief', and Francine suspected that before the evening was over she would be asked to entertain the guests with a couple of songs, and that it could well be the early hours before she was free to go 'off duty' and return to the small room she'd been allocated in an old-fashioned women-only hotel conveniently close to Shaftsbury Avenue.

She didn't mind the extra hours of work. They helped her to stop thinking about Marcus. She'd thought she'd known all there was to know about emotional pain but she'd discovered that she'd been wrong and that each heartbreak was different and unique and unbearably painful in its own individual way.

What hurt most about losing Marcus was that she didn't know if she had lost him because of the way she had been wrongly portrayed to him and accused of deliberately deceiving him by someone else, or because he himself had decided that he didn't after all care for her as much as he had allowed her to think. Either way, the result was the same – she had lost him – but not knowing why was like a constantly

289

running sore that she was beginning to think would never heal. The loss of her son, not once but twice over, had been unbearably painful, but Marcus's understanding of what she had gone through and his apparent acceptance of the fact that she had borne Jack out of wedlock and been forced to hand him over to Vi had done a great deal to ease a part of that pain. That Jack had been killed when a bomb had fallen on the Welsh farmhouse Vi had sent him to against Francine's own wishes was a different kind of pain and, like the one she felt for Marcus, a pain that she knew could never be wholly eased. All she had wanted for Jack was happiness, and she had truly believed that by allowing Vi to adopt him she was doing the best thing for him. They had had such a very brief time together, not long enough for her to win his confidence sufficiently to be able to tell him the truth: that she was his mother. He had, though, she hoped, known that she loved him, and they had shared some happiness together during those few brief days when she had had him all to herself.

'Fran, you ready yet?' The voice of Tom Gardner, the theatre manager, from outside her dressing-room door brought her back to reality.

'Just about,' she told him, reaching for her evening bag and checking that the navy-blue chiffon gown, with its sprinkling of sewn-on crystal beads – made in Egypt from fabric she had bought there when they had been on tour – hung properly, before opening the door and stepping out into the corridor.

'You'll certainly wow everyone tonight,' Tom told her appreciatively, 'although all the other women are bound to be green with envy, and not just because of your gown,' he told her gallantly.

Francine gave him a wide smile. She knew that Tom, debonair in his dinner suit, his fair hair slicked back, for all his flattery and man-about-town airs, preferred his own sex to hers, and was in a long-term and very discreet relationship with another man.

'What's tonight's do all about?' Francine asked him as she placed her hand on the arm he had crooked for her.

'A welcome party for some American airmen, sponsored by the Eagle Club, even though they're holding it at the Savoy. Major status, I would guess, rather than generals,' Tom told her.

Francine knew the name. The Eagle Club for Americans had opened in London in 1940.

'I suppose they're over here because of these talks Winston Churchill is having with their president?' she commented as they stepped out into the street, and miraculously Tom managed to secure them a taxi.

'Shush, mum's the word, remember?' he teased her, quoting one of the popular slogans the Government used to warn the general public to be discreet in case they were overheard by 'spies'.

It was one of those damp November evenings with fog oozing from narrow streets to make the city look even more run down and war worn than ever, and Francine shivered as she got into the taxi.

It had given her a shock, Francine admitted, to return to England and discover how badly London had been bombed. From all accounts Liverpool had suffered just as much if not more, although she hadn't as yet had time to go north to see her sister Jean and see for herself.

Dear Jean, who had always been so kind to her,

and who, the minute Francine had let her know she was back in England, had written to tell her that she hoped Francine wouldn't mind but she had loaned some of the clothes Francine had left behind to Katie, Luke's fiancé. Francine smiled, remembering the charming letter she had received from Luke's Katie after she had written back to Jean assuring her that she did not mind in the least, and that Jean and Katie and Grace were to consider the trunk and its contents their own.

The truth was that Francine had changed so much from the young girl who had bought those clothes in America that she no longer wanted to wear them. They belonged to a different life, a life before being reunited with Jack, and a life before loving and losing Marcus.

Marcus . . . there she went again, letting him into her thoughts when what she ought to be doing was keeping him out of them and out of her heart as well.

The Savoy was busy with couples obviously intent on having a good night out, war or no war, many of the men in uniform whilst the women were wearing smart dresses, carefully preserved, Francine suspected from the style of them, from pre-war wardrobes. Guessing that made her feel a bit guilty about the elegance and style of her own evening gown. In Egypt there was no rationing or restrictions. However, if English women could not buy new gowns they were certainly compensating for that by wearing their best jewellery. Of course, the clientele of the Savoy was, in the main, top drawer, well born and wealthy – the kind of women who would have good jewellery – although

Francine had seen one or two girls clinging to male arms who seemed to suggest that the age-old practice of rich men squiring pretty young actresses was still common currency.

A small smile touched Francine's lips as she wondered what people looking at her would make of her and where they would place her in the Savoy's clientele hierarchy. She was a singer, not an actress, and she certainly wasn't a girl any more, or looking for a 'sugar daddy', to borrow a phrase from her Hollywood days. But then neither was she out of the top drawer, or even out of a middle drawer, even if she no longer spoke with her original Liverpool accent.

Only those members of the Savoy's staff from before the war who were over the age for service still remained at the hotel, their manner courteous and very British. Tom asked where they might find their party and was told that it was being held in the River Room.

'Mmm, perhaps I was wrong and it is generals,' Tom grinned as he and Francine made their way there.

A couple of smartly uniformed young American servicemen were on duty outside the doors to the River Room, although it was a tired-looking British civil servant who checked their names off against his list, the light shining equally unkindly on his bald head and his well-worn suit, as he indicated that they were free to go in.

It was a senior official from ENSA who was responsible for their invitation, and luckily he was standing close enough to the doors for Francine and Tom to find him without any difficulty.

'Good, you're here. Let me introduce you both to a few people. There are a couple of uniforms I want you to meet,' he told them. 'They are part of a contingent of political and military personnel over here on some hush-hush business that can't be discussed but we've been given orders to make sure that they are well entertained. I dare say the hush-hush business has something to do with Winston's talks with the Americans about what kind of help they're prepared to give us whilst remaining neutral.'

The fact that the Americans had so far remained neutral was something of a sore point, but Francine knew better than to let her nationalistic feeling show when she and Tom mingled with the other guests and played the roles they were there to play.

A young man in air force uniform had attached himself to them – little more than a boy really, Francine thought ruefully, for all his swagger and pride in his country and in himself.

'Take care of your young admirer,' Tom told her during the few minutes they had together for private conversation. 'His father's a very, very rich banker and his mother is from one of American's first families.'

'So what's he doing in uniform over here instead of helping his father count their money?' Francine asked, as she sipped her White Lady cocktail.

'Apparently he enlisted before his parents could stop him, and he got himself over here to join the Eagles.'

The Eagles were a group of young American airmen who had taken it upon themselves to ignore their country's neutral status and come over to Britain to form their own fighting unit.

'The American press have got hold of the news that he's joined the Eagles and have turned him into a bit of a hero, so his parents can't put any pressure on the American Ambassador to get him shipped back home. Instead the Ambassador's got him working at the Embassy as a sort of go-between, liaising between the Embassy and the Eagles in an attempt to keep everyone happy.'

Francine could understand any parent wanting to keep their children safe, especially when, after all, it wasn't America's fight.

'So when are you going to let me take you out for dinner?'

Francine put down her cocktail glass and looked the young American in the eye. He had been pursuing her all evening. His name, she had learned, was Brandon Walter Adams the third, and his burning ambition, apart from taking her out to dinner, was to fly with the famous Eagles. He was very good-looking in that clean-cut Ivy League way of a certain type of upper-class young American, with thick wheat-blond hair, good skin, bright blue eyes and the height and breadth of shoulder of a young man used to playing sport. He was also slightly arrogant and overconfident, and far, far too young for her, Francine decided.

'Are you sure you're allowed to stay up that late?' she mocked him deliberately. She had learned a long time ago that the best way to depress the attentions of a certain type of young man was to make him feel small. However, the scarlet colour that washed his face made her feel so guilty that instinctively she reached out and touched his arm, saying gently, 'I'm sorry, that was very rude of me. I am extremely flattered by your invitation but truthfully I am far too old for you to take out to dinner. If you're feeling lonely why don't you speak with your Ambassador? I'm sure he knows some suitable young girls you could ask out.'

'Sure he does,' Brandon agreed. 'But the girl I want to take to dinner is you. Come on, you wouldn't want to see a guy starve, would you, because I promise you I'm not eating until you agree to eat with me.'

The thought of a young man as large and as muscular as this one was not eating was enough to make Francine burst out laughing.

'Good, so that's a yes then,' Brandon told her, seizing on her laughter so swiftly that Francine was caught off guard. Before she could even shake her head in denial he was making arrangements, and somehow or other Francine found herself in the ridiculous situation of having agreed to have dinner with him the following evening, even though that was the last thing she really wanted to do.

Pink cheeked and scrubbed clean, her hair washed and braided; and wearing the pretty floral nightdress and dressing gown set Bella had given her, Lena started to eat the supper Bella had prepared for them.

At least the girl looked less like a tart now, and she had surprisingly good manners, Bella acknowledged, watching Lena eat.

'Did Charlie tell you anything about me?' she asked Lena abruptly.

Finishing her mouthful of food, Lena shook her head.

'I only saw him the twice,' she admitted. 'A proper

fool I was an' all to think that he loved me. I know that now.'

'You won't be the only girl to be taken in by someone like Charlie whilst this war's on,' Bella assured her. 'I was married to a man who made a fool of me and who would have gone on doing so if he hadn't been killed by one of Hitler's bombs.'

Charlie's sister was a widow? That must be how she came to have this beautiful house all to herself. Lena couldn't imagine what it must feel like to have not just a room but a whole house. She'd never been in anywhere as smart, nor filled with such nice things. She had wanted to stay wrapped in the thick fluffy bath towel Bella had given her forever – until Bella had given her the beautiful nightdress and dressing gown she was now wearing, along with a pair of what she had described as 'old' slippers, but which to Lena, who had never been able to replace the slippers she had lost when her parents' house had blitzed, were wonderful.

Now, clean and warm, sitting in this beautiful kitchen, eating a big bowl of soup, which Bella had told her her mother had made, Lena felt almost as though she had somehow or other ended up in heaven. Already everything Bella said and did was beginning to fill her with innocent admiration that bordered on hero worship. How could it not do when Bella had been so kind and generous to her?

Tears filled Lena's eyes at the thought of that generosity, causing Bella to frown and demand, 'Now what's wrong?'

'Nothing,' Lena told her. 'It's just that I've never met anyone as kind and good as you are. No one has ever been as kind as this to me before, and I know I don't deserve it, what with what I've done with your Charlie an' all.'

Already, although neither to them had noticed it, Lena, a natural and instinctive mimic, was modulating how she spoke so that it was closer to the way Bella spoke and less like that of a girl from the slums.

No one had ever told Bella before that she was either kind or good, but when she looked suspiciously at Lena she realised that the girl not only meant what she said but actually believed it. Poor little thing, Bella thought, protective instincts she hadn't known she possessed suddenly aroused. She could just imagine how easily she would have fallen for Charlie, and how fatally. Not that Bella for one minute approved of Lena's current situation, of course. Certainly not. But there were plenty of tales circulating about young married women going off the rails in the absence of their husbands, and babies being born within the sanctity of marriage, but fathered outside it, so to speak. Lena had the misfortune to be too young and too naïve to know how to protect her own interests.

'I'm ever so grateful to you,' Lena told Bella fervently. 'I really am. You've got a heart of gold and no mistake.' Lena had to blow her nose on the clean handkerchief Bella had given her and Bella found that she too was in danger of being overcome by emotion. She wished that those who thought they knew her, like Jan Polanski and his family, for instance, were here to witness Lena's praise, but of course Jan was married now, and his sister and mother had left Bella's roof to move in with some other Poles. Bella wished that they would leave Wallasey altogether. That way she wouldn't need to be reminded of Jan, but Bettina, his sister, now worked in an official capacity within Wallasey Council as a liaison officer between the council and the Polish refugees billeted in the area.

Lena stifled a yawn.

Bella told her, 'You might as well go up and get a good night's sleep. After all, you'll have to fend for yourself from tomorrow, and I've got some paperwork to do anyway.'

Lena's eyes widened and darkened with open respect at Bella's reference to her work. What a wonderful person she was to make time for her when she had so much to do.

'So about this dinner date of ours?'

Francine couldn't help laughing even though she shook her head firmly. 'We have just had dinner together,' she pointed out.

'Ah, but that was just so as we could discuss having a proper dinner date,' Brandon told her, unabashed.

Had she been ten years younger it would have been very easy to be seduced by that energetic and oh-so-American go-getting confidence that came from good looks and wealth, Francine admitted, but since she was not, she was ruefully aware that it was very easy to remain unmoved by Brandon's determined attempt to win her over.

'If your Ambassador gets to hear that you are trying to date an ageing British singer, he'll be on the telephone to your parents faster than you can imagine and then we'll both be in trouble. I value my job far too much to want to lose it because an irate American parent thinks I'm about to cradle-snatch their son.'

Francine smiled and kept her voice light. The words

299

and the threat of parental intervention should be enough to deflate the largest of young male egos.

'You're right,' Brandon agreed promptly. 'My dad would probably be on the next flight over.'

Francine smiled her relief, only to realise that she had been overoptimistic when he added with a wickedly male smile of his own, 'And once he saw you he'd understand exactly why I want to date you.' He reached across the table and took possession of Francine's hand before she could stop him. 'I'm not going to stop asking until you say yes, even if that means staying here all night, so you may as well give in now.'

EIGHTEEN

Bella assessed Lena critically. She was certainly looking a lot more respectable this morning than she had done when Bella had first brought her home. Her hair was styled and brushed neatly, and wearing the smart maternity two-piece in navy, with its white collar and navy and white spotted bow, which Bella had given her, she looked not just passably respectable but actually very smart, Bella recognised. She certainly had more of a look of someone who would make a good worker than those girls she had been interviewing for that new position as a nursery maid-in-training, which would be coming up once the crèche was expanded. It wouldn't be a bad thing for her to have someone she could trust working with the other nurses either. That way she could make sure that any potential problems were dealt with the minute they cropped up instead of not finding out about them until they had begun to fester. Laura had had terrible trouble with two nursery nurses who had had a falling-out about something when they had first opened. Bella certainly didn't want that happening to her.

It would mean Lena having to stay on here with

her, of course, but Bella admitted to herself that she had actually woken up with an unfamiliar sense of anticipation this morning, knowing that she had someone living with her who actually admired her. And then there was the fact that this child Lena was carrying would be her own niece or nephew. Not that anyone could ever know that, of course.

Lena had finished her breakfast – porridge, which Bella had insisted she was to have, and a cup of tea too – yet another sign of Charlie's sister's kindness and generosity. She got up from the table, carrying her used crockery over to the sink where she proceeded to start washing up.

Bella's eyes widened thoughtfully. She'd already noted how neat Lena had left her room, and how anxious she was to win her own approval. The house had felt empty since the Polanskis had left – not that she missed them for one minute, but with those empty bedrooms she was bound to have the billeting people round soon. In fact, there were so many reasons why it made good sense for her to have Lena here that Bella decided not to waste any more time merely thinking about it.

'I'll go up and get my things,' Lena began. Her voice was husky, her head turned away from Bella so that Charlie's sister wouldn't see her tears. She felt so special and privileged to have been brought back here by Bella and looked after the way she had looked after her, and she didn't want to repay Bella's kindness by getting all upset now when she had to leave.

'I've been thinking.' Bella stopped her. 'Seeing as it's Charlie's child you're having – although of course you are to promise that you will never ever tell anyone

302

that – and since there is a vacancy coming up at the crèche – for the right kind of girl who knows how to conduct herself and be a credit to the person who recommends her – and with me already having a spare room here, you might as well stay on.'

All the blood left Lena's face. She stared at Bella, speechless with disbelief and hope, and then stammered, 'You mean that I can stay here, with you, in this house, and work at the crèche?'

'For a probationary period,' Bella confirmed. She didn't want to leave herself with no get-out if things didn't work out after all.

'Oh! Oh, I can't believe that anyone could be so kind.' Now Lena's face was as flushed as it had been pale, burning with awe and thankfulness as she sobbed out her gratitude and then, to Bella's shock, put her arms around her and hugged her fiercely.

Bella had never before been hugged by another girl, and certainly not by one whose baby she could suddenly feel giving a little kick as though of approval and joy. For a second she didn't know what on earth to do. Then, feeling awkward and yet at the same time somehow proud and elated, she hugged Lena back rather gingerly.

'Oh, you are so good. A true saint. I don't know what I've ever done to be lucky enough to have met you,' Lena sobbed to Bella as they stepped back from one another. 'Oh, I shall have to sit down for a minute. I've come over all funny.'

'We'll need to register you with a doctor,' Bella announced, suddenly very aware of her new responsibilities, 'and we'll have to start buying things ready for the baby. When is it due?'

'The middle of January,' Lena told her.

She couldn't believe her good luck. It was like a dream come true, as though somehow Bella had known that when Lena had been lying in Bella's beautifully comfortable and clean bed last night she had said a prayer that she might never have to leave.

'I've got to go to work in a minute. I'll take you with me and get one of the other nursery maids to show you what you'll be doing,' Bella announced, reverting to practicality. She'd have to speak with Mr Benson, of course, she decided. She didn't want any problems later with people saying she was showing Lena favouritism. And she'd have to explain away her presence in her own home as well. Bella thought for a minute and then had a brain wave.

'I think it's best for now that we just say that my auntie in Liverpool asked me to take you in on account of what's happened to you and her being in the WVS.'

That explanation sounded vague enough to work, Bella decided. After all, with the war causing so much upheaval people didn't have time to ask too many questions any more. Her own mother was bound to make a fuss, though. Bella gave a small inner shrug. She would just have to make it then, wouldn't she, and she, Bella, would just have to remind both her parents how poor Lena had come to be in trouble in the first place.

'Are you and the twins going to the Grafton this Saturday?' Carole asked Katie as they shared their morning coffee break.

'I expect so.' Katie knew that Jean preferred it if the twins had someone to keep an eye on them when they went out dancing, and there was very little that Katie wasn't prepared to do for Luke's mother.

'Can I come with you then?'

'Of course you can.'

'I'm hoping to get an air-mail letter card this week. It's bin nearly a month since I got the last one.'

'They're only allowed one a month,' Katie reminded her. The air-mail letter cards were restricted to one per month per man, and since they were private they were much more popular with men serving in the Middle East then open aerograms.

'Andy writes ever such cheeky stuff in his sometimes. Proper saucy,' Carole giggled.

Katie smiled back. Luke's letters, whilst ending with tender words of love for her personally, were the kind she could read out aloud to his family, and Katie made sure that she kept him up to date with all the family news when she wrote back to him. Of course, there were normal sea-mail letters as well, but they took six weeks or even longer to get through, and it was in these that Luke wrote rather more intimately of how much he missed her and how much he ached to hold her, and how much he hoped she was remembering that she was engaged to him and that she was letting other men know that she was officially 'taken'.

She did miss him, of course, and she worried for him too. The desert was such a long way away, and she knew how anxiously Jean and Sam listened to the news for reports on what was happening out there. She, though, had Luke's family to comfort and support her.

Jean had initially hoped that Luke might be home for Christmas but Katie had guessed that Sam had more realistically doubted that this would be the case.

'He'll only just have landed before he'd have to come back,' Sam had warned Jean. 'And there's no way the army would send men out there only to bring them back again after two or three weeks.'

'Well, I wish they would,' Jean had returned. 'This will be the third Christmas of the war, Sam, and the first one that Luke hasn't been at home.'

A lump had come into Katie's throat when she'd seen the way Sam had put a comforting arm around Jean to draw her close. One day she and Luke would be like Jean and Sam, and they too would have their children to love and worry about – and their children's grandparents too, of course, Katie hoped.

NINETEEN

Seb was waiting for her as she got off the train, and Grace went straight into his arms, for once ignoring the fact that it was hardly a 'proper' thing to do. She'd caught the train from Liverpool straight after her shift had finished, so that they could have their two full days off together rather than lose half a day with her travelling in the morning.

'And how's my best girl?' Seb asked her huskily after he had released her and they were walking arm in arm out of the station, Grace cuddling up close to his side for warmth, their breath making puffs of white vapour in the cold November evening air.

'Your best girl?' Grace teased him. 'Your *only* girl, I hope you mean. Oh, Seb, I've missed you so much, but it won't be long now until we can be properly together. I've got my final exams at the end of the month, and then . . . We'll need to sort out getting the banns read. Mum's going to have a word with our vicar for me, but you'll have to sort out doing that down here.'

They had to break off their conversation to say 'good evening' to Mr Thompson, probably on his way to his billet. He was in overall charge of operations

307

at The Old Rectory, as the building requisitioned by the Government to house the Y Section was known.

It was so cold that Grace was glad when they reached the little teashop, which luckily was still open. They had just settled down at one of the tables tucked into a corner so that they 'had' to sit close together and so could surreptitiously hold hands, when the teashop door opened and a group of girls quite clearly dressed up for a night out came in. Initially Grace thought nothing of it when they looked over in their direction, but then one of them, slightly older than the others, with dark hair and hard pebble-brown eyes, detached herself and sauntered over, practically ignoring *her*, Grace thought indignantly. She then produced a cigarette and leaned across the table to ask Seb for a light, obviously without giving any thought to the fact that she was intruding and that the intrusion might not be welcome.

Worse was to come, though. Keeping her back to Grace, she perched on the edge of the table and told Seb, 'I hope you aren't going to let me down at the dance tomorrow night, and that you'll be there.'

'I let you bully me into buying two tickets, didn't I?' Seb answered her with a smile, ignoring the sharp look Grace was giving him.

'So you did,' the brunette agreed in a knowing tone that instantly got Grace's back up even further. 'I'll look forward to having that dance with you.'

With that she stood up and sashayed back across the floor to join the other young women, who were now sitting down at two of the other tables.

'Who was that?' Grace demanded, up in arms. 'What did she mean about you buying dance tickets and promising to dance with her?'

Grace could see from the surprised look that Seb was giving her that he was taken aback by her angry reaction.

'Her name's Sybil and she and the other girls have been down here on a training course for Y Section work. She's good,' Seb added, so approvingly that Grace's hostility to the other woman immediately intensified.

'She certainly seems to be good at ignoring the fact that you're an engaged man and that your fiancée was sitting right next to you whilst she was trying to make up to you.'

Seb laughed. 'Don't be silly. That's just her way. It doesn't mean anything.'

'I am not being silly and it does mean something – to me.' Tears filled Grace's eyes – tears of anger she assured herself, and the person she was most angry with was Seb because he didn't seem to understand not just how rude Sybil had been, but, more importantly, how he should have dealt with the situation by stating very firmly that he would not be dancing with any girl other than his beloved fiancée.

'Well, I think we've almost got everything now and that Baby will arrive to a properly equipped nursery,' Bella announced in a pleased voice as she and Lena found a table in Joe Lyons and Bella summoned one of the café's nippy waitresses.

They'd been in Liverpool all Saturday morning shopping for baby things, to add to the impressive number of essential items, as Bella referred to them, already waiting in Bella's house.

'And that's all thanks to you,' Lena said gratefully.

In Lena's eyes now there was no one as wonderful as Bella, and no one who could ever come anywhere near being as wonderful. She had almost literally picked Lena up out of the gutter, and given her a home and a job, and, even more importantly as far as Lena was concerned, given her her friendship as well.

In the handful of days Lena had been living with Bella, she had already not just put on some much needed weight, she had also started to model herself on Bella, not wanting her heroine to be ashamed of her.

It was lucky that Lena had such good table manners Bella reflected approvingly. She knew all of Lena's life story now, and about the mother who had been in service, married and then regretted that marriage. Bella's own mother had of course been furious when Bella had called round to tell her what she had done, and Bella had half expected to have to face a row with her father. However, she hadn't heard a word from him. Not that she would have paid any attention even if he had objected. Bella was enjoying having Lena living with her far more than she had expected.

Take last night, for instance, when they'd sat chatting after supper about the crèche, and in no time at all it had been nearly midnight and Bella hadn't noticed the time passing, she'd enjoyed their conversation so much.

And then there was the coming baby. Bella's family doctor had examined Lena and pronounced that both she and the baby were doing very well, although Lena needed to put on a little bit more weight, and Bella couldn't help but be flattered by the way in which Lena turned to her for advice and approval.

Lena had hardly been able to believe it when Bella had managed to talk the owner of the beautiful coach-built pram they'd gone to look at into letting them have it even though it was really promised to someone else.

'They'll be so disappointed,' Lena had argued guiltily, but Bella had stood firm and pointed out that Lena's baby would be disappointed as well if there was no pram for it, and of course her argument had won the day.

'Look, I know you're tired,' Bella told Lena once she had had her cup of tea, 'so why don't you stay here and wait for me whilst I pop back to Lewis's and just make sure that they haven't got another pair of rubber pants tucked away.'

'Oh, Bella, no, you've spoiled me enough already,' Lena protested, but Bella shook her head.

'You'll need at least two pairs – I know that from the crèche.'

One thing Bella had been scrupulous about was not 'borrowing' any of the baby equipment that rightly belonged to the crèche. She didn't allow the girls who worked there to do that and that same rule had to apply to Lena as well.

Bella had been gone only five minutes and Lena was just pouring herself a second cup of tea when a familiar voice announced, 'Lena, it is you, isn't it?'

It was Gavin, the young apprentice tugboat pilot who had been so kind to Lena when she had had to join the trekkers. Lena blushed and then hung her head slightly, well aware of how much her pregnancy now showed.

'Are you on your own?' he asked, looking round.

'No, I'm with a . . . a friend.'

He thought she meant she was with a man, Lena realised immediately. A mixture of guilt and determination filled her. It was no use, she was going to have to tell him the truth. She wanted to tell him the truth, she admitted. She hated being deceitful and pretending to be something that she wasn't.

'I'm not married on . . . or anything,' she told him determinedly.

Gavin didn't know what to say. It was obvious that she was pregnant and now with her comment he was beginning to wish that he'd simply walked past without speaking to her.

'You're shocked, I can see,' Lena acknowledged. 'And I dare say you think that I'm a bad lot who deserves to be in trouble.'

'No I don't,' Gavin denied, realising as he spoke that it was true, and that although he was shocked he also felt sorry for her and oddly rather protective of her.

'It was that soldier – Charlie – the one me auntie threw me out over. He's the father. I don't know why I ever let meself by taken in by him, I really don't. I should have known he didn't mean it when he said that he loved me, and that we were going to be married, especially with him being posh and me being like I am. But I thought he meant it, you see. I thought he did love me and that he'd come back for me and marry me, otherwise I'd never have let him—' She broke off, looking ashamed and miserable, and very young. 'You'll think even less of me now than you did before, I dare say, and don't say you didn't because you did, I could tell.'

Gavin flushed uncomfortably.

'It's all right, I'm not saying that I blame you,'

Lena surprised him by saying, 'especially not with the way I am now. Lied to me good and proper, he did, telling me it was me he wanted when all the time he was engaged to someone else. Married to her now he is, an' all.'

She sounded so forlorn, more innocent and naïve than the experienced worldly sort he'd originally had her down as. He heard his own mother saying often enough that it was often decent girls who got themselves into trouble and not them as knew what was what. Lena certainly wasn't coming across as someone who knew what was what right now. Her honesty had touched him and made him feel sympathetic towards her. More than that, it had made him feel protective towards her, he recognised, almost as though she was someone he ought to worry and concern himself about, like a member of his family. His feelings confused and alarmed him. He didn't want to get involved with or feel sympathy for her. It was the war that was to blame, he comforted himself. It changed things, forging bonds between strangers in a way that could never happen in peacetime.

'You're all right, are you?' he heard himself asking reluctantly. 'I mean, you've got somewhere to live and that, and—'

'Yes, I'm fine. No, really I am,' Lena insisted when she saw the dubious look he was giving her. 'Bella, that's Charlie's sister, has taken me in and she's sorting me out with a job. Been ever so good to me, she has. A proper angel, she is and no mistake. Not like that brother of hers.'

'Well, that's all right then.' Gavin exhaled in relief. He told himself that he was glad that any duty he might have felt he had towards Lena was cancelled out by someone else stepping in to help her out, but at the same time he felt strangely reluctant to end their conversation and walk away from her.

She was so young and so very naïve, Gavin thought, but that wouldn't protect her from people's disapproval, and worse – even though it took two to create what she'd so obviously got in her belly. A woman's guilt was plain for the whole world to see whilst a man could ignore and even deny his if he chose to do so.

'I got thrown out of my job and my billet,' Lena continued. Somehow he felt like an old friend and someone she could trust, which was just plain daft, seeing as she'd only seen him twice before. 'And then Bella took me in. It was like a miracle had happened to me.' Her eyes filled with tears.

Gavin had heard the warnings his own mother had given his sisters and he knew how angry she would be if one of them ended up in Lena's situation, but he knew too that she wouldn't turn her back on them or throw them out. But then Lena didn't have a mother.

'Bella's been ever so good to me. A proper saint, and no mistake. I don't know what I'd have done but for her. Ended up having to give up my baby, I expect, and I wouldn't want that. I suppose you think that's wrong of me, me not having a husband or a wedding ring or anything,' she went on. 'I suppose I'd think it myself if it was someone else and not me, but, well, I just know that I don't want to give me baby away.

'What about you and your schoolteacher?' Lena asked him, remembering her manners.

'She's engaged now – to someone else.'

'Oh, I'm ever so sorry.' Lena's face was scarlet.

Gavin shook his head. 'There's no need for you to be. We were never more than friends, despite what my grandmother liked to think.'

Dolly! 'How is Dolly?' Lena asked him more eagerly.

'She's fine, although she's giving my mum a hard time.'

He broke off, stepping to one side of the table as Bella arrived.

She had seen Lena talking to the young man the minute she'd entered the restaurant, and she wondered protectively who he was and what he wanted. As Bella knew from her own experience, a pretty face attracted a lot of male attention.

Now, though, as Lena introduced them in a slightly flustered and anxious manner, Bella realised that 'Gavin' was the person Lena had mentioned when she had been telling her about her experiences with the trekkers, and remembering how much Lena, with her way of describing things, had made her laugh with her description of Dolly, Bella was actually smiling when she shook Gavin's hand.

'Gran will be put out that it's me that's seen you and not her,' Gavin told Lena, and then to his own astonishment he heard himself saying brusquely, 'Look, why don't you give me your address? I know that Gran often talks about you and wonders how you are going on.' It wasn't exactly a lie, even it wasn't exactly the truth either, Gavin assured himself.

'Oh, yes.' Lena's face lit up but then she looked uncertainly at Bella, hesitating in case Bella disapproved of what Gavin was suggesting.

Such an obvious desire to have her approval made Bella feel very much in a position where she had to do the right thing by Lena. Had this Gavin been the sort she thought would take advantage of Lena she would naturally have suggested that Lena refused, but he seemed decent enough, and perfectly respectable. Taking charge in a businesslike manner, she gave Gavin her address. Witnessing Lena's pink-cheeked pleasure and Gavin's own male approval, she felt, Bella recognised with a small start of surprise, as though she had passed some kind of unexpected test.

And she had managed to persuade the saleswoman to sell her a second pair of precious rubber baby pants.

Inviting Gavin to join them for a pot of tea, Bella told Lena about her Lewis's triumph, adding, 'All we need to do now is to find someone to paint the nursery for us.'

'Well, I can do that,' Gavin offered before he could stop himself.

'Oh, Gavin, could you?' Lena was thrilled at the thought of being able through someone she knew, to remove at least one of the preparations for her coming baby from Bella's shoulders.

Bella thought for a minute. Knowing an able young man who could turn his hand to various domestic tasks would be a bonus she'd be a fool to turn down, and it would also prove, just in case anyone might think to query it, that she was not misusing her position at the crèche to get things done at home.

Yes, she decided approvingly, when Gavin had taken his leave of them after insisting on paying for their shared pot of tea, the trip to Liverpool had been an extremely profitable investment of time, what with getting two pairs of rubber baby pants and finding a personable-looking man who was willing to come round and paint the nursery.

'I dare say that your friend will even know the best place to get his hands on some distemper for us,' she said to Lena cheerfully when they were seated together on the ferry taking them back across the water.

Lena nodded enthusiastically and felt proud that Bella approved of Gavin, as well as grateful to Gavin himself for his kindness to her.

The weekend hadn't gone anything like as well or been as happy as Grace had expected, and all because of that horrible, horrible Sybil, who seemed to haunt their footsteps almost as though she was deliberately following them, even though when Grace had said as much to Seb, and Seb, who never, ever criticised her, had taken her completely aback and hurt her too by saying tersely that she was being silly and exaggerating the situation out of all proportion.

That had been over an hour ago now, but just thinking about it still made her feel like having a good cry. Not that Seb would notice if she did, not with it pouring with rain like it was, and them not even being able to cuddle up together under an umbrella because there was a market on in the town and the streets were packed with farmers and their families who had come in to join the townsfolk. They hadn't even been able to get a table in the café, never mind a nice bit of lunch in the pretty pub where Grace had been looking forward to sitting nestled next to Seb in front of an old-fashioned open fire. But what hurt most of all was the fact that not only did Seb not seem to understand why she was so upset by Sybil's behaviour, even worse, he actually seemed to be cross with her instead of supporting her and agreeing that it was Sybil whose behaviour was unacceptable.

But then if he had supported her in the way that a loving fiancé should support his girl when another girl tried to attract his attention, none of this misery would have happened in the first place, Grace thought. Surely last night when Sybil had come up to their table and perched there for all the world as though Grace simply hadn't existed whilst she flirted with Seb, Seb should have clearly, very firmly and publicly put her in her place and told her what was what – that he was an engaged and soon-to-be-married man and that he wanted nothing whatsoever to do with her.

Grace had said as much to Seb later on when her landlady had allowed them an hour alone together in her front room before announcing that she wanted to lock up for the night and that it was time for Seb to leave. But instead of agreeing with Grace Seb had said that it was both unnecessary and impossible for him to take that kind of attitude. Unnecessary because in his opinion Sybil meant no harm and her manner was just her way of behaving, and impossible because as Sybil's superior it would undermine his own authority if he had to start complaining about her natural friendliness.

'It's just her way,' he had kept on saying, 'and best ignored.'

'You mean like she was ignoring me?' Grace had demanded, and Seb, who had been on the point of taking her in his arms, had drawn back from her to

318

say quietly, 'This isn't like you, Grace, and I have to say that I'm a bit disappointed. Surely you know how much I love you?'

'Yes, of course,' she had told him immediately.

'Then I don't understand why you are getting so cross about Sybil. What harm can she possibly do to us, after all?'

She had felt obliged to agree with him, and she had woken up this morning determined to put last night behind her, and determined as well to insist despite Seb's having bought two tickets for the dance that was apparently being held at the church hall, that they did not go.

Because of this wretched Sybil they had hardly spoken at all about the wedding or their own plans, and now Seb had just announced that despite everything she had said he felt that they really ought to go to tonight's dance.

'How can you say that?' Grace demanded.

'You'll enjoy it, and besides, what else would we do?'

'I thought the whole idea of me coming here was so that we could have some time alone together,' Grace reminded him, almost in tears.

'Well, yes, but it isn't as though it's summer and we could go for a long walk, is it? Mrs Philips has made it plain that she doesn't want us occupying her front room, and I can hardly take you back to my billet. Come on, don't be a crosspatch, Grace. You'll enjoy it if you'd just let yourself.'

'I'd enjoy it a lot more if Sybil wasn't going to be there.'

Seb exhaled loudly, and then swung round to face her.

'Darling, please, do stop being so silly about poor Sybil. She doesn't mean any harm really.'

How could he possibly believe that? Grace felt as though her throat was choking on the unfamiliar mixture of anger and disbelief that Seb could be so dim.

She would have said what she thought to him, only someone trying to get past them jostled her, causing her to grab hold of Seb's sleeve to steady herself.

'Come on,' Seb coaxed her with a smile. 'At least if we go dancing I'll be able to hold you close.'

'Are you sure it is me you want to hold close?' Grace challenged him. 'How do I know that you don't secretly want to go to this dance just because Sybil's going?'

The humour had died out of Seb's gaze and Grace's heart gave a frightened little flurry of beats. He was so easy-going, was her Seb, that she sometimes forgot that he was also very strong-willed and determined. In the past she had only ever seen that strong will and that determination used to her advantage, but now suddenly she had a feeling that reminded her of the fear she had felt the night the hospital had been bombed at the height of the blitz.

Driven by that fear she continued, 'When you first told me you were coming down here you never said anything about you being put in charge of any girls.'

'I've already explained that to you. They only arrived a few days ago and they are only here temporarily. It is my job to help train them, Grace, and I'm sorry if that upsets you but that is my job and part of my duty to my country.'

What about your duty to me? Grace wanted to ask him, but somehow she couldn't.

Was she really getting too old to enjoy dances any more, Katie wondered as she sat sipping her shandy, whilst keeping a watchful eye on the twins, who were both up on the floor, Sasha, all smiles and pink-flushed cheeks, dancing with Bobby Lyons, the young bomb disposal sapper, who had made a beeline for her the minute he had arrived, and Lou dancing nothing like as enthusiastically with one of his friends, or was it simply that she was missing Luke too much to want to enjoy herself?

Luke wouldn't really like her being here, she knew that much, but even he would have to admit that she could hardly have refused his mother's hint that she would feel much happier about the twins going to the Grafton if Katie was with them to keep an eye on them.

Carole certainly seemed to have no qualms about what Andy might think of her going out dancing. She was on the floor and in the arms of a young man Katie didn't recognise, but who she guessed must have asked her to dance whilst Katie had been in the ladies.

It was no fun coming here and being asked to dance with one of Bobby's friends just so that he could dance with Sasha, when really she would much rather have danced with her twin, Lou thought miserably. But then life was no fun at all at the moment in her eyes. She hated the telephone exchange and thought the work they were learning to do was the dreariest thing imaginable. Mrs Withers, the stern supervisor who was in charge of them, had made it

plain that she didn't like her and was always criticising her and finding fault with her whilst praising
Sasha, even if Lou was deliberating getting things
wrong and sabotaging her own success. Once she
and Sasha would have giggled together about that,
sharing the secret of what she was doing, but even
Sasha was frowning disapprovingly at her when she
failed to make the right connections in the boards.
She could have been just as good as Sasha if she'd
wanted to be, but she didn't want to be. The work
was dull and boring, and the place was stuffy and
dark, and she longed for the kind of excitement and
adventure that was not limited to a Saturday night
dance at the Grafton with a gawky UXB sapper.

Out of the corner of her eye, and over Bobby's
shoulder, Sasha watched Lou anxiously. It made
her feel all squeezed up inside and tight with misery
just thinking about her twin these days because
that meant acknowledging how much things had
changed between them. What would happen if they
went on changing? Would they end up like their
mother and Auntie Vi, who were also twins but
who were not close at all? Was that what growing
up meant?

Deep down inside Sasha knew that there was much
more to the widening distance between them than
just growing up. She loved working at the exchange,
and living at home, she enjoyed knowing that on
Saturday evening she would be coming to the Grafton
and that Bobby would be there, and that he would
ask her to dance and that one day when they were
both old enough he would ask her to be his steady,
but Lou was just the opposite. That she hated working
at the exchange and was doing everything she could

to get herself dismissed really upset and frightened Sasha. If that happened then for the first time in their lives they would end up being properly separated, unless she left with Lou, and she admitted to herself, she didn't really want to do that.

Growing up was so very difficult. She didn't want to betray her twin by telling their mother just what Lou was doing at the exchange, but neither did she want Lou to be dismissed. She'd talked to Bobby about it and he'd offered to have a word with Lou on her behalf but Sasha knew that she couldn't let him do that. Even so, it had pleased her that he had been so keen to help her. He was ever such a nice lad and her parents liked him as well.

Katie sighed to herself when she saw Carole returning to their table accompanied by not just one but four young men. Giggling, she introduced them all to Katie, ending her introduction with, 'And this is Danny.'

Katie found herself face to face with an extra-ordinarily good-looking young man with thick almost black curly hair worn longer than the military male haircuts she was used to seeing, his deep green eyes framed by thick long lashes any girl would have envied. When he spoke it was with a soft Irish accent and a look of admiration in his eyes that had the colour storming Katie's face just as much as the way he was holding on to her hand for conspicuously too long. A little anxiously she looked for the twins, half wishing they would return and half hoping they would not. This was exactly the sort of situation Luke had warned her against, and Katie was bit cross with Carole for putting her into it by bringing over these boys, especially this far too wickedly handsome one whose gaze said much more than it should on such a short acquaintanceship.

'So is it true then that you're sitting there all day reading other people's love letters?' he asked, as soon as they were all seated, with him sitting at Katie's side.

His manner was so engaging that Katie couldn't object, but nevertheless she gave Carole a reproachful look. They were not supposed to talk about their work.

'I dare say then that you'll know all about those things a fella says to a girl when he wants to sweet-talk her?' Danny continued, even though Katie hadn't answered his first question.

'Pay no attention to our Danny,' Mick, one of the other young men, told Katie, his Irish accent flavoured liberally with Liverpudlian intonation.

'Or his Irish accent. He just puts that on to impress the girls, don't you, our Danny?' put in Liam, another of the young men.

A look seemed to pass between the men.

'It comes of living with Mam's family for a few years when I was a little 'un,' he defended himself, giving Katie another smile.

'You're none of you in uniform, then?' Katie couldn't stop herself from asking, and she knew from the frown that Mick was giving her that her voice sounded slightly accusatory.

'We're working down the docks, love, doing our bit for the war effort that way,' Barney, the fourth member of the quartet, who had been dancing with Carole and who seemed to speak for all of them, answered.

'So come on then,' Danny was trying to cajole

Katie. 'Tell us all about them love letters you get to read. Maybe we can pick up some hints.'

Katie was relieved to see the twins approaching the table. She stood up and told Carole, 'I promised Jean that I wouldn't keep the twins out late, so we'd better make a move, I think.'

Carole's mouth fell open. She looked as though she was about to object but Katie had no intention of allowing herself to be talked into staying. And just as soon as she got Carole on her own she was going to have something to say to her about letting on to the lads about their work. Not that people didn't know that the mail was censored – you only had to get a letter from someone overseas to know that it was – but officially they were not supposed to talk about even the innocent side of what they did, never mind all the rest of it.

'Enjoying yourself?'

Francine gave Brandon a wry look. The truth was that she should not have been enjoying herself since she had tried her best to refuse his invitation to this reception at the American Embassy, but the reality was that she was enjoying it very much indeed. But then during the short time she had known Brandon she had come to learn that he was adept at over-turning her preconceptions about a wide variety of things, not least the fact that on every single one of the dates he had either tricked or coaxed her into accepting, he had not so far made a single move on her sexually. Rather than feeling offended as she might have done had she been younger, she actually liked knowing that their dates were not going to end in an unseemly scuffle, Francine admitted. What was more, she liked Brandon and enjoyed his company as well. On the outside he might be a brash young American 'fly boy', all too willing to boast about his success with the Flying Eagles, but on the inside Brandon showed an awareness of the problems faced by humanity, and spoke about them so directly and from the heart that Francine often found herself choking up a little listening to him.

Had Jack lived, Brandon was the kind of young man she would have wanted to see him grow into, and although the age gap between Brandon and herself was nowhere near big enough for her to have been Brandon's mother, she did feel rather like a 'big sister' towards him, especially on those occasions when, as she had done when he had called for her this evening, she had noticed how tired he looked. So tired, in fact, that although she had not been able to smell alcohol on his breath he had almost stumbled as he had escorted her to the waiting taxi. Luckily she had managed to hold on to him whilst he steadied himself, and it had been a poignantly sweet sensation to feel him leaning against her as a child might lean against its mother, again making her think of her own Jack.

The reception had gone on longer than planned, and she guessed that it would be close to midnight before they were able to leave. Francine shrugged inwardly. She was used to late nights.

Locked in the ladies' lavatory, trying not to cry, Grace reflected miserably that the evening had been even worse than she had dreaded. Of course, it wasn't Seb's fault that the only place to sit had been at large tables, and it wasn't his fault either that Sybil and her pals had chosen to sit at their table, not with so many of the others being occupied by locals, and several of Seb's male colleagues already having claimed chairs round the table with her and Seb. She probably couldn't even blame him for the fact that Sybil had leaned over her in the way that she had to ask Seb for a light for her cigarette and had then 'accidentally' knocked over Grace's drink, which had soaked the skirt of the new pewter-grey wool frock she and Katie had worked so hard together to make, from one of the lovely lengths of fabric that her mother's sister Francine had brought home from Egypt and had sent up from London for them. With long sleeves, with white cuffs and a little Peter Pan collar, the dress perhaps wasn't exactly a dance frock – she hadn't after all expected to be dancing – but Grace had been so thrilled and proud when she had put it on. With its neat fitted body and its gently shaped skirt cut so as to use as little of the precious fabric as possible, and worn short as the new fashion dictated, Katie had clapped her hands together the first time she had pinned it on Grace and said that she had the perfect legs for such a style.

The wool would dry, of course, but the drink – even if had only been lemonade – was bound to leave a stain. Even worse, though, in Grace's eyes than the damage to her lovely new frock was the damage that had been done to her heart. Perhaps it was only natural that when Sybil had dropped her cigarette before Seb had had time to light it for her, his glance should have followed it and thus taken in Sybil's exposed cleavage in her low-necked sweater, but Grace still had not liked it, and she had liked it even less when only half an hour ago Sybil had pulled Seb to his feet without a by-your-leave, to demand that he dance with her. And she was a good dancer, Grace was forced to admit.

She wished desperately now that she wasn't here alone in Whitchurch and that she had one of her own female friends with her to support her – one of the other nurses or, even better, Katie; someone who could keep Sybil occupied and away from Seb. But at the same time part of her felt hurt that that should be necessary, and angry too, because if Seb really understood how she was feeling he should have brought an end to Sybil's behaviour himself. When Sybil had grabbed his hand like she had and insisted she wanted a dance, he could have told her to go and dance with one of her friends because he only wanted to dance with his fiancée.

Grace heard the door to the outer ladies' room opening and then the sound of female voices. She couldn't stay in here for ever, she warned herself, but before she could open the door she heard one of the women outside saying, 'Honestly, some girls just can't take a hint, can they? You'd never catch me trying to hang on to a chap by his engagement ring when he didn't want to be held on to.'

Grace couldn't move. She just knew that the girl outside was talking about her.

'That's the trouble with this war, if you ask me. You get these girls grabbing all the best men because the chaps feel obliged to propose to them, because there's a war on.'

'It's the poor men I feel sorry for.'

That was Sybil's voice, Grace recognised.

'They tell you in confidence that they are just desperate to escape and have some fun but they can't bring themselves to be the one to break things off.

Personally, if it was me in that situation and my fiancé was showing any sign of wanting to end things, I'd be the first to tell him he was free to go, but some girls just haven't got any pride or self-respect at all. Come on, you two, hurry up. I don't want to miss the next dance.'

Grace could hear some good-natured grumbling, the snapping shut of handbags, then the opening of the door and finally, to her relief, silence.

The powder room was empty when she emerged from the cubicle. The mirror threw back to her an image of herself she hardly recognised. Her face looked pale, her eyelids swollen and faintly pink, whilst her mouth was trembling so much it took her three attempts and the wastage of some of her precious new 'Pretty Pink' Yardley lipstick – another gift from Egypt from Francine – before she had redone her lips. She couldn't go back out there after what she had just heard, but she knew that she had to. Was it true that Seb wanted to end their engagement? Grace was no fool – after all, she had worked with members of her own sex for three years now and she knew both how kind they could be and how unkind. She was pretty sure that Sybil had somehow engineered the conversation she had just overheard as a way of taunting her. The old Grace, the Grace she had been before Seb had been transferred to Whitchurch, would have come out of the lavatory and laughed at the absurdity of anyone even suggesting that Seb didn't love her any more. But that was the old Grace, and the new Grace, the Grace who felt so insecure and afraid that Seb wasn't really her Seb at all any more, felt more like hiding herself away in shame.

TWENTY

Well, that was another hurdle successfully managed, Bella congratulated herself, as she unlocked her front door and bustled Lena – dressed in the bold checked wide swing coat Bella had fortuitously bought the previous winter, and which she had put away virtually unworn because she had then seen something she had liked more – protectively inside ahead of herself, after their morning attendance at church.

Thanks to her position with the crèche Bella had been able to speak with the vicar's wife and alert her to Lena's situation, and naturally, given the somewhat fictionalised version of events Bella had relayed, Lena had been welcomed into the congregation sympathetically with a discreet veil drawn over her supposed 'bigamous' marriage.

Sadly, without Maria there was no lovely smell of roasting meat to greet their return. Bella and Lena were having to make do with mince, mash and veggies. Bella was no cook and she had had to turn to the cook at the school for help in her determination to follow the doctor's advice that Lena and the baby she was carrying were to be well nourished.

Bella had been considering hinting to her mother

that she and Lena had their Sunday lunch with Bella's parents, but her mother, whilst outwardly supporting Bella's fictionalised version of Lena's supposed marriage and pregnancy, had been tight-lipped and hostile with Lena herself when they had come out of church. Fortunately the dank November weather had meant that no one wanted to linger for chat, so her mother's omission had gone unnoticed.

Of course, she could understand that her mother would be thinking of Charlie and the potential damage it could do to him if the truth were to get out, Bella acknowledged fair-mindedly as she bustled about, instructing Lena to stay in front of the gas fire and keep warm whilst she sorted out their lunch, but that wasn't going to happen and it wasn't Lena's fault that Charlie had lied to her and treated her so badly.

'There's Wilhelm.'

Emily tried not to colour up self-consciously, and act as though she hadn't already seen the German when Tommy, waving with one hand, tugged on her coat sleeve with the other to draw her attention to the prisoners of war lined up waiting for their transport back to the farms on which they were billeted, as they emerged from church.

Emily had as good as expected when summer came to an end that the farmer would feel that her vegetable garden no longer merited Wilhelm's attentions three times a week, but the farmer's wife had laughed at her for being a townie and had told her that there would be autumn and winter crops to be sown and the ground to be put in good heart for the spring, and that it would quite simply be bad husbandry and unpatriotic for her not to allow Wilhelm to keep on tending her garden.

'Hmm, more like bad for their bank balance,' Emily's neighbour had announced when Emily had told her all this, 'seeing as she'll be claiming money off the Government for feeding him and giving him a bed, whilst it's you that really gives him his meals.'

'Oh, I don't mind doing that,' Emily had been quick to assure her neighbour. 'It's more than worth it to me to feed him when he's doing such a good job on the vegetable garden. He's even managed to get that little greenhouse that was falling to bits sorted out.'

It wasn't just gardens Wilhelm was good at maintaining, though, as Emily had discovered that day the iron had stopped working and then again when one of the kitchen taps had started dripping.

If Sunday hadn't been the Sabbath and it not strictly right for anyone to be working, Emily would have invited Wilhelm in to share her and Tommy's Sunday dinner with them, as a thank you for all that he did, but since she could not do that, she now made sure instead that she cooked her Sunday roast on a day when Wilhelm was there, and if either he or Tommy thought if was odd to be sitting down to a good roast dinner on a weekday, neither of them had embarrassed her by saying anything about it.

'Come on we'd better get back before this damp air gets on your chest,' Emily urged Tommy, his wave in Wilhelm's direction enabling her to smile and lift her own hand without feeling that she was doing anything out of the ordinary or risking making a fool of herself.

*   *   *

Grace was feeling so desperately unhappy, what with last night and the fact that she and Seb had hardly had any special time together at all, that she almost missed noticing Tommy as he turned to wave to Wilhelm.

Her eyes widened as she grabbed hold of Seb's arm and whispered urgently, 'Seb, look over there, that's him. That boy I was telling you about that looks like Jack.'

Seb did his best to do as Grace was asking, but Emily and Tommy were several yards away from them and then Seb's boss caught up with them and wanted to ask Seb his opinion on some staff rotas, and by the time Seb had answered him Emily and Tommy had gone.

'It couldn't possibly be Jack,' Seb pointed out to Grace later as they chewed their way through an unappetising Sunday dinner in a local hotel – a meal that was supposed to have been a special treat but which in no way compared with Jean's Sunday dinners.

As they ate their dinner Grace noticed Seb looking surreptitiously at his watch. Why? Because he was fed up with her and was looking forward to it being time for her to leave so that he could enjoy some of the 'fun' that being engaged to her was keeping from him?

She had hardly slept last night after what she had heard in the ladies at the dance. Instead of feeling close to Seb and loved by him, she felt more as though she was an outsider and unwanted. She had heard about couples breaking up because of the pressures of war but she had never thought that that would ever happen to her and Seb. She had been confident that their love for one another would withstand anything and everything, but now she was beginning to question if she had been too confident.

Bella and Lena had just settled down to listen to a wireless programme together when the telephone rang. When Bella went to answer it the exchange put the call through and Bella heard the voice of her mother's neighbour saying unnecessarily, 'Bella, it's me, Mrs James from next door to your mother. I think you should come round as quickly as you can. Your poor mother is in a dreadful state.'

Muriel James had replaced the receiver before Bella could ask her any questions, leaving Bella irritated and half inclined not to do anything as she suspected, given her mother's behaviour after church, that she had worked herself up into a state over Lena.

However, her promotion to crèche manageress meant that she had a certain position to maintain, Bella acknowledged. Impatient though she was inclined to be with her mother, she certainly didn't want Muriel James setting it about Wallasey that she, Bella, was not a fit person for the promotion she'd been given because she neglected her own mother.

'I shan't be very long,' she told Lena, adding, 'And make sure that you keep warm and that you don't overdo things.'

Lena gave Bella a grateful smile. If she could have chosen anyone in the whole world to rescue her she could not have chosen anyone better than Bella, who had been and was being so very kind and lovely to her.

*   *   *

334

It didn't take Bella very long to walk round to her parents' house. The gates were open and her father's car was in the drive.

As though she had been watching for her from behind the net curtains at her front-room windows, the door to Muriel's house opened and she beckoned to Bella from her front step, telling her in a hushed voice, 'Your poor mother, such a terrible shock, no wonder she's in the state she is. Who would ever have thought it?' before going back inside her own house and closing the door before Bella could ask her what was going on.

Bella still had a key to her parents' house, and she used it now, her parents' raised angry voices so loud, even through the closed door to the kitchen, that they drowned out the sound of Bella's arrival. As she stood in the hall Bella could hear every word they were saying.

Her mother's voice was shrill with fury as she demanded, 'How could you do such a thing? You, a member of the council, and as for that . . . that slut . . .'

'Pauline is not a slut, she's the future Mrs Firth,' Bella heard her father retorting, 'and a far better Mrs Firth than you've ever been.'

Bella stood in the hallway, rooted to the spot as the enormity and the reality of what her parents were saying began to sink in. Her father was having an affair with his assistant – no, more than an affair if he was talking about her being 'the future Mrs Firth'. Nausea and anger churned together inside Bella's chest. She might have grown irritated and annoyed by her mother since she had started working at the crèche, seeing her in a new light and recognising that

335

she wanted more from herself than her mother had ever asked from herself, but Vi was still her mother. Bella shook herself out of her shock and went to open the kitchen door.

Her father was standing facing the back door with a bulging suitcase on the floor at his feet whilst her mother was standing in front of him barring his exit.

It was Vi who saw Bella first, exclaiming, 'Here's Bella. Now you can tell her what you've done and see what she has to say about it.'

'I don't give a damn about what either you or Bella have to say about anything any more, Vi, and you'd better understand that. Pauline is right, the pair of you are costing me thousands and I've been a fool to put up with it. Well, I'll tell you something: I won't be putting up with it any longer. Just as soon as my divorce is through—'

'Divorce? You can't divorce me. I won't let you.'

'Oh yes you will. Pauline's a respectable young woman and, like she says, I owe it to her to make sure that she's treated properly and that means her having a wedding ring on her finger.'

'What about treating Mum properly, Dad?' Bella stepped in, pointing out acidly, 'After all, Pauline does already have a wedding ring on her finger, and I dare say those who know her well won't be too surprised to hear that she's been helping herself to another woman's husband's affections. After all, she's quite plainly that type— Ouch!'

Bella's hand flew to her cheek to sooth the pain caused by the hard slap her father had just given her. Edwin had always had a nasty temper, but he had never hit Bella before and for a minute she was too shocked to do or say anything.

'I'm not having you speaking like that about Pauline.'

'Edwin, Bella is your daughter – how could you?'

'Some daughter, going and getting herself married to that wastrel and expecting me to go on paying her bills. Pauline's right, I've spoiled the lot of you rotten. Well, I won't be spoiling you any more. It's high time you stood on your own feet, Bella. Look at Pauline and take a leaf out of her book. She's supported herself ever since she lost her husband.'

'Yes, and we all know how, don't we, Daddy?' Bella couldn't resist saying, but this time she stepped out of reach of her father's violence and watched from a safe distance as his face turned puce and a vein throbbed in his forehead.

Ignoring Bella, Edwin turned to Vi and told her coldly, 'I'm warning you, Vi, you'd better agree to divorce me because if you don't I'll make sure that you wish that you had. You'll be out of this house, for a start, and Bella out of hers as well. After all, they both belong to me by rights, and you can forget about me paying you anything. Of course, you can always go and ask one of your friends to take you in – or Charlie's in-laws, perhaps.'

Bella could see that her mother was looking more distressed with every word that her father was uttering. Vi was a terrible snob and Bella knew what her mother would be thinking and how much she would be dreading the shame and gossip that a divorce would cause.

'You can't do this to me, Edwin. You can't and I won't let you. Just because that . . . that slut has turned your head . . .'

'Pauline is more of a lady than you ever were

Vi,' Edwin announced brutally. 'I'll come back in the morning when you've had time to see sense. Like I've already said, I'm prepared to do the decent thing by you if you agree to divorce me. You can move in with Bella, and I'll give you a bit of an allowance for your pin money.'

Bella gave her father a sharp look, which he returned with one of angry determination.

'Pauline reckons that there's no need for the pair of you to have a house each and I agree with you. Me and her can move in here until the war's over, and your mother can live with you.'

'You can't really expect Mummy to have to put up with you and Pauline living in her house,' Bella told her father, genuinely shocked. 'I'm surprised that Pauline would want that herself.'

Bella suspected from her father's shifty look that she had caught him on the back foot. From what she had seen of Pauline, Bella doubted that her expect-ations were limited to moving into her predecessor's home. Bella knew that her father was making a lot of money, Pauline knew that too, and Bella had no doubts whatsoever that Pauline would be expecting that money to be lavished on her.

'I'd have thought she'd want to live somewhere like the Wirral.'

'It doesn't matter where she wants to live, because I am not giving up my home and I'm going to divorce you either, Edwin,' Vi said, adding virtuously and vehemently, 'It's for your own sake, Edwin. You'll come to your senses, I know you will, and when you do you'll thank me for stopping you from making a fool of yourself over that . . . that slut . . .'

'You're the one who's making a fool of yourself,

338

Vi, if you think that anything you say can change my mind. I'm leaving you and one way or another you will divorce me.'

Edwin had gone before either Bella or Vi could say anything else, leaving Vi to collapse onto one of the kitchen chairs, and Bella to put on the kettle.

An hour later, Bella had had the full story from Vi of how Edwin had arrived home just after Vi had got back from church, to announce that he wanted Vi to divorce him so that he could marry Pauline.

Vi went into hysterics just relaying to Bella what had happened, and Bella could well imagine just how her mother would have reacted to her father's shocking and, as far as she could see, totally unexpected ultimatum.

Vi was adamant that nothing would make her agree to a divorce. Edwin was *her* husband and he was going to remain her husband. Not because she loved him, Bella suspected, but because of the social stigma and shame that would attach to her if they were to be divorced.

In the end Bella had had to summon the doctor, who had given Vi a sedative and said that he would call to see her again in the morning. She had also gone round to see Muriel to ask her if she could possibly keep an eye on Vi for her overnight, and to her relief Muriel, who was widowed, had offered to stay and sleep in the spare room.

Bella suspected that Muriel was probably enjoying all the drama but nevertheless she was still grateful to her.

Now that she'd got her mother settled, Bella intended to go to see her father. He would be down at his office, she suspected – either there or at

Pauline's. She'd try the office first. She guessed that she would not be able to persuade him to change his mind about leaving her mother, but she intended to make sure that both she and Vi kept their homes and that her mother got a decent amount of money out of him. And, of course, she knew just how to do that, Bella decided grimly.

Grace looked at Seb. The November afternoon was fading fast into a wet grey bleakness that shrouded the buildings of the small town, and yet at the same time left the couple with nowhere to be on their own and have the privacy that Grace felt they so desperately needed.

Now, sitting with Seb on a sofa in the front room of his billet, she could almost feel him willing the minutes away until he could take her back to the station. She couldn't lose him; she loved him so very much and he had loved her as well. She wasn't going to let someone like Sybil come between them.

She took a deep breath and then said quickly, 'Seb, about Sybil . . .'

Immediately he stood up and walked away from her, saying sharply, 'For goodness' sake, Grace, don't let's start all that again.' He thrust his hands deep into his trouser pockets, keeping his back to her.

Grace felt as though her heart was being squeezed in a vice. The clock in the hall struck the hour, breaking into the tension.

Grace stood up and told Seb quietly, 'I think we'd better set out for the station.'

Surely now he would say something, or do something to comfort her. Tell her that he loved her and only her; take her in his arms; beg her forgiveness and understanding. But no, he was doing none of those things.

Feeling sick with despair, Grace put on her coat whilst Seb picked up her small case for her. She knew what she had to do.

They walked to the station in silence, Grace tucking her hand into the pocket of her coat instead of reaching out for Seb's hand to hold. The station loomed up ahead of them out of the foggy dusk.

Seb caught hold of Grace's arm. 'There's something I've got to tell you,' he began.

Grace's heart slammed into her ribs. This was it. This was the moment she had been expecting and dreading since she had overheard that conversation in the cloakroom. She shook her arm free of Seb's hold.

'Wait until I'm on the train,' she stopped him quickly. That way he wouldn't see her tears as it took her away from him and left him free for Sybil and fun.

As luck would have it the train was early and already waiting on the platform. Grace hurried over to it immediately, leaving Seb no choice other than to follow her. As soon as she reached the train Grace mounted the steps to one of the carriages, taking her case from Seb and putting it down inside.

Then with tears in her eyes Grace pulled off her engagement ring and held it out to him, telling him, 'I don't know whether or not Sybil meant me to overhear what she was saying to her pals, but I did overhear it and I know that when she talked about engaged girls holding on to fiancés who no longer wanted them and felt that their engagement had been a mistake and that they would rather be

341

free to have fun, she was talking about me – and you. I'm sorry, Seb, for doing that to you, but you see you're partly to blame yourself because you did say that you loved me. Doing this is breaking my heart but I won't keep you engaged to me when you'd rather have your freedom.'

The guard was walking towards them, closing the doors, his red flag at the ready.

Grace could see Seb reaching out towards her. Blinded by her own tears and the smoke from the engine, Grace just had time to press her precious ring into his palm, closing his fingers over it before the guard slammed the heavy door, separating them. She could hear Seb calling out her name but she couldn't see him. There was a terrible wrenching feeling inside her chest as though someone was literally ripping out her heart. The pain was terrible and unbearable, but somehow she must bear it.

She had done the right thing, the decent thing, the only thing in setting Seb free. She had been strong for him and now she must be strong for herself.

TWENTY-ONE

Bella knew exactly what she was going to say to her father, and exactly what she was going to make sure that he did, as well, and she certainly wasn't going to allow herself to be intimidated by Pauline. She and Bella's father might consider her to be as good as the next Mrs Firth but right now, in Bella's eyes and the eyes of the world, she was merely a woman who was trying to steal another woman's husband. Not that Bella had any illusions about persuading her father to return home to her mother, and if she had had any, she admitted that they would have burst like soap bubbles the minute she walked into her father's office.

He immediately placed his arm protectively around Pauline, announcing curtly, 'If you've come to tell me that your mother has come to her senses then you can stay. If you haven't then you can leave.'

'What about if I've come to do you a favour and tell you a very good reason why you should sign over the house to Mummy, and mine to me, and make Mummy a decent monthly allowance for the rest of her life?'

As Bella had known he would, her father looked

343

as though he was about to explode with rage whilst Pauline tittered contemptuously.

'Sign over nothing, that's what I shall be doing. You and your mother should be thanking your lucky stars I've bin as generous as letting you have the one house, never mind giving you them both.'

'Too generous in my opinion, Edwin. Heavens, what young woman with any sense of decency expects her father to buy her a home and provide her with an income? That's what husbands are for.'

'Which is, of course, why you've needed two of them, Pauline,' Bella shot back immediately. 'One obviously was not enough to keep you in the style to which you'd like to become accustomed. Well, I'm sorry but Mummy got there before you and Daddy owes her a very great deal. Everyone knows that.'

'He certainly does,' Paule agreed mockingly. 'He owes her two children who between them couldn't make one decent one.'

'Which is why you're planning to make sure that you do, is that it?' Bella asked sharply, having just noticed the small telltale swell not quite disguised by Pauline's loose top.

It was plain that her words had caught both her father and Pauline off guard.

'No wonder you're so keen to get Mummy agree to divorce you, Daddy. Pauline won't want her little bastard being born as exactly that, will she?'

Her father looked as though he was about to burst a blood vessel, Bella thought unkindly, wondering if it might not be a bad idea if he did and then died, leaving her mother a very rich widow. Such thoughts, though, were hardly daughterly, and despite the fact that right now she did not feel as though she loved him one single little bit she certainly didn't want his death on her hands. As that thought formed Bella acknowledged with a small sense of shock how much she seemed to be changing. Once, and not so very long ago either, she would never even have thought to feel guilty. It must be the effect Lena, who had elevated her to the state of something approaching sainthood, was having on her, she decided ruefully, before returning to the attack.

'I must say, Pauline, that I'm surprised that you're willing to settle for a house in Wallasey with all the money that Daddy is making by inflating those Admiralty contracts the way he does. I'd have thought you'd be wanting something much more swish out on Wirral.'

Bella almost felt slightly sorry for her father as she saw the way Pauline was looking at him, her mouth compressing and her eyes hard.

'Of course we won't be staying in Wallasey,' she told Bella coldly. 'Edwin would never expect that of me, would you, Edwin darling?'

'No, no, of course not . . .'

'Then Mummy and I may as well stay in our houses. Or were you thinking of your cousin living in one of them perhaps, Pauline, the one that looks after your son?'

An angry red colour was heating Pauline's face.

'For your information – not that it's any business of yours – me and your father are going to let the house out. There's plenty of people would pay good money to rent it whilst this war's one and then once it's over we can decide what we want to do with it.'

Bella widened her eyes and she said mock sweetly, 'Oh goodness, how clever of you to think of that.

Pity that you've wasted your time, because I know that Daddy, being the kind, generous person he is, is going to sign the house over to Mummy and that he's going to go with me to his solicitor first thing in the morning to do so. Because if you don't, Daddy, then I'm afraid I'm going to have to—'

'If you're going to threaten to get your father into trouble – again – over his costings, let me tell you, Bella, that you're wasting your time. Who are you going to tell anyway? Who'd listen to you, a silly hysterical girl who's behaving badly and out to cause a lot of trouble for her father out of spite? The Head of the Admiralty?' Pauline mocked Bella with a tinkling little laugh, before turning towards Edwin and smiling up at him.

'No,' Bella told her sweetly. 'Actually it's Mr Benson from the Government who I'd be telling.' She paused for a moment to enjoy the speed with which the smile disappeared from Pauline's lips and her father shrugged his mistress's hand off his arm.

'Now see here, Bella' he blustered. 'A joke's a joke and you've had your bit of fun.'

'I'm not joking Daddy,' Bella stopped him. 'To be honest I have been feeling very uncomfortable about the fact that my own father is cheating the Government out of money it so desperately needs for the war effort, and I've worried a lot about what I should do. As a daughter, of course, I have my loyalty to you but now that we are at war we all have to think beyond our personal duties to those closest to us and think instead of our greater duty to our country and to all those men – our boys – who are risking their lives to protect it and us. Well, that's what I think, anyway.'

Pauline was giving her a look that was pure vitriol, Bella recognised happily.

'*You* think about "our boys"? That will be the day,' Pauline announced viciously. 'You've never given a thought to anyone other than yourself from the day you realised what a thought is. Well, if you think that me and your dad are going to let you blackmail us then you can think again.'

Pauline's voice had become unpleasantly shrill, but Bella had momentarily stopped listening as she battled against the sudden sharp and unfamiliar stab of pain caused by Pauline's accusation. So what if she was as Pauline had described her? Why should she care what Pauline or anyone else thought or said?

'Anyway,' Pauline continued acidly, 'you can threaten to tell whoever you like but you can't prove a thing.'

'Oh yes I can,' Bella told her. Turning to her father she pointed out, 'You've always said how important insurance is, Daddy, so naturally when you were so unkind to me about my own house I decided to take your advice and take out some of my own. I copied the details of some of your best-paying contracts from your books – you know, the ones you used to keep at home and not here in the office – and I've got the details of your special bank accounts as well – you know, the ones you pay all that lovely extra money you earn into.'

'None of that means anything. It's just figures,' her father blustered.

'Figures that I am sure will be very interesting to the Ministry, Daddy, and very interesting to Mr Benson as well.'

'I'm your father,' Edwin protested. 'And when I think of what I've spent on you and given you—'

'Mummy is your wife,' Bella reminded him pointedly. She could see the flicker of unease in her father's eyes and she was tempted to go to him and plead with him – beg him, if necessary – to forget about Pauline and go home to her mother.

'Mummy loves you,' she told him, 'and she's dreadfully upset, Daddy. The doctor had to come out and give her something to help her sleep. If you do force Mummy to divorce you, no one will ever have the same respect for you, Daddy, and I dare say you'll even lose your place on the council.' Bella knew how much that meant to him. Far more than her mother, she suspected.

For a moment Bella thought she could see him wavering, but then Pauline moved closer to him and said gently, 'Edwin, darling, I know what an honourable man you are and if you really feel that you would rather be with Vi than with me and our child then I won't stand in your way. I know I can trust you to do the right thing by us, and if all those things we've talked about and planned can't happen because you feel it's your duty to be with Vi, then I will understand.'

Pauline's voice was soft, and her appeal exactly right to have the most effect on her father, Bella knew.

'I've made up my mind, Bella, and nothing you or anyone else can say will change it. Me and Pauline have plans for the kind of future together I could never have shared with your mother.'

'A future built on Mummy's unhappiness and financed by cheating the Government,' Bella pointed out sharply.

'Now look here, my girl, you aren't doing either yourself or your mother any favours by taking that kind of attitude, you know.'

'I'm not the one who has stolen money from the Government,' Bella pointed out doggedly, 'and there's another thing as well, Daddy. I dare say you won't want there to be much of a delay before Mummy gives you your divorce, not with Pauline in the condition she's in. You know what Mummy's like if she's feeling stubborn. If I were you I'd be doing everything I could to make sure she agrees, and not the opposite, but then maybe I'm missing something and you aren't really as keen to marry Pauline as she seems to think.'

'Of course Edwin wants to marry me,' Pauline told Bella in a hostile voice. 'You don't think I'd have permitted him the intimacies I have if that hadn't been understood right from the start, do you?'

'I don't know,' Bella answered. 'I wouldn't have the first idea how a person like you thinks, I'm afraid.'

'I've risked my reputation for your father and my love for him. I dare say there will be plenty who will blame me for Edwin leaving your mother when they should blame her for not being a better wife to him.'

'My mother has always supported my father, and if he's told you any different he's a liar, but then you already know that he is a liar, don't you?'

Pauline's face was burning an angry red, but Bella didn't feel any sympathy for her despite her pregnancy. She was pretty sure that Pauline must have set out right from the start to promote a relationship between herself and Bella's father, and now that she had succeeded Bella didn't see why she should sympathise with her because she was going to have to face social hostility and criticism.

'Very well then, Bella, I shall have a think about what you've said and give you my decision in a couple of days.'

'Oh no, Daddy,' Bella told her father firmly. 'That won't do at all. I think it would be much better if you came with me tomorrow to see your solicitor to make over the house to Mummy, along with a proper allowance, or I shall go straight to see Mr Benson. Besides, I'm sure that Pauline will be able to see the sense of your treating Mummy generously. A man in your position and a woman in hers can't afford to lose what little reputation they've got left, can they?'

They were both furious with her but there was nothing they could do as both they and she knew, Bella acknowledged.

Her feeling was confirmed when Pauline said angrily, 'Oh I suppose you'd better do what she says, Edwin, otherwise we're never going to get rid of them and they'll be hanging around you for ever, trying to spoil our lives. After all, we've got plenty to look forward to, me and you, and she's right about the Wirral. I reckon we could get ourselves a real bargain out there now whilst this war's on.'

Watching her father whilst he glowered at her, Bella knew that she had won but there was none of the triumph she might once have felt at that knowledge. Instead she felt more like crying. Not that she intended to let either of them see that, she decided as she ignored her father's baleful look and left his office.

TWENTY-TWO

By rights she ought to be sleeping, Grace knew. After all, she was starting night duty tonight, but she couldn't sleep, not after what had happened.

All she could do was simply lie here, her eyes wet with her tears as she went over it all again and again; every word, every look, every kiss. Even now she could hardly believe that it had actually happened. She looked down at her left hand, where Seb's ring was back in its rightful place, and fresh tears flowed.

With a cold railway carriage all to herself for the return journey to Liverpool after she had left him in Whitchurch, she had cried the whole way, knowing that no matter what her future might hold it could never hold a man she could love as much as she loved Seb, nor a pain as bad as the one she was now feeling.

Only her pride had had her dabbing at her eyes when the train had finally pulled into Lime Street, and adding a touch of lipstick to lips that were still trembling with misery and loss. Hugging her winter coat around herself she had kept her head down as she made for the barrier, so that she hadn't seen Seb at all and had no idea that he was there until he reached for her hand – but miraculously, as they had

351

both said to one another, she had known immediately that the hand reaching for hers belonged to him. She had stopped dead where she was, of course, unable to believe it was humanly possible for him to be there. She had left him in Whitchurch, after all.

But before she had been able to say a word or ask any questions, Seb had placed his finger to her lips and then with his other hand he had slid her engagement ring back on her finger and told her, 'How could you possibly think that I don't love you and only you, and that more than anything else I want to make you my wife? I could shake you, Gracie, I really could, but instead the minute I get you to myself I'm going to kiss you silly instead, and then I'm going to make you promise me that you will never ever take off our ring again.'

To which Grace had only been able to reply breathlessly, 'Oh, Seb . . .' before giving in to her overwhelming need to hurl herself into his arms and hold him as tightly as she possibly could whilst she wept a few tears and gave a small laugh, and then shamelessly, or so she told herself now, flung her arms tightly around him and kissed him for all she was worth. It had taken the wolf whistle of a grinning soldier to break them apart and even then Seb had kept an arm wrapped tightly around her as they had left the station and Grace had cuddled as close to him as she could whilst asking him the questions that tumbled from her lips.

'How on earth did you get here before me?' she marvelled, to which Seb had grinned and said, 'Come and let me show you,' before guiding her outside the station to where he'd paid a young boy of about twelve years old to stand guard over the motorcycle that he explained to Grace he'd borrowed from a colleague.

'I told him that it was a matter of life or death, the life or death of my heart,' Seb had told her tenderly, before asking her in disbelief, 'How could you ever think that I wanted to end our engagement?'

'It was because of what I'd overheard Sybil saying whilst I was in the ladies,' Grace had admitted, going on to explain to him exactly what had been said and then pointing out quietly, 'You did seem to enjoy her company, Seb, and whenever I tried to tell you how unhappy she was making me feel you didn't really seem to want to know or, even worse, you were cross with me.'

'I did behave selfishly and unfairly,' Seb admitted, 'and I want to ask your forgiveness for that, Grace. It never occurred to me that you'd think what you did. It was just that I've been having a bit of a problem with this new temporary superior I've got whilst Jim Langdon is in hospital having that bad leg of his sorted out. Rory has been making things a bit difficult for me, throwing these girls on me and telling me that the powers that be have said that it's very important that they are made to feel they want to come and work at Whitchurch, and telling me that if they start saying they'd rather work somewhere else, it will reflect on me. I suppose I was trying to give them the same leeway I'd have given Sasha and Lou if it had been them I was training, hoping that I'd be able to win them round to be good workers. I'm afraid I was worrying more about what Rory was going to do than what Sybil was doing. I never dreamed that Sybil would start acting like she did.'

His admission softened Grace's heart even more.

'It was really mean of Rory to be like that with you, and so unfair.'

'Well, he's got a bit of a chip on his shoulder, I think. He isn't really a service chap. He's someone who's been drafted in, but he is still my superior.'

'Why didn't you tell me all this?' Grace asked.

'Because I didn't want anything to spoil our weekend,' Seb had answered her so ruefully that Grace had started to laugh, and then so had Seb, so that they'd ended up laughing their heads off and then hugging one another all over again, and then, of course, kissing one another all over again until the boy watching over the motorcycle had objected, 'Hey, mister, you said you was only going to want me to look out for yer bike for half an hour.'

After Seb had paid off the boy, naturally Grace had insisted that Seb must come back with her to her parents, and after snatching a wonderful precious hour together in her parents' front room, they had rushed out again to make the evensong service so that, at Seb's insistence, they could see the vicar together and make arrangements for the banns to be read for their late December wedding.

Seb had even told her that he had decided to ask for a transfer back to Liverpool, even if that meant losing his promotion, but Grace had vigorously rejected the very idea.

'I'll be qualified by then, with a bit of luck,' she had pointed out, 'and I should be able to get a transfer to Whitchurch, to that hospital they've got down there, and seeing as you are already living out I dare say we'll be able to rent somewhere there more easily than we can here, even if it's only one room.'

'All I want is for us to be together and for you to be happy,' Seb had told her, and Grace had known that he meant it.

Fresh tears filled her eyes. She was just so lucky; the luckiest young woman she knew, and all that she felt for Sybil now in place of her earlier bitter jealousy and misery was pity.

TWENTY-THREE

'I want us to be married.'

Francine couldn't have been more astonished or appalled if Brandon had suddenly grown two heads.

They were in the American Bar at the Savoy, where he insisted on taking her even though she kept on telling him that the prices were outrageous and that he should be spending his money on impressing someone much younger and more suitable for him than she was. She should have ended things between them after their first date, she knew, but the truth was that she liked Brandon and felt ruefully protective and fond of him in exactly the same way that she would have done someone like her elder sister's son, Luke. Just like Luke, Brandon was old enough to squire a more mature auntie around but at the same time far too young for their relationship to be anything other than that of a sisterly inclined older woman towards a charming well-mannered young man. And although she was less happy about admitting it, his company helped to ease the loneliness she felt both for Jack, her lost son, and Marcus, her lost love. They both held places in her heart that would be forever empty without them. They were irreplaceable, but too many long lonely hours spent alone grieving for what she had lost had made Brandon's company a temptation she had wrongly given in to. Wrongly for his sake, she recognised guiltily, rather than for her own.

She had wondered why he continued to pursue her when not once had he made any attempt to institute any kind of physical intimacy between them. For a while she had even wondered if he might be homosexual, but nothing he had said or done whilst in her company had indicated that that was the case.

He had taken her to events at the American Embassy, he had treated her with respect and he had shown great affection for her; he would, if she had allowed him to do so, have lavished far too much money on her by way of expensive treats and gifts, but although he had claimed virtually all her free time since they had been introduced she had never for one moment been expecting anything like this.

She leaned towards him and told him lightly but firmly, 'That is the most ridiculous suggestion I have ever heard.'

'I mean it,' Brandon returned. 'I need you to be my wife, Francine.'

It was the word 'need' that warned her that there was more to his outrageous and unwelcome proposal than he had so far told her.

'Need?'

She could also see him relaxing slightly, as though her question was the one he had been hoping for.

'Yes, need. You see, the thing is, well, I may not be around much longer.'

Francine's eyebrows shot up, and she gave him a pained look. This was the kind of line that every

357

young would-be Lothario in uniform, and some who weren't, handed out to girls naïve enough to be seduced by it and them, and she had thought better of Brandon than to have to listen to him trying such a line on her.

'I realise the Eagles have a reputation for taking risks, but you've said yourself that you've been grounded on your father's orders.'

'I'm not talking about buying it via Hitler,' he told her abruptly. 'That was why I joined the Eagles originally, it's true, but it looks like fate isn't going to do me any favours and make things easy for me, and now Dad's got me grounded anyway. Besides, the other guys don't like it when they've got a guy on board who's got a death wish. They say it puts a curse on them all, so I guess for their sakes it's best that I don't fly missions with them. I was just running scared, though, at first – at first.' He gave a jerky sound somewhere between a laugh and a sob that tore at Francine's heart. 'What do I mean "at first"? I still am and I guess that the coward that I am I will be right up until the end. That's what all this is about, France.'

'France' was his nickname for her and one that no one else had ever used.

'You see – and you won't like this – there's enough of my dad in me to have me going all out for what I want. OK, when we first met I just thought you were a fine-looking woman but then there was something about you that kinda drew me closer to you, and since I'm one that believes in fate – well, I've had to, I reckon – I did a bit of checking-up on you and I found out about your boy Jack, and about your major. More fool him for dropping you like he

358

did – on account of your past, I suppose – and not realising what he was losing.'

Francine didn't bother to correct him; she was too shocked and angry to say anything. The thought of him digging into her past alienated her and made her feel she wanted to get up and walk out of the bar without looking back, but something, some sense of maternal duty that she felt could only have been invoked by his use of Jack's name, kept her where she was despite the revulsion and dislike she was feeling.

'I can guess what you're thinking,' he told her. 'It's not nice to go digging into people's private lives, not even for Americans, although my dad does it all the time – that's what being a billionaire does for you. He even had my mom investigated after he'd divorced her in case she was spending his alimony on another man. Not, of course, that their divorce stopped him spending money on the girls he was squiring around, but then he'd been doing that behind her back before they were divorced so I guess he felt it was OK anyway.'

He had already told her about his parents' divorce and the enmity that now existed between them, intensified on his father's side at least by the fact that *his* father, Brandon's grandfather, had left his will in such a way that it meant that the billions Father was now enjoying had to be passed on to his own first-born male child. And only to him.

'Dad's sworn he won't marry a fourth time, but I reckon he will once he knows the truth – he'll have to because I'm not just his eldest son, I'm his only son. His other kids – at least the ones he's prepared to acknowledge – are all girls, and once this thing

359

that's eating me away inside finally gets me and I'm gone, that will mean there's no one to inherit under Granddaddy's will.'

So at last they had come to it and it was there, out in the open between them. Something that felt like a slimy cold octopus seemed to have wrapped its tentacles around Francine's heart, squeezing it so painfully that just feeling its irregular beat hurt.

It had to be impossible – some sort of stupid joke, surely – that this healthy, fit strong-looking young man seated opposite her could really mean that he was terminally ill and about to die, but when Francine looked at him she could see the shadow in his eyes that told her that it wasn't a joke and that it was real and happening.

She took a deep breath, suddenly very much in the role of a mother, as she questioned him firmly, 'Are you sure things are as bad as you think? Sometimes doctors say—'

'I'm sure. I've been to every expert there is, including a couple in Switzerland, and there's no mistake. It's a form of brain disease – rare and incurable, so all the experts have told me. Of course, my mom will blame my dad, and he will blame her, but the truth is that there is no one to blame – not them, not me and not even God. It's just the luck of the draw and I drew the wrong card, that's all.

'I had hoped to take a short cut and get it all over with – get shot down or, better still, shot up and go in a blaze of glory kind a thing. Better for my folks that way: to lose a son who's halfway to being a hero and not one that's gone all the way to being a coward and who's going to die in a mental hospital bed with his mind gone.'

'There must be something that the doctors can do.'

Francine wished she hadn't spoken when she saw the tears gather in his eyes, along with a look of helpless grief and despair, as he shook his head.

'Nothing. There is no cure, no anything.'

'You must tell your parents. They love you, they—'

'Yep, they love me but they love themselves more. If I told my mom she'd have a breakdown on the spot, and if I told my dad he just wouldn't accept it. He's a billionaire and he thinks he can buy everything and everyone he wants, but you can't buy your way out of something like this and you can't buy life. Until I met you I didn't know what I was going to do. I'd thought of jumping out of a plane without my parachute or, even more effective, perhaps trying to cross Piccadilly during the blackout.'

He waited, so obediently Francine responded to his weak joke with an attempt at a smile.

'But then when I met you I knew that God had answered my prayers and that he'd sent you to me to be with me; to be my strength and my succour, if only I could persuade you to be those things for me. I need you, France. I can't do this alone. I'm so damned afraid. Please help me. Please tell me that you'll be there for me, that you'll be my mind when my own has gone and that you will see right done by me with dignity and all those things that you Brits are so damned good at. I need you. There is no one else. There is only you.

'The reason I want us to be married is that that will give you certain rights. It will enable me to name you as my chosen next of kin so that when the time comes – and it isn't far off, I know – that I can't do

361

things or make decisions for myself you can make the decisions for me that I want to have made. I want to die here, in this country, Francine. I want to die in the arms of someone who cares and who understands, not in some nameless hospital surrounded by medics whilst my mom is locked away in a padded cell somewhere and my dad is out fucking his latest girl in a desperate attempt to get another son. I'm already weaker than I was. I guess you must think it strange that I haven't taken you out dancing since we met or made a move on you. The truth is that when we say good night I go back to my hotel room and I'm done.'

There were tears in his eyes and his hands were shaking.

Francine looked at him, her heart aching with pity and understanding. Here, in the man boy, she would have the care of both the boy she had lost in Jack and the man she had lost in Marcus. Here, in Brandon, they met, and she, the woman who had lost her son and her love, could out of those losses give to this boy growing into a man, who would never become that man, the comfort of a mother's love and the tenderness of a woman's love. She reached for his hand, and squeezed it gently.

'Very well then, I will marry you.'

The relief she could see in his eyes compounded her appalled pity.

'It will have to be soon – as soon as we can – and I'll make it worth your while, France. I've already made my will and you—'

Immediately she released his hand and shook her head, telling him fiercely, 'No, I can't be bought and I won't be. Leave your money to whoever or whatever you choose, Brandon, but please don't burden me by leaving it to me.'

'Mmm, I think it needs to be just a touch more golden, sort of like the yolk of an egg only a teeny bit lighter,' Bella pronounced, standing back to study the neat one-foot square of yellow distemper Gavin had just applied to the walls of the smallest bedroom, soon to be the nursery.

'But it must be Lena who decides,' said Bella generously. 'After all, the nursery is for your baby, Lena.'

'A second coat of paint will deepen this,' Gavin assured both young women with a calm male certainty.

'Well, I do know what you mean, Bella,' Lena agreed – Lena thought so highly of Bella that she knew she would agree with whatever Bella said – 'but I don't want to put Gavin to too much trouble,' she added hesitantly.

'Who said anything about it being any trouble? Not me,' Gavin assured them both.

'Oh, well, in that case I do think that Bella is right and that it does need to be just a touch more golden.'

'That way it will pick out the yellow of those little teddies in that fabric I just happened to come across the other day,' Bella smiled approvingly, without going on to say anything about the fact that far from coming across the fabric, she had actually already had it, having bought it when she had expected to be having a little one of her own. It would only upset Lena to hear about Bella's lost baby, and there was no way that Bella wanted to do that. As the girls who worked with Lena were always saying, she was like a little ray of sunshine with her smile and her happiness, and she lifted the spirits of everyone who came in contact with her.

Everyone, that was, except Vi, Bella reflected ruefully, her heart sinking with a mixture of guilt and dread at the thought of having to leave the happy atmosphere of her house to go round and check that her mother was all right. It was her duty to do so, though, and Bella – the new Bella she had somehow almost miraculously become from that very moment she had stopped in the street to help Lena – would not have dreamed of ignoring that duty, no matter how onerous she might find it.

She gave a brief discreet look in the direction of Lena and Gavin, both of them now poring over the second patch of distemper Gavin had applied to the wall. Although perhaps neither of them was aware of it as yet, Bella somehow sensed that they were two people who were beginning to share a closeness that could become special. Bella wasn't naïve. The very best thing that could happen for Lena and her baby was for Lena to marry a kind, generous man who would love both her and Charlie's baby and who she could love back in turn. But if that happened it would mean that she would lose the special closeness that had developed between the two of them, she knew. In Lena she had found someone who had brought into her life a love that was the combination of the best kind of friendship and the deepest kind of sibling love. But more probably, having watched the way in which Gavin watched Lena, Bella thought if they married then she was bound to lose that special place she now had in Lena's life and heart. It would be the easiest thing in the world for her to drop hints in Lena's ears about the problems that could occur when a very pretty and charming young girl, who had already shared intimacy with one man – dangers that included jealousy and even the risk of physical violence – attracted the interest of a new young man. Lena held her in high regard, Bella knew that, and it was only natural that she in turn should want to protect her. No one would blame her if she urged Lena to be cautious and pointed out to her that she and her baby would always have a home with her and that there was no need for her to feel she needed to marry anyone. Lena was already unconsciously mimicking the way Bella spoke, her manners were excellent, she was bright and quick. In a few more months she would easily be able to pass herself off as a girl from the middle classes rather than a girl from the slums. Then there would be no reason why she shouldn't stay here in Wallasey for ever. She and Bella could bring the baby up between them and he or she (and Bella was hoping it would be a girl) would want for nothing, especially not love.

In order to make all that happen all Bella had to do was simply gently and kindly warn Lena that she felt it might not be such a good idea for Gavin to keep on coming round. Lena would accept what she said, Bella knew that, and as yet what she, Bella, could see flickering into life between them was something she was quite sure neither of them had recognised. There would be no broken hearts, no feeling of betrayal or hurt. It would all be so very easy. And, Bella decided painfully, so very wrong.

She exhaled on a shaky breath and told them with a smile, 'I'm going to see my mother now.'

'I'd better go myself then,' Gavin offered straight off, like the well-mannered, considerate young man

Bella already knew him to be. She hadn't been trying to test him but the knowledge that he was ready to put Lena and her situation first underlined everything that Bella had already been thinking.

'I'm going to get a key cut for you, Gavin,' Bella rewarded him with another smile, 'then you can come and go as you please whilst we are out at work. There is no one I would trust more to do an excellent job, and it eases my mind knowing that you do have a key, especially for when Lena is here at home and I'm at the crèche.' Bella could almost see Gavin's chest swelling with pride along with Lena's eyes growing luminous with hero worship for her.

Lena was so easily pleased, her gratitude and her joy in the smallest and simplest of kindnesses constantly making Bella aware of how generous and loving Lena's heart was.

Leaving them both in the nursery-to-be, Bella went downstairs and put on her coat and her boots ready for the walk to her mother's.

A sharp wind off the estuary had blown away the morning's cold grey blanket of thick wet mist, leaving the sky ice blue and the wind with a sharp knife edge of cold that made her shiver, despite her warm clothes, and huddle deeper into the warmth of her fur-collared coat, whilst walking that little bit faster. Lena's baby was due to be born in January, one of Bella's least favourite months of the year, poor little thing, and it had already been arranged that Lena would go to the country to a special mother and baby nursing home to give birth. Bella had asked lots of anxious questions of both her doctor and the young mothers who brought their children to the crèche to make sure that the best possible nursing home had been selected.

Despite the sharpening keenness of the wind, Bella found her walking pace slowing the closer she got to her mother's. It didn't seem to matter that Bella had done so much for her mother to keep her financially secure in her own home, Vi still complained so bitterly when Bella visited that sometimes it was almost as though Vi was blaming Bella for the fact that Edwin had left.

There was one thing she was doing, though, and it was that one thing that was in part responsible for Bella's increasing reluctance to visit, even though at the same time it was also causing her to worry about her mother. And that thing was the fact that Vi had become very argumentative and verbally offensive, especially after a couple of G and Ts, when her complaints would become vitriolic criticisms of Bella and Lena, and of course 'that woman', which would then descend to heartbreaking outbursts of angry tears that left Bella almost as exhausted as they did Vi. It might only be a matter of a few short weeks since Edwin had left but Vi's drinking had escalated during those weeks to the point where Bella had felt obliged to discuss her concern with her mother's doctor.

His grave warning, that he too felt her mother *was* drinking too much and that he was concerned that Bella had no other family members whose company might have helped her to keep her mother too occupied to dwell on her situation, had not reassured Bella.

There was Charlie, of course, but the only response Bella had had to her letters to him telling him what their father had done had been a laconic and typically Charlie comment that he was surprised the old man was up to that sort of thing at his age.

Bella was pretty sure that Charlie would not find the situation so amusing should Pauline give birth to a son or two, to displace Charlie in their father's affections and potentially his will.

This being a Saturday, Bella was free to visit her mother earlier in the day than normal. The first thing she noticed as she unlocked the front door and stepped into the hallway was the silence. Her heart-beat quickened as she headed first for the kitchen where the sight of her mother lying fast asleep in a kitchen chair with her head on the table, whilst she snored gently, did nothing to dispel her anxiety. Also on the table were an empty glass, an almost empty bottle of gin and a half-full bottle of tonic. Bella's heart did a slow somersault, fuelled by mingled guilt and anger.

She could hear someone knocking on the back door. Before going to see who it was, instinctively she picked up the glass and the gin bottle, thrusting them out of sight behind the bread bin that was on top of the metal dresser, which was her mother's pride and joy.

When she opened the door her mother's neighbour was standing on the step, trying to peer over Bella's shoulder and into the kitchen.

'Ever so glad you've come, I am, Bella, and no mistake,' Muriel James announced, so obviously intent on coming in that Bella was obliged to step back to allow her to do so. 'I'd thought about telephoning you but you know what it's like with those girls on the exchange: they know everyone's business and of course they are forever gossiping, everyone knows that. I didn't want to embarrass your mother by having to say how worried I was about her and why. She was waiting on the step earlier for the grocer to deliver, you know, and it wasn't her usual shop she'd ordered from either. This man came up to the door carrying a box of veggies and that, and – well, I wasn't trying to look or anything – but you just couldn't help seeing it. There was a bottle of something or other. And more than one. Two, I think, stuck in with the greens. Black market, I dare say. Your dad always did have good connections in that regard, didn't he? I remember how envious we all were last Christmas when your mother managed to get those wonderful puddings from America. Anyway, like I was saying, this chap who was delivering in this dirty old van kept on looking over his shoulder the whole time and then your mother paid him and he put the box down, and after he'd gone I saw her carrying in the bottles from it and then the veggies. Poor thing. I do really feel ever so sorry for her, Bella, with all that she's had to go through. Who would have thought that a decent upstanding man like your father would go off the rails like that? And as for that dreadful woman—'

'Yes, thank you, Muriel,' Bella tried to stop the other woman. 'It really is kind of you to be so concerned.'

'Well, how could I be anything else? Like I said, who would ever have thought of something like this happening? I remember when you all first moved in here, your mother was so proud of you, and so full of plans. We all marvelled at the way she set about changing things in the house, and getting all those workmen in to put in a new bathroom. And such a pity that you are having to deal with this all on your own, Bella dear, what with Charles newly married, and in uniform and living so far away. It's at times like this that a person needs a family to rally round and help out.'

From behind her Bella could hear the sound of her mother groan as she woke up.

Anxiously she turned to look at her, her heart sinking at what she saw. Her mother had lost so much weight that she now looked pinched and thin, her skin a yellow greyish, liverish colour.

By the time Bella had managed tactfully to persuade Muriel to leave, Vi was on her feet and weaving her way towards the stairs.

'I don't know why you've come round here, Bella,' she announced, spacing out her words very slowly and carefully. 'I've got a WVS meeting to go to in a few minutes.'

'It's dreadfully cold outside, Mummy. I really do think it would be better if you stayed at home and kept warm.'

What Bella really longed to say was that her mother was in no fit state to go out, and that if she did manage to get to her WVS meeting her fellow volunteers would be so shocked by the fact that she had so obviously been drinking that she would probably be asked to leave the group. But of course she couldn't. She was too afraid of what her mother's reaction might be. Not for her own sake – she had after all already withstood a drunken husband and a bellicose and violent father, and her mother in her present frail state was hardly likely to cause harm to anyone other than herself – no, what Bella feared was the humiliation her mother would suffer at the memory of her current behaviour when she eventually got back to normal and stopped indulging in too many G and Ts.

'It can't be that cold. You've walked here, after all.'

'Mummy, it is very cold. I wrapped up well and walked fast, and—'

'I am not a child, you know, Bella, and I am perfectly capable of—'

When her speech was suspended by a huge hiccup Vi leaned against the wall looking astonished.

'Come along, Mummy,' Bella urged her. 'Let's get you upstairs so that you can have a nice lie-down.'

Bella had taken her mother's arm, but Vi pulled back from her, shaking her head like a petulant child whilst she told Bella crossly, 'No, I don't want to lie down. I want to go out.'

'The doctor said that you must rest,' Bella reminded her mother desperately, hoping that the mention of the doctor would carry enough authority to persuade her mother to let Bella help her up to bed.

'Did he? When did he say that?'

Bella suppressed a sigh. 'He said it when he came to see you the other week, Mummy. He said that you must have lots of rest and keep warm.'

'He gave me some medicine.'

'Yes, that's right,' Bella agreed brightly. 'He gave you some pills to make you sleep, and a tonic because he thought you were rather low and not eating properly.'

So far neither of them had mentioned Edwin, and Bella hoped that she didn't have to.

She had no idea how to deal with what had happened when talking to her mother. She was afraid of mentioning her father in case it sparked off one of the terrible scenes there had been in the first weeks of her father's departure, during which Vi had sobbed and reviled Edwin and Pauline, using language that Bella had no idea her mother had known, never mind ever expected to hear her use.

In the end it took Bella well over an hour to persuade her mother to go upstairs and lie down on her bed. She stayed with her until she was sure that Vi was soundly asleep and then went back downstairs to tidy up the kitchen. Washing up was so much more fun when it was shared with Lena instead of being done alone, but knowing how house-proud Vi really was, Bella didn't want to leave the kitchen in the untidy state it had been in when she had arrived, with the sink full of dirty dishes.

Bella also emptied what was left in the gin bottle down the sink, telling herself that she was doing it for her mother's sake, whilst hoping that Muriel had been mistaken about her mother having found a black market supplier who was prepared to deliver gin direct to the house.

The afternoon was turning into a cold grey dusk when she eventually started to make her way home, the December light already starting to fade. To cheer herself up Bella tried to focus on Christmas instead of worrying about her mother This year *she* would be cooking Christmas dinner, having decided that that would be more comfortable for Lena than the two of them going to her mother's. Now, in view of what she had seen today, she was glad that she had made that decision.

Lena had confided shyly to her that she felt very self-conscious about the fact that Bella had all those books and she had never read much at all, adding with that natural sweetness that was so much a part of her nature, that she 'didn't want Baby growing up ashamed of its mother because I hadn't had a proper education', so Bella had been going round second-hand shops and stalls whenever she was out, bargaining for the kind of books she had most enjoyed when she had been growing up. Books such as the 'Chalet School' stories, *Little Women*, *Pride and Prejudice*, and several others. It gave Bella a really warm glow inside to buy things for Lena that she knew Lena would appreciate. They could read them together in the long winter evenings whilst they waited for the baby, and still listen to their favourite wireless programmes. Lena loved popular music and sang well, and she and Bella often entertained themselves by pretending that they were Gracie Fields or Vera Lynn, their impromptu concerts almost always finishing in fits of shared giggles.

Bella started to walk faster, not so much this time because she was cold but because she was eager to get home to the bright warmth of her own house. Poor Mummy, it was terribly sad that Daddy had left her, sad and cruel, but Bella did wish that her mother would not drink. In the initial days after Edwin had gone Bella had suggested to Vi that she move in with her and Lena for a few days so that she wouldn't be on her own, but Vi had announced that she was certainly not going to sleep under the same roof as the 'little tart' who had tried to make so much trouble for Charles.

That, of course, had got Bella's back up and if she

were honest she had been relieved not to have to have her mother to stay.

In another couple of weeks it would be Christmas, the third Christmas of the war, and all the mothers who used the crèche were saying how sorry they felt for their children with no toys to be bought, and no treats to be had because of rationing, and how much they wished that things were different. Many of them had husbands who were overseas fighting, and Bella couldn't begin to imagine how hard it must be for them, trying to make Christmas special for their little ones whilst they were worrying about the men they loved who were so very far away.

She had said as much to the most senior nurse at the crèche and suggested that maybe they should try to cheer everyone up by having a small party for the mothers and the children.

Mrs Walsh had been enthusiastic and full of praise for Bella for making such a suggestion, which Bella personally felt was undeserved, but she had put Lena in charge of thinking up games for everyone to play whilst she herself had been firmly but tactfully working on their suppliers to try to get a few extras in their grocery orders, whilst she had coaxed Cook into offering to pare down the meals a little bit so that she would have enough left over to do a proper Christmas party buffet for the crèche.

Christmas – how fast it had come round again but this year there would be no chance of Luke making it home to share it with them, Jean acknowledged as she sat at her kitchen table looking at the list she had made. She'd got the turkey ordered, and she'd had to go back to that rascal she always seemed to end

374

up ordering from even though she was sure he overcharged.

The back door flew open and Grace almost tumbled into the kitchen, her cheeks flushed with happiness and excitement, as she exclaimed, 'Mum, I've passed, and with flying colours. I'm a fully qualified nurse.' She did a few dance steps of joy and twirled round, laughing with relief and excitement.

Putting down her list Jean went over to her and hugged her tight.

'Oh, I'm that pleased for you, love,' she told her.

'So am I,' Grace admitted breathlessly. 'I've run all the way from the hospital to tell you. Matron only sent for me after dinner, and then Sister said that I could have a bit of extra time for my tea break so that I could come home to tell you. I telephoned Seb from the hospital.' Grace, who hadn't yet stopped to draw breath, chuckled and continued, 'He knows now that there's no chance of the wedding being cancelled, so he's lost his last opportunity to escape.'

'As if he'd want to,' Jean chided her eldest daughter. 'I've never known a man more eager to walk his girl down the aisle on his arm as his wife than Seb.'

Grace gave her mother a happy smile. What she had said was after all true. Since that dreadful weekend when they had so nearly parted Seb had made sure that Grace and everyone else knew just how much she meant to him and how much he loved her.

'Seb's going to go ahead now and rent that little cottage I was telling you about, and Matron has said that whilst she doesn't want to lose me, she's prepared to recommend me to the new hospital near to

375

Whitchurch they've set up for the war. And Auntie Fran saying that she's brought me a wedding dress back from Egypt just makes everything perfect.'

Jean forced herself to smile. She knew she was going to miss Grace when she moved to Whitchurch but she didn't for one moment want to cast any shadows over her daughter's happiness, and she certainly wasn't going to tell her how shocked she had been by Fran's casual declaration in her last letter that she was now a married woman, married to some American she had known only a matter of weeks.

At least Francine was coming to the wedding so Jean knew that she'd have an opportunity to check for herself to see whether or not her younger sister was truly happy. She hadn't, though, said whether or not she would be accompanied by her husband. But then there was nothing strange in that: a man in uniform wasn't always free to attend family events. He had his duty to perform, after all. An American, though. Her Sam would have something to say about that, Jean was pretty sure.

Grace looked at her mother. She knew how hard it would be for her parents not to have her brother, Luke, there either for Christmas or for her own wedding, and hard too for Katie who, along with the twins, was going to be Grace's bridesmaid.

'I wish in a way that we hadn't had to invite Auntie Vi and her family,' Bella told Jean, trying not to sound as reluctant as she felt to have her mother's twin sister and her family at her wedding. 'You know what Auntie Vi is like. She's bound to find fault with everything.'

'I know what you mean, love, but it wouldn't have been right not to invite them,' Jean pointed out,

'And I certainly don't want them thinking that we haven't invited them owing to some daft tit-for-tat nonsense because we weren't invited to Charlie's wedding.'

Grace looked worried. 'You don't think I should have asked Bella to be a bridesmaid as well, do you? I wouldn't want to be rude or upset her, and she did ask me when she got married.'

'Upset Bella?' Jean didn't have a very high opinion of her selfish and overindulged niece, but it was kind of Grace to have thought of her cousin.

'Since she's been married she couldn't be a bridesmaid, she'd have to be your matron of honour, and that would set her over Katie and the twins, and I don't think that would be fair really. After all, it will be Katie who will be doing the most to help you get everything ready.'

'So you don't think that I need to ask her then?' Grace established, feeling relieved.

'No, I don't, love.'

'I'd better get back, Mum. It was really good of Sister to let me come out at all. Oh, and the others that were in my set when we first started, and haven't dropped out, have passed as well.'

Two of the original six in the training set Grace had started with had left without finishing. One of these was the girl who had pursued Luke and then dropped him for a young doctor, who had then dropped her, and the other was a girl who had missed her family so much that she had left to go home.

'All we need now is for the twins to get taken on full time once their probationary period is up,' Grace announced gaily as she hugged her mother.

Jean nodded. She didn't want to spoil her elder

daughter's moment of excited happiness by telling her that Sasha had already confided to her that she was worried because Lou had been told off so often by their supervisor for making mistakes. When Jean had tackled Lou about Sasha's worried comments Lou had lost her temper and had accused Sasha of telling tales behind her back, complaining that her twin had changed since she'd 'gone all soppy' about that UXB lad Bobby.

Jean was a twin herself and her heart had sunk as she had listened to Lou. She and Vi might never have been as close as Lou and Sasha but it had still hurt her when she and Vi had gone their separate ways. At the same time Jean also recognised that it was important that as young women the twins did have lives independent from one another. She had, though, also hoped that Sasha and Lou would keep some of the closeness they had always shared. There were, after all, some things that happened in a woman's life than even the best of husbands could not always understand in the way that a loving sister, especially a twin sister, could; all those small domestic anxieties that women worried about so much, especially when they involved the health and happiness of their children; problems as a young wife and mother that a tired husband coming in for his tea after a hard day's work might not have the patience with that a twin sister would.

'Oh, and will you tell Katie for me as well, Mum, please?' Grace sang out halfway through the back door. 'I feel ever so sorry for her, I really do, with Luke so far away and Christmas just round the corner.'

Jean agreed. Katie was someone else she was

worrying over. Katie was by nature a quiet girl, who didn't say anything unless she had something to say, but it seemed to Jean that she had been even quieter than usual just lately. She didn't want to pry, of course, but she genuinely did have a special place in her heart for her son's fiancée and it upset her to think of Katie being unhappy in any way for the girl's own sake. She knew that Katie and Luke had had their moments. Luke was a wonderful son, but there was no getting away from the fact that he was inclined to be a bit jealous as well as naturally protective of Katie, and Jean just hoped that there hadn't been some upset between them in their letters. She had tried to coax out of Katie if anything was wrong between them but Katie had just given her such a wonderfully radiant smile as she shook her head that Jean knew she ought to have been reassured. But somehow she wasn't.

TWENTY-FOUR

'And Gavin said to tell you that if you still don't think that the yellow is deep enough then he can mix it a bit deeper,' Lena told Bella.

They were in the nursery studying the still damp wall that Gavin had industriously painted whilst Bella had been with Vi. Even on a horrible grey day like this one the yellow distemper gave the room a lovely sunny glow, like the inside of a buttercup, Bella thought as she admired it.

'You've had a visitor as well, ever such a nice man. He arrived just as Gavin was leaving and explained that his mother and sister used to billet with you. I was a bit worried about letting him in at first but Gavin really took to him so I knew it would be all right,' Lena informed Bella happily.

Jan. It could only have been Jan who had called, but what on earth for, Bella wondered, her pleasure in the yellow wall fading to be replaced with an edgy defensiveness she hadn't felt for so long that for a few seconds she didn't really know just what it was that was making her so cross and anxious.

'I can't imagine why he called here,' she told Lena sharply, 'or what he could have wanted.'

'I think he just wanted to see you. He asked how you were and said that he'd heard from his sister about how you'd been promoted at the crèche. Perhaps he's sweet on you,' Lena suggested, watching Bella to see how her friend would respond.

Lena often wondered why someone as special and marvellous as Bella didn't have a man in her life, and when she had opened the door to the handsome Pole who had come round asking after Bella she had immediately wondered if they were romantically involved, and had even felt a bit disappointed that Bella had never mentioned him to her.

'Sweet on me?' Bella just about managed to stop herself telling Lena that Jan loathed and despised her. 'I hope he isn't,' she said as robustly as she could, 'seeing as he's married.'

Lena would certainly never make a good card player, Bella thought ruefully, because she was no good at hiding what she was thinking. An expression of open disappointment was clouding her eyes, and she burst out, 'Oh, what a shame. I thought he was so perfect for you. You are so very pretty and he is so good-looking, and he was really interested when I told him all about how kind you've been to me.'

Bella groaned inwardly. Oh, yes, she could just imagine how interested in that Jan would have been. Right now he was probably reporting everything Lena had told him to his sister, who was as cynically contemptuous of her as he was. No doubt the two of them were having a good laugh at her expense. Well, let them. She didn't care.

'I hope I haven't done the wrong thing?' Lena was asking, looking crestfallen.

Bella smiled reassuringly at her and then went over

and gave her a hug. Lena was getting larger by the day and Bella's arms wouldn't go right around her now, which caused them both to giggle.

'Of course you didn't . . .' Bella began to say, and then stopped and told Lena, 'Oh, he is definitely going to be a footballer, Lena. He's just kicked me twice!'

'Oh, he hasn't, has he? He was ever so active last night, keeping me awake and kicking away like mad.'

They had both taken by now to referring to the baby as 'he' without actually having made a decision to do so, and his energetic kicks kept them both amused.

'Anyway,' Lena told Bella, her expression softening with genuine love, and admiration, 'I only told that Jan the truth when I said how you saved me and the baby, and how special you are and how much you've done for me.'

Seeing Lena's eyes fill up with tears, Bella told her briskly, 'Now that's enough of that. I don't want my head getting so swelled that I can't get through the doorway.'

Lena giggled but Bella felt her own tears weren't very far away.

Lena's comment had, though, reminded her of her duty to Lena's future and that of her baby, and so she said as lightly as she could, 'Talking of people being sweet on people, it seems to me that a certain young man isn't coming round here just to paint nursery walls.'

Lena blushed hotly and looked uncomfortable.

Bella frowned slightly and said, 'I thought you liked Gavin.'

'Yes, I do,' Lena admitted, 'but I wouldn't want you or him getting the wrong idea, Bella. I mean, it's very kind of him to come round like he does and not accept any payment for painting the nursery but he's only doing it because it's what his grandma has asked him to do. He's told me that.'

Bella frowned. She certainly hadn't got the impression that Gavin was practically haunting the doorstep because he wanted to please his grandmother, but she didn't want to put Lena in a position where the younger girl felt obliged to say she cared more for Gavin than she actually did because she thought that was what Bella wanted her to say.

As Bella had quickly come to learn, along with the pleasure of having Lena admire her so much had come the responsibility of making sure that Lena didn't do things she didn't really want to do just to please her.

'Well, if he's told you that then I'm sure it must be true,' she said as lightly as she could.

Lena gave a vigorous nod of her head and tried to smile, but in reality she didn't feel much like smiling. She had been so happy earlier in the afternoon, sitting watching Gavin paint and then giving him her opinion of the colour when he asked her for it. It had felt so cosy and lovely, him in his overalls painting, her sitting on what Bella called a 'pouffe' watching him, just like a proper family where girls who were having babies also had husbands and those husbands loved them.

Thinking that had somehow or other led to her saying happily to Gavin, 'It's really nice having you here. It makes me feel ever so happy, Gavin.'

'Well, it's me gran that said that I should come and give a hand, and of course she's always wanting to know about how you're going on,' he had responded, and Lena had known from the tone of his voice and the way he kept his back to her as he spoke that somehow her comment had not been what he wanted to hear and that his answer to her was a warning to that effect.

She had felt ashamed of herself for the way her eyes had filled with tears and she had gone all shaky and unhappy, so she had stood up and given him a smile and had told him as brightly as she could, 'I'd better get back downstairs. Bella had a letter from her brother this morning and she said he asked her about me and the baby in it.'

Gavin's only response had been a disinterested grunt, so Lena had fled to the kitchen where she had tried to cheer herself up by singing along to the wireless. It wasn't after all a lie that Charlie had asked after her, and it was no one's business but hers if she didn't tell Gavin that Charlie had gone on to say that he wanted nothing whatsoever to do with her or the baby and that he'd only mentioned them in the first place to warn Bella not to write anything about them in any letters in the future.

Not that she was bothered about that. She could hardly even remember what Charlie looked like now, never mind anything else, but she certainly didn't want Gavin getting the wrong idea. After all, it would be downright silly of her to think that a decent respectable lad like him could ever think of getting involved with a girl like her who had let herself down good and proper and who was going to have a baby without a husband, to prove it.

'Oh, come on, what harm will it do?' Carole demanded as she and Katie leaned on the rail of the packed ice rink, watching the twins skate.

Katie frowned as she turned to her friend and

pointed out uncomfortably, 'I'd really rather not, Carole. It doesn't seem right, with Luke and Andy so far away and fighting for this country, for us to be going out dancing with two Irish lads who aren't even in uniform.'

Katie could see that her friend wasn't at all pleased to hear what she had said. It was her turn to frown now and not just frown but look a bit cross as well.

'I suppose you're afraid that one of those twins of your Luke's mother's will go writing to him telling tales.'

'I am not afraid of any such thing,' Katie snapped at her, pink-cheeked. 'Jean would never send a letter to Luke saying something she thought might upset him, and neither would the twins, just as I would never do anything that would upset him.'

'Liam said that you'd be too scared, but I told him that he was wrong, and now you're letting me down by proving that he was right.'

Katie could feel her heart sinking with genuine distress at the growing discovery of how differently she and Carole thought and felt about the responsibilities that went with being engaged, and a sharp touch of anger that Carole should think she could manipulate her by making such a silly and obvious comment.

'I'm not the one who is letting anyone down,' she pointed out firmly. In addition to her unease and anger, there was another issue here that went beyond her personal feelings. It was one that Katie had been wanting to raise with Carole ever since she had begun to realise how much Carole was enjoying the company of the young Irishman she had met. But it was also one that was getting harder with every week that passed, with

385

Carole continuing to sing Liam's praises and do her utmost to persuade Katie to get as eagerly involved with Danny as she was with Liam. That issue was one of the duty they owed their country; a duty that, so far as Katie was concerned, was all the stronger because of the confidential nature of the work in which they were involved.

It was true that Danny had never made any comments about her work other than continually to tease her about the fun she must have reading saucy messages meant for other eyes, but even those kind of comments were the sort that Katie didn't really care for herself, and ones she knew Luke would consider far too intimate to be passed from another man to her, his girl. If Seb had not been transferred to Whitchurch she suspected that she would have been tempted to confide in him and ask for his advice, as he had once told her she must feel free to do, should the need arise.

Where other boys were concerned Katie knew where to draw the line. She wasn't remotely interested in Danny, good-looking though he was, or anyone else. How could she be when she was already committed to Luke? But the Irish boys' habit of managing to materialise at their table whenever Katie went dancing with the twins was causing her to feel uncomfortable, and all the more so because of the way Carole was increasingly encouraging them. Carole's present suggestion, that they should in effect agree to let the Liam and Danny partner them to the Grafton's Christmas Eve Dance, was in many ways enough to make Katie consider whether or not she ought to be direct with her friend and tell her that she preferred not to continue a friendship with someone who would accept a date when she was as good as engaged. But Andy, Carole's fiancé, was not just one of Luke's friends, he was also one of Luke's men, and just as Luke took his responsibility as a corporal seriously where his men were concerned, so Katie felt that she as his fiancée was in a sense responsible for Carole and needed to look out for her, and for her relationship with Andy.

'And what's that supposed to mean?' Carole demanded, obviously taking umbrage at Katie's comment.

'You are as good as engaged to Andy, and Luke and I are engaged,' Katie felt obliged to remind her.

Carole bristled and said crossly, 'It's just a bit of fun, Katie, going to one of the Christmas dances as a foursome and with a partner. The Irish boys know that we're coupled up. There's no harm in it. Anyway, Liam says that he reckons that our lads won't be holding back over there in Cairo over Christmas when there's dances on and plenty of girls around to have fun with.'

'You *told* Liam that Luke and Andy are in Egypt?' Katie couldn't conceal her shock.

Carole tossed her head dismissively but her face went bright red, as she retaliated, 'Well, and what if I have? Everyone knows that we're out there fighting the Germans. Anyway, why shouldn't Liam and Danny know where they are? We're all on the same side, after all.'

Katie desperately wanted to remind her friend that Ireland was neutral but she suspected that to do so would provoke even more sharp words from her, and the last thing she wanted to do was instigate a row.

She wasn't going to agree to Carole's plans for the Christmas Eve Dance, though.

'Well, are you going to come to the Grafton then?'

387

Carole challenged her, adding, 'You'd better, because I'm going to look a real idgit if you don't.'

'Idgit' was one of Liam's favourite words and it gave Katie a horrible feeling in her tummy to hear Carole using it in an automatic imitation of Liam's soft accent. A person didn't do that unless they were already getting involved with someone.

'No, I shan't be going,' she told Carole quietly. 'After all, it was at the Grafton last Christmas Eve that me and Luke met up for the first time, just like you and Andy,' she felt obliged to remind the other girl.

'Well, please yourself, but I'm going and I think you're a fool for staying in when you could be going out having fun. Like Liam said, I'll bet that Andy and Luke won't be sitting in their camp thinking about us.'

'Perhaps not,' Katie agreed coolly. 'After all, for all we know they could be out in the desert fighting for us and for this country.'

Without waiting for Carole to respond she waved her hand in the direction of the twins and walked along the side of the ice rink in front of the seats, leaving Carole standing on her own.

Since the twins possessed only one pair of skates between them, Katie had loaned Lou her pair so that she and Sasha could skate together. They came skimming across the ice towards her now, taking hold of the rail as they leaned in to her. Sasha was glowing with happiness, her cheeks pink and her eyes alight with enjoyment. Lou, though, wasn't smiling at all.

Jean may not have said anything directly to her but Katie had guessed that Jean was worrying about the twins and the way they were growing apart.

'Are you and Carole going to the Christmas Eve

Dance at the Grafton, Katie?' Sasha asked eagerly. 'Only I don't think that Mum and Dad will let us go on our own, and we're longing to go. It will be our first proper grown-up Christmas dance, after all.'

'You speak for yourself,' Lou cut in curtly. 'I'm not longing to go at all. It's you that wants to go, not me, and you only want to go because Bobby will be there.'

Katie felt a sharp tug of sympathy – for Sasha, who quite plainly was becoming keen on the very nice and respectable young bomb disposal sapper, who had helped to save her life when she had been trapped beneath an unexploded bomb, and also for Lou, who equally plainly was horrified and miserable at the thought of losing her twin to a proper grown-up relationship.

Jean herself had said that whilst she worried that Sasha was still too young to be going steady properly, if one of the twins had to start walking out with someone she would prefer it to be Sasha because she was so much steadier than Lou. They had all seen how her near-tragedy had matured Sasha, and there was no denying that Bobby was a sensible and trustworthy young man.

'If you both really want to go to the Grafton on Christmas Eve and your mother is willing to give her permission then I'm happy to go with you,' Katie told them half truthfully. She was happy to go with them, but she was not happy at all to go and then be forced to sit at a table with Liam and Danny. She hesitated and then decided that as the twins were growing up and bound to notice anyway, she might as well mention something to them about the fact that she and Carole would not be going to the Grafton together – and why.

'You'll both have to put up with me all evening, though,' she warned them, 'seeing as it looks as though Carole will be going with a . . . a friend.'

'You mean that Irishman she's always talking with,' Sasha guessed straight off.

'Liam. Yes, that's right.'

'What about the other one? Did he ask you to go with him?'

'Well, not exactly. They do both know that I'm engaged to Luke, and that Carole is going steady with Andy,' Katie felt she had to point out. 'And Liam has only asked Carole if he and Danny could join us at a table, but, well, I don't feel right about it so I've said no. Now,' she told them both more briskly, 'you'd better get your skates off otherwise we'll be late back for tea, and your mum won't like that.'

'I think Katie was right not to agree to sit with those Irish boys,' Sasha told Lou as they sat down on one of the benches several yards away from where Katie was waiting for them, to remove their skates. 'After all, when a girl's given her promise to a boy and they're engaged—'

'Oh, stop going on about people being engaged, will you?' Lou interrupted her twin angrily. 'It's all you ever talk and think about these days.'

'No it is not.'

'Yes it is. You were all over Sandra Willis at work the other day when she was showing off her ring, oohing and aahhing and acting all daft and soppy.'

'I was just being polite. That's what you have to do when you're working with other girls. That's what

390

Mrs Noakes, the new supervisor, told us all when she held that meeting that you missed because you'd stayed at home with a bad headache. She said that it was important that we all got on with one another and that we worked as a team and helped one another, just like our men do when they are in uniform. She said that our role in the war effort was a really vital link in the chain of communication and that—'

'Did she say anything about the work being so boring that it makes you want to fall asleep and that all you'll ever hear is dozens of stupid rules?' Lou interrupted her twin angrily.

Sasha's face went bright pink.

'No she didn't, because it's not like that at all, and you're not being fair. You've been determined to not like the exchange ever since we started and you've done everything you can to put me off. Well, I haven't been put off and I like working there.'

'And I don't.'

'Everyone can see that, Lou. I dare say it would have been different if it had been your idea that we applied to work there. Then you'd have loved it. But because it was my idea and not yours you were determined not to like it right from the start.'

'That's not true.'

'Yes it is.'

They glowered at one another, Sasha's expression one of righteous indignation whilst Lou's was more sullen and obstinate. But inside Lou was the one battling shocked tears of rejection and the recognition that it wasn't just a lad that that was coming between them and was now more important to her twin than she was, it was the exchange as well.

'Oh, Lou, please don't let's fall out with one

another,' Sasha suddenly begged, putting down her skates to give her twin a fierce hug that brought fresh tears to burn the backs of Lou's eyes. 'I so much want us both to be asked to stay on at the exchange when our probationary period ends next week. You could work everything much better than me if you wanted to – you know you could. I do wish you hadn't gone and deliberately got the supervisors' backs up like you have. Mum is going to be ever so upset if they don't keep us both on, and so am I. You can still do it.' Sasha reached for Lou's hand and gripped it tightly. 'Please will you, Lou, just for me? I don't want us to have to work at different places. I want us to be together.'

Sasha's words were a balm to Lou's sore heart, but it wasn't in her nature to simply give in without claiming her own personal victory.

'All right then,' she told Sasha. 'But you've got to promise me first that you'll stop seeing that daft UXB lad that's always hanging around wherever we go.'

'You want me to stop seeing Bobby?' Sasha's voice as well as her expression betrayed how shocked and how upset Lou's demand made her. She couldn't understand why Lou would ask her to do such a thing. This wasn't like it had been with Kieran, when they had each believed that he preferred her to her twin because he was buttering them both up behind each other's back. Bobby had made it plain right from the start that it was her he liked, and she liked him too.

'Don't be silly, Lou. You know I can't do that,' Sasha protested. 'I owe him so much, after all. He did save my life, remember.'

Lou's mouth tightened. Hadn't she also helped to

save Sasha's life? But that obviously didn't matter any more, just like she didn't matter any more.

'Come on,' she told Sasha unceremoniously. 'Katie's waiting.'

Sasha gave her twin a worried look as Lou walked off ahead of her without turning round. Why was Lou sometimes so awkward and difficult? She had been inclined to be like that all the time they had been growing up, but then it hadn't mattered like it did now. Sasha could remember how Lou had always been the one to choose who they would be friends with and who they wouldn't, even though she, Sasha, was actually the elder. Well, she wasn't going to stop being friends with Bobby just because Lou was being a bit scratchy about him. She did wish though that Lou would pull her socks up a bit at the exchange. She had had several tellings-off in Sasha's hearing, and Sasha knew – because Lou had told her so herself – that she had been warned that she would not be kept on if she didn't make more of an effort.

It was unthinkable that they might be separated and have to work in different places, and all because Lou was being stubborn and awkward. Lou might go on about the exchange being boring but what else was there that suited them so well and was so convenient for home? There wasn't anywhere. They were getting ever such a good training and they'd still be able to work at an exchange even if the war ended tomorrow.

There was a horrible, miserable feeling burning Lou's insides, like a tight ball that somehow made her throat and her chest hurt. Sasha obviously expected her to do what she wanted them to do, but when it came to Lou asking Sasha to do something for her, she wouldn't. She, Lou, would never ever, she just knew, put some stupid boy before her twin, and if their positions had been reversed and Sasha had asked her to give up seeing a boy for her sake then she would have done so gladly.

Sasha looked at Lou, who was hanging back from her and Katie, suddenly feeling conscience-stricken and guilty when she saw that Lou had her head down and was dragging the side of her shoe on the ground just as she always did when she was upset about something. Hadn't she and Lou promised themselves after all that business with Kieran Mallory that they would never ever fall out over a lad again?

But Bobby wasn't just any lad, he was the person who had saved her life, and he was stuck here in Liverpool all on his own with his family far away in the Northeast, whilst he was doing a horribly dangerous job. So dangerous, in fact, that the men who worked in the UXB units had the shortest life expectancy of all the men in uniform.

Sasha hung back too, waiting until Lou had caught up with them to touch her arm and say, 'Don't let's fall out over Bobby, please, Lou.'

Lou nodded as though in acceptance of Sasha's plea, but inwardly she didn't and couldn't accept it. Her twin was just trying to trick her into doing what she wanted and get her back in their supervisor's good books so that she'd end up spending the rest of her life working in the exchange, because that was what Sasha wanted. Well, it wasn't what she wanted, and she wasn't going to do it.

TWENTY-FIVE

'There's someone here to see you.'

Bella, who had been leaning down to retrieve a file that had slipped off her desk and so had her back to her open office door, suppressed a small sigh as she smiled in acknowledgement of the announcement from the harassed young nursery nurse. Her somewhat unprofessional style wasn't the nurse's fault, after all. What Bella really needed was a properly trained deputy but she was loath to spend any of her precious budget on clerical staff when they were so desperate for more trained nursery nurses for the children.

The nurse had gone back to her duties. Jan's heart-joltingly familiar male hand reached over her own to pick up the file, and his even more heart-tearingly familiar male voice announced, 'I just wanted to call and say hello before I set off back for camp. I did call round at the house but your young protégée told me that you'd gone to see your mother.'

How had it happened that her eyes and her ears had registered and remembered these things about him without her even knowing, and certainly without her wanting them to do so?

'I can't imagine why you'd want to bother to call and see me,' Bella told him abruptly, as she snatched back the file and put it on her desk. 'Unless it was just so that you could tell me all over again how worthless I am and how much you despise me.'

Ignoring the challenge in Bella's voice, Jan told her quietly, 'Lena introduced herself to me when I called round. She thinks the world of you, Bella. She couldn't stop singing your praises to me.'

'But you, of course, know me better than she does? Yes, I do know that, Jan, and if you've come here to remind me of all my faults and failings, then—'

'No, I haven't come here to do that.'

Now that the shock of seeing him so unexpectedly was over and she could look at him properly, Bella saw what she had not seen before and that was that his face was thinner and drawn, and that he looked almost haggard, a look of pain and defeat darkening his eyes. Against her will she was curious, and worse, anxious about the cause of the change she could see in him.

'How are Bettina and Maria?' she asked him reluctantly.

The smile illuminating his face told her that whatever he was worrying about it was not his mother or sister.

'They are very well. Bettina loves her work here in Wallasey, and she and my mother are now renting a house large enough for them to take in refugee billetees themselves. They are both very happy. Bettina is walking out with my friend from the Polish Air Force.'

'How nice.' The tone of Bella's voice was decidedly brittle. 'Your mother must be feeling very pleased that you could both end up married to fellow Poles . . . Why have you come here, Jan?' she asked him abruptly. 'What do you want? She didn't have the stomach or the stamina for playing a who dares wins game with him that she knew she was bound to lose.

'What do I want?' His mouth twisted in a painful smile, the look he gave her bleak with an expression she could not analyse.

'What I want is what I have wanted for a very long time and what I know I cannot have. Come and walk with me, Bella. I can't talk properly to you in here.'

Walk with him? Bella looked towards the window. Outside, the December sky was heavy and sullen with the threat of rain. She took her responsibilities very seriously and she never left her desk on a whim. But she hadn't taken a lunch hour for weeks, eating at her desk instead, and she knew that if she refused and let him go without finding out what was wrong she would end up wishing that she had not done so.

Walk with me, he had said, and her stomach was a mass of wing-flapping butterflies more suited as a response to an invitation to a wonderful evening out – with a man who was free to make her such an invitation, rather than a cold walk with a man who despised her. It was just curiosity that was motivating her, nothing more. After all, she was hardly stupid enough either to think that Jan could possibly want to talk to her for any personal reasons or to want him to do so. Her whole body still burned with shame every time she recalled the humiliation she had suffered when she had thrown herself at him and

397

been rejected. That horrible experience had taught her a lesson she would never ever forget.

'I can't be out for very long,' she warned him, reaching for her coat, and then tensing as somehow he had managed to remove it from its peg before she could do so and was holding it open for her. How had he managed to move so quickly? Normally she liked men to be polite, but now the lack of space in her office and the fact that Jan was holding her coat forced them into a proximity she would have preferred them not to have had. Just the act of standing close to him whilst he slipped on her coat for her somehow had become an act of almost shocking intimacy that made her tremble so much inside she was afraid that he would notice. She could feel his warmth behind her, but the old Bella, who would have been so convinced of her own female power and so used to using it that she would have thought nothing of turning round and smiling seductively up at a man she wanted to tease and torment, had died savagely and painfully when Jan himself had rejected her, and now the last thing she wanted to do was to be anywhere near him or any other man. Now the mere fact that she was aware of his body heat, the smell of his cologne, the male pressure of his hands on her shoulders as he helped her into her coat, made her feel so acutely vulnerable that she almost wanted to bolt out of the room. Not that she would do that, of course. It simply would not be fitting, given her professional status, so instead she thanked him brusquely without turning round, and then marched through the open door, telling the first nursery nurse she saw that she was going out for an hour if anyone should ask for her.

Lena, who had seen Jan arrive, watched as they left together, thinking what a handsome and well-suited couple they made. What a pity it was that he was married to someone else. She had thought him so nice and just perfect for Bella.

The raw December weather with its east wind whipped up Bella's blonde curls round the brim of her pretty fur-trimmed hat – a prewar buy that these days she wore for warmth rather than for admiring glances – causing her to lift her hand to keep her hat secure.

Watching her, Jan thought how beautiful she looked, all the more so in his eyes because now the true beauty – a beauty of spirit and soul he had always known she possessed – shone so clearly from her. Just watching her made his heart ache with pride, and with love and regret.

She really had no idea why she had agreed to come out in this bitingly cold wind. Bella tried to make herself feel cross but only succeeded in increasing her nervousness. She had felt much safer – from herself – inside the school than she did out here where she was alone with Jan and her own secret and shameful vulnerabilities.

'It's far too cold to walk about aimlessly,' she announced, turning round, intending to go back inside.

But to her dismay Jan simply took hold of her arm insisting, 'Then let's go to your house. We can talk properly there, and knowing you I dare say you have a nice warm fire banked down.'

'I have to keep the house warm for Lena,' Bella defended herself. 'Her baby's due in a few weeks and the circumstances of the early weeks of her pregnancy mean that she needs cosseting.'

'Something that, according to what my mother and sister have heard, you are excelling at doing for her.'

Was that really an almost indulgent gentleness she could hear in Jan's voice? Bella turned to look at him and then wished that she had not done so. He was so very handsome, and so very married, she reminded herself sharply. And even if he had not been married, he had made it plain what he thought of her.

'That was a very courageous thing for you to do, Bella, taking her in like you did.'

Praise for her and from Jan. Bella tussled with both pride and her new-found realism.

When realism won she told him firmly, 'Helping a young woman in difficult circumstances is hardly courageous, Jan. It is men like you – all those men who are risking their lives to save this country and its people – who deserve that accolade. Had I truly been courageous she would not have been in such a dire situation. In the circumstances I could do nothing other than help her. I would not say this to anyone else and I must ask you to respect this confidence. The father of Lena's child is Charlie. He has behaved appallingly towards her and so have my parents. I should have helped Lena when she first came asking for help.' Bella bent her head, her voice so low that Jan had to bend his to catch what she was saying.

'Lena tells me every day how lucky she believes she is because I have helped her but she is wrong. I am the one who is lucky, because I was given a second chance to do the right thing by her. If I had not been given that second chance, and something had

400

happened to her and her baby, then that would in part have been my fault. After . . . after what happened to me with . . . well, when I . . .' Jan's small squeeze of her hand told Bella that he knew exactly what she was trying to say about her own lost baby, and somehow or other she was now allowing her hand to rest in the comforting warmth of his.

'You were so kind to me then and I felt . . . that is . . . I wanted to pass on that kindness,' she told him with great dignity. 'I wanted to be better than I was, and better than everyone thought me, and Lena has helped me to do that. Do you know, Jan, never once has she said anything bad or unkind about Charlie, and never once has she shown me anything but love. She has taught me so much, made me feel that I must try to be the person she seems to think I am and that you more than most know that I am not.'

'You must not say that, because it is not true.'

As always when his emotions were aroused his accent had become more noticeable. He had stopped walking so that Bella was obliged to do the same.

'Of course it is true. And you were the one, who said . . . You were the one who made me see that . . .'

Jan was walking again, and so fast that Bella was almost having to run to keep up with his long strides, and was out of breath by the time they were standing inside her nice warm hall with the front door shut, the house cocooning them in its warmth and privacy.

'I'll put on the kettle,' Bella announced.

'What, with your coat and hat still on?' Jan teased her gently.

'Oh . . . yes . . .' Bella reached up to remove her hat and put it on the shelf above the coat stand, and then began to unbutton her coat, her fingers trembling because she was so conscious of Jan standing behind her waiting to take her coat from her.

His, 'Why are you trembling?' was both ungentlemanly and a reminder of how much he had already hurt her, Bella acknowledged.

'Probably because I am cold,' she had been going to say, but somehow the lie would not be spoken and to her horror she could feel her eyes filling with tears so that all she could do was shake her head and make to dart past Jan so that she could take refuge in the kitchen. Only he stopped her and caught her up in his arms and then kissed her with such longing and passion that everything she should have done and said meant nothing, and all that mattered was clinging to him whilst her body trembled and her heart sang, and against his lips she whispered his name over and over again.

'Thank you for marrying me, France. It means so much to me – everything, in fact – knowing that I'll have you – someone of my own – to be there with me, right to the end.'

Brandon's voice was gruff as he covered her hand with his own. Francine smiled tenderly at him. Was it her imagination or could she see a change in him already, a thinness to his face that had not been there this time last week, an unsteadiness in his step? Poor, poor boy. She had been with him now to see the eminent Harley Street specialist who was treating him and had heard from Professor Whiteford's own lips the exact prognosis that Brandon had already given her. She had tried to persuade him to contact his parents and discuss the situation with them but he had flatly refused and, even worse, he had become so agitated and upset that Fran had felt she had to drop the subject. She rather suspected that the American Ambassador did not entirely approve of their marriage, but Brandon had shrugged aside her concern, saying that there was nothing that either he or anyone else could do, and that his marriage was his own business and *he* very much approved of it.

What Fran was trying to do, having spoken at length with the professor, who had told them both of the suffering experienced by other families who had often young children who were afflicted with the same condition as Brandon, was to urge Brandon to use some of his money to set up a charity – a foundation, as Brandon called it – to help other sufferers, and she felt that the work involved in establishing his foundation was giving him something to hold on to: a purpose that he could cling to during these last remaining months – or weeks – of his life.

'I have to go to my niece's wedding, Brandon. My sister will be hurt if I don't.'

'Of course we must go.'

Fran smiled at him. 'There is no need for you to come with me. I don't expect that of you.'

'Then you should,' he told her robustly. 'I am your husband, after all, and your family will expect it – unless you haven't told them about our marriage.'

'I have told them but I wasn't sure that you'd want to meet them.'

'I'm proud to have married you, Fran, and I shall be proud to meet your family.'

Fran knew that what he was really saying was that he didn't want her to leave him behind in London on his own. Her sister Jean would be rather shocked to discover that she had married a man so much younger than she was herself, Fran suspected, but Jean had only ever wanted her happiness, and provided she was able to convince her that she was happy then Jean would accept her marriage and be pleased for her. Jean, bless her, made allowances for her because 'she had been to Hollywood', Fran knew. And because she had lost Jack. Now she was going to mother and lose another 'boy' – was that always to be her role in life?

Another Christmas would soon be here. Her second with Tommy. Emily's heart swelled with love and pride. Away from Liverpool and here in Whitchurch, apart from that funny incident when they had first moved here, Tommy had come on by leaps and bounds and was now doing so well at school that his teacher was talking about him being one of her cleverest pupils. When he got back from school today she and Tommy were going to finish writing the Christmas cards they had made together the previous weekend. Emily felt obliged to send one to Con, just as she also felt obliged to write to him every week. Not that he always wrote back to her, except when he wanted something. Emily always felt a bit guilty when she realised not only just how little she missed her husband but, even worse, how little she actually cared about him at all.

For her and Tommy this Christmas would be very different from last year's. This year they knew and understood one another a lot better than they had then. Tommy still never mentioned his past, but Emily had no wish to force him to disclose to her what had happened to him or how he had come to be on his own. Deep down inside she knew that she was afraid of discovering that somewhere there were those who might have more claim on him than she had. Tommy had chosen to be with her, she reassured herself, and if that was good enough for him then it was good enough for her.

Emily had already ordered her goose from the farmer's wife, and out of good manners rather than anything else she had invited her neighbour to come and have dinner with them. She would much rather have invited Wilhelm, who had done so much for her with all his hard work in her garden, and especially her vegetable plot, but of course that was not possible. Wilhelm would be having his Christmas dinner with all the other POWs in their camp several miles away. Emily had been relieved to be told when she had questioned him anxiously about their camp and the way they were treated that in Wilhelm's opinion their English guards treated them very well indeed.

Jan and Bella were together on the plush fabric-covered sofa in Bella's front room. Its maroon colour toned perfectly with the striped burgundy-red and off-white striped Regency wallpaper. The heavy burgundy velvet curtains, with their bobble trip of cream, had been closed, ostensibly to keep in the warmth from the fire. Behind the larger of the two armchairs stood a standard lamp with a striped burgundy and cream lampshade. The smart blond wood radiogram and matching cocktail cabinet gleamed in the soft light from the fire, and the wheels of the tea trolley had sunk into the thickness of the handsome burgundy and cream floral-patterned carpet.

Neither of the occupants of the sofa had touched the tea that Bella had made or cared much about the room's décor, though. Instead they were seated facing one another, Bella's slim delicate female hand held fast between Jan's two much larger and stronger male hands.

'But I don't understand,' Bella protested shakily. 'How can you say you love me now when before . . . ?'

'I lied before,' Jan told her simply, adding thickly when he saw her expression, 'Ah, my love, please don't look at me like that. It is true, I swear to you. I loved you from the first moment I set eyes on you but I knew then that if I had given you my heart you would have crushed it and broken it, and me.'

'You said you felt sorry for me. You said you despised me . . .'

'Not you, Bella, not the true sweet wonderful you I knew you really were underneath – it was only the things you were doing – things you were being made to do because of what others had taught you – that I questioned. Here, though, in my heart where I have known the real you I have loved you more than it is possible for me to find enough words to say, and I always will.'

Bella's eyes smarted with loving tears. Everything that had happened had come as such a shock, a sweet thrilling realisation of shock, it was true, but a shock none the less. She wanted to reach out and touch Jan to make sure that she wasn't merely dreaming. She wanted to relive every precious heart-beat of those wonderful moments she had just spent in his arms when he had whispered so passionately to her of his love for her and she had felt her heart beating so fast that it had been as though it had wanted to burst out of her chest to give itself into his hold. Once all of that would have been all that mattered, but she was not that Bella any more and there was something that mattered very much indeed, and that something was the fact that Jan was married to someone else.

Bella took a deep breath and turned to face him.

'You say these things to me, Jan, lovely wonderful things that I'm not even going to pretend that I haven't wanted to hear, because I have and I do.' She gave him a smile that touched Jan's heart with its sweet sadness and made him want to reach for her and hold her safe against all the world's pain and difficulties for ever. But as though she knew what he was feeling she shook her head and continued shakily, 'But the reality is that you are a married man and as a woman I know it is my duty to respect that woman and your marriage, just as I would want and expect another woman to respect me and my marriage if our roles were reversed. When you married you gave her a lifelong promise to be her husband. I cannot and I will not allow you to break that promise with me.'

The shudder that took her body showed how much she wished things were different, even without the tears Jan could see in her eyes.

'I should never have married,' he told her sombrely.

'But you did marry her,' Bella pointed out quietly.

'I felt I had no choice, Bella. She was so vulnerable and so afraid so . . . so much in need, and her family such close friends of my own. Unhappily what I had believed to be merely the effect of the natural fears of a young woman who experienced at first-hand the horror of her country being invaded and overrun by the enemy, has turned out to be something far more serious.'

Bella frowned, her own despair pushed to one side by a surge of protective female love for this man as she recognised the very real anguish and hopelessness in Jan's voice. Instinctively she reached out to him, and then tried to pull back when she saw the fierce burn of passionate longing in his eyes. But it was too late, she was in his arms and unable to stop herself from responding to his kiss with all the pent-up love in her own heart.

'I love you so much.' Jan's voice held a raw edge of passion. 'I've dreamed of holding you in my arms like this so often. I've been such a fool.'

'Shush, you are not to say that,' Bella protested softly. 'And you are not a fool. You are the man I love, the only man I will ever love. Oh, Jan!' He was so dearly familiar, so already known to all her senses and yet at the same time her intimacy with him felt new and exciting. Dangerously so, she recognised as their kisses became deeper and more intense, neither of them holding back from showing their love. She wasn't a girl any more. She was a woman; she had been married; carried a child; her body was a woman's body, her love a woman's love and the intimacies she craved with Jan went far beyond mere kisses, no matter how passionate.

But that could not be. Jan was married and the new Bella she had evolved into so painfully would not allow them to do something they would both regret. It took all her inner strength to end the kiss and push Jan away, denying them what they both wanted.

'I want you so much, but we mustn't,' she told him when he tried to gather her close to him again. 'You're married, Jan.'

'Married, yes. But I do not have a wife, and even if I did she would not be you; she would not be the woman I love.'

The look he gave her turned her heart over inside her chest. It was the look of a man in torment. Something was very obviously wrong with Jan's wife, and in his marriage.

Bella's heart lurched with real pain for him, as she pressed him anxiously, 'Jan, what is it? What's wrong?'

'We don't really know. The doctors we have seen – and by "we" I mean her father and I, as she refused to accept that there is anything wrong, even though she refuses to so much as allow me to share with her a bedroom or its bed – believe that the trauma of her mother's death has somehow become associated in her mind with the German invasion of Poland, and because of the brutality she witnessed she has developed a fear and loathing of any kind of marital intimacy. And yet ironically she has also become so fiercely jealous that she cannot witness me having a conversation with my own sister without flying into the most dreadful rage, during which she tears at her own skin with her fingernails. I feel so dreadfully sorry for her, Bella, and so guilty. If I had not married her perhaps her hold on normality might have strengthened, but it is as though her marriage to me has pushed her over an edge into some terrible dark abyss from which she cannot find the way back. The doctor believes that her poor mind is irreversibly damaged by what she witnessed when the serving girls were dragged from the house and raped by the German soldiers, but we cannot be sure as no one really knows exactly what it was that set off this terrible mental affliction that has taken her over.'

'Oh, Jan, how dreadful for you, and for her as well. What a terrible thing to have happened to you all.'

'It is my mother and her father who feel it the most, as they were the ones who brokered our marriage and who had such high hopes of it. My mother feels dreadfully guilty, and all the more so I think because I suspect she has guessed how I feel about you.

'I hadn't planned to tell you any of this. I hadn't even planned to see you but somehow I found myself walking down your road and then I was knocking on your door and feeling more disappointed than I could bear to admit because you were not here. I am a coward and worse for coming to you as I have when I know I can never have any right to your love, and when I know too that for your sake I should be encouraging you to give it to another and a better man who can give you his love with honour and a promise of marriage.'

'There is no other man I could ever want,' Bella told him fiercely and truthfully, 'but as much as I love you, Jan, and I do, we must not see one another again.'

She could feel his pain and see it in his eyes, dark now with tears as he gripped her hand so hard his hold was almost hurting her.

'It is for the best,' she told him bravely, 'and because I love and respect you. We cannot sink to the level of conducting an illicit relationship behind your wife's back. You are too honourable a man for that, and I have my own responsibilities now – to the crèche and to Lena as well. She has been so very brave over Charlie's dreadful behaviour, but her reputation is bound to be damaged by her husband-less state and if it were to be known that I was having an affair with a married man her reputation would be further damaged and that would not be fair to her. She is such a darling girl, and so bright and clever, and so eager to make something of herself that . . . well, I want to set her the best example I can. If I could have had a little sister, then Lena would have been the sister I would have wanted.' Bella bowed her head, knowing that somehow, she who had always done exactly what she wished without any regard for others, was now going to do the exact opposite and put the needs of those she loved above her own. She also knew that it was going to hurt – an awful lot – and that it was a pain she would have to carry with her for the rest of her life. Was this what people meant when they said that the war was bringing out the best in people, she wondered grimly, as she tried to swallow against the dry misery gripping her throat.

'We can't see one another ever again, Jan,' she said miserably, 'not even to say hello or to hold hands, not even when we are with other people. It would be wrong now knowing what we both do about our feelings. And besides,' she took a deep breath, looked straight into his eyes and then held her breath against the sheer agony of the pain that felt like a knife being struck straight into her heart, 'if I were ever to see you again I couldn't promise that I would not revert to the old Bella and demand that you have your

411

marriage set aside and annulled so that we could be together.' She couldn't help it: as soon as she had finished speaking the tears rose up and spilled down from her eyes, splashing on their locked hands.

'Oh, my love, my love, I should never have come here and unburdened myself to you. I have been selfish and weak, a coward who was unable to resist his own longing to see you and be with you, and because of that I have hurt you terribly.'

'No,' Bella stopped him fiercely. 'You must not say that because it is not true. You are brave in so many different ways, Jan, and I respect and admire you for that just as much as I love you. Your gift to me of your love is what will give me the strength to carry on, because I knew secretly that I loved you and it hurt so terribly knowing that you did not love me back. I can bear the pain of not sharing my life with you far more easily than I was bearing the pain of loving you and believing that you despised me. My main regret is for you.' Bella lifted her hand and touched the side of his face in a gentle, almost maternal caress. 'I wish with all my heart that your wife could be healed and your marriage made whole. I never knew before that real true love meant putting the happiness of the person you love above your own happiness, but I do understand that now.'

Jan reached for her hands, holding them tightly as he lifted them to his lips, kissing them passion-ately, his emotions overwhelming him so that his tears fell on her skin leaving the long dark lashes she had always resented a mere male possessing, damp and clumped together, his thick dark hair falling over his forehead as he looked at her with a mixture of helpless longing and despair. This was how their child would have looked at her at those times when he was hurt and afraid and, just as though Jan were their child, Bella gathered him in her arms and rocked him gently against her own body, whispering tender words of love and solace over the dark head.

TWENTY-SIX

'Oh, Mum, look, isn't it gorgeous?' Grace laughed out loud with happiness and delight as, in her old bedroom, she held the wedding dress in front of her and then twirled round in an excited pirouette, whilst Jean nodded her head, too overwhelmed by her own maternal emotions to trust herself to speak.

When Francine had first written to say that she had taken advantage of the shops in Cairo to bring back a wedding dress and trousseau for Grace, along with a bridesmaid's dress for Katie, fabrics for brides-maids' dresses for the twins and an outfit for Jean, and that she hoped her family wouldn't feel offended, Jean and Grace had both been speechless with delight and relief.

It was possible to hire wedding gowns, or to borrow them if one had a friend who had one, but the gift of a beautiful new wedding gown like the one that Francine had brought back was luxury indeed.

The gown had a French label sewn inside it and, knowing her younger sister, Jean knew that Fran would not have skimped on the cost. Even in the dull December light the tiny pearls and diamanté drops sewn all over the beautifully fragile net over-dress, which went over the gown's supple white slipper satin, bias-cut Hollywood-style skirt, glowed and twinkled so much that Jean, never normally fanciful, felt as though the dress had captured some flavour of the love and joy that every bride should feel.

'Let's get it on you then, to make sure it fits,' she instructed Grace in a practical voice, pushing aside her own uncharacteristically romantic thoughts.

The parcel Fran had sent from London had arrived only that morning, and the eau-de-Nil gown that Fran had chosen for Katie was already hanging up on the wardrobe to allow the creases to drop out of the slipper satin. Fran had written that she had chosen eau-de-Nil because she had bought the gowns in Cairo, and because she knew the colour would suit both Katie and the twins. Katie's gown was a less dramatic version of Grace's wedding dress, an evening gown really, Jean guessed, with its bias-cut skirt and strapless top, but Fran had bought with it the pret-tiest bolero jacket in marabou dyed to match the gown itself.

Because she hadn't known the twins' size, Fran had brought back eau-de-Nil fabric for their gowns, and that, along with some of the other fabrics Fran had also bought, had arrived a couple of weeks ago and was already with a local dressmaker, who had offered to make the twins' gowns for free in return for a length of the lovely fabric as payment.

Grace slipped off her tweed skirt and pale blue twinset, shivering slightly – more from excitement than cold – as she stood in her satin bra and camiknickers Jean and Katie had made from a cut-down old dress, waiting for Jean to help her into her precious, wonderful gown.

It took them a good five minutes to get the dress on and fastened, but even before she had seen her own reflection in the old-fashioned pier glass, Grace knew how perfect her dress was from her mother's expression and the combination of a shaky smile and the maternal tears she could see on Jean's face.

She shed a few tears herself, along with a gasp of delight, when she did see her own reflection. Surely she wasn't really as slender and so, well . . . bridal-looking?

She swung round, a look on her face that every loving mother hopes to see on her daughter's face when she tries on her wedding gown, her lips trembling as she repeated in a choked voice, 'Oh, Mum . . .' before slipping off the dress to put it down carefully on the bed, and then hugging Jean tight, whilst Jean hugged her back, sniffing away her own happy tears.

As it was to be a winter wedding, and given the problem of getting fresh flowers, Grace had seized on Katie's hesitant suggestion that maybe just a few flowers twined with lots of ivy – something she remembered seeing done at a society wedding break-fast held at the Savoy – might work, and several eager neighbours' children had been dispatched on ivy-hunting missions with strict instructions not to remove it until closer to the big day.

The wedding breakfast was being held in the church hall. Everyone who had been invited, which was most of the church congregation and their neighbours, offering to help out with 'a plate of something', whilst Jean planned to make a trifle using some of the fruit from Sam's allotment that she had bottled earlier in the year.

It wasn't so much Grace's wedding that she and Jean spoke of, though, as they carefully replaced the gown in its tissue paper, but Fran's unexpected marriage.

'She says that she is coming to the wedding and that she's bringing her husband with her, so I suppose he must be all right,' Jean confided to Grace, who burst out laughing and said teasingly, 'Well, of course he will be all right, Mum, otherwise she wouldn't have married him. 'I just wish that Luke could be here for my wedding. Katie looks so sad sometimes although she never complains.'

'I think she might have had a falling out with that girl she works with,' Jean told Grace. 'Has she said anything to you about her? Only Sasha mentioned that the last time they went to the Grafton Carole didn't sit with them like she normally does. Mind you, Sasha also said that Carole seems to have taken up with a couple of lads, even though she's as good as engaged, so I can't say as I blame Katie for keeping her distance.'

'Katie hasn't said a word to me, Mum, but I wouldn't worry too much. I'm sure she would tell you if there was anything really wrong.'

Jean hoped that Grace was right. She loved Katie for her own sake and she was going to miss her this Christmas, but it was only fair that this year Katie should go to London to spend Christmas with her own parents and the friends with whom they shared a house. Hopefully next Christmas this war would be over and Luke would be home safe for good, but Sam had told her only the other day not to get her hopes up. The war, he reckoned would go on for a fair time yet. Like a long debilitating illness, the conditions of living in a country at war were grinding them all down now. Somehow they had found the strength to survive the shock of going to war, and then of Dunkirk, then they had had their spirits lifted by the Battle of Britain before being plunged into the horror of being blitzed, but now, even with the blitz behind them, the prospect of another winter of rationing and going without was dragging everyone down. You could see it in people's faces, grey and pinched with the constant struggle to 'manage' and the constant ache of hunger that came from trying desperately to make the increasingly small rations stretch, with mothers willingly sacrificing their rations for their children and their husbands, and yet somehow having to find from somewhere the energy not just to care for their families but in many cases also having to do their bit for the country as well.

Unaware of the bleak nature of her mother's private thoughts, Grace hummed happily under her breath. It was almost impossible for her to believe that in just over ten days, on the Saturday before Christmas, she and Seb would be married. Her lovely wedding dress could do double duty as an evening gown for those few precious days of their honeymoon in London staying at the Savoy Hotel, where, thanks to the good offices of Katie's father, Seb had been able to book them a room and a table for the Savoy's special dinner dances, a treat to which Fran had added an extra gift – as though she had not already done enough – by getting them tickets for some of the city's best shows. But best of all, better than anything else, no matter how thrilled and grateful she was to everyone for their kindness, was that soon now she would be able to wake up in the arms of the man she loved – her wonderful Seb – her husband.

Grace was thrilled with the cottage she and Seb would be moving into in Whitchurch, tucked securely down at the bottom of a narrow lane, but still close enough for him to be able to cycle to The Old Rectory where he was working. It had two spare bedrooms, three in all, which meant that her family could come down and stay with them.

Grace had also had a letter from the matron of the local hospital, offering her a post as a qualified nurse. The hospital treated local people and had a separate military wing as well.

And almost like icing on the cake, Seb had told Grace that Sybil and a couple of the other probationers and been turned down as not being suitable to continue with their training.

Katie looked sideways along the large desk she and all the other girls in her group at the censorship office shared, to where Carole was seated next to her, and then tried not to let her heart sink even further when she saw that, far from responding to her small overture, Carole was deliberately ignoring her and trying to pretend that she hadn't seen Katie look at her and, even more hurtful and upsetting, that she wasn't aware of why Katie was doing so. They had been so close that Katie had never dreamed that something like this could happen. She had thought that Carole was as committed to Andy as she was to Luke. She felt torn between her loyalties and her own sense of what was right and what was wrong. If she had said nothing and gone along with Carole's plans with regard to the Irish boys, their friendship might still be intact, but how could she have done that and not felt that she was betraying Luke, when she knew how he would feel about her getting friendly with another man? And then there were the Irish boys themselves, with their questions about their work and the discomfort and unease that had brought her. No matter how many times Carole told her that she was being silly when she said they should not discuss their work with them, Katie could not shake off her own belief that it was wrong. And wrong too of the boys to press them so persistently. Perhaps they simply didn't realise the difficult situation they were putting her and Carole in, but what if they did? What if their interest in their work had more to it than simple curiosity and a male desire to tease them?

It had come as a shock to Katie to realise how differently she and Carole felt. She had assumed that because they did the same work that they would feel the same way about it, but Carole's attitude had made it plain that she did not share Katie's sense of responsibility towards the secrecy of their work. Katie had kept to that rule of secrecy even when she had feared that doing so would come between her and Luke, because she had felt it was her duty to do so. Carole, though, seemed to have no such qualms. She had shrugged dismissively when Katie had tried to tell her that she wasn't happy with the Irish boys' questions.

Katie knew that she should have been able to talk about all of this with Carole but Carole got so cross whenever she tried to do so that she had felt obliged to drop the subject.

Now, though, Katie was unhappily aware that

Carole was very cross with her anyway, despite all the efforts she had made to keep the peace.

Carole had made that more than clear, turning her back on Katie whenever Katie tried to talk to her, sitting with someone else at tea break and lunchtime, and generally making it plain that she wanted nothing whatsoever to do with Katie.

Now Katie was in the horrible position of feeling she had to delay going for her dinner so as not to further anger Carole by trying to go at the same time. Her pleading look at her, ignored by Carole, had been a desperate attempt to try to mend things, but it was plain that Carole was so angry with her that she had no wish to repair their damaged friendship.

Now Katie had to sit pink-cheeked with embarrassment as Carole got up and slipped her arm through that of one of the other girls, chattering away to her nineteen to the dozen as they went for their dinner whilst Katie felt obliged to remain where she was, blinking desperately so as not to humiliate herself any further with silly tears.

'Katie?' She had been so wrapped up in her thoughts that she hadn't realised that Anne, who was in charge of their table, had got up and come over to her, the gentle warmth of Anne's hand on her shoulder making her jump.

'I don't want to pry,' Anne told her, slipping into Carole's vacated seat, 'but as table leader naturally I want our table to work together well. It's obvious that something has happened between you and Carole. Would you like to talk about it? I don't want to pry but the two of you were such good friends, and anything that affects the good working of my table is of concern to me.'

421

'There isn't much to talk about really,' Katie answered her uncomfortably. 'I've tried to make things up with Carole but she won't even look at me, never mind let me say anything.'

'Make things up? So you had a quarrel then? That doesn't sound like you, Katie. You're such a kind level-headed sort of girl. What was the quarrel about? Not boys, obviously, since you are engaged to Luke and Carole's as good as engaged to Andy.'

The small tremor that shook Katie's body gave her away even before she felt obliged to say uncomfortably, 'It is sort of about boys. That is to say . . . well, I know that Carole doesn't mean any harm, and there's nothing wrong in wanting to have a good time and go out dancing, but, well, I know that Luke wouldn't like it if he thought that I was going to the Grafton to meet up with someone, even if it was just to dance with them, but Carole doesn't see it that way. Not that I'm saying what she's doing his wrong,' Katie defended her friend determinedly, 'but Andy's different from Luke, and, well, I know I wouldn't like to think that my Luke was meeting up with another girl when he's on leave overseas, even if Liam and Danny say that he and Andy are probably doing that.'

'Liam and Danny?' Anne pressed.

Katie nodded. 'That's these boys that Carole wants us to go dancing with.'

'Well, it is hard when your own chap is far away, and you want to have a bit of fun and go dancing,' Anne sympathised, 'but I do agree with you, Katie, that it isn't very fair to wear a chap's ring and then go out with someone else. As for what your Luke is doing abroad, well, I dare say he feels exactly the same about you as you do about him. Where did you meet these boys?'

'At the Grafton. Jean, that's Luke's mum, had asked me if I'd go with Luke's twin sisters to keep a bit of an eye on them, and then Carole asked if she could come with us, and of course I said yes. Then she met these Irish boys there.' Anne's unquestioning sympathy was such a relief that it was easy for Katie to confide in her and spill out all her pent-up worries. 'And that makes it worse somehow – them being Irish and not in uniform – although I know that that's only because they're working down at the docks.'

'I'll bet they've silver tongues and good looks if they're anything like the Irish I've met,' Anne laughed.

Katie gave her a grateful look. 'Yes, they have, and I suppose that's why Carole told them—' She stopped abruptly, her face burning with guilt and discomfort.

'That's why she told them what?' Anne pressed.

'Oh, nothing, really,' Katie denied.

For a minute there was silence and then Anne said gravely, 'Katie, I know that Carole is your friend and naturally, as a good friend to her you want to protect her. I know too that you aren't the kind of girl to go talking about anyone behind their backs, but we are at war, Katie, and in a war situation a person's loyalty to their country must come before everything and everyone else. Now, is there something that, having searched your heart and your conscience, you think I should know that you have not yet told me?'

Katie bit her lip and then admitted reluctantly, 'Carole met the boys first. There were four of them then, although it's only Liam and Danny that come and join us now. When she first introduced Danny to me he started to joke with me about reading people's love letters.'

'So he knew that you worked here?'

Katie nodded, adding quickly, 'But that doesn't mean that it was Carole who told him.'

They were not after all supposed to tell anyone about their work.

'Have these young men asked you any other questions about your work?'

'They've tried to, but I said straight out that I wouldn't talk about it.'

'And you'd have preferred to have nothing more to do with these young men, but Carole wants to and she's quarrelled with you because you won't, is that it?'

Unhappily Katie agreed. 'I feel so bad about it all, especially now that I'm telling tales on her, and—'

'You have nothing to feel bad about, Katie. Now, why don't you go and get yourself some lunch?'

TWENTY-SEVEN

As she stood in her mother's kitchen on the opposite side of the table from the doctor, her hands on the back of a chair to support herself, and listened to what he had to say, Bella knew that she had been wrong to think that in facing up to the fact that she could never truly be with the man she loved and who loved her, and that their love must be sacrificed in the name of honour and duty and marriage vows already made, she had faced the worst thing she ever would have to face; the most personally intimately emotionally painful, perhaps, but there were other kinds of pain, as she had just discovered.

When she had received a furious telephone call at work from her father, demanding that she come and remove her mother from his office, 'otherwise I'll call the police and she'll end up in a cell,' Bella had dropped everything immediately to go to telephone for a taxi to take her down to her father's office. Having bribed the taxi driver very generously indeed to wait for her, she hurried inside, where she had found her mother, wearing her dressing gown and her slippers, and very obviously the worse for drink, raging at both Pauline and Edwin between bouts of hysterical screaming and sobbing.

Somehow Bella had managed to persuade her mother to get into the car and had brought her home, having had to telephone her own house, where thankfully Gavin had been working finishing off the nursery, to ask him to come round and help her with her mother whilst they waited for the doctor.

It had been her mother's violence that had made her think of ringing Gavin, and now Bella's cheekbone was swelling with what would be a bruise where her mother had lashed out at her when Bella had been bundling her into the car.

Very discreetly and tactfully Gavin had offered to take Lena, who had insisted on accompanying him 'in case I can help', home, to give Bella privacy to talk to the doctor about Vi, but Lena had refused to leave, taking hold of Bella's hand and saying stoutly, 'I'm not leaving Bella to have to deal with this on her own, Gavin, not after all that she's done for me.'

The doctor had nodded approvingly, despite Bella's protests that Lena needed to think of herself and her baby and not worry about her.

Now the four of them were in the kitchen, and Vi was upstairs in bed, and very soon a private home nurse would be arriving to sit with her overnight to make sure that she didn't come to any harm.

'I can't believe that Mummy actually walked all the way down to Daddy's office in her night things, like that. She's always been so particular and so proud. She was even refusing to go to my cousin Grace's wedding because she doesn't want her sister to know what's happened. I just don't know what to do, Doctor. Somehow she's still managing to get hold of some gin, on the black market, I suppose.' Bella shivered, thinking of the risks her mother must be running dealing with black market crooks in her openly vulnerable state. 'I suppose the best thing would be for me to move Mummy in with me and then see if I can find someone to look after her.'

That was the last thing Bella wanted, but duty was duty, and Vi was her mother.

'I think for the moment that the best thing for your mother, Bella, would be for her to be admitted to The Sisters of Our Lady Nursing Home, where she can be properly looked after and rested,' the doctor announced firmly.

And where there would be no alcohol and twenty-four-hour-a-day nursing care to make sure that she could not go out as she had done today, Bella recognised.

'I don't want to think that Mummy is being punished, Doctor. After all, it's really Daddy's fault that she's doing what she is.'

'There is no question of that, Bella, but we do need to get your mother's health back to normal.'

A ring on the front doorbell heralded the arrival of the nurse, a no-nonsense middle-aged woman in a uniform so starched that it crackled, and yet who, whilst looking rather fierce, somehow managed to reassure Bella with her manner that her mother would be in good hands.

'How long will Mummy need to be in the nursing home for?' Bella asked the doctor anxiously. 'Only if it is for any length of time I should really tell Charlie. Not that he will do anything. He's not even written to her since Daddy left.'

427

'I hope not for too long,' was the doctor's ambiguous response, as he picked up his bag and headed for the hall, where Bella handed him his coat and then waited whilst he put on his hat.

When Bella returned to the kitchen it held that kind of silence that said that its occupants had been discussing the situation in her absence.

This was confirmed when Lena looked at Gavin and then at Bella and then said determinedly, 'Me and Gavin have just been talking, Bella, and we both think that you should have a word with your mum's sister.'

'Auntie Jean? But she and Mummy hardly ever speak to one another, and Mummy didn't even want her to know about Daddy leaving.'

'Well, maybe your mum doesn't want her to know, but what about you needing someone in your family that you can turn to, Bella? It's not right that you're having to cope with your mum carrying on like she is on your own, and I reckon from what you've told me about your auntie that she'd want to know anyway, what with her and your mum being twins.'

Lena did have a point, Bella admitted, and besides, Jean would have to be told something. After all, Bella could hardly turn up at Grace's wedding without her mother without saying something, and if she didn't go at all that would be an awful insult.

'I'll think about it,' she promised Lena.

Katie felt dreadful. She felt she should not have confided in Anne, even if both Anne and the supervisor had insisted that just the opposite was the case. She knew that.

Certainly Carole felt that she had betrayed her and let her down. Not that Carole had said so directly to Katie. And now it was too late for Carole to tell her anything because not only had she been dismissed, she had also been sent home and warned not to make or receive any contact from the young Irishman whose company she had enjoyed so much that she had been prepared to put her relationship with Andy at risk.

There had been a horrible incident after she had been summoned by their supervisor and before she had been escorted out of the building and, so it was rumoured, to her auntie's to collect her things, and from there to a new billet and job in some remote part of the country.

Katie, unaware initially that Carole had been summoned by their supervisor, had not known what was happening until Carole had been marched back to her desk virtually under escort, and had then burst out bitterly in front of everyone else at the table that Katie was a traitor to their friendship and that she had deliberately lied about her to get her into trouble, and that she, Carole, intended to make sure that Katie paid for that disloyalty.

What had made things so much worse had been that despite her nastiness, Carole had been crying and Katie had known immediately just how hard her former friend had been hit by the discovery that her friendship with Liam was going to be stopped by a far higher authority than that of a mere over-seas boyfriend. Carole had been distraught at the thought of never seeing Liam again and Katie had recognised with a sinking heart that Carole's rela-tionship with the young Irishman had become far more intimate and intense than Katie had been allowed to know. It was all horrible and awful. They had been such good friends and Katie felt bereft without that friendship, as well as terribly guilty about poor Carole's fate.

This dreadful war . . . She longed for it to be over. It was nearly six months since Luke had been sent overseas, as long a period as that during which she had known him and spent with him. Sometimes, no matter how much she gazed at his photograph – one that she had taken herself before he had left, and in which he was smiling at her with those lovely bright blue eyes of his, even if the photograph did not show their colour – she felt panicky and afraid that somehow her memory was losing him and that he and their love were slipping away from her. They might write to one another of how strong their love was, but writing those words wasn't like holding one another and whispering them. Even the Luke smell of the woollen scarf she had teased from him before he had left had gone from the wool, so that now when she buried her face in it with her eyes tightly closed, and tried to imagine that she was breathing in the scent of his skin, all she could really smell was the carbolic soap smell of her own hands.

She needed him so desperately now to comfort her and to tell her that she had done the right thing. But had she? Luke was fiercely loyal to his men, and what was Andy going to think and feel when he found out what she had done?

War was so confusing and muddling at times. Of course Katie knew that her loyalty was to her country above and beyond everything and anyone else, but right now that felt like a cold treacherous loyalty that had involved her in hurting someone who had been a good friend, and no amount of reassurance from anyone at work could ease the pain of that feeling.

TWENTY-EIGHT

Bella took a deep breath as she got off the ferry, and looked up towards the city of Liverpool itself. Her tummy was churning with nerves, and despite the bone-chilling cold of the wind whipping across the wave-laden grey water of the Atlantic beyond the Mersey bar, her face was burning with apprehension. What if Auntie Jean wasn't in? What if she refused to see her? What if . . . ?

But she mustn't think of those things. Those were the kind of thought the old Bella would have had, and she wasn't that Bella any more. So much had happened to her to change her these last few months that Bella could scarcely remember exactly what the old Bella had been like. She certainly knew that the old Bella would never for a moment have felt humbled and grateful for the love of a man so dear to her that he meant everything, whilst at the same time knowing that that love could never be publicly acknowledged or privately given. And yet the gift of Jan's love had brought to her heart a peaceful joy that had eased so many sore places inside her that she could only rejoice in it with a quiet dignity and delight that needed no public recognition. It was

431

right and proper that Jan should support and look after his poor unhappy wife. Bella knew that having seen and known so much of the pain that came from broken vows, she could never live happily knowing that she was responsible for the destruction of another's marriage, and wisely she knew too that it would not sit easily with Jan's sense of honour to do so either.

She had had a visit from Maria – on her own, without Bettina – and whilst at first she had feared that Jan must have confided in his mother and that she had come to berate her, Maria had quickly made it plain that she had come in the spirit of friendship and a new start. Jan had indeed told his mother of his feelings for Bella, and of Bella's own decision that they must put their love for one another to one side for the sake of his marriage.

'You are a good person. You must be if my Jan loves you,' Maria had told her in her heavily accented English. 'And now you have proved this with your sacrifice of your own happiness.'

'I am sure that Jan's wife will realise how lucky she is and that . . . that she will want to become a proper wife to him,' Bella had responded, squeezing out the words from a heart that felt as though it was being crushed at the thought of Jan being happy with someone else and not knowing how she could bear it, whilst also knowing that for Jan's sake and the sake of his marriage she must.

'I had not thought well of you but now I see that I was wrong. You are a woman of great love and great courage,' Maria had said to her, touching her hand and then her face as though she genuinely cared about Bella's own feelings and understood them, and Bella knew that in Jan's mother she now had an ally and not an enemy.

It wasn't a particularly long walk from the terminal to her auntie Jean's house, but although Bella had initially stepped out briskly, as much to escape the cold wind as anything else, by the time she had reached the pre-Christmas bustle of St John's Market, with its long queues of housewives eager to take advantage of Churchill's edict that every family was to have the benefit of a traditional Christmas dinner, her walking pace had slowed, hampered by her growing anxiety about how she might be received. Her auntie Jean had no reason to welcome her, after all. Bella could think of a dozen and more instances when she had given her mother's twin sister every reason to dislike her intensely, and something in Bella's own growing sense of awareness made her worry about the moral rightness of her asking her aunt for help now at this time of her mother's need when Vi had been so eager in the past to look down on her less materially well off twin.

But somehow or other, even though she was dragging her footsteps, she had reached her auntie's street, and with her heart in her mouth Bella walked down it until at last she was opening the neat white-painted wooden gate and walking up the path to the front step to ring the front doorbell.

When Jean opened her front door to find her niece, Bella, standing on the step she was so astonished that for a few seconds she just stood there staring at her without saying a word. This was, after all, the first time that Bella had ever paid them a visit, but then when Jean saw the anxiety in Bella's eyes and registered the way she made to step back from the door, ducking her head in exactly the same way that Lou did when she felt abashed, Jean reacted instinctively to the need she sensed in her niece and reached out to put her hand on Bella's arm, saying warmly, 'Bella, how lovely to see you. Come on in.'

Her aunt's kindness was almost too much for Bella, and she had to search in her pocket for her handkerchief as she followed Jean into a warm cosy hallway.

'Goodness, it's cold out there,' Jean shivered. 'Let me take your coat and then I'll put the kettle on. You won't mind if we go into the back room, I hope, Bella, only it's warmer in there.'

Obediently Bella handed over her coat and her hat, unable to stop herself from contrasting her auntie Jean's behaviour with that of her own mother. Jean had natural maternal warmth about her that felt like being wrapped in a cosy blanket, Bella acknowledged as she followed Jean into the back room with its warm comforting smell of home-made soup from the pan simmering gently on the gas stove.

'You must be wondering what I'm doing here,' Bella began as soon as Jean had coaxed her into a chair. 'It's about Mummy, Auntie Jean.' Bella couldn't help herself, the strain of the last few weeks brought sharp tears to her eyes, revealing to Bella herself the full weight of the burden she had been carrying as her emotions overwhelmed her.

Jean lifted an anxious hand to her chest where her heart had started to pound. She and Vi might not be close any more and indeed there were many occasions on which her twin exasperated and even annoyed her, but Vi was still Jean's twin, for all that there were many things she had done and many sadnesses for which she was responsible that Jean deplored.

'Something's happened to Vi?' Jean demanded shakily.

Bella bit her lip. This was so very hard to do. She felt both like a traitor to her mother and very conscious of the fact that her visit could be interpreted as a way of getting out of her own responsibility towards Vi.

'It's nothing for you to worry about, Auntie Jean. I know how busy you'll be, with the wedding and everything, it's just that I thought, well, it was Lena who said I should come and see you really. She's got ever such a sensible head on her shoulders, despite her being so young . . .' Bella broke off and gave her aunt a rueful smile. 'Here's me going on about Lena and I dare say you won't even know who she is. She's a girl that Charlie got into trouble and then abandoned. She's living with me now, though, and she and the baby will be properly provided for, no mistake about that.'

Whilst Jean was still struggling to take this surprising information on board, and the even more surprising discovery that Bella, the niece she had always thought of as the most selfish and uncaring young woman there could possibly be, had somehow been transformed into someone who had taken upon herself such a heavy responsibility, Bella continued bleakly, 'I know that Mummy doesn't want you to hear about this, and I do feel mean for telling you, but, well, the fact is, Auntie Jean, that Daddy has done the most dreadful thing. He has left Mummy to go and live with his assistant. He's making Mummy divorce him. I've done my best and I've managed to get the house out of him for her, and a decent allowance, but, well, you can imagine how she feels.' Bella gave a sad shake of her head. 'She's taken it so very badly – the shame of it, you know, and people knowing, even though she isn't the one who has done anything wrong. But that's not really why I've come. You see, poor Mummy has started drinking, and our doctor has had her placed in a nursing home so that she can be properly looked after. She will be able to get well again, but of course she won't be at Grace's wedding and . . .'

Before Bella could say any more Jean went over to her and took her in her arms, holding her tightly.

'Oh, Bella, love, when did all this happen?'

'A while ago,' Bella admitted tearfully. Her aunt smelled of warmth and lavender water, and somehow weirdly of Bella's own childhood, and a sudden memory came to her of being a little girl sitting on her auntie's knee in a sunny back garden.

'And you've been struggling with all of this on your own,' Jean reproached her.

'Lena's been a total brick even though baby is due towards the end of Janaury. She was the one who urged me to come and tell you.'

'I should think so as well. What about your Charlie?'

'I've told him about Daddy leaving, but he hasn't come home or anything. I dare say he won't want Daphne's family knowing, and neither, of course, would Mummy.

'It was horrid having to get her from Daddy's office, Auntie Jean. She had gone all that way there in her dressing gown. I've tried to stop her getting any more gin, but . . .'

'Oh, Bella.' Jean felt guilty as well as shocked. Surely as Vi's twin she ought to have sensed that something was wrong, and it went against everything that Jean as a loving mother believed in that someone of Bella's age should have to deal with such a situation all by herself.

'I'm so frightened for Mummy, Auntie Jean,' Bella admitted, voicing her fear for the first time.

'Don't be, love. We'll sort something out. Where did you say she was? Only I'd like to go and see her if she's allowed to have visitors.'

Bella shook her head. 'It's a nursing home in Wallasey, run by nuns, but Mummy isn't allowed any visitors at the moment. She won't be coming to the wedding, of course . . .'

'But you must come, Bella, please. I'll worry about you if you don't,' Jean told her firmly, not hesitating to use the emotional blackmail she would once have thought would have no effect on her niece what-soever. But Bella had changed, Jean could see that, and now in the new maturity she could see in Bella's pretty face Jean could see a far greater resemblance to her own Grace.

'The Ambassador has said that seeing as we're going to Liverpool, he wants me to show my face at some high-level security place they've got up there, and give a bit of support to one of our generals who has been invited to attend some kind of official recep-tion party.'

Fran understood. She was perfectly happy to support Brandon in his role as a young American airman attached to the American Embassy in an unnamed diplomatic role, all the more so because she suspected that his health was deteriorating faster than he was prepared to admit. He had lurched into her a couple of times when they had been walking together recently, the lurch of a young man who might have had too much to drink, perhaps, in the eyes of the outer world, but to Fran one of the signs of the progress of his illness the specialist had warned her to be on the lookout for. It had surprised her how protective she had become of her young husband and how very deeply involved with him she was – not as a wife or as a lover, but more as a cross between an older sister and a mother. It made her heart ache for him to know that his own parents had virtually turned their backs on him to such an extent that he felt they would reject him outright if they knew of his condition. His father would never tolerate anything or anyone that was not first rate and perfect, Brandon had told Fran, and his mother would throw a hysterical fit and then blame him for being ill and distressing her. Neither of them would give him the emotional support Fran knew he needed. But if he didn't have them at least he did have her, and she was determined to be with him through everything, no matter what.

Lou stared blindly at the shop window. She had no real recollection of having walked here from the exchange but obviously she had done. There was certainly nothing in the shop window – a run-down haberdasher's – to merit her fixed gaze. Her heart was pounding and there was a horrid sick feeling in her tummy. She had really gone and done it now. The supervisor had said as much when she had torn a strip off her and told her in that frosty voice of hers that she was jeopardising Sasha's chances of being given a permanent position, never mind her own with her bad behaviour. Sasha had cried afterwards and begged her to try harder, but she had tried, she really had. However, the harder she tried the more she hated working at the exchange and the more she wanted to run away from everything that working there meant. Sasha didn't understand that, though; she didn't care about how she, Lou, was feeling because all Sasha cared about now was that stupid boy Bobby.

Lou turned round, apologising as she bumped into two smart-looking girls in WRAF uniforms, her heart twisting with fresh misery. How happy they looked in their uniforms. How exciting their lives must be compared with her own. Only the other week one of the girls they'd been at school with, whom they'd bumped into at the Grafton, had been full of how a cousin of hers had joined the WRAF and was actually flying aeroplanes from factories to RAF bases in England. Just imagining having a job like that, and getting away from the exchange and Liverpool and all those things that were making her feel so miserable, including Sasha. Lou knew that she ought to go back to the exchange. She had, after all, walked out without asking permission, but she just couldn't bring herself to do so. She looked down the street, her attention caught by a second group of young women in WRAF uniform, coming out of a recruitment office further down the street. How she envied them.

TWENTY-NINE

Fran smiled at the commanding officer in charge of Joint Operations at Derby House, the headquarters of the North-West Approaches, whilst keeping her arm tucked discreetly through Brandon's. They had arrived in Liverpool earlier in the day, and despite the fact that the train journey had resulted in him being dreadfully unwell, Brandon had still insisted on them meeting Jean and Grace, and Grace's husband-to-be, Seb, at Lyons Corner House for afternoon tea.

Fran had seen the way Jean's eyes had widened when she had realised how young Brandon was, but tactfully her sister had not said anything, not even when she and Fran had gone to the cloakroom together, other than to ask Fran if she was happy.

'Very,' Fran had told her promptly, and surprisingly she had discovered that it was true. It was as though Brandon's need of her had given her a purpose in life that had somehow taken away some of the pain of her loss of Jack and Marcus.

She hadn't said anything to Jean about Brandon's illness. There would, after all, be time enough to explain all about afterwards.

And now here they were at this very military reception, with all the top brass lined up to greet their guests, and the American general, who had initially simply been in England on a diplomatic visit, was now anxious to talk to a fellow American, especially one with American Embassy accreditation, about the bombing of Pearl Harbor by the Japanese on 7 December.

The attack had shocked America, propelling the country towards war, and patriotic young men were rushing to join up for military service. Brandon had been filled with helpless anger when they had heard the news, plainly desperate to do his bit and yet at the same time knowing that his health would mean that he could be putting those men he was serving with at risk.

Fran had slipped into her official role as the wife of a very wealthy and patrician young American with the ease that came from years of being in the public eye as a singer. Working for ENSA had honed her existing small talk skills so that she was easily able to converse with the military top brass whilst at the same time sympathising with the American general over the language difficulties he was encountering.

'Two nations divided by a common language,' Fran quoted to him with a smile.

To which he had nodded his head and announced emphatically, 'Now ain't that just the truth, ma'am.'

'Career soldier,' Brandon murmured in her ear, as they stood to one side, 'and definitely not WASP, not with that accent.'

'Don't be such a terrible snob,' Fran whispered back teasingly, managing to look at ease and sound light-hearted, whilst at the same time keeping a careful eye on Brandon, whom she was sure was feeling far from well, even though he was refusing to admit it.

She was just about to suggest to him that they use the excuse of Grace's wedding in the morning to make their escape when the door to the large room opened and a fresh group of uniformed men came in. Since she was facing the door Fran had a good view of them and her heart rolled over like a boulder crashing into her ribs when she saw that one of them was Marcus. A leaner Marcus, perhaps, and not as tanned as he had been in Cairo, but his dark hair was still as thick, and still in need of a cut, whilst his height and the breadth of his shoulders set him apart from the other older men he was with.

Marcus. Her heart felt as though it had been seized in a giant vice, but she had no idea that she had said his name until she heard Brandon querying brusquely, 'Marcus?' before he turned to stare at the new arrivals.

'Ah, here's Colonel Stafford, who is in charge of our liaison group here,' the CO exclaimed. 'Do let me introduce you.'

It was too late to escape. The American general was turning towards the colonel and extending his hand. Naturally, Brandon had to follow suit, as the colonel strode towards them, followed by his entourage, which of course included Marcus.

Fran was guided forward, with a professional smile and a firm hand in the small of her back from one of the smartly turned-out and very pretty WRAFs who were on 'hostess' duty, and introduced as, 'Mrs Brandon Walter Adams.'

The colonel, bluff and burly and red-faced, took her hand and held it briefly as though afraid to shake it in case he broke it. Fran had already noticed that American military and diplomatic men gave a much harder handshake that their British counterparts, accompanied by a much wider smile, although as yet she had not come to any conclusions as to whether they were 'just being American' or making a point of showing their superior strength. Having worked in Hollywood she tended to think it was the former – after all, everything in America was 'bigger' than its British equivalent.

'Major Marcus Linton.'

It couldn't be avoided, and somehow Fran managed to hold her gaze steady as Marcus took her hand and she forced herself to say calmly, 'Marcus, how nice to see you again.'

'Oh, you've already met.' The WRAF looked slightly put out.

'I was with an ENSA group in Cairo and the major had the unrewarding task of shepherding us around safely,' Fran explained with one of the bright professional smiles she had learned long ago to use to protect her real emotions.

'You were with ENSA?' The WRAF's tone and glance were speculative and assessing, but Fran ignored the subtle challenge in the younger girl's manner. What did it matter to her now what another girl, who obviously felt a proprietary interest in Marcus, should think about her?

The light from the unexpectedly extravagantly illuminated chandelier fell on Fran's left hand, sparking a riot of flashing colour from her engagement ring – a gift from Brandon that she had told him he should not have given her but which she wore to please him.

She could see Marcus looking down at it, and she

was not surprised as, when the WRAF was called away to talk to someone else, the minute they were left on their own Marcus said pointedly, 'No need to ask how life is treating you, obviously.'

Holding on to her anger and her pain, and conscious of Brandon's presence and the reality of their marriage, Fran told him quietly, 'When I was younger I used to feel envious of those people who are able to make such absolute judgements of others on the strength of what lies on the surface. Now that I'm older, though, I tend to feel rather sorry for them because I've grown to realise that their judgement is as superficial and shallow as their own emotions, with no real depth or understanding. Please excuse me. I must rejoin my husband.'

It was over, done; and only she would ever know how much, instead of walking away from Marcus, she had wanted to throw herself into his arms and beg him to hold her there for ever.

Lou felt dreadfully sick and shaky, and yet excited at the same time. She had had to hold her breath whilst she had lied about her age in case she was challenged but she hadn't been, and now it was done and she had joined the Women's Royal Air Force.

At the beginning of December, Mr Churchill had announced that all young men and women of sixteen had to register their names as a first step towards going into uniform, and all unmarried women between the ages of twenty and thirty were to be called up to serve in the police, the fire services and the armed forces, whilst married women and single women up to the age of forty had to register as available labour.

Because of that her dad wasn't going to be able to put his foot down and refuse to give his permission for her to join the WRAF, as she knew he would have done before the new rules had been brought in. It was true, of course, that girls were supposed to be at least eighteen before they could go into uniform, but no one had made any comment to her about her age when she had been interviewed. The country needed girls like her, she had been told approvingly.

She had been given an address to go to on Monday to be measured for her uniform and to go through the rest of the enlistment process, but there was definitely no going back. Not now that she had signed on the dotted line.

Her father would be furious and her mother would cry, but what about Sasha? Would she secretly be glad that they were going to be separated? It would certainly mean that she could spend as much time as she wanted with her precious boyfriend, Lou thought miserably, the shock of what she had done suddenly bringing her down out of her clouds of euphoria at her daring, to the harsh reality of what her actions actually meant.

Panic mixed with pain filled her, but then another girl emerged from the recruitment office and smiled at her, exclaiming in a jolly way, 'Golly, I never thought I'd really have the guts to do it, but I have. I keep telling myself that it will be spiffing fun, especially if I get to learn to fly, although only a few of the girls do get to do that.'

'That's what I want to do as well,' Lou agreed firmly.

THIRTY

Jean sighed in semi-protest at the sound of yet another caller knocking on the front door. She'd had that many people coming round these last few days as the wedding day drew closer, that her voice was hoarse from reminding everyone not to leave the back door open too long and allow the precious heat to escape. Not that the house was likely to get cold with all the cooking and baking that had been done, and all the rushing about that was going on.

'Go and get the door, will you, Sasha love?' Jean instructed, carefully measuring a precious spoonful of cooking sherry into the juice from the bottled pears she was planning to put in the trifle. She'd had neighbours coming round virtually all week bringing their cut-glass trifle bowls, and spare plates, along with offers of whatever other help they could give.

At least one of the benefits of a winter wedding was that she didn't need to worry about any of the food going off, Jean acknowledged, as Sasha returned, accompanied by Amy Preston from several doors away.

'My, but it's lovely and warm in here, Jean,' Amy announced. Her own nose was pink from the late December cold.

'Sasha, take that dish from Mrs Preston, and her coat so that she can sit down and get a bit of a warm. I'd offer you a cup of tea, only my Sam will be back soon and I want to get this on the trifle sponges before he comes in. You know what men are like. He'll be expecting his tea, wedding or no wedding,' Jean warned her visitor tactfully, not wanting to be rude or ungrateful for her offer of help but not wanting to encourage her to stay for a long chat either, when she had so much to do.

'Bertha from across from me said as how you were wanting some extra trifle dishes, so I thought I'd pop down with one,' Amy told Jean as she handed over the dish, and then her coat to Sasha, before settling down on the kitchen chair Jean's last visitor had left pulled up close to the warmth of the oven.

The kitchen smelled of the ham Jean had been roasting earlier in the day. Sam, along with several of the other allotment holders, was part-owner in a pig, and with Grace's wedding to cater for Sam had managed to claim a good-sized gammon joint as his part of the animal.

There was also a pressed tongue in the larder, cooked earlier in the week and now weighted down ready to be carved up for the buffet.

First thing tomorrow morning Jean and some of her neighbours were going to go to the church hall to give it a thorough clean through before they started to decorate it for the wedding breakfast.

'I suppose you'll have to have one of them cardboard wedding cakes?' Amy asked Jean.

Jean agreed. 'Them's the rules now, so we don't have any choice, and my Sam's a stickler for not buying anything on the black market.'

447

'Good for him,' Amy said stoutly. 'I admire a man of principle, and heaven knows them poor lads in the Merchant Navy shouldn't have to put their lives at risk for a bit of black market stuff.'

Later on that evening, Jean intended to try on her own wedding outfit, if she could make five minutes to do so, since Grace had insisted that she wanted to see her mother in her finery. The hospital had given Grace a few precious extra days off and she would be coming home this Wednesday evening to stay until the wedding on Saturday.

Tomorrow, though, she was going to Whitchurch, where she and Seb were giving their new home a coat of fresh distemper and arranging the furniture they had been buying, as and when they could, keeping it stored down at the depot where Sam worked. A friend of a friend of Sam's had offered to take their bits and pieces down to Whitchurch for them, and in addition to paying him for his trouble Grace and Jean had agreed to give his wife a length of the twins' bridesmaids' dress fabric for their daughter's twenty-first birthday.

Fran, bless her, hadn't forgotten Jean in her shopping expedition in Cairo, including a lovely coat and skirt ensemble for her, complete with a blouse and accessories. The fabric was so luxurious that Jean was worried about catching the delicacy of the pretty chiffon blouse. Her hands had gone that rough with all the extra work and cooking the wedding involved. Jean remembered that her grandmother had always sworn by goose grease for chapped dry hands, but even if she had been able to get hold of some, Jean didn't fancy smelling of goose grease all through her daughter's big day.

Whilst she listened to her neighbour's chatter and answered her questions, Jean was mentally going over her list of things to be done. Grace, normally so calm and practical, had started to get bridal nerves and worry that everything wouldn't go according to plan. If she'd asked Jean once she'd asked her a hundred times if she was sure that everyone would fit into the church hall and that they'd have enough food.

'They're coming to see you married, not get a free meal,' Jean had told Grace firmly. 'They won't be worrying about that and you shouldn't either. Besides, thanks to everyone helping out we'll have plenty to go round.'

Seb's landlady had generously offered Seb an un-expectedly spare room in her house for his parents, and so naturally Jean had felt obliged to add her name to the guest list, which seemed to be growing by the day as neighbours and friends came round to offer their help. Seb and his parents would be travel-ling up from Whitchurch on the first train of the morning, and out of respect for the tradition that the groom should not see his bride until she walked down the aisle to him on her father's arm, Seb and his parents would be going from the station to the home of one of Jean and Sam's neighbours to change into their wedding finery before making their way to the church.

Jean was keeping her fingers crossed that Saturday would be a fine dry day. With petrol being as scarce as it was, and Sam having the feelings he did about the nation's resources, it had been decided that everyone, including Grace and Sam, would walk to the church, which was after all only just past the end of the road.

A neighbour had produced from her attic a dark

449

red velvet hooded cloak that she had worn as Rose Queen years ago in her youth, and Jean had taken advantage of the steam produced when she had preboiled the ham and the tongue to bring the pile back on the velvet before hanging it up in the bathroom for a final steam over bowls of water containing bags of lavender from the allotment, to ensure that it smelled sweetly of summer rather than strongly of cooking meat.

With so many people putting themselves out to help them, they had ended up virtually having to invite the whole street to the wedding.

Not that Jean minded. The more people that came to wish Grace and Seb a happy future, the better, as far as she was concerned.

Sasha had barely shown Amy Preston out of the front door when Katie came in through the back door, announcing, 'I've brought you this, Jean. They were selling them in Lewis's. They'd just had a delivery, and I thought you might like it as an early Christmas present, with all the extra work you've been doing.'

Jean could have cried when she saw the small pot of hand cream that Katie was holding out to her. Sam had also arrived home and was suggesting that they might try a slice of the ham with their tea just to see how it was, causing her to insist vehemently, 'Sam Campion, you'll do no such thing!'

Jean was known for the excellence of her baked ham, roasted to her own special recipe of honey and brown sugar spiced with cloves, and before the war no big party had been complete without one of Jean's baked hams, but such treats had become a rare luxury now.

By the time Grace had arrived a little later in the evening, Jean had decided that since she was going to have to try on her outfit for Grace to see, they might as well have a proper dress rehearsal and all try on their finery, although she instructed the twins to wash their hands first.

Sam was instructed to stay in the kitchen with his paper, whilst the first floor of the small house rang with excited female voices, dropping to an awed hush after Grace had been helped into her gown first. Naturally, there had to be that little moment that they all shared, when they all looked at her and then at one another, and no words were needed to tell of their pride and their love.

Then Jean was bustling the twins into their dresses, shaking her head a little ruefully at the way they were now several inches taller than she, tall and leggy with narrow waists and small bosoms, and then brushing away a few maternal tears when she saw how grown-up they looked in their gowns, not girls any more but proper young women, with their slim figures and their brown hair shining like burnished conkers under the electric light. Katie too looked lovely in her dress, her manner everything that a bride's main female supporter should be, calm and loving, as she organised the twins and helped Jean to check that the bows at the back of their sashes were tied properly and Grace's train smoothed out.

'Come on, Mum,' Grace urged her. 'You've got to put yor outfit on as well.'

Jean had never had an outfit as expensive or as elegant as this one. She had known the moment she had seen it that it was something very special. The blouse was ecru chiffon with a high ruffled

451

neckline and tiny pearl buttons that fastened all the way down the pintucked front and up the sleeves. The peachy brown coat and skirt she was to wear with it were in the finest silkiest wool she had ever touched – cashmere, Grace had said it was, looking knowledgeable and awed. The skirt was narrow, somehow making her look much slimmer than she was, the coat that went over it three-quarter length, with a soft swing to it. The front of the coat and the collar were trimmed in chocolate-brown velvet frogging, and the chocolate-brown velvet hat that went with it was decorated with matching frogging. Jean could hardly believe she was to wear such a wonderful outfit. It was totally impractical – something she could never wear again in her everyday life – and yet despite her normally practical nature she was as excited as though she was still a little girl at the thought of wearing something so very pretty.

Fran had thought of everything, because there were even chocolate-brown lizard-skin shoes and gloves, and a matching handbag.

Very carefully Jean changed into her outfit, her skin going faintly pink when she saw the way that even the twins' eyes widened in admiration once she had everything on.

It was left to Grace to speak, her voice breaking slightly as she put her hand on Jean's arm and said, 'Oh, Mum . . .'

The final two days before the wedding passed in a haze of scrubbing the church hall floors, dusting chairs and ironing loaned tablecloths and even white sheets to cover the slightly shabby trestle tables, whilst the younger ones busied themselves decorating the hall with trails of ivy, ornamented with some white ribbon a neighbour had found tucked away in a drawer and offered as her contribution to the big day.

It was hard work, but the tasks were broken up with shared laughter when they all stopped to eat the meat-paste sandwiches Jean had made and drink tea from one of the borrowed urns.

The local hairdresser had promised to fit Jean in for a shampoo and set the night before the wedding, leaving the early morning of the wedding day free for Grace and her bridesmaids.

Jean would have liked to have invited Seb and his parents over for a family meal on the Friday night before the wedding, but they had all agreed that it would be impractical with the travelling involved. She and Seb's stepmother had been corresponding with one another ever since Seb and Grace had become engaged. Photographs had been exchanged, and shared goals for their children's future established, and Jean had no qualms about the warmth of the reception Grace would receive from her in-laws. As for Seb, well, she and Sam already thought of him as a member of their family.

Finally, by Friday teatime, everything was ready: the church hall transformed and the tables laid with immaculate white cloths and borrowed cutlery and china.

The top table – a long trestle table covered in two white sheets and a tablecloth – was decorated along the front with more garlands of ivy, whilst a last-minute addition – a pair of five-branched silver-plated candelabra, loaned by yet another neighbour – held pride of place on the top table, ivy twined round the silver, 'pretend' candles made from cardboard painted white, taking the place of the completely unavailable real thing. She'd have to make sure that no one forgot and tried to light them, Jean acknowledged, as she gave the silent, waiting room a final anxious look before closing and locking the door.

All she had to do now was go home and have a quick bath, and then get to the hairdresser's. Everyone bar Grace had to have their bath tonight, leaving the bathroom free for Grace in the morning prior to going to get her own hair done.

The weather simply could not have been better, Jean decided, as she took her place in the front pew, preening herself just a little in her beautiful new outfit, knowing from the way the guests had craned their necks to get a glimpse of her that it looked wonderful. They had woken to blue skies and sharp winter sunshine, and now Jean's heart was thumping with a mixture of pride and nervousness as she waited alone for Sam and Grace to arrive.

Jean guessed that every mother felt as she did on her daughter's wedding day: filled with a mixture of love and pride and loss, and that every mother too thought that her daughter was the most beautiful bride ever, her heart swelling with the pride that had swelled Jean's earlier this morning when she had finally stepped back from fussing with Grace's veil and had felt her heart catch on a stab of maternal love so intense that it had robbed her of breath.

Now standing in the front pew of their church, knowing that at any minute Grace would be coming down the aisle on Sam's arm, Jean dabbed at her eyes with her handkerchief, remembering the sheer luminous joy and expectation she had seen glowing from Grace's face earlier. Yes, her daughter had a beautiful gown and was a beautiful girl, but it was her love for Seb that had illuminated her face with the happiness that had touched Jean's maternal heart.

As she had said to Grace before she had finally given in to Katie's gentle urging that they should leave for the church, 'There'll be good times and bad ahead of you in life, Grace love, but remember always to hold strong to the way you feel about Seb today.'

'Oh, Mum,' Grace had returned, going to hug her, but Jean had shaken her head, reminding her daughter of the need not to crush her veil, and now here she was in the front pew, with a space left for Sam, and on her other side, Bella, who had just given her hand an unexpected little squeeze. Next to Bella were Fran and her new husband.

On the other side of the aisle were Seb's family, his parents as happy with the marriage as she and Sam were, whilst Seb himself was standing proud in his uniform, not with Luke at his side as his best man, of course, much to Jean's regret, but with an old friend from his schooldays who had also joined the RAF.

Behind them, on both sides of the church the pews were packed with Jean and Sam's friends and neighbours, along with Grace and Seb's friends, young people in uniform, Grace's fellow nurses, some of whom had given up their precious hours of sleep to be here.

Unlike the church where Bella had been married, St Thomas's did not have an organ but the pianist was doing them proud with her rendition of Handel's

'The Arrival of the Queen of Sheba', and Jean could already hear beneath the rustle of fabric and the gasps of admiration that told her that Grace was on her way down the aisle.

How lucky Grace was to be marrying the man she loved and who loved her, Bella acknowledged, but she had warned herself before coming out that she must not think those kind of thoughts today, and that she must instead hold on to the happiness she had felt at knowing that Jan loved her, even if they could not be together.

She hoped that Lena wouldn't overdo things. She and Gavin were going out Christmas shopping and Gavin had assured Bella that he would take good care of Lena. Vi was still in the nursing home, and furiously angry about the fact. She had raged at Bella when Bella had gone to see her, insisting that she was to go home, but the doctor had warned Bella that it would be some time before he felt that Vi was well enough to leave the nursing home.

How different this wedding was from her own, Fran thought tiredly. She hadn't slept well, but she was too much of a trooper to let it show. Seeing Marcus had left her feeling dreadfully low, and guilty because of that when Brandon's every thought was naturally for his country and his fellow countrymen after Japan's attack on Pearl Harbor. All Brandon wanted to talk about was the fact that now America would be forced to enter the war and how much he wished he could be part of what he knew would ultimately be an Allied victory.

Even so, she had been caught off guard this

morning when Brandon had said quietly over break-fast, 'You still love Marcus, don't you?'

'I'd be a fool to love a man who would rather believe the lies of others than trust me to tell him the truth,' she had responded, but she had known that Brandon wasn't deceived. He was such a dear boy, so very brave and so deserving of all the love and loyalty she had to give him.

Fran closed her eyes to suppress the ache of her threatening tears. She was a fool, a fool who loved a man who had traded his proclaimed love for her for contempt. It was Brandon she needed to think about now, Fran reminded herself. Brandon who needed her so very much, and who was so very afraid of dying. As she was of living?

Sam and Grace were standing in front of the vicar. The proud and happy tears in Jean's eyes blurred her daughter's white-gowned image.

All that was missing to make this day perfect was Luke. Jean had been thinking of him the whole time they had been getting ready, trying to work out what time it would be for him and what he would be doing, hoping that he was not in combat and that the love she was sending him would reach him.

Katie bent discreetly to straighten the short train of Grace's veil. It had been Bella who had stepped in and insisted that Grace must have the pretty tiara and veil that she herself had worn, and it did go perfectly with Grace's dress.

This morning in all the excitement of getting ready, Grace had still found time to tell Katie, 'I mean to take care with the dress, Katie, 'cos it won't be long, I know, before you'll be wearing it.'

Katie had hugged her and blinked away her tears. She was missing Luke dreadfully today, despite the busyness of her role as chief bridesmaid. As for them getting married soon, though, Luke hadn't made any mention in any of his letters about coming home any time soon. It must be wonderful to be in Grace's position, Katie thought wistfully, but then fair-mindedly she reminded herself of the dangers Grace and Seb had both already experienced during the blitz and tried not to feel too envious.

She was never going to get married, Lou decided. It was all such a fuss. Sasha, on the other hand, loved every minute of the day, and had been going on as though being a bridesmaid was the most exciting thing that had ever happened to her. That was when she wasn't going bright red at the thought of her UXB beau having been invited to the wedding, just like they were a proper young couple, even though her mother had stressed that he was being invited because he had saved Sasha's life and had no family in Liverpool, not because of any imagined special friendship between him and Sasha, who was, after all, far too young to be walking out seriously with anyone. Well, Lou didn't care about Sasha or getting coupled up. She was going to be doing something much more exciting soon. She and Gemma, the girl she'd got chatting to outside the recruitment office, had agreed to meet up there on Monday and go to be measured up for their uniforms together, and Lou just couldn't wait. There was, though, an uncomfortable squirmy feeling in her tummy at the thought of telling her parents what she had done, even if Mr Churchill was calling for more girls to go into uniform.

* * *

'Hey, steady on. Bella said you weren't to do too much rushing around, remember,' Gavin cautioned Lena as she darted between the stalls at the busy St John's Christmas Market.

'Oh, pooh,' Lena laughed up at him, shaking her head as he made to take her arm. 'I'm only having a baby.'

The truth was that she would have loved to have taken Gavin's arm, and she would have loved it even more if she could have proudly held on to it and to him with the right that came from being his wife and the mother of his child. Lena had seen the smiles their appearance together had attracted as passersby obviously looked at them and thought them a young couple expecting their child. She was so enormous now that Bella's big swing-back check coat barely fastened over her. Gavin was such a lovely man, and so very kind. She had been out with him before several times. In fact, earlier in her pregnancy, when he had taken her to Lyons to have tea with his mum and his gran, or to the pictures, with Dolly sitting between them, giving a loud running commentary on the film, she had known that she felt safe and happy being with him, but she had not known what those feelings really meant. Then she had still been thinking like the silly girl who had been so taken in by Charlie and who had thought of falling in love as something that came out of nowhere like a big explosion. Now, though, she knew better; now she knew that the best kind of love came quietly and filled you up with a warm happy glow; that real love made you feel safe and comfortable, and that it was the most natural thing in the world to tuck your hand through a man's arm and put your head on his shoulder, but of course she could not do any of those things with Gavin, because of what she had already done with Charlie. Lena suspected that if things had been different and there was to be no baby and there had been no Charlie, then she might have had a chance with Gavin, but there *had* been Charlie, and there *was* to be a baby, and she couldn't for all the world wish the poor little thing away, not even if doing so meant that she might win Gavin's love. The poor little mite was going to have a hard enough time of it as it was, with no dad and no proper name, so it would need all the love she could give it.

Gavin looked down at Lena's dark head. He too had seen the smiling looks they had attracted and his own heart had contracted on a surge of sadness and regret. The poor kid was going to have such a hard time ahead of her, with no husband and a baby. He felt for her, he really did, because there was bound to be gossip, no matter what story Bella had fabricated to try to protect Lena. Bella had been wonderful to Lena, but Gavin feared that the posh folk of Wallasey would never really accept Lena as 'one of them'. Not that it was his problem. He wasn't the one who'd gone and got her into trouble, and if he had, she'd have been wearing his ring by now and nothing said about the baby coming a couple of months or so early.

They were just heading for a stall selling roast chestnuts when it happened. Lena turned to look before crossing the road and then froze as she saw her aunt and her cousin standing right across from her.

They'd seen her too, and before she could do or say anything, her auntie had marched across the road to confront her, announcing in a loud voice, 'Well, look who it isn't, and flaunting herself as bold as brass too, just like the shameless hussy she is. Come on, Doris,' she told her daughter, 'I'm not staying here whilst her sort's parading herself about.'

As Gavin tried to step protectively in front of Lena, her aunt gave her a deliberate shove as she pushed past her. All might have been well if the cobbles underfoot hadn't been greasy and damp, but they were and her aunt's deliberate push, combined with the bulk of her pregnancy and the slippery cobbles, caused Lena to lose her balance. Gavin reacted immediately, trying to catch her as she fell, but Lena's cousin was in the way, and Lena gasped in shock as she felt the cold sting of the cobbles against her knees.

'I'm all right, really I am,' she was still protesting to Gavin ten minutes later after he had helped her to her feet and taken her to Joe Lyons, where she had gone to the powder room to inspect the damage to her thick lisle stockings and her knees. Both were grubby, and her knees stung a bit, but thankfully her stockings were intact or would be once she had darned the scuffed knees.

Physically she was all right, but the incident had left her feeling vulnerable and weepy, and Gavin was well aware of the tears she was trying so bravely not to let him see.

'As soon as you've finished your tea, I'm going to take you home,' Gavin told her firmly. Lena's face clouded with disappointment and distress. She'd been enjoying herself so much just being out with him and now it was all spoiled.

'I'm sorry if you were embarrassed by my auntie,' Lena began to say, and then stopped, her mouth going into a round 'Oh' of shock and her face going a bright red.

'What is it?' Gavin asked her anxiously.

'I dunno, exceptin' that I've gone and wet meself,' Lena told him, reverting to her original accent in her shame and distress.

She hadn't said anything to Gavin about those funny little pains she'd been having ever since she'd fallen, but now they were getting stronger, and she felt really peculiar.

One of Gavin's mother's neighbours had been the local midwife, and he knew enough from overhearing the conversation in his mother's kitchen from his schooldays to guess what had happened.

Several thoughts filled his head at the same time. He needed to get Lena to the nursing home pdq. Bella would have his guts for garters for not looking after her properly, and right now, much as he wanted to find and give that aunt of hers a piece of his mind, looking after Lena was far more important than anything else.

'You may kiss the bride.'

Grace looked up at Seb, her breath catching as she saw the sheen of emotion dampening his eyes as he looked at her with so much pride and love that her heart turned over.

This was the beginning of a new life for them both, a life as a married couple, and this moment one so special and so filled with happiness that not even the hardship of the war could dim the joy she felt.

The vicar was indicating that they needed to follow him to sign the register. Grace looked towards her parents, her father standing tall and trying to look stern, but in reality looking as proud as a man could be, whilst her mother was dabbing at her eyes with the pretty handkerchief that Katie had bought for her just for today.

Dear Katie, Grace couldn't wait for Luke's fiancée to join her in the ranks of new wifedom. It would be such fun to have a sister-in-law whom she liked so very much.

Well before they had reached the ferry terminal, Gavin had begun to worry that they wouldn't have time to make it to the nursing home, so instead he had taken Lena to the only place he could think of at such short notice, his own billet, all too relieved to be able to hand Lena over into the capable care of his landlady. Mrs Stone, swiftly judging the situation, had sent him at a run to Mrs Lewis at number thirty-two, who was the area's midwife, whilst coaxing Lena upstairs to her back bedroom where she stripped the small spare bed at speed, thankful that she still had the rubber sheets she had used when her grandchildren had been small, virtually throwing them down onto the bed, whilst trying to time Lena's contractions as she did so.

Gavin's landlady had had five children of her own and was the grandmother of eight, and she was at home enough with the process of giving birth to make Lena comfortable. A pilot boat captain's wife knew a thing or two as well about keeping calm in a crisis, especially when there was a war on, and by the time Marion Lewis came panting up the stairs, Vera Stone had comforted Lena out of her panic and fear with her brisk firm manner, whilst keeping to herself the

463

fact that she suspected that Lena's baby was in a bit too much of a hurry to be born.

Downstairs Gavin paced the small kitchen with all the anxiety and sense of helplessness of any man who knows that the girl he loves is suffering and that he can't do anything for her.

Gavin had, of course, known for some time that he had fallen for Lena but he was a sensible, responsible young man whose mother had made sacrifices to bring her children up decently and who had certain expectations of them. His mum had been that thrilled when she'd thought he might marry a teacher, and that disappointed when she'd realised that he wouldn't. Someone like Lena, not wed and with another man's baby, wasn't the kind of wife she'd want for him, even though she'd been kind enough to Lena when she'd met her. And then there was his own pride. What right-thinking man wanted a wife who'd gone and behaved like Lena had with someone else? He'd be letting himself in for a life of misery with other men getting to know and going on about it, and some of them even thinking that they could try their luck with Lena because of her past. He didn't think he'd be able to stomach anything like that. Gavin was ambitious, and he'd got plans. First he wanted to get his Master's certificate, then command of his own pilot boat – that meant long hours of studying and long hours of working, and that meant that he'd need a sensible down-to-earth sort of wife who could hold her own and hold a home together whilst he was working, not a girl who needed looking after and protecting.

He could hear groans and gasps from upstairs that tore at his own insides.

*   *   *

The register was signed and the pianist struck up the soaring triumphant chords of Mendelssohns's 'Wedding March'. Seb, beaming with a proud husbandly air, escorted Grace back down the aisle and past the traditional nativity scene set up at the back of the church close to the font, to where, outside, eight of his fellow RAF chums had formed a military arch for the newly married couple to walk under, whilst everyone else pelted them with confetti made from minced-up privet leaves soaked in white distemper. A sharp beam of sunshine broke up the leaden grey of the late December sky. Suddenly, Grace thought back to the dreadful bombing blitz of the previous December and then turned to look at Seb, who squeezed her hand tightly as though he too was sharing that painful memory.

Brandon was looking so pale that Fran would rather have got him back to their hotel than gone on to the wedding breakfast, but she knew he would balk at any attempt by her to mollycoddle him in public, and so instead she simply moved protectively close to him, her face shadowed with the anxiety that her commitment to him had brought her.

Watching Sasha looking all coy as Bobby reached for her hand made Lou scowl and scuff the side of her shoe on the ground. Well, she wouldn't have to put up with their soppiness for much longer, thank goodness.

A few flakes of snow drifted down from the heavy grey sky, making Katie shiver. It was almost a year to the day since she had first met Luke. She looked down at her engagement ring and wished with all her heart that he could have been here, and not just for her own sake. She knew just how much Jean

465

would be missing her son on such a special occasion. How different her Christmas was going to be this year from last year. Then she had been shyly looking forward to spending Christmas with the Campions, not knowing that Christmas was going to bring her the gift of Luke's love. This year she would be spending it with her parents in Hampstead.

Bella looked up at the grey sky. Was Jan up there somewhere on an op, or was he off duty and with his wife, planning Christmas with her and their families, whilst knowing that she herself must be without him?

She must not think such thoughts. They were forbidden and far too painful, and besides she had promised herself that she would not do so. It was just seeing Grace looking so in love and so loved in return that had brought such thoughts to the fore. She would be better as soon as the wedding was over and she was back at home. She just hoped that Gavin hadn't let Lena overtire herself.

Gavin was in midpace when he heard it – a silence followed by a long-drawn-out sound of pain and then suddenly a sharply mewling cry that had him taking the stairs two at a time, only to be barred from the bedroom by his flushed and delighted-looking land-lady, who thrust a towel-wrapped bundle into his arms, telling him, 'Just keep hold of her for a minute whilst we get Lena sorted out, will you, Gavin?' before closing the bedroom door firmly in his face.

A girl. Gingerly Gavin eased back the blanket and then stared in mute awe at the tiny baby with her damp dark curls, her long eyelashes, and her delicate rosebud mouth. She was just like Lena, Gavin thought

466

dizzily, sitting down on the top stair, the better to hold her protectively.

When she yawned and then opened her eyes and looked up at him, he felt as though his heart were being wrenched out of his body on a surge of fiercely protective paternal love for her. Tears filled his eyes as he held her. She was so beautiful, so precious, and he was never ever going to let anyone hurt her in any kind of way.

Lena smiled gratefully at the two women who had helped bring her baby safely into the world, as they sponged her down and tidied her up. Thankfully, because the baby had been a month early, there'd not been any tearing, despite her hurry to be born, and as the midwife had said, Lena was the right shape for motherhood, with good child-bearing hips.

'Right, I think what we all need now is a good strong cup of tea,' the midwife announced once Lena had been helped back into the newly made-up bed. 'I think I've got a spare laundry basket at home for the baby for now, if you haven't got one, Vera,' she told Gavin's landlady.

Lena laughed, thinking of the lovely cradle waiting in the nursery at Bella's, and then asked a bit anxiously, 'Where is she, my baby?'

'I gave her to Gavin to look after whilst we sorted you out,' she was told. 'I'll go and get her.'

When Mrs Stone opened the door, Lena could see Gavin sitting on the top stair, cradling the towel-wrapped bundle as carefully as though she were the most precious thing in the world.

After one look at Gavin and another at Lena's face, Gavin's landlady touched the midwife on the arm and said meaningfully, 'I could do with a hand getting them sheets and that downstairs, and I've got a nice bit of shortbread, if you fancy a piece.'

The midwife frowned and then nodded as she too recognised the emotions she could see on both young faces.

It wasn't the done thing at all to let a man into the room so soon after a birth, not even when he was a husband, so some said, but she'd had enough experience over the years to know that there were some rules that were made to be broken – on certain occasions.

As she followed Mrs Stone across the landing she tapped Gavin on the shoulder and told him, 'You'd better take that little 'un to her mum, seein' as you can't provide what she's going to start yelling for any minute.'

Very carefully Gavin got up and walked towards the bedroom, hesitating at the doorway, until Lena held out her arms, and then stepping inside.

The room smelled of cold sea air, as the midwife had opened the windows after the birth, and then closed them again to keep Lena warm, and old polished furniture.

There were dark shadows like bruises beneath Lena's eyes, and those curls round her forehead that had escaped from the neat plait done by the midwife, were damp still with the sweat of her labour.

'She looks just like you,' Gavin told Lena, carefully handing over the baby.

Lena smiled at him and then at her daughter, her eyes filling with gentle tears when the baby reached out as Gavin tucked the towel round her to grasp his finger with her tiny baby hand.

'Lena, I've bin thinking . . .' Gavin's head was bowed and his voice gruff.

Lena looked up from gazing in adoring awe at her daughter's perfect features to look instead at Gavin's down-bent head.

'We get on well together, you and me, and what with the baby coming and her not having a dad of her own, and you and me getting on like we do, well, I was thinking that perhaps you and me should think about getting married so as she can have a proper mum and dad to look after her – that's if you'd like us to get married.'

Lena could feel her love for him flowing gently and calmly through her like a placid river unperturbed by any tumultuous demands of the tide, strong and sure in itself and content to be as it was. That was what real love was, she decided suddenly, feeling very grown up.

'I'd like that a lot,' she told him. 'I really would, Gavin, but I don't know what your mum will have to say, me being a bad lot like I was, and doing what I shouldn't have.'

'Don't worry about Mum. She'll come round once she sees I've made up my mind. I love you, Lena, I really do, and I promise I'll be a good dad to our little 'un.'

'Oh, Gavin, I don't deserve to be so lucky and to have you to love me. It's like a dream come true. There's me knowing how much I love you all these weeks and thinking you could never love me back 'cos of me having a baby, like I have done, and now here you are saying that you love me and that you want to be a proper dad to Baby, just like she was your own.'

Their kiss was tremulous and uncertain, and brought to an end by the rattle of teacups outside the bedroom door, but neither of them could bear to release the other's hand, and the looks they were exchanging fair brought a lump to her throat, Mrs Stone told the midwife when she went back downstairs.

'We'll get married as soon as we can get the banns called,' Gavin told Lena, 'and when it comes to putting down the little 'un's name on the birth certificate, it's my name I want to see you putting there, Lena, seeing as I'm going to be her dad.'

Grateful tears filled Lena's eyes. She was so lucky. First there had been Bella's kindness and generosity, and now this, the gift of Gavin's love – not just for her but for her baby as well.

'What are you crying for?' Gavin asked her anxiously, fearing some complication from the birth.

'Because I'm so happy,' Lena told him. 'And because I love you and you love me, and because I'm just the luckiest person in the whole of Liverpool.'

man (1967) asks: "The important scientific problem is this: Is the taboo on suicide so intense that even psychoanalysts are reluctant to expose their case materials and personal experiences in this area?" (p. 327).

To penetrate this "taboo," Litman (1965) conducted interviews with some 200 therapists who had had patients who committed suicide during treatment. Many of these therapists were reluctant to be interviewed, and many who did speak to Litman evidenced considerable difficulty in working through the loss. Apart from Litman's general report, only a few therapists have discussed their reactions to the suicide of a patient. Levinson (1972), in a paper on "sudden death," provides a vignette depicting some of his reactions to the suicide of an adolescent boy he had been treating. He points to the necessity—and difficulty—of mourning the loss and indicates how the therapist's aggression toward the deceased patient can interfere with a satisfactory working through of the loss.

The theme of aggression toward the patient is reiterated in a paper by Alexander (1977), who candidly describes some of his difficulties in accepting the suicide of his patient. Alexander emphasizes that aggression in the *preloss* relationship to the patient, if not recognized, can complicate the therapist's mourning of the patient. Kolodny and her associates (1979) also discuss some of their individual reactions to a patient's suicide. What comes through in their brief and frank reminiscences is not only a feeling of anger at the lost patient, but a sense of personal failure; they all felt that they had let down their patients, and themselves.

In contrast to these reports, Binswanger (1944/1967) notes that he reacted to the suicide of a patient with calm and philosophical acceptance. Binswanger discusses the case of "Ellen West" primarily to delineate the philosophical stance of existential psychoanalysis. Thus, he writes: "As a young woman Ellen West had already become old. . . . The suicide is the necessary-voluntary consequence of this existential state of things. And just as we can only speak of the gladness of old age as the 'most intimate and sweetest anticipatory relish of death' when the existence is ripening toward its death, so too in the face of self-induced death only gladness and a festive mood can reign when death falls like a ripe fruit into the lap of existence" (p. 295).

Such calm—to say nothing of "festive"—acceptance of the suicide of one's patient is not common. Litman (1965) states that he failed to find a single instance of this kind of philosophical acceptance among his interviewees. Rather, the suicide is more likely to prove deeply troubling, if not traumatic, for the therapist, and the typical reactions are likely to involve mourning, including pathological expressions of mourning. These reactions are what I want to focus on here, with the intention of amplifying and adding to the discussion begun by others. Let me begin by briefly describing the background of my patient, a man I shall call T.

In his early 40s, T. was an intelligent, intense person, who on first impression, struck me as someone still in search of himself—a search that had something quietly desperate about it. Partly motivating T.'s lifelong search was his hope of winning approval from his father, a hard-drinking, rough-hewn, successful salesman. Throughout his life, T. had struggled—vainly, he believed—to find ways of demonstrating his manliness. In high school, he had tried sports, only to be rejected by the football coach for "lack of aggressiveness"; as a young man, he opened a boating supplies business, only to go bankrupt; and just before his death, T. had decided to become a professional clammer, only to find the work too physically strenuous.

T. had been married for eight years and had one child (a son) but had been separated from his wife for two years before entering treatment. He said that his wife had left him because of his moodiness and his drinking sprees, and he added that he did not blame her. Shortly after the separation, T. lost his boating supplies business; in utter despair, he isolated himself in his apartment and drank himself into near oblivion. He wound up comatose in the local hospital. Released after a six-week stay, he continued psychotherapy at the low-cost clinic where I was working.

I saw T. once a week throughout the next one and one-half years. He arrived at his sessions regularly and on time, and he conscientiously tried to produce relevant material. He declined, however, to increase his sessions to two a week, a suggestion I made about six months into the treatment. He said he was living on his meager savings and simply could not afford it; besides, he felt he was already making progress.

Indeed, throughout most of T.'s treatment, he did seem to be progressing. His moodiness waned, he became less reclusive, he found a job as a bank teller, and he stopped drinking altogether. My only reservation—which was a major one—concerned T.'s persistent maintenance of polite distance from me. This stance had a schizoid quality, and I found myself struggling with a reciprocal coolness. My suggestion that he attend sessions twice a week was an effort to alter this mutual aloofness. In explaining my recom-

mendation, I indicated awareness of the distance between us and wondered whether it could be better
addressed with more frequent contact. Although T.
did not accept the recommendation, he politely acknowledged my observation.

T.'s suicide did not occur altogether unexpectedly. During the month that preceded it, he had
experienced several serious reversals in his life circumstances. His wife had decided to divorce him so
she could marry another man. His girlfriend also
seemed to be pulling away from him. His job as a bank
teller fell through, and then he injured his back
trying to support himself as a full-time clammer.
Predictably, he became severely depressed. He began
to ruminate about killing himself. "This time," he
said, "there will be no half-hearted attempts." I told
him that he seemed to be a danger to himself but did
not press him when he declined hospitalization or
even a psychiatric consultation for medication. Ten
days later, after a session during which T. said he
would never return to the hospital, he went to the
basement annex of the local university medical
school, tied a rope to an iron ceiling beam, and
hanged himself.

Working Through a Patient's Suicide

Even when a therapist has been aware of a patient's potential for committing suicide, the therapist's initial reaction
is nonetheless likely to be one of shock. To this day, more
than six years after my patient committed suicide, I viv-
idly recall the clinic secretary's expressionless voice as she
reported to me of reading in the morning newspaper that
T. had hanged himself. I was stunned. Despite my aware-

ness of T.'s threat to himself, my immediate reaction was, "No, this isn't so."

In working through the loss of a patient, the therapist encounters a number of obstacles. Litman (1965) and Kolodny and colleagues (1979) suggest that the therapist frequently views the suicide of a patient as a sign that he has failed. Even when the therapist recognizes his patient's suicidal potential from the outset, he will probably feel he is a failure if the patient commits suicide. Nonetheless, I believe that colleagues should not hurriedly reassure a therapist whose patient has committed suicide. It is not helpful to be told, "It was in the cards for so-and-so, after all." The therapist, either consciously or unconsciously, is unlikely to feel that the patient's suicide was inevitable. The therapist must be allowed to work through—slowly, and often painfully—any feelings of failure or narcissistic injury.

Working through this loss is difficult in part because the therapist cannot expect to arrive at an absolute conviction about whether and, if so, when he erred. Binswanger (1944/1967), in his existential approach, implies that some patients are headed irrevocably toward suicide. He is undoubtedly right, and the therapist must accept this possibility in evaluating particular patients. But the therapist must also accept the possibility that his errors and failings played a role in a patient's decision to commit suicide.

With regard to T., I am certain now that I should have urged, if not insisted upon, a medical consultation and probably hospitalization. I do not mean to imply that my urging would have saved the day or, if it had done so, that T. would not have committed suicide at some later date. One can never know. The ambiguity remains—always.

Two factors affect the therapist's ability to accept this ambiguity and work through the loss: (1) the degree of omnipotence in the therapist's therapeutic strivings, and (2) the nature of the therapist's relationship to the patient. As might be expected, the more omnipotent the therapist's sense of what he can and should do for the patient, the more difficulty he will have accepting the feelings of failure engendered by the suicide. This omnipotence can manifest itself in excessive denial of guilt and narcissistic injury or, alternatively, in a sense of worthlessness as a therapist. In brief, therapists who are characterologically inclined toward excessive narcissism or depression—both involving components of omnipotence—are apt to have great difficulty working through the loss.

The more the therapist–patient relationship is colored by hostility, and especially unconscious hostility, on the therapist's part, the more difficult it is to work through the loss. As both Levinson (1972) and Alexander (1977) indicate, when a patient commits suicide, the therapist may feel anger toward the patient. Alexander emphasizes that the therapist may feel abandoned by the patient, whom he has come to regard as a valuable love object. I would add that the therapist possibly—if not probably—will experience the suicide of his patient as a narcissistic injury. The greater the therapist's sense of omnipotence, the more profound is this sense of injury and the more extreme is the therapist's aggression toward the lost patient.

Moreover, a well-known motive in committing suicide is to inflict injury on those caretakers who "failed" to help the patient. It was evident to me (though not to T.) that he was extremely angry at the people in his life who had failed to nurture him as he unconsciously wished they would. His choice of location for committing suicide, the local medical school, was probably not accidental. Rather, I think that he was symbolically pointing an accusatory finger at his caretakers, including me. Such "accusations" arouse guilt and, generally, aggression toward the patient. The therapist may deny this aggression or deflect it elsewhere, such as toward the patient's family or toward the clinic or hospital. These maneuvers can be expected as initial ways of dealing with the aggression, but eventually the therapist must become aware of and accept his aggressive feelings toward the patient.

Even more fundamental than the aggression toward the patient for committing suicide, however, is the level of aggression, especially unconscious aggression, that existed toward the patient in the preloss relationship. As it happens, the same patient who would go so far as to commit suicide is likely to be one who arouses aggression in others—in therapy, as in life. Consequently, the preloss relationship may well be colored by aggression on the part of both patient *and* therapist.

With T., who maintained an aloofness throughout much of the treatment, I was occasionally as aloof and rejecting as he. I seldom felt that I connected with him, and I sometimes found his inaccessibility hard to bear. In short, countertransference aggression was there, and sometimes abundantly so; however, I believe that my awareness of this aggression increased my ability to eventually work through the loss. I was unaware at the time— and only later painfully realized—that I may have failed to urge medication or hospitalization because of negative countertransference feelings. In a word, if T. felt I lacked concern for him, and that I even wished to be rid of him, at that time he was undoubtedly correct.

This realization caused me to feel acutely guilty. And what further added to my sense of guilt (and shame) was an awareness that for quite a while I did not feel any sadness over T.'s death. I was eventually able to feel sad for T., and for how his search had ended in such utter failure, though the truth is I never did feel a sense of missing him. I struggled with this awareness for many months, and I must admit that during this time I was plagued with a sense of myself as an uncaring therapist (and person), and I wondered at times whether I should have chosen another profession. What helped me work through these feelings were my consultations with a colleague, as well as a reassuring awareness that others had undergone similar experiences in the aftermath of a patient's suicide (Alexander 1977, Kolodny et al. 1979).

Symptomatic Expressions of Pathological Mourning

When the therapist is unable to work through the suicide of a patient, he remains caught up in what can be called "pathological mourning." Let me highlight what I believe to be the most usual types of pathological mourning responses. Most often, perhaps, are "depressive" manifestations of mourning: exaggerated feelings of guilt, expectations of severe judgment and recrimination from colleagues, and pervasive ruminations on one's worth as a therapist or on the value of therapy in general. Less obvious are the therapist's "narcissistic" manifestations: denying guilt and feelings of failure, lacking any grief, and placing all blame elsewhere (on the patient, the patient's family, the therapist's colleagues, or the clinical setting). To some degree, I believe the therapist may expect to experience both depressive and narcissistic responses in the months following the loss of a patient. When these responses are exaggerated and unremitting, however, they signal that the therapist is caught up in pathological mourning.

Apart from these affective responses, the therapist's behavior toward other patients may be influenced by pathological mourning. For some time after the suicide of a patient, the therapist may expectably be unwilling to accept referrals whose suicidal potential is evident from the outset. The therapist often needs time to absorb the loss and may be wise to refuse such referrals for a while. Moreover, the therapist must deal with the impact of the suicide on other work with current patients who also may be suicidal. A significant negative effect I have noticed in myself and in some colleagues is the tendency to become overly anxious and overly cautious when confronted with suicidal ideation in another patient.

As Winnicott (1974) has noted, some patients, usually those with disorders based in early childhood, regress in the course of therapy to the point where suicidal ruminations may assume a frightening and real aspect; these patients may, in fact, become suicidal threats. Therapists who cannot tolerate deep, anxiety-provoking regression are unlikely to be able to help these patients benefit fully from treatment. In retrospect, I believe that for about a year after T.'s suicide, I inadvertently warded off such regression. Also, other patients who expressed relatively harmless suicidal ruminations caused me undue anxiety, which, in turn, undoubtedly elevated their anxiety as well.

A Framework for Working Through the Loss

In light of the difficulties inherent in working through the suicide of a patient, therapists should have colleagues who serve as consultants. I have noticed, however, that therapists who lose a patient through suicide often attempt to sort out the trauma entirely by themselves. In clinic and hospital settings, a therapist whose patient commits suicide may be questioned briefly by administrative staff, often to determine obvious criminal negligence. Otherwise, the therapist's colleagues frequently leave him to himself, no doubt in an attempt to be tactful. The therapist in private practice may have even less impetus to explore the case.

My own experience with T. leads me to believe that it is helpful, and perhaps even necessary, to bring the case into supervision with colleagues. Without such supervision, I doubt whether I could have sufficiently worked through the trauma. For this reason, I would recommend that within hospital and clinic settings a therapist whose patient commits suicide should have, as a matter of standard procedure, an available forum (a colleague and a supervisor, for example) for reviewing the case. This type of forum should exist separately from any administrative effort to determine negligence and should be available immediately after the event and at intervals during the following year. Finally, this forum should ideally include another therapist who has already worked through the suicide of a patient. Without this type of support, therapists may be inclined to deal with the event privately and perhaps inadequately.

My purpose here has been to suggest some potential risks for the therapist who does not work through the loss of a patient. Yet it is also true that in coming to terms with the patient's suicide, the therapist stands to learn from it—about the case, about himself, and about his work with other patients. When this happens, the suicide of a patient may ultimately, if tragically, have some redeeming value.

7

Countertransference with Borderline Patients

This chapter will explore an aspect of the psychotherapy of borderline patients that has received relatively little attention in the literature—namely, the therapist's loving feelings and fantasies about these patients. Among the many useful papers published in the past decade or so regarding countertransference with borderline patients, the predominant focus has been on the various forms of "hate" or "aggression" that arise in the therapist during the treatment. I believe that these investigations (to be discussed later) have proved enormously helpful to many therapists. Personally, I have found them to have a liberating effect on my work with borderline patients. However, an unfortunate side effect of these investigations has been a tendency to obscure, or even downplay, the importance of the therapist's countertransference "love" in the treatment of these patients.

By countertransference "love," I have in mind the gamut of the therapist's libidinous affects and attitudes toward the patient, including sexual feelings of all sorts, neediness, omnipotent concern, as well as the more subli- mated reactions of fondness, appreciation, and admira- tion. It is my belief that the therapist's recognition, comprehension, and therapeutic management of his countertransference love toward the borderline patient also plays a significant role in the treatment process. This chapter will discuss two essential uses of the thera- pist's countertransferential loving feelings and fantasies: (1) the "silent" use—that is, the use of such data as a source of information about the patient and the ensuing transference-countertransference matrix; and (2) the "open" use—that is, the therapist's selective disclosure of this data as part of the therapeutic process.

Before proceeding, let me briefly define which pa- tients are included in the category of borderline patients. I am employing Kernberg's diagnostic notions (1975, 1976), whereby borderline patients are characterized by certain manifestations of ego weakness (lack of anxiety tolerance, impulse control, and developed sublimatory channels); specific defensive operations (above all, splitting); and a typical pathology of internalized object relationships (fail- ure to meld all-good and all-bad self and object images into "whole," or integrated, images of self and others).

While accepting Kernberg's view that borderline pa- thology involves a failure in separation-individuation as described in the developmental schema of Mahler and her associates (Mahler et al. 1975), I am less inclined to em- phasize constitutionally based aggression as a crucial de- termining factor in borderline pathology. I view the child's real interaction with the mother during those years as a far more important determining factor. Diagnosti- cally, I also find that Kernberg stretches the category of borderline personality somewhat too far. While I would include, as he does, a wide range of character disorders under the general rubric of borderline personality, I would consider narcissistic personalities as a separate diagnostic entity, as do Epstein (1981), Masterson (1981), and Rinsley (1980).*

Countertransference Hate

By now it has become quite acceptable for therapists who treat borderline patients to acknowledge frankly the travails of working with these individuals. One has only to attend a case seminar at an analytic institute, or listen to the conversation in the staff room at a mental health clinic, to hear a colleague groaning openly and exasperatedly over his current predicament with some borderline patient or other. This was not always so. Until the 1950s, benign neutrality was what was expected of the therapist, and what the therapist expected of himself. The probability that the therapist might at some point find himself hating the patient, and that this hatred might serve some useful purpose, is a concept that has gained acceptance only gradually in the last 35 years. It remains, at bottom, emotionally difficult for many therapists to accept totally their negative feelings, especially as they find themselves suddenly and painfully in the midst of a countertransferential maelstrom. But we have come a great distance in our willingness to explore these feelings and accept (at

*The principal reason for considering narcissistic personalities as a distinct entity is that the cohesive constellation of the "grandiose self" would seem to require an alternate technical approach—one that employs aspects of Kohut's technique (1971, 1977), particularly in the earlier phases of treatment. Elsewhere, I have discussed the treatment of narcissistic personalities in more detail (Gorkin 1984).

least intellectually) that occasional bouts of barely controlled rage are part of the occupational hazard of working with borderline patients.

We owe a debt of gratitude, I think, to some of the early investigators, such as Winnicott (1949) and Little (1951, 1957), whose initial work on the treatment of preoedipal disorders challenged the view that benign neutrality was the only acceptable therapeutic stance. Their work was outlined in Chapter 1, so their positions will not be reviewed here. But perhaps quotes from the works of Winnicott and of Little will suffice to capture the essence of their then-iconoclastic views.

In his seminal essay, "Hate in the Countertransference," Winnicott had this to say:

> If the analyst is going to have crude feelings imputed to him he is best forewarned and so forearmed, for he must tolerate being placed in that position. Above all he must not deny hate that really exists in himself. Hate *that is justified* in the present setting has to be sorted out and kept in storage and available for eventual interpretation. . . . A main task of the analyst of any patient is to maintain objectivity in regard to all that the patient brings, and a special case of this is the analyst's need to be able to hate the patient objectively [1949, p. 70; italics are Winnicott's].

In her pioneering essay " 'R'—The Analyst's Total Response to His Patient's Needs," Little declared:

> To feel real hate of a patient for weeks on end or to be suddenly flooded with rage is extremely painful, as it is accompanied by guilt. It makes little difference whether the feelings are due to the patient's projec-

tions or whether they are objective and called forth by the patient's actual behavior. Real damage can be done if they remain unconscious, but there is little danger if they become conscious. Recognition of them alone brings some relief and the possibility of either direct or indirect expression [1957, p. 244].

In the years since the early and courageous papers of Winnicott and Little, there has been a steady and increasingly sophisticated exploration of the totality of the therapist's negative countertransference as it regularly emerges in the treatment of borderline patients. For example, investigators have discussed the emergence of feelings and attitudes such as violence and rage (Epstein 1977, 1979, Poggi and Ganzarian 1983, Searles 1965, 1979, Spotnitz 1976), greediness (Ogden 1979), confusion (Giovacchini 1981, Kernberg 1975), hopelessness and despair (Bollas 1983, Nadelson 1977), the sense of being driven crazy (Ogden 1979, Searles 1965, 1979), boredom, sleepiness, and narcissistic withdrawal (Kernberg 1975, Khan 1963, McLaughlin 1975). These dysphoric reactions have been recounted in illuminating and poignant detail in the recent literature, with the net effect that today we are no longer quite so guilty when we feel ourselves embattled with the borderline patient.

Much of the value of this literature has been to elucidate just how these countertransferential responses may be put to use as a barometer in understanding the vicissitudes of the patient's transferences. By sensitively monitoring the countertransference—and with awareness of one's "personal equation," as Racker (1957) phrased it—it has been demonstrated that the therapist can acquire valuable information regarding the internal imago or role in which the patient has cast him. Thus, when caught in a countertransferential bind, the therapist today typically stands back and asks himself the following questions: Why am I responding to the patient in this way *now*? Who among the various dramatis personae of his life, or which part of himself, am I being called upon to play? How, in word and deed, is the patient exerting pressure on me to enact this imago or role? The recent literature, as discussed in Chapter 3, has been extraordinarily helpful in providing the intellectual tools for grappling with these questions.

To reiterate, the notion of "projective identification," originally outlined by Klein in 1946, has been overhauled and honed to the point where it is commonly employed by Kleinians and non-Kleinians alike in conceptualizing aspects of the countertransference (Kernberg 1984, Ogden 1979). And the less frequently mentioned, though also valuable, notion of "role-responsiveness" (Sandler 1976) has similarly proved useful in explaining the emergence of certain countertransference reactions. In sum, with the aid of these conceptual tools, therapists working with borderline patients have been able to create some order out of the not infrequent countertransferential chaos, and they have thus gained an additional degree of freedom in the treatment of these individuals.

While the majority of therapists today subscribe to the "silent" use of countertransference (as a source of information about the patient), there remains considerable controversy as to what, if anything, of this countertransference might be disclosed to the patient. Inasmuch as the principal focus has been on the negative countertransference in the treatment of borderline patients, questions have been raised as to what, when, and how the therapist might openly let the patient know of his countertransferential hate (anger, despair, boredom).

Winnicott was one of the first to propose that the patient has a need to be told, *when* his ego can tolerate it, that the therapist has hateful feelings toward him. Winnicott believed that patients sometimes require this kind of countertransferential interpretation in order to trust in the genuineness of the therapist's emotional reactions to them. He further argued, in bold and iconoclastic fashion, that the therapist might also need to give vent to some of his hateful feelings simply in order to go on working with a hate-inducing patient.

Winnicott's advocacy of the therapist's disclosure of hate in the countertransference has been reiterated by several more recent investigators. Among the more articulate and enthusiastic proponents of selective disclosure of countertransferential hate in the treatment of borderline patients are Searles (1965, 1979), Spotnitz (1976), Epstein (1977, 1979), and Bollas (1983). In a clearly expressed statement of this point of view, Epstein (1977) has delineated four reasons that disclosure of the therapist's hateful feelings can be helpful to the borderline patient: (1) It demonstrates the therapist's credibility and genuineness, (2) it reassures the patient of his interpersonal impact, (3) it diminishes the patient's guilt and paranoia by making apparent the real and not fantasized impact of his hatefulness, and (4) it diminishes the patient's envy, since the patient need not feel he is the only "bad" person in the room. Epstein makes it clear that the manner of delivery must not be a spontaneous outpouring of venom, but rather a metabolized and measured dose of the therapist's feelings.

This particular use of the therapist's negative countertransference in the treatment of borderline patients is honored, I suspect, far more often in the privacy of the office than it has been in the public forum of journal articles. In the latter domain, the majority position continues to be that open disclosure of the countertransference places an excessive burden on, or provides gratification for, the patient, and is in any case likely to muddy the transference. These arguments and counterarguments have been put forth in Chapter 4, and I have already indicated my belief that selective disclosure can be useful. Regarding the disclosure of the negative countertransference, I am substantially in agreement with the point of view of Winnicott and Epstein. However, this chapter will focus on the value and use of, not hate, but love in the countertransference. Accordingly, I will discuss some of the theoretical and technical issues concerning the therapist's countertransferential love of the borderline patient, including the questions of when, how, and why the therapist might usefully communicate to the patient aspects of his loving feelings and fantasies.

Countertransference Love

In employing the phrase "countertransference love," I am including a wide range of libidinal feelings and attitudes toward the patient, just as other investigators have employed the phrase "countertransference hate" to denote a gamut of aggressive feelings and attitudes toward the patient. In particular, I intend to explore the following responses of the therapist: (1) sexual responses toward the patient, (2) omnipotent concern for, and neediness of, the patient, and (3) admiration of the patient's qualities, and fondness for and delight with the patient. These libidinal feelings and attitudes are called forth or engendered in the therapist by the nature of the borderline patient's transferences and personal qualities; further, just as it is at times important to disclose aspects of the therapist's countertransferential hate, so it is helpful to reveal aspects of the therapist's countertransferential love.

I do not believe that the countertransference must be disclosed on a regular basis. By far, the more frequent use of the therapist's countertransference is one of silently evaluating the experiences, and then making statements about what he senses is going on inside the patient. Nonetheless, an occasional and timely disclosure of what is going on inside the therapist can be valuable in the treatment of the borderline patient.

Just as it is sometimes necessary for the patient to be made aware of the impact of his hate on the therapist, so does he need to know the impact of his love. The patient needs to know that the more primitive and instinctualized aspects of his love (for example, his desire for symbiotic fusion, and certain erotic wishes) are manageable by the therapist; in other words, the patient needs to know that the therapist can tolerate his wishes even though he does not intend to comply with them. In addition, it seems to me that the borderline patient also needs to find that certain of his more sublimated, though also intense, loving feelings toward the therapist (for example, fondness, admiration, and delight) are in substantial measure reciprocated by the therapist. This is particularly so as the treatment progresses. As the mutual hatefulness is lived through and integrated by both participants, the latter affectional ties tend to become reliably and consistently present in the interaction. The terms "physicianly concern" or "dedication" or "unconditional acceptance" do not adequately capture the intensity or depth of some of these affectional feelings. I believe that in a fully realized therapy, the borderline patient must become pleasurably (and not defensively) comfortable with his own affectional ties to the therapist; for the patient to do so, he needs to know that the therapist has come to relish the development of such feelings in himself toward the patient. The patient's awareness of all this, including his awareness of the therapist's management of his more primitive forms of loving, is facilitated in many ways. The therapist usually does not need to talk about what is going on inside himself. But sometimes there is no other way, or no better way, for the therapist to clarify what is happening than to disclose aspects of his countertransferential love; and then he must be prepared to do so.

Much of what I am suggesting here has been noted or alluded to by others. In his own way, in the final years of his life, Ferenczi was similarly trying to clarify just which aspects, and how much, of the therapist's countertransferential love could be usefully revealed to the patient (1930, 1931, 1933). He went a good deal further in his recommendations than what I am proposing. He was inclined, for instance, to communicate his loving feelings not only in words but in actions, including various enactments of his omnipotently curative wishes and his desire for some physical contact with the patient. He placed himself at the beck and call of some of his patients, inviting them home on social occasions, and bestowed kisses upon them (see Balint 1968, pp. 112–117, Jones 1957, p. 174). These crude enactments of the countertransference and gross departures from the therapeutic frame have been roundly condemned from Freud onward—and rightly so. But I do believe that what was valuable in Ferenczi's approach was his then-unprecedented view that some patients have a therapeutic need to experience aspects of the therapist's countertransferential love.

One can also find among some members of the British object relations school the notion that more disturbed patients require the experience of, and perhaps even the open acknowledgement of, aspects of the therapist's countertransferential love—in particular, the therapist's intensely affectionate feelings. Implicit in Little's two contributions on countertransference (1951, 1957) is the assumption that the therapist's loving feelings will often be aroused by the more disturbed patient. And much as the therapist must be forthcoming in his acknowledgement of anger and hate, so is it valuable at times for the therapist to apprise the patient of his loving response to him.

Winnicott, too, in his seminal contribution on countertransferential hate (1949), implies that the severely disturbed patient needs to feel the therapist's love for him. Indeed, part of the reason for revealing countertransferential hatred, it seems, is to render believable the therapist's opposite set of feelings—that is, his love. Winnicott stated: "If the patient seeks objective and justified hate he must be able to reach it, *else he cannot feel he can reach objective love*" (p. 72; italics are mine). It is not clear whether Winnicott openly disclosed aspects of his countertransferential love as he did his hatred, or whether, quite literally, he let it go without saying.

Among more recent contributors, Searles (1965, 1979) has provided illuminating and sensitive accounts of the therapist's use of countertransferential love. Searles's principal field of interest is the treatment of schizophrenia, but he makes it evident that many of his observations apply to borderline patients as well. He discusses a wide range of libidinal feelings and attitudes toward his patients—including oedipal love, symbiotic relatedness, and omnipotent concern—and he states that these feelings occur regularly and predictably in the course of treatment. In Searles's view, the therapist must open himself to experience these diverse feelings if he is to understand the patient, and if he is to make emotional contact with him. In a manner quite similar to Little and Winnicott, Searles insists that the patient must know that the therapist has made contact with him on a deep level; he must know that the therapist has come at times to hate him, and also to love him. Like Little, Searles does not hesitate, when he deems it necessary, to disclose aspects of his countertransference to the patient.

Sexual Responses to the Patient

It is well known that borderline patients often present profound disturbances in sexual functioning, including "polymorphous perverse sexual trends" (Kernberg 1975). In order to protect the relationship to the therapist, the patient may attempt to avoid focusing his feelings and fantasies on the therapist, and may instead direct such inclinations toward another person in his life. Eventually, however, these sexual aims need to be brought into the patient–therapist relationship; if the patient is to take this risk, he must have an intuitive sense that the therapist can tolerate being the target of these sexual expressions. Chapter 5 outlined how various sexual aims of the patient tend to arouse specific and corresponding sexual countertransferences in the therapist. Several observations provided in that chapter are certainly applicable to the treatment of borderline patients. As was previously stated, the therapist's awareness of the induced sexual feelings can provide him with both an emotional understanding of the patient and clues as to significant early experiences in the patient's life; the therapist's resistance to, or lack of awareness of, his sexualized countertransference may lead to a prolongation or short-circuiting of the sexualized transference.

This chapter will focus on an aspect of the borderline patient's sexualized transference that was not emphasized in the earlier discussion. In more classical parlance, this aspect would be generally referred to as the "oral" sexual aims of the patient. In the lexicon of the British object relations school or interpersonal school, this aspect would be described as the patient's needs for "holding" and "handling." Such terminological preferences notwithstanding, it is widely agreed that in the borderline patient these early aims or needs have been profoundly mismanaged by the mothering one(s). The patient remains seriously disturbed in his expression of these aims or needs, and he brings his disturbance into the arena of his transferential relatedness to the therapist. As is the case with the expression of other aspects of the patient's sexuality, the expression of his needs for holding and handling, as well as his conflicts about these needs, tend to arouse a related set of countertransferential responses in the therapist. Some examples will illustrate what I have in mind here.

I had an early clue as to J.'s problems in this area when I noticed within myself an unusual fascination with her appearance, accompanied by a wish to touch her—*not* with any warmth, but rather with curiosity, to see if she were real or inanimate. There was something so studiedly made-up about J. that she struck me almost from the beginning of treatment as a figure from Madame Tussaud's famous wax museum. In the hundreds of times I saw her in the first years of our work together, she never wore the same outfit. When I openly mentioned this one day she smilingly affirmed that she had enough clothing in her house to fill a good-sized clothing store. This affinity for clothing, she explained, had come from her mother who, from the time J. was an infant, had dolled her up for public presentation. What her mother never did, however, was to hold or cuddle her. J. stated that she did not really mind because she herself never liked being touched—not by her ex-husband (with whom she had had a perfunctory sexual relationship), and not even by her own daughter. In fact, it became apparent that J. had repeated the same pattern with her daughter, never holding or cuddling her, and yet proudly attending to every detail of her appearance. The daughter had escaped the schizoid fate of her mother by turning to the paternal grandmother for cuddling and bodily warmth.

In another case, it was a quite different physical response to the patient that first alerted me to her conflicts in the area of holding and handling.

L., a female patient in her mid-twenties, had a manner of occasionally curling up in the armchair across from me in an almost fetal position. On such occasions, she refrained from her usually outspoken and energetic recitations of her chaotic daily life, and instead would sit there drawn up, woebegone, softly crying. In reaction to this palpable mood of hers, I would frequently experience a strong urge to cuddle her and stroke her lightly as if she were an infant. But shortly after I would enter the fantasy of doing so, I would imagine her suddenly bolting from my embrace in a frantic effort to get away from me. It became clear that I would enter into this countertransference-transference matrix with L. on precisely those occasions when she teetered on the verge of some piece of frighteningly independent behavior—for instance, when she planned to move to a new apartment, or take a job in New York City, which involved commuting by train from her suburban town. At these times, she seemed suddenly to collapse.

I was eventually able to discover how our pattern had its antecedents in what took place between L. and her mother. The latter, also apparently a borderline woman, had managed to convey to her that the world outside their house was forbiddingly bedevilled. From early childhood on, L.'s efforts at moving away from her mother's grasp were subtly and pervasively undermined. In moments when she did try to assert her budding independence, she would invariably collapse, and long for nothing more than to curl up in "someone's, anyone's" arms. But, in fact, as a child she never did curl up in anyone's arms, she recalled, and especially not her mother's. "I feared," she said, "that she'd just hold me there forever. I wanted so much to have her touch me and hold me, but I never dared let myself go to her in that way."

Unlike the two cases just described, some patients will express unambivalently the wish for holding and handling. This may occur relatively early in the treatment, or it may take place after many years have elapsed. At times, as with neurotic patients, the wish will remain on the fantasy level, while at other times the patient may demand unabashedly some form of holding or handling as part of the treatment. The timing, manner, and circumstances in which these wishes are expressed all contribute to the countertransferential response that will be stimulated in the therapist. The therapist may thus find himself responding with varying degrees of reluctance and annoyance, or temptation and wishes to comply.

As unsettling as it may be to find oneself repelled by a patient's wish for holding and handling, it may be no less anxiety provoking for the therapist to sense within himself a deep wish to reciprocate. In fact, in my observation, therapists nowadays are often *more* uncomfortable with the emergence of these positive countertransferential feelings than with their negative countertransferential responses. The literature on countertransference has prepared us far more to expect and deal with our negative feelings. We are less ready for the emergence of countertransferential urges to lovingly hold and handle the patient, especially when these urges arise with some intensity.

And yet, of course, they sometimes do. Induced (and at times seduced) by the patient's longing for physical contact, we may find ourselves, in fantasy, wishing to reciprocate. What the patient usually wishes for in his desire for contact of this sort with the therapist is to capture or recapture a reassuring sense of physical closeness that was either missing or prematurely disrupted when he was a young child. He longs to be in touch with the all-good, soothing parent (usually the mother), and at the same time to ward off the experience of the therapist as a disappointing, withholding, or traumatically unavailable parent.

When these longings arise later in the treatment, especially in the context of the patient's reliving of his experience of the parent's emotional and physical unavailability, it is not unusual for the therapist to experience some wish to comply, by holding, stroking, or cuddling the patient. What is essential, then, is for the therapist to accept and manage these feelings in himself—that is, to accept and manage the patient's projectively identifying him as the all-good, physically responsive parent.

I do not believe it is helpful for the therapist to enact the countertransference by actually making physical contact with the patient. Nor do I believe it is likely to be helpful *at times like these* for the therapist to disclose his countertransference to the patient. Enactment, or disclosure without physical enactment, run the risk of interfering with the patient's experience of the physical unavailability of the parent, and therefore can impinge on the mourning process. But what I would argue is that the therapist's unexpressed, but silently experienced, physical responsiveness to the patient often forms an integral part of his lovingly empathic presence for the patient, and this presence must be felt by the patient for him to dare to fully reexperience his parents' traumatic unavailability. In these circumstances, if the therapist resists the emergence of his physical responsiveness to the patient, what can happen is that his attitude and stance toward the patient will be affected, and detrimentally so.

Chapter 5 discussed in some detail a form of holding and handling that is occasionally requested of the therapist, and that is often unsettling to him: the request for sexual intercourse. This request, sometimes described as the "erotized transference," seems to fall into the category of oral needs, or holding and handling, because the patient's overriding wish is not for genitally related satisfaction, but rather to recreate a symbiotic oneness with the therapist. In this Garden of Eden, hate and despair are denied as patient and therapist are entwined in a timeless (not just 50-minute) embrace. This fantasy, which assumes delusional proportions in the erotized transference, can be quite unsettling. I think this is sometimes so not only because of the patient's evident disregard or disdain for the therapist's way of doing things, his therapeutic method, but also because the demand can be presented over time in such a way as to induce in the therapist, at least in some measure, a delusional wish to comply.

In Chapter 5, I provided an example of this type of occurrence from my work with a borderline woman in order to demonstrate that the temporary arousal within myself of longings to enter this Garden of Eden—that is, the emergence of a delusional countertransference—was ultimately useful in allowing me to establish a deep emotional understanding of this patient. Obviously, when the therapist enters into this kind of fantasy, both he and the patient are in some danger of the fantasy becoming actualized, in subtle ways if not in an overt, treatment-destructive, "magically curative copulation" (Searles 1979). I do not wish to minimize this danger. Yet, there is another type of danger that is seldom discussed, but that I have noticed both in my own work and in that of some supervisees: When the patient presents the wish for holding and handling in the form of a request or demand for sexual intercourse, the therapist may find himself recoiling in a defensive and hurtful way. In the name of "reality," the therapist may provide a premature or abrupt interpretation that has the effect of short-circuiting the developing transference in all its aspects. Some patients may initially express the wish for a "holding environment" concretely, in these erotic terms. The wish for the "adult" form of erotic holding may serve as a defense against more "infantile" dependency wishes and, in particular, the wish for symbiotic fusion with the therapist. The therapist therefore needs to be able to sit with relative ease with such a request, which means that he must be able to manage the gamut of feelings that may arise within himself, including his fantasies of compliance. The therapist who is accepting of his countertransference is then able to decline the erotic request in a manner that is neither too abrupt and hurtful ("You wish to have sex with me because you have no faith in the treatment I am offering you"), nor too seductive ("Your offer is appealing, but . . ."). The patient is slowly enabled to relinquish the erotized claims without precipitously foreclosing the more basic transference wish for emotional holding, and specifically, the wish for symbiotic fusion with the therapist.

A difficult technical question regarding the therapist's sexual countertransference in the treatment of borderline patients is what, if anything, can be usefully disclosed to the patient. In principle, it seems that if one espouses the view that disclosure of hate is at times useful, then disclosure of love, including aspects of sexual love, might also prove useful. The ultimate test depends, however, on clinical experience. As stated in Chapter 5, I have not found that the disclosure of erotic feelings—wishes to fondle, caress, or penetrate the patient—is likely to prove useful to the patient. A few unfortunate attempts at such disclosure have inclined me to believe that the patient is liable to be unduly frightened or stimulated. The impact has seemed roughly akin to that of an unmodulated, vituperative release of hostility. The patient suspects that some action is forthcoming—an expectation that burdens the treatment. On occasion, though, when I have inadvertently become involved in a disguised enactment of the sexual countertransference, I *have* found that an abbreviated or indirect form of disclosure can be useful. For instance (as mentioned in Chapter 5), I felt it necessary to acknowledge to a masochistic patient (B.) that I had unwittingly become caught up in a teasing pattern with her which, I came to understand, repeated the sexually provocative play that had taken place between the patient and her brother. Having enacted an aspect of the sexual countertransference, I felt it was helpful to acknowledge it and discuss my enactment with reference to her incestuously tinged relationship to her brother. To be sure, the treatment would have been better served if I had merely experienced internally the wish to banter sexually with her, without enacting this wish.

Finally, it has been my experience that the disclosure of certain wishes to touch a patient in an affectionate, but not especially erotic, manner can sometimes be of value. For example, with the borderline woman (L.) who would curl up in the armchair, thereby arousing both my ambivalent wish to stroke her as if she were an infant and my fantasy that she would immediately bolt away, it might have been useful to discuss this countertransference with her. As it was, I never did so. But what did happen is that, some four years into the therapy, her manner and character had shifted appreciably from that of the woebegone child who might bite the hand that held her to that of a far more healthy and endearing young woman whom I was now unambivalently fond of. In this period, during our last year of work together, I would occasionally experience a fatherly wish to give L. a hug and plant a kiss on her forehead, which I now imagined she would accept unambivalently. Thus, one day, when she had just finished talking about her mother and her boyfriend (now in far more realistic and compassionate terms), I said, "If it were my custom to touch patients, I would hug you and kiss you on the forehead." L.'s response convinced me that what I had said was worth saying. She smiled warmly and acceptingly, and after a pause added: "Yep, I think I like myself better these days too."

In sum, then, as a generalization I would say that there is a place for disclosure of *some* sexual countertransferences in the treatment of borderline patients—not raw erotic feelings, but the more sublimated, affectionate wishes for contact. A fuller exploration of precisely when, where, and how these disclosures can be employed would seem to me of interest and value. At present, however, this particular area of technique remains taboo, with discussion of such matters not yet receiving the public exposure that is needed.

Omnipotent Concern for, and Neediness of, the Patient

While the precise etiology of borderline pathology is still a matter of debate, it is widely agreed that a crucial precipitating factor is the mother's inability to assist and accept her child's separation and individuation from her. In order for the child to move out of the symbiotic orbit with his mother and relinquish his claim to omnipotent involvement with her, he must be eased out gently in an optimally frustrating manner. The mother must neither push him out too abruptly nor hold onto him too long out of her own needs or concerns. This is a tall order for any mother; for the mother of the borderline child, it is an order that, for pathological reasons of her own, she simply cannot fill.

As a result of this failure, the borderline child is unable to relinquish his wish for exclusive, omnipotent possession of the mother, a wish that, nonetheless, is often fraught with ambivalence. In his experience with other people, and now with the therapist, the borderline individual brings to bear this wish for omnipotent involvement, and his fears of just such involvement. For his part, the therapist will certainly feel the prod of the patient's transference, as the patient choreographs for him his internal imago(s) of this mother whom he so longs for, and whom he so fears and hates. Or, otherwise stated, in his countertransferential response to the patient, the thera-

pist will keenly feel at times as if he were the pathologically impaired mother of this borderline child.

So much has been written about the borderline patient's excessive aggression that it can easily be overlooked that the history of this early relationship with the
mother is frequently not one of anger and hatred alone.
Thus it is often not only the mother's hostility that under-
cuts the child's ability to separate, but also her great
neediness of the child, her omnipotent concern for him,
and in general her destructive way of loving him. Accordingly, as part of his countertransferential responsiveness
to the patient, the therapist will frequently be pushed and
prodded not only into hating the patient, but also into
reacting—if only in his internal experience—in a manner
of omnipotent concern for, and neediness of, the patient.
In the treatment of neurotic patients, an even-keeled "physicianly concern" is relatively easy to maintain; the therapist treating a borderline patient, on the other hand, often
finds himself buffeted back and forth between periods of
hostility and withdrawal, and then periods of profound,
and even omnipotent, concern for the patient.

Unlike the neurotic patient, the borderline individual
very often collapses—"goes down in a heap," in Stern's
apt description (1938)—when confronted with the slings
and arrows of daily fortune. He goes through prolonged
periods of returning to the therapist for emotional refuel-
ing, his tank on or near empty. He requires, even demands, soothing, and sometimes he demands this at all
hours of day or night. Or, rather than clinging to the
therapist, he seeks, consciously or unconsciously, to engage the therapist through one form of acting out or
another; self-destructive behavior is very common among
these patients.

In all of this, the patient seeks to draw the therapist

into his life in a pattern of omnipotent concern. He projects onto the therapist the imago of the all-good, completely devoted mother, and the therapist feels internal pressure to play out this role. This is not all the therapist experiences, of course, but I think it is sometimes overlooked in discussions of countertransference with borderline patients that deep wishes to rescue, care for, and cure another are regularly engendered—so much so that the therapist may experience the sense (in part reflecting his omnipotent strivings) that what is "best" in himself is being called for by the patient. That is also part of the reason the therapist can begin to hate or withdraw from the borderline patient. For having wished to offer, or perhaps even having attempted to offer, that which is "best" in himself, the therapist can easily be put off by the patient's rejecting it or finding it inadequate; that is, the therapist may find himself reacting to being abruptly demoted from the "all-good" to the "all-bad" mother. The therapist is then likely to experience the patient as insatiable, greedy, or incorrigible, and he will be inclined—if only in his internal experience—to castigate or withdraw from him. In sum, the borderline patient gets under the skin of the therapist not simply by projective identifications of negative aspects of the self or mother imago, but often by a pattern of alternating these negative projections with projective identifications of the all-good, omnipotently concerned mother or self.*

It becomes essential for the therapist to accept and manage the feelings of omnipotent concern, neither resisting these feelings, nor enacting them in inappropriate and

---

*By projective identification of the omnipotently concerned part of self, I have in mind that part of self that wished to minister to or cure the needy mother (see Searles 1979, pp. 380–459).

destructive ways. I have noticed, for example, that some
therapists are prone to resist the emergence of these feelings and instead coolly experience the patient's verbalized
and enacted desperation as "just manipulations." For characterological reasons, or out of a conviction that "neutrality" is to be maintained at all cost, the therapist persistently avoids the internal experience of profound concern
and the wish to rescue the patient from his desperation.
His demeanor, as well as his internal experience, remains
one of detachment. The result of this countertransference
resistance is that the patient feels out of contact with the
therapist and believes—realistically, and not just transfer-
entially—that the therapist is uninvolved with him and
insufficiently concerned about him. This belief, in part
reality-based, can lead to the patient's terminating treatment or escalating his self-destructive efforts to gain the
therapist's involvement. Parenthetically, I want to add
that this particular type of countertransference resistance
needs to be distinguished from the *induction* of withdrawal
or aloofness. An example of the latter, presented in Chapter 6, is when the therapist has the *unusual* internal experience of detachment, even as the patient ruminates about
committing suicide (or any other blatantly self-destructive
act). In this case the patient has projected onto him the
imago of the pathologically withdrawn and unconcerned
mother.

The opposite, and perhaps more common, countertransferential problem that arises vis-à-vis the patient's
efforts to induce omnipotent concern is that the therapist
becomes so caught up in these feelings that he enacts them
in treatment-destructive ways. The therapist may thus
comply with chronic breaks in the therapeutic frame: He
repeatedly answers telephone calls at all hours of the day
and night, spends more than the allotted treatment time,

and reschedules appointments. Or, the therapist continues to avoid hospitalization or auxiliary treatment despite repeated self-destructive acts on the patient's part (suicide attempts, self-mutilation, or substance abuse). In other words, the therapist refuses to accept limitations in his own ability to care for and cure the patient. To be sure, here I am touching on areas of technique that may reflect clinical judgment and not just countertransference issues. Nonetheless, when these patterns are carried on repeatedly and in the extreme, I am inclined to suspect that the therapist is enacting the imago of the omnipotently concerned mother that has been projected onto him by the patient, and that for his own pathological purposes the therapist has taken on, or even invited. Enactment of this omnipotent concern usually does not relieve the patient's desperation, but rather leads to an intensification of the acting out.

Closely related to the sense of omnipotent concern is another of the therapist's libidinally determined attitudes toward the patient: his neediness of the patient. It has been pointed out by several investigators that the mother of the borderline patient typically needed to bind the patient to her when he was a child (Masterson and Rinsley 1975, Saretsky 1977, Searles 1979).

The mother's neediness may have been openly expressed in an anaclitic manner or, more commonly, it may have been expressed unconsciously and covertly. In the latter pattern, the mother projectively identifies her child with the helpless-hopeless part of her self, and through her actual behavior she pressures him to play out this role which, tragically, he takes on as his own. The mother may accomplish this by various means: by inculcating in her child a vision of the world outside the home as so forbidding and dangerous that he requires mother's vigilance as he attempts to sally forth independently; or alternatively, by withdrawing from the child as he moves away, in a covert effort to undermine this separation; or perhaps most often, by switching back and forth between these behaviors in a bafflingly inconsistent manner. The aim of all this is to enable the mother both to maintain a sense of powerfulness and proficiency and to consciously feel how much her child needs her. The truth is that she needs him (as a receptacle of this projective identification) every bit as much as he needs her. Similarly, it is this particular type of neediness for the patient that arises countertransferentially, in some measure, in the treatment of many borderline patients. In the long and arduous treatment of these cases, the patient often comes to stand, to some extent, for the therapist's hopeless-helpless self (Searles 1979). The patient invites this response from the therapist, and the therapist, depending upon his own "personal equation," will be more or less tempted to use the patient in this way.

In this connection, I would note a countertransferential development that occurs in the treatment of many borderline cases. When the patient, after considerable turmoil and vascillation, finally begins to take some daring steps toward separation (finding a new job, for example, or entering a new relationship), the therapist may find himself experiencing feelings other than clear-cut delight in this healthy development. In an echo of the patient's pathogenic mother, the therapist may sense within himself a certain meddlesome and excessive worrying about the patient's plans, particularly if the patient uncharacteristically fails to consult with him about these plans. Or, as the patient enthusiastically flexes his independence, the therapist may sense a kind of petulant wish to withdraw from him. Several months ago, for example, I noticed the emergence of some of these countertransferential responses in myself during a phase of my work with F., a young borderline man.

I had worked with F. for four years, during which time he had managed with great turmoil to move out of his mother's home and, in fact, take up residence near my office. He worked in a menial job that was considerably beneath his capacity, and he found it very difficult to make and maintain social contacts. I, as a stand-in for his mother, had become his principal contact. I was quite aware of how much I meant to him, but I seldom experienced a conscious sense of what he might mean to me. Rather, I often felt my involvement with him to be agonizing, as he repeatedly called upon me to provide my "best," although it rarely seemed good enough.

Then, some months ago, in what felt like a surprise, F. began to take genuine pleasure for the first time in spending time with two or three new friends. As a child he had always felt—realistically, it seemed to me—that his mother had intruded on his friendships, usually by disparaging them in one way or another. Thus, when the patient now began to get involved with these new "buddies," as he called them, it was a significant move for him.

I knew that I should have been inwardly delighted, and in part (the healthy part of myself), I truly was. But I also experienced a palpable hesitation. I sensed this hesitation in my unspoken, smotherly concern about the "character" of one of these friends. I also sensed this hesitation in my cool response to his arriving twenty minutes late one evening because he had been "out with (his) buddies," and again a few weeks later when he telephoned to cancel an appointment because he had spontaneously decided to go see a hockey game in Manhattan with these friends, something he had never done before. I sensed an aloofness in my tone of voice on the telephone, and afterwards I found myself wondering how I would respond to his anger (actually, my projected anger) when he realized that he would be charged for the session.

As it turned out, F. was not at all angry at being charged for the session; he volunteered immediately that he knew he had to pay for the session, "but it was worth going anyway." He added, however, that *I* had seemed put off. Having recognized and worked on my countertransference in the interim, I chose to disclose to him that he was right. I further stated that while I was truly happy for him in his new-found ability to go off with friends, there was apparently also something within me that hesitated to see him go, much as his mother also had not wanted to see him go. I further suggested that perhaps the manner of his going—announcing his new independence by missing a session—may inadvertently have been a way of getting me to oppose this very independence, just as his mother did. And I added that "I guess both of us are going to have to get used to your new independence."

This disclosure appeared helpful to him. It led first to a discussion of his concerns about missing the session and his awareness that it might annoy me. Afterwards, it led to a further exploration of his relationship to his mother and a clarification of his mother's need for him. It did not seem to hinder his separation from me, which has continued to proceed, I believe, with minimal interference from me.

I am aware that characterological features of my own contributed to my hesitation in envisioning this patient's emerging independence. Yet I would also argue that this borderline patient, and others, "objectively" tend to create a transference-countertransference matrix in which this kind of neediness on the therapist's part is a feature. If the borderline patient's mother needed the patient to be hopelessly dependent upon her, then the therapist is likely to feel invited and pressured—again, if only in his internal experience—into a similar use of the patient. The therapist's ability to be sensitive to and work through this countertransferential response is crucial to the treatment and ultimately helps the patient to separate from the therapist. I suspect that in many cases in which borderline patients remain "lifers," a contributing factor is the therapist's failure to work through this type of neediness for the patient.

Admiration, Appreciation, and Fondness for the Patient

Some researchers in the treatment of borderline pathology have indicated that it is possible to substantially help, even fundamentally cure, the patient without developing positive feelings toward him (Epstein 1977, Spotnitz 1976). It may be true in some cases that one can effect *some* worthwhile changes without ever coming to like the patient in any way whatsoever. What I have found far more usual, however, is that over the course of treatment of the borderline patient, the therapist develops an increasingly reliable admiration, appreciation, and fondness for the patient. Furthermore, the emergence of these more sublimated positive feelings in the therapist, and the patient's realization that the therapist so regards him, is a valuable aspect of the overall treatment. I would even claim that in a fully realized therapy of the borderline patient, it is *necessary* for the patient eventually to accept pleasurably (not defensively) the emergence of mutual, positive feelings between the therapist and himself. This development is part and parcel of the patient's growing ability to see himself and others in an integrated manner—that is, as "whole objects." By extension, a treatment that ends with the patient unaware of these mutual feelings—perhaps because they never arose—is a treatment, I suspect, in which the patient's capacity for "whole object" relatedness remains somewhat impaired.

In the course of treatment of a given borderline patient, as with any other patient, I frequently find qualities or characteristics that I appreciate or admire. Sometimes these qualities are recognizable from the start, but more often it is in the long process of getting to know the patient that I find myself deeply appreciating him. Indeed, the more fully I know the patient, as with any other person, the more fully I can see how intertwined are some of his shortcomings and virtues. Part of the process of enabling the patient to gain a more realistic and integrated view of himself is precisely one of drawing his attention to the nature of this intertwining.

Let me give some examples of what I have in mind. In the process of tracing the relationship of the borderline patient to the mother, I am often struck by the intense loyalty with which the patient clings to her. It frequently seems that the tie that binds the troubled patient to his troubled mother is not just his excessive hatred, but his (typically unconscious) wish to minister to her, to somehow soothe or calm her. The patient may be attempting to revive the mother from a withdrawn state (see Guntrip's fascinating account of his own analysis [1975]), or attempting to relieve her depression by serving as a scapegoat. Or, as previously indicated, the patient may be presenting himself as helpless and hopeless so that the mother can feel powerful and proficient. In all of these situations, the patient attempts in his own way to "cure" the mother (Searles 1975). The patient seldom realizes that this is part of his bind to the mother. He feels stuck, caught in the undertow, to the mother. He generally underestimates the degree to which he has, in a sense, stood by her, as well as the degree to which he unconsciously equates growing up and away from the mother as a betrayal of her.

It is very important that the therapist be able to understand and respect this quality in a patient when he finds it; the therapist must appreciate how not only the patient's "badness" (hostility) but also his "goodness" (loyalty) has led, tragically, to the patient's inability to separate from the mother. It may take quite a long while before the patient can accept this goodness in himself; usually, he and the therapist must first become thoroughly acquainted with the badness. As the patient finally does move to separating from his disturbed mother, however, the sense of loyalty and betrayal are closest to the surface. On these occasions, it is often therapeutic for the therapist to let the patient know, usually in an indirectly admiring way, that he has become aware of the loyalty that the patient possesses.

An additional quality of some borderline patients, which has often struck me as both exasperating *and* admirable, is their hypersensitivity. At its worst and most obnoxious, this quality emerges as a "paranoid-style scanning" (Rinsley 1980, p. 130). At its best, though, this same quality can be seen as an almost uncanny facility for fathoming the unconscious surfaces of others. The borderline patient, enmeshed as he is with his pathologically disturbed mother, often develops a laser-sharp sensitivity to specific nuances of mood. He is especially sensitive in those areas in which his security was, and is, threatened—for example, when the mother, and now anyone else (including the therapist), withdraws, intrudes, criticizes, patronizes, or becomes angry. The mother was generally unable to corroborate the patient's accurate perceptions when as a child he brought his sensitivity to her attention. Consequently, the patient grows up with a sometimes righteous or mystical or eerie awareness of his sensitivity to certain nuances of mood and behavior in other people.

In helping the patient to become realistic about this special sensitivity, the therapist's own perspective and attitude become crucial. Once again the therapist must recognize not only pathological and "paranoid" elements, but also the uncanny accuracy with which the patient's antennae pick up subtle signals. In short, if the patient is to accept the paranoid element (that is, the distrustfulness) of his scanning, he must know that the therapist corroborates and even respects his exquisite sensitivity in some areas.

A further virtue that one finds in abundance among some borderline patients is the elusive quality of courage. Any patient who seriously engages in psychoanalytic psychotherapy requires at least a modicum of courage. This is all the more true for the borderline patient because what he must face about himself and his past is especially devastating, and the odds of significantly repairing the damage are, as he so often senses, not in his favor. Yet some of these patients press on with a courage that, if difficult to comprehend, is nonetheless manifestly present.

For years I have attempted to understand what it is that makes some of these people so brave. Sometimes this courage seems intertwined with various pathological features. The patient's enormous capacity to withstand psychic pain seems fueled at times by his masochistic courting of pain; or, his unwillingness to give up the struggle seems linked, in part, to a persistent longing for the lost paradise of the all-good mother. These explanations alone have never seemed adequate to me, however, and in the end I am left with the thought that there might also be some constitutional basis for this quality of courage. Just as some seeds planted in an awkward part of the garden will reach for the light more tenaciously than others, so too do some individuals seem to have more of a thrust toward individuation than do others. In any case, when I notice this quality in the patient, and over time become convinced that this is a part of who he is, I eventually tell him so. Interestingly, while some borderline patients are aware of possessing this quality, others seem never to have regarded themselves in this light. In either case, the therapist's observing and commenting on the patient's courage, if properly timed, can be reassuring and validating. Although the therapist's appreciative acknowledgement is gratifying to the patient, to withhold such an observation is to deprive the patient of a valuable aspect of the therapist's perception of him.

I have mentioned here some of the qualities commonly found in borderline patients. Naturally, each patient will be endowed with his own unique characteristics and virtues. The principal point I wish to make is that, as part of the treatment, the therapist will need to convey, directly or indirectly, his awareness of these qualities. Awareness and exploration of the patient's negative qualities must eventually be accompanied by an exploration of the patient's virtues.

Finally, I would claim that by the time one reaches the closing phase of treatment of a borderline patient, the

predominant feeling toward the patient is likely to be one
of fondness, and even delight. This countertransferential
attitude is not unlike what occurs in the treatment of
neurotic patients. Yet there is something especially uplift-
ing when this development takes place with a borderline
patient, for the journey has generally been much more
difficult. The therapist has had to overcome deep swings
of feeling about the patient—hating him, wishing to save
him, despairing about him, and hating him again. The
reliable sense of fondness that the therapist is finally able
to feel toward the patient has been hard-won. His experience of the patient has changed, just as the patient's
experience of him has shifted. In both participants there
has been a shift toward experiencing the other in a more
integrated fashion, and for both participants this is an
enhancing and reassuring development. It is a fundamentally curative experience for the borderline patient to
know that the formerly distrusted therapist whom he now
regards so fondly has come to regard him with a similar
fondness. When this ultimately does happen, I will sometimes mention it aloud to the patient, or if he has stated it
first, I will confirm it gladly. This confirmation is not
overly stimulating, but rather feels warmly comfortable—
to both participants. It is, quite simply, an idea whose time
has come. To put this matter another way, I would embel-
lish slightly the title of Bettelheim's book (1950): Love is
not enough, but with the borderline patient, hatred is not
enough either.

8

Countertransference in Cross-Cultural Psychotherapy

The cultural background of the therapist vis-à-vis the patient seldom emerges as a potential barrier to psychotherapeutic treatment. This is so for the simple reason that both participants usually share similar backgrounds. When this is not the case, however, divergent cultural values and assumptions may invade the treatment, sometimes undermining it altogether. This chapter will focus on some of the countertransference issues in cross-cultural psychotherapy, with reference to one specific, and in some ways unique, therapist–patient dyad: the Jewish (Israeli) therapist and the Arab patient.

The Jewish therapist–Arab patient dyad has received no attention in the literature, largely because Arab patients in Israel have only recently begun to seek modern forms of outpatient psychotherapy. Today, Arab Israeli patients are increasingly appearing at outpatient clinics, especially in areas with large Arab populations. They are also appearing at the university-based psychological services, and they are beginning to turn to private psychotherapy.

These patients are usually treated by Jewish therapists, inasmuch as there are only a few trained Arab therapists in Israel. During a two-year stint as a psychotherapy supervisor at the Student Counselling Services of the Hebrew University in Jerusalem, I supervised several Jewish therapists who were treating Arab patients. In addition, I consulted with therapists who worked in other facilities. Their struggles, and those of their patients, provide the data on which this chapter is based.

A number of researchers have delineated some of the more frequent countertransference problems that arise when the therapist is treating patients from a different culture (Abel and Métraux 1974, Basch-Kahre 1984, Devereux 1953, Ticho 1971, Tseng and McDermott 1972). In the last two decades, countertransference issues in interracial psychotherapy have received particular attention (Griffith 1977, Jackson 1983, Schacter and Butts 1968, Wohlberg 1975). Some of their findings are germane to this study, but rather than outline them here, I have chosen to discuss them by way of comparison with some of my observations. Suffice it to say at this point that while the countertransference issues that arise in the Jewish therapist–Arab patient dyad are similar to those in other cross-cultural psychotherapies, the extreme nature of the ongoing political struggle between these two peoples tends to exacerbate the countertransferential difficulties—sometimes to the extent that the therapist can no longer continue to work with the patient. But this is not usually the case. Most treatments do go on—to the enormous credit of both participants.

A point that needs to be made explicit from the outset, especially in discussing cross-cultural psychotherapy, is that the therapist may at times respond inappropriately for reasons that are not due to his internal conflicts, but rather are due to a lack of knowledge about the patient's culture. Perhaps an example will elucidate this distinction.

> P., an unmarried Arab woman with masochistic features, informed her therapist that she had just discovered she was pregnant. She knew that she must have an abortion and was thinking of asking her sister and a friend from her village about where she might go for the procedure. The therapist, a Jewish male, encouraged P. to go right ahead and consult with her sister and friend. He completely overlooked the fact that his patient might be in danger if her parents, particularly her father, were to discover her mishap, which in their village would be regarded as an unpardonable disgrace for the family.
>
> The therapist failed to recognize that a course of action that would be sensible in his culture was for his patient probably a hazardous expression of her masochism. This oversight did not issue from any countertransferential sadism. It was simply, though dangerously, an initial failure to grasp the cultural meaning of the patient's intended action. Fortunately, the therapist was able to undo his error in time and to follow up with a useful exploration of the patient's masochism.

There is, however, a category of misunderstandings or misreadings that generally do reflect the therapist's underlying subjective countertransference—namely, those

global misreadings known as "stereotypes" and "prejudices." As Ticho has stated, both stereotypes and prejudices
are "projections of ambivalence toward various cultural
values and ideals" (1971, p. 314). They provide a framework in which countertransferential problems are expressed. Some contamination by stereotypical or prejudicial perceptions is probably unavoidable in the *initial*
phase of cross-cultural psychotherapy. It is the failure to
reevaluate these prejudicial and stereotypical perceptions
over the course of treatment that alerts us to the likeli-
hood of underlying countertransference issues.

An example of an especially harmful stereotype sometimes held by Jewish therapists is the perception that Arab
patients are not sophisticated or psychologically minded
enough to benefit from insight-oriented psychotherapy.
Some therapists pointedly told me that they believed it
was "impossible" to do insight-oriented treatment with
Arabs. It is true that many Arab patients enter treatment
with expectations of receiving advice, directives, and con-
crete forms of help, but it is patently untrue that these
expectations are rigid and impervious to change—and it is
just as inaccurate to portray Arab patients as incapable of
introspection or psychological-mindedness. These stereotypes obviously undermine the possibility of carrying out
insight-oriented treatment. Interestingly, they are the
same misconceptions and stereotypes that are occasionally
held by white therapists with regard to black patients
(Jackson 1983, Wohlberg 1975).

Common Types of Countertransference

Several of the more common countertransference issues
for Jewish therapists working with Arab patients will be
delineated next. The aim is not to be exhaustive but rather

to focus on some of the more typical and troublesome issues. Examples from several cases will be introduced for illustrative purposes.

Excessive and Ambivalent Curiosity about the Patient's Culture

One of the typical areas of countertransference difficulty is the therapist's pervasive, and occasionally hovering, curiosity about the patient's cultural background. The therapist seizes upon the opportunity to meet a representative of this intriguing foreign culture, and in the process loses sight of the therapeutic task. Cultural material is explored more for its intrinsic interest than for its immediate relevance to the patient.

This type of countertransference problem has been discussed by other researchers (Abel and Métraux 1974, Devereux 1953). Devereux, a psychoanalyst with an avid interest in American Indian cultures, reveals his occasional difficulty in restraining his curiosity when dealing with Indian patients. He points out that the patient may come to resent the impersonal nature of the therapist's interest; or the patient may feed into this interest, plying the therapist with cultural data in lieu of exploring more personal areas of difficulty. Devereux suggests that perhaps the only way to avoid the pitfalls of excessive curiosity is to familiarize oneself with the patient's culture before beginning the treatment.

In the psychotherapy of Arab patients, Jewish therapists also occasionally fall prey to the countertransferential problem of hypercuriosity. Most of the Jewish therapists with whom I had contact were not widely familiar with Arab culture. None of these therapists had ever had an Arab as a close friend, most had never paid a social visit to an Arab village, and only one had a fluent knowledge of

Arabic. Yet most of these therapists had the desire to know more about Arab culture. The opportunity to treat an Arab patient was thus sometimes regarded as an opportunity to learn first-hand about Arab culture. A few Jewish therapists openly acknowledged choosing to work with Arab patients for this reason.

Not surprisingly, this type of curiosity sometimes led to sidetracking of the therapy. There was, for example, an occasional rambling exploration of the Arab extended family or of village life in general; or in one instance, a rather prolonged examination of sexual taboos in Arab culture. For the most part, however, these bouts of excessive curiosity, mingled as they were with an appropriate wish to understand the patient's cultural background, did not seem to cause great or enduring harm to the treatment.

What did greatly interfere with the treatment was the therapist's vacillation between a wish to understand the meaning of the patient's Arabness and an intense aversion to this Arabness—that is, curiosity interwoven with ambivalence. The matter of countertransference aggression will be discussed more fully later in this chapter. The point here is that in some instances, the therapist's curiosity seemed to be suddenly impeded by a wish (usually unconscious) to distance himself from all that was Arab in the patient.

As can readily be imagined, this countertransference problem is enhanced by the long-standing political antagonism between Jews and Arabs. This dilemma does not emerge with such poignancy in Devereux's examples of white therapist and Indian patient, nor even in the many reported cases of black–white interracial psychotherapy. Yet it seemed to be a troubling countertransference reaction for some Jewish therapists treating Arab patients. On occasion, when I had a chance to explore this issue with a therapist, what seemed to emerge was a vague but deep-seated fear about close contact with "the enemy," in spite of consciously held liberal and egalitarian political notions. This approach–avoidance seesawing had deleterious effects on the treatment, and unless it was addressed (usually in supervision), the therapy faltered.

Making an "Island" of the Treatment Situation

Sometimes allied with the above countertransference difficulty is another issue, which can be categorized as making an "island" of the treatment situation. In light of the political antagonism between Jews and Arabs, it is understandable that at times both therapist and patient may attempt to avoid discussion of their cultural differences. What happens in this instance is that each of the participants cues the other that matters of cultural difference are extraneous or, in any event, beyond the pale of exploration.

Therapists who participate in this type of obfuscation may do so under the guiding philosophy that, as Sullivan stated, "everyone is much more simply human than otherwise" (1953, p. 32). Few would quarrel with this view. But it is also true that therapists may foster and cling to this philosophy as a resistance. Occasionally, for example, I consulted with therapists who had been treating Arab patients for periods of a year or more and who reported that cultural differences never emerged as a topic for discussion. When asked about this, a common response was, as one therapist phrased it, "For me, the Arab patient is just another person."

In discussing interracial psychotherapy researchers have pointed to the importance of neither over- nor under-emphasizing the matter of race (Bernard 1953, Griffith

1977, Jackson 1983). If the patient attempts to avoid the topic, the therapist is advised to explore this avoidance. Failure to do so is viewed as countertransference resistance. Similarly, the Jewish therapist needs to recognize the meaning of the patient's Arabness for him, and the meaning of his Jewishness for the Arab patient. Any avoidance of this disquieting material by the therapist, in an effort to make an island of the treatment situation, is indicative of countertransference difficulties.

Some therapists attempt to make an island of the treatment situation in a narcissistic manner. They attempt to portray themselves as somehow above the cultural and political influences of their own society. They present themselves as exceptions. They may also subtly attempt to induce their Arab patients to behave as exceptions. The patients, of course, need not be passive recipients in this cover-up; they may initiate and try to evoke a response of "exceptionalism" in their therapists, who may in turn fail to confront it.

In two cases with which I am most familiar, it was the Jewish therapists (one man, one woman) who attempted to present themselves as free of cultural and political antagonisms and prejudices. Both therapists were actually something of outsiders within their society, and both held anti-Zionist views. In attempting rather early in treatment to cue their patients that they were exceptions within Jewish society, however, they aroused suspicion and rejection. Their patients wanted no part of this rapid intimacy; it was the therapist's need, not theirs. Moreover, the patients seemed to understand intuitively that creating this type of island would foreclose any possibility of discussing in a genuine way culturally and politically related conflicts.

Regrettably, only the woman therapist was able to manage her countertransference satisfactorily. She was able to see that she had allowed herself (as a woman and therefore, in her view, a second-class citizen) to overidentify with her Arab patient. She had sought to make an island with a fellow "victim"—a misalliance from which she eventually was able to disentangle herself. No such disentangling took place for the male therapist, who as a lower-class Sephardic Jew was similarly overidentified with his patient. He could grasp intellectually what was happening to him, but he could not avoid the undertow of his countertransference. The patient predictably did not last long in treatment.

Manifestations of Guilt

One of the most important and recurrent areas of counter-transference difficulty for Jewish therapists treating Arab patients involves the intrusion of guilt into the treatment arena. Consciously or (more often) unconsciously, guilt reactions to the Arab patient seemed to enter, at some time or another, into nearly all cases that I witnessed. It is well beyond the aim of this chapter to discuss the "realities" of Israeli–Arab politics. What is important, though, is that most of the therapists who treated Arab patients did believe that Israel had—knowingly or not—caused some harm to its Arab citizens, and beyond that, to the larger entity referred to as "Palestinians," with whom many Arab Israelis identify. As a consequence, guilt reactions (or defenses against them) were easily triggered by the treatment situation.

For instance, all the Jewish male therapists served in army reserve units. Depending on the unit in which they served, they might have to absent themselves from treatment once to three times a year, for periods of several weeks. Since this was the era of the Lebanon War, a few of these men were serving there. When it came to informing their Arab patients that they would be absent, some of these men experienced considerable guilt. They might state that they would be absent but, in contrast to their behavior with their Jewish patients, they did not state the reason, and they found themselves hoping that the Arab patients would not inquire. Or occasionally they would forget to mention the impending absence at all.

One therapist neglected to tell his Arab patient of his impending reserve duty until the last moment. The patient, in treatment only three months, had been working quite effectively, having established an idealizing transference to the Jewish therapist as a father figure (his own father had died when the patient was a young boy). For his part, the therapist was concerned—perhaps overconcerned—about "disappointing" the patient. Consequently, when he was called for reserve duty, he was most hesitant to inform the patient. When he finally did so at the session before his departure, the patient responded with an extended silence. Then, several minutes later, the patient's associations turned to Israeli–Arab politics, and specifically to his admiration of the Palestine Liberation Organization and its leader, Yassir Arafat, whom he described as the "father of the Palestinians." The Jewish therapist became immediately and intensely uncomfortable, but he was unable to sort out his feelings sufficiently to formulate a response. He left for reserve duty feeling guilty, not at all confident that he would still have a patient when he returned in three weeks.

The Arab patient generally senses the Jewish therapist's guilt. The patient's response to this countertransference will depend upon the nature of his character and pathology. Not uncommonly, the patient will evoke the therapist's guilt, in part as a means of camouflaging his personal difficulties.

A highly intelligent university student with a narcissistic disorder used treatment for a long while as a place to vent his frustrations with Israeli society. He recounted episode after episode of his mistreatment at the hands of Jews. His female Jewish therapist sensed that even if the episodes were true—and she tended to believe they were—the patient was nonetheless hypersensitive to injury and insult; he expected tribute from others and was easily wounded when it was not forthcoming. But the therapist found herself unable to intervene or in any manner address the patient's narcissistic vulnerability. She believed that the patient would respond with political flag-waving should she confront the repetitious nature of his recitations. Beyond this, she was unable to intervene because the patient's recountings and semidisguised accusations had evoked within her a sense of irritation and, above all, a paralyzing sense of guilt. She could not bear being perceived by her Arab patient as "an unfeeling Jew," as she put it.

It is perhaps worth noting that part of what fostered the therapist's difficulty was her temporary inability to evaluate the "subjective" and "objective" elements of her countertransference. She understood that the patient was at least unconsciously aware of inducing uneasiness in her by citing episodes of Jewish injustices. Yet she had great difficulty using the informational content of her predictable (objective) countertransference to formulate an appropriate response because she also sensed that her reaction was exaggerated and unremittingly intense; that is, there were significant subjective elements. She was not only reacting but overreacting, and not only identifying but overidentifying (above all, as a victim). It took her quite some time to work through her intense reaction, at which point she was finally able to address—without feeling guilty—the patient's hypersensitivity and his need to make others feel as uncomfortable and ashamed as he himself inwardly felt.

Occasionally, when the therapist is beset by guilt, he acts out by attempting to compensate the patient. This may be done in specific ways: The therapist may allow the sessions to run overtime or be lax in setting and collecting fees. More globally, the therapist may find himself becoming—as did the aforementioned female therapist—uncharacteristically and hollowly supportive. It is as if the therapist took on personal responsibility for undoing the wrongs perpetrated upon the patient. This attempt to engineer a "corrective emotional experience" is sooner or later likely to misfire and lead to further difficulties.

One of these difficulties is that the therapist feels under pressure to avoid any confrontation or negatively tinged interaction with the patient; such interactions would only make the therapist feel more guilt. But, of course, the therapist cannot avoid negative feelings toward this patient who is repeatedly arousing guilt. A vicious circle thus evolves: guilt leading to aggression, leading in turn to more guilt and further attempts to compensate the patient.

Manifestations of Aggression

Guilt and aggression are often intertwined in countertransference reactions. Each fosters the other. Accordingly, in the various manifestations of aggression that will be described next, guilt is a common accompaniment.

One example of this aggression- and guilt-tinged countertransference reaction is when the Jewish therapist finds himself experiencing, in spite of his egalitarian ideology, persistent feelings of superiority toward the Arab patient. The therapist wants to regard the patient as an equal, and yet consciously or unconsciously he feels that the patient is from an "inferior" culture. This kind of demeaning stereotype frequently intrudes when the therapist comes from the dominant or majority culture and the patient is from a minority culture. Several studies on interracial psychotherapy point to this prejudical attitude in the white therapist (Griffith 1977, Jackson 1983, Thomas 1962). Furthermore, such prejudice is sometimes shared by the black patient (Griffith 1977).

In the Jewish therapist–Arab patient dyad there is the additional factor of the ongoing war, in which the Jews have been winners and the Arabs losers. Both Jews and Arabs tend to attribute this political result, in part, to the supposedly superior qualities of Jewish society; the Jewish society is seen as more advanced or progressive. The mere fact that Hebrew is the spoken language in virtually all Jewish therapist–Arab patient psychotherapy further enhances this sense of social dominance and superiority.

These prejudices are sometimes brought into the treatment by *both* participants. For the Arab patient, seeking psychotherapy may represent a wish to participate in the benefits of this "progressive" society. The Jewish therapist is then idealized as a representative of that society. For the Jewish therapist who aspires to an egalitarian outlook, such idealization and all that it implies may well cause him discomfort, evoking a melange of guilt and vaguely felt triumph.

The political dominance of Jews vis-à-vis Arabs in Israel is conducive to another form of countertransference aggression. Until a sturdy therapeutic alliance is formed, the Arab patient is generally quite passsive with the Jewish therapist. He hesitates to assert himself in any manner. His aggression usually takes the form of passive-aggressive maneuvers, such as noncompliance with the treatment framework (lateness and absences are examples) or vague complaints about treatment. A frequent consequence of this behavior is that it engenders an over-assertive and negatively tinged countertransference.

One female Jewish therapist reported in supervision that she found herself becoming unusually active and confrontive with a male Arab patient. The therapist was not as a rule disposed toward therapeutic activism, nor did she have a confrontive style. As we examined the case material, which spanned several months, it became apparent that the patient was extremely passive with her, and beneath his seeming uncooperativeness was a pervasive mistrust. While the patient never said so explicitly, the therapist had the sense that she was regarded, as she put it, "as the Grand Inquisitor"—a role which she felt she had enacted at times by doggedly probing her evasive patient for more information. It thus became apparent that in his passivity, which at times bordered on passive aggression, he had evoked countertransferential hyperactivity, even aggression, from the therapist. This countertransference had both objective and subjective elements. In brief, the therapist not only was reacting to the patient's provocative passivity but also was influenced by her negative feelings about passive and unavailable men. Once the therapist was able to contain and manage her countertransference aggression, she began to explore in a nonconfrontive manner some of the patient's mistrust. It was almost a relief for her when he blurted out dramatically, "You see what is happening to the Palestinians in Lebanon; next thing you Israelis will be coming after us in Israel!"

A final type of countertransference aggression that deserves mention is one that arises out of deeply held differences of belief between therapist and patient. To be sure, this can happen in any kind of psychotherapy, but the extreme nature of the political conflict between Jews and Arabs makes this pernicious development all the more likely. The Arab patient may hold political beliefs that are anathema to the Jewish therapist. Or the patient may be directly or indirectly involved in political activity that is felt as threatening by the therapist. In either case, the therapist winds up struggling with negative feelings, even hatred, toward the patient. In extreme cases, the therapy simply cannot go on.

In one poignant example, the therapist was a concentration camp survivor whose political views generally tended toward liberalism and dovishness on Israeli–Arab questions. She had already treated three Arab patients when she was presented with the case of a young Arab intellectual with avowedly pro-PLO sympathies. She had little difficulty empathizing with the patient and his personal difficulties during the initial months of treatment. One morning, however, as she arrived at her office at the Hebrew University, she noticed a demonstration on campus by a group of Arab students protesting Israeli government policies toward Arabs. Her immediate thought was "I wonder if my patient is demonstrating there." And then,

"Why in hell am I helping an Arab when one day he may turn against me?"

She realized that she was in countertransferential difficulty but was not sure how to address the issue with the patient. Much to her relief, when her patient arrived for his appointment that afternoon, *he* raised the issue. He was openly sympathetic to the demonstrators but had not personally demonstrated. The therapist, sensing that the patient wanted to explore their cultural and political differences, acknowledged that the demonstration had made her uncomfortable. This led to a candid discussion of their different political sympathies. They reached no resolution, yet each felt there had been some clearing of the air. In retrospect, the therapist felt certain that if she had attempted to avoid the issue and had not been somewhat self-disclosing, the patient would have dropped out of treatment. As it was, the patient stayed on, and the therapy continued to a satisfactory conclusion some two years later.

This case raises the issue of how the therapist can most effectively use countertransference in the service of treatment. What should be told to the patient? How much self-disclosure is useful? And what is the correct timing for such interventions? In the final section of this chapter, these technical issues will be further explored.

The Management and Use of Countertransference

In treating a patient from a very different background, the therapist is prone to countertransferential errors that reflect his cultural assumptions and values. He is also likely to err at times in understanding or construing the meaning of some of the patient's statements and behavior. There is no way of completely avoiding these problems. Yet, the therapist has open to him some ways of minimizing the difficulties.

One of these, as indicated by several researchers, is that before treating a patient from another culture, the therapist should attempt to familiarize himself with that culture (Bernard 1953, Devereux 1953, Griffith 1977, Jackson 1983, Ticho 1971). Realistically, the therapist cannot expect to develop a thorough expertise, but he can hope to gain some access and awareness through reading and discussion with others. I have noticed that in those instances in which the therapist has made this kind of preparatory effort, the patient often seems to sense it, and it appears to strengthen the treatment alliance.

An additional facet of the therapist's preparation for working with patients of another culture is the need to examine candidly his motives for choosing to do so, especially those motives that may interfere with treatment. In short, the therapist is wise to examine the extent to which he might be bringing to the treatment situation countertransference predispositions: excessive curiosity, or aggression, or the wish to prove himself above prejudices, or the need to expiate feelings of guilt. The therapist may discover that his countertransference predispositions are of such magnitude that he would be ill-advised to begin a particular cross-cultural psychotherapy. More often, he is likely to discover what Racker (1957) has called a "personal equation"—namely those areas of countertransferential difficulty that potentially are most likely to emerge, albeit in manageable form, once the treatment is underway. These are the areas that the therapist will need to scrutinize throughout the course of therapy.

An important technical problem in cross-cultural psychotherapy is whether and when the therapist needs to initiate with the patient an exploration of their cultural differences. Is the therapist wise to wait until the patient alludes to their differences, or until obvious transference or countertransference problems arising out of their cultural differences impinge upon the treatment? Or should the therapist take up the matter at the outset of treatment, thereby alerting the patient that he believes cultural issues are likely to bear on the treatment? In this connection, several researchers on interracial psychotherapy have indicated that early discussion is advisable, even necessary (Griffith 1977, Schacter and Butts 1968, Tseng and McDermott 1972). In recommending early discussion of racial issues in interracial psychotherapy, Griffith states: "It sets the stage for openness in the therapeutic interaction and conveys the message that this crucial issue is not taboo" (p. 38).

These considerations also apply to the Jewish therapist–Arab patient dyad. Yet, in my observation, early discussion, especially in the initial session or two, was seldom initiated by the therapist. There is little question that the reluctance of the therapist to do so was fraught with countertransferential meaning in many instances. On occasion, however, it did seem that the therapist was reluctant to immediately confront the issue of cultural differences, primarily out of a tactful awareness that these matters were too threatening for the patient and that, rather than setting the stage for openness, early discussion would have engendered only paranoid-like resistance. Thus it sometimes did seem more constructive for the therapist to wait for the patient's transferential allusions to the therapist's Jewishness.

Although it is clear that sooner or later (and *usually* sooner) it is important for the patient to exlore the meaning for him of the therapist's cultural differences, it is less clear just how self-disclosing the therapist needs to be in this regard. Should the therapist's self-exploration be a "silent" one, or should he share some of this exploration with the patient? I am inclined to believe that in the initial phase of treatment, the therapist's self-exploration probably needs to be carried out silently. Having decided to raise the issue of cultural differences in the intake session or shortly thereafter, the therapist should then focus on the patient's thoughts and feelings. In my view, the therapist need do nothing more *at this point* than acknowledge the possibility of occasional misunderstandings due to cultural differences and *if asked*, acknowledge whether or not he has treated other patients from that culture. But the focus must be on the patient's concerns. The questions of the therapist's countertransferential predispositions and his general motives for working with the patient are a matter for his silent review; open discussion of them at this early stage would likely prove burdensome to the patient.

Once the treatment is underway, countertransference difficulties arising out of cultural differences often occur. Sometimes the therapist becomes aware of these difficulties before he acts them out; more often, however, he has already begun to act out. Indeed, it is usually his acting out that first alerts the therapist to the existence of countertransference problems. The question is then one of what should be said to the patient.

There is no absolute answer to this question. So much depends on the relationship of a particular therapist to a particular patient, as well as the nature of the counter-transference problems and just how and when they arise. In general, though, it has seemed to me that therapists have erred on the side of ignoring or attempting to deal "silently" with countertransferential impingements, rather than on the side of excessive self-disclosure. I am not suggesting that the therapist ought to engage in an exaggerated mea culpa. But it does seem that once the countertransferential impingement has become obvious to the patient, or once the patient indicates an unconscious awareness of it (such as in dreams or transference allusions), the therapist needs to acknowledge, and up to a point discuss, the impingement, with a focus on its meaning for the patient.

The only valid evidence of the value of such technical suggestions comes from the examination of specific cases. Let me illustrate, then, from some of the case material already presented, what I take to be correct or incorrect handling of countertransference impingements.

The male therapist who forgot until the last moment to tell his patient that he was leaving for reserve duty mismanaged the countertransference. The therapist realized that his guilt had interfered with making the announcement, as well as with his responding to the patient's veiled hostility (and disappointment) once the announcement was belatedly made. The therapist left for reserve duty without having addressed these matters. Even when he returned he failed to address them, although the patient immediately made transparent references to the therapist's sudden departure and supposed military activities. The therapist encouraged the patient's exploration of these "fantasies" about the departure, but he did not allude to his own countertransferential difficulty. He chose to deal "silently" with his countertransference.

In my view, the therapist's silence was in this instance neither helpful nor advisable. The therapist needed not only to focus on the patient's fantasies about the departure but also to acknowledge his own difficulty in announcing the absence. I believe that had the therapist acknowledged his own difficulty, it could have led to a fruitful exploration of transference and reality elements in the patient's perceptions, and it might have enhanced the treatment alliance between patient and therapist. Unfortunately, we will never know. What did happen is that the patient slowly veered away from the subject. Then, several weeks later he suddenly, and irrevocably, announced that he would be discontinuing treatment.

This case can be contrasted with the example of the woman concentration camp survivor who found herself overwhelmed by aggression toward her Arab patient as she contemplated a political demonstration of Arab students. She realized that she had to manage these feelings in order to go on working with her patient. When the patient came to his session the same day and mentioned the demonstration, he was obviously concerned about not only his feelings but hers as well. She could have chosen simply to explore his feelings and fantasies. She, after all, had not sufficiently worked through her countertransferential aggression. (I suspect that the patient may have sensed this.) Yet she chose to talk about her discomfort and her fantasy of the patient's participation in the demonstration. This was a bold thing to do, but she believed in retrospect that refusal to explore her countertransference would have proved deleterious to her relationship with the patient and to the treatment. I am inclined to agree with her. But again, we will never know. All we do know is that her intervention seemed to lead to a clearing of the air, and not to any signs of resistance on the patient's part.

These two examples are presented to demonstrate how some countertransferential difficulties might be technically dealt with by the therapist. While they are suggestive of the occasional usefulness of the therapist's self-disclosure, each case must be examined on its own terms. The question of just when, how, or if to openly explore countertransference issues is not one that lends itself to facile generalizations.

In summary, one more point should be emphasized: In cross-cultural psychotherapy, the management of countertransference is a technical matter of special meaning. In such therapy, the usual problems of trust and empathy are often sharply accentuated. This is all the more true in the milieu of modern-day Israel, where antipathy and distrust between Arab and Jew are the norm. Countertransference problems arising out of cultural and political differences are almost certain to occur in this situation. The therapist's adequate management of these problems— including, if necessary, self-disclosures—often seems to make the difference between successful and failed treatment. All of this is a difficult task for the Jewish therapist and imposes great demands on him—and on the Arab patient, too. But the fact that some treatments do reach a most satisfactory outcome is quiet, and perhaps even edifying, testimony that such a task can be accomplished.

9

Countertransference in Supervision

Just as therapists over the past thirty-five years have learned to pay increasing attention to their countertransferences in the treatment of patients, so too has it become apparent that supervisors need to monitor the emotional phenomena that arise within themselves as they engage in the supervisory process. These emotional phenomena, or countertransferences, can serve as either a hindrance or a useful tool in the supervisory process, much as the therapist's countertransferences can impede or inform in the treatment process. This chapter will explore some of the ways in which the supervisor's countertransference experiences vis-à-vis the therapist can either help or hinder the supervisory work.

Among the beneficial uses of the supervisor's countertransferences, I especially wish to discuss "parallel" and "triangulation" processes, phenomena which, when understood by the supervisor, can be enormously helpful as a means of gaining insight into what is transpiring

221

between the supervisor and the therapist and, in turn, between the therapist and the patient. On the negative side of the ledger, the chapter will delineate some of the more typical "blind spots," or "subjective" countertransferences, that supervisors themselves sometimes introduce into the supervisory situation—in particular, countertransferential issues involving (1) the supervisor's position and authority within a given institution, (2) the supervisor's problems with envy of the supervisee, and (3) the supervisor's attitude of omniscience. Finally, some technical comments will be offered regarding the supervisor's disclosure of countertransference experiences to the supervisee as a means of enhancing the supervisory process and, by extension, the treatment process.

Parallel Processes in the Supervisory Situation

As outlined in Chapter 1, the period of the late 1940s and early 1950s witnessed a significant broadening of views with regard to the role of the analyst's emotional responses to the patient in the treatment situation. For the first time, it was emphasized by a spectrum of analysts (Cohen 1952, Heimann 1950, Little 1951, Racker 1953, Weigert 1952, Winnicott 1949) that these emotional responses could serve a useful purpose in understanding the patient. By observing the feelings engendered in himself, it was argued, the therapist could gain valuable information as to the patient's inner world and transferences. It is perhaps not surprising that, as this innovative notion began to impress itself on the minds of many therapists, it was soon extended to the supervisory process as well. Thus, in 1955, Searles published his landmark essay "The

Informational Value of the Supervisor's Emotional Experiences." In the opening paragraph of that essay, he put forth his thesis: "The emotions experienced by a supervisor—including even his private, 'subjective' fantasy experiences and his personal feelings about the supervisee— often provide valuable clarification of processes currently characterizing the relationship between the supervisee and the patient" (p. 157).

Searles referred to this phenomenon as the "reflection process," by which he meant that a given emotion evoked in the supervisor *may be* a reflection of what was earlier evoked in the therapist by the patient. In describing the process, Searles wrote:

> With convincing frequency I have seen that a therapist who during an occasional presentation appears to be lamentably anxious, compulsive, confused in his thinking, or what not, actually is a basically capable colleague who, as it were, is trying unconsciously, by this demeanour during the presentation, to show us a major problem-area in the therapy with his patient. The problem-area is one which he cannot perceive objectively and describe to us effectively in words; rather, he is unconsciously identifying with it and is in effect trying to describe it by way of his behaviour during the presentation [p. 170].

Subsequent investigators have refined Searles's original notion of the *reflection process*, giving this phenomenon a new name and, more important, extending our awareness of how and where and why it occurs. Ekstein and Wallerstein (1958) were the first to dub this phenomenon a *parallel process*—a phrase that has since been widely employed by others. In addition, Ekstein and Wallerstein

demonstrated that parallel processes need not be unidirec-
tional—as Searles had stressed—but may flow in both
directions; that is, the therapist may not only play patient
to the supervisor, but he may also play supervisor to the
patient. Recent investigators (Doehrman 1976, Gediman
and Wolkenfeld 1980, Winokur 1982) have further elaborated this theme of multidirectionality in parallel processes, emphasizing that it is sometimes quite difficult to
tease out who is providing what impetus to the pathological interrelatedness of supervisor–therapist–patient. The
additional questions of why the various participants go
about instigating a parallel process, and when they are
most likely to do so, have also received some attention in
the literature (Caligor 1981, Gediman and Wolkenfeld
1980). So, too, has there been a deepening of our theoretical understanding of the mechanisms by which the various
participants engender these parallel processes (Arlow
1963, Bromberg 1982, Grinberg 1979). These observations
will be discussed in more detail later. At this point, however, it might be useful for illustrative purposes to introduce a case example in which a parallel process was rather
obviously at work.

> I was conducting a case seminar at the Student Coun-
> selling Services of the Hebrew University in Jerusa-
> lem. There were seven psychologists in the seminar,
> all of whom I had supervised individually the pre-
> vious year. The woman who presented that day, V.,
> was a skillful clinician known for her animated way of
> capturing the essence of a case. Nonetheless, as she
> recounted the background of the case she had se-
> lected for supervision, her manner was distinctly low-
> key and withdrawn. After a year of twice-a-week ther-
> apy with her patient, S., she believed they had come

to an impasse, and she added that she found herself "exhausted and depleted from the effort of trying to reach S."

As it turned out, S., a 32-year-old woman, was also "exhausted and depleted" in her own way, although this was not immediately evident from the external facts of her life. S. was, to all appearances, successful and well-adapted, combining with great efficiency a career as a graphic artist and an active family life. (She had married early and had four children before she was 30.) In addition, S. found the time to participate in a well-known local choral group.

What had brought her into treatment was a sense that something was amiss. S. vaguely sensed that in spite of her considerable involvement with people, she was disconnected from them and experienced no real pleasure in their company. On occasion—"my black days," as she called them—she withdrew from everyone, ostensibly ill, and remained in bed. These "black days" were especially frightening to S. because they reminded her of what her mother had done when S. was a child. S. had tried with great effort to reach her mother during these bouts of depression and withdrawal, but with little success. As a child, S. had intuitively sensed that her mother's depression was linked to the latter's experience of some years in the Auschwitz concentration camp. Her mother had always withdrawn to bed, for example, around the time of Holocaust Day, when Israelis remember those who died in concentration camps. Not unusually, however, her mother rarely spoke of her years in Auschwitz, and S.'s father, a native-born Israeli, had advised her never to bring up the sub-

ject—advice which S. followed scrupulously, even
though she tried in every other way to minister to her
mother during *her* black days.

In fact, a pattern that became evident in hearing
the case presentation was that much of S.'s childhood
had been spent in trying to please her mother, to
make a warm connection with her and in a sense
bring her back to life. S.'s successes in school and her
early interest in art and music seemed to be partially
motivated by a wish to please her mother, who, prior
to her concentration camp experience, had pursued
similar interests. Superficially, the mother had encouraged and welcomed her daughter's accomplish-
ments, but on a deeper level these efforts failed to
bring mother and daughter warmly together. "No
matter how interested she appeared," S. had recalled,
"I never felt I made her really happy—*I never felt I
could truly reach her.*"

In the above quotation from the patient, I have
taken the liberty of underscoring the last phrase because it was exactly this wording that V. also used in
summarizing her relationship to S. In spite of her
great desire to "reach" S., in spite of her considerable
probing for details, clarifying patterns in S.'s life, and
interpreting genetic and transferential material, V.
felt she was getting nowhere. V. had become not only
"exhausted and depleted," but also—as was obvious
to some members of the group—frustrated and furious with S. In her guilt over this anger toward S., she
had redoubled her efforts to reach her and continued
to ply her with more and more elegant observations
and interpretations. Significantly, the one area that
V. scrupulously had avoided discussing was S.'s feelings and fantasies about her mother's incarceration

in Auschwitz. She no more dared to push S. to elaborate upon this material than S. had dared to push her
mother to reveal what had happened there. This fact
was noted by one of the members of the group, who
gingerly stated that V. was overlooking the issue of
Auschwitz and its impact on the family. But this
observation, while acknowledged by V., obviously did
not register with her. And the rest of the group did
not pick up on it either.

Indeed, the group picked up on no theme with
any consistency. Rather, just as V. had doggedly plied
S. with more and more observations and interpretations, so too did the group now doggedly pursue V.
Their observations were astute, yet V. could not at
that moment use any of them. She listened politely
and (I thought) with feigned interest, while sinking
ever more visibly into her armchair, shielded by a
cloud of cigarette smoke. Gone was any semblance of
the usual animated V., who had so often stimulated
and amused the group. Now, instead, the group
members—every one of them, I noticed, as I looked
around the room—sat on the edge of their chairs,
leaning toward her, as if attempting to reach and
revive her. Finally, one of the members looked
around and stated loudly and exasperatedly, "I give
up; no matter what we say, tonight we just are not
going to reach V.!"

It was at this point, with the advantage of being
something of an outside observer of this "uncanny"
phenomenon (Gediman and Wolkenfeld 1980), that I
chose to point out the parallel process that seemed to
be happening in V.'s therapy with S. and, in turn, in
her relationship to the group-cum-supervisors. Generally, I noted that S. had managed to get V. to expe-

rience during the therapy an important aspect of how she, S., had originally felt with her mother; in turn, V. had managed to get the group to experience this same important aspect that she felt with S. And specifically, I observed that revivification of a withdrawn and depressed person was the principal theme in these parallel interactions, with Auschwitz remaining a taboo topic to all. It would take me too far afield to discuss in detail the ensuing interaction in the group, but I think the reader will not be surprised to know that for V., as well as for some others in the group, there had been a similar life experience of having a parent who was a concentration camp survivor. As a child, each of these therapists had apparently attempted to "reach" this parent and somehow restore him or her to life.

In the group, on that evening at least, I did not attempt to discuss the theoretical issues involved in this parallel process. I would like to turn to some of these issues here, however, with specific reference to the foregoing example. Regarding the question of directionality of the parallel process, it seems clear that this case falls into the category of cases described by Searles: The therapist plays out the patient to the supervisor, and not vice versa. In order to alter this pathological pattern, the supervisor would need to begin relating to V. *not* in this parallel pattern—that is, not as V. related to S.—but in a different and more constructive manner. If and when the supervisor(s) were able to so relate (for instance, by relaxing their frenzied resuscitation efforts but *not* avoiding the topic of Auschwitz), then the directionality of constructive influence could be said to flow from supervisor to therapist to patient; in other words, a benevolent parallel process could occur (Doehrman 1976).

In this example, the group-cum-supervisors became caught up in a destructive parallel process, repeating with V. what V. had enacted with S. If we ask why the group members became caught up in this enactment, we can point to two broad categories of influence: (1) the real and palpable (or "objective") pressure that was exerted upon them by V. to relate in this way; (2) the largely unconscious and conflicted (or "subjective") predisposition on the part of several of the group members to take on this role in relation to V. Even those group members who were not as subjectively predisposed to take on the role of revivifier found themselves more or less doing so, though perhaps with greater conscious awareness that they were succumbing to an undertow (for example, the group member who finally stated his exasperation about not being able to "reach" V).

I too experienced this "objective" pressure to try to reach and revivify V. I can remember thinking in the early part of V.'s presentation that she seemed disconnnected that night, and later the thought passed through my mind that "I've *got* to help her, but anything I say will fall on *dead ears*." It was this phrase, coupled with the sensation of an exaggerated wish to help V., that alerted me to begin evaluating what might be transpiring between V. and me, and also between V. and the group. I was able to stand back and observe because I was neither as caught up in the group process as were the members, nor as subjectively predisposed to assuming the role of revivifier with V. as were several of them.

This fortuitous sense of distance is not always attainable, of course, and sometimes the supervisor remains quite caught up in the parallel process, unable to find his bearings for weeks on end. This is particularly so when, for unconscious and subjective reasons, he is predisposed to enact a given role with the supervisee. Or, as Caligor puts it, "The parallel process occurs more dramatically when the patient, therapist, and supervisor have a juncture or crossing of blind spots with resultant heightened disjunctive anxiety and decline in empathy" (1981, p. 22). In these circumstances, when enactment by the supervisor has been ensuing for some time, it may be quite difficult, if not impossible, to determine whether a given parallel process was initiated in the patient–therapist dyad or in the supervisor–therapist dyad, and it may require considerable self-exploration for the supervisor to unravel his own pathological contribution to the parallel process enmeshment.

By what psychological mechanisms are such parallel processes transmitted? The most satisfying conceptualization of this phenomenon, in my view, is that expressed in terms of multiple projective identifications. Thus, in this example, it can be said that the patient, S., projected the part of her self that felt disconnected from her mother and longed to revive her, onto her therapist, V. By means of verbal and nonverbal cues, S. induced V. to experience this frustrated and painful part of her self. Because of her own subjective inclinations, V. became overwhelmed by this experience—so much so that she could not contain and examine it, but instead, in her interaction with the supervisory group, she too projected this imago of self as cut off and futilely engaged in revivification. And in their turn, the group members took in and became overwhelmed by this projection, to a point at which they too could not contain and examine it. It may be argued (Ogden 1979) that both patient and therapist employed the mechanism of projective identification, not only for the purpose of ridding themselves of a stressful part of self and/or introject, but also for the purpose of communication—that is, letting another person know of an important aspect of internal experience and, hopefully, receiving some help with it. This manner of conceptualizing parallel processes was anticipated by Searles in his original contribution (1955).

In the case illustration presented here, I chose to openly apprise the group of the ensuing parallel process as I understood it. I began by drawing their attention to the most obvious manifestion of the parallel process: the observation that everyone at that moment was leaning toward V., who was reclining in withdrawal. I elaborated this theme of revivification of a withdrawn, depressed person, and explained how my initial awareness of this theme had developed from my own similar response to V. In addition, I explicitly stated that, in parallel fashion, all seemed to be avoiding the taboo topic of Auschwitz.

As with any intervention—by supervisor or therapist—the timeliness and fit can best be judged by the response. The fact that a good deal of personal and meaningful self-revelation ensued, with the result that V. was finally "reached," led me to feel that the intervention had been appropriate. (I was further convinced some weeks later, when V. reported a similar shift in her relationship with S.; she was not working quite so strenuously and impatiently, and the topic of Auschwitz was being discussed.) In retrospect, I have no question that in *this* instance it was helpful to discuss openly my countertransference, that of the group, and that of V.; it was important to explore the parallel process. I was on firm enough footing with the members of the group—there was a good "learning alliance" (Fleming and Benedek 1964)—and the various members, most essentially V., were all sufficiently self-aware to absorb the data. In other circumstances, it may be necessary to use one's awareness of the parallel process only as a source of information; open discussion may prove too disturbing to the supervisee. In this example, however, open discussion proved to be a beneficial first step in undoing a destructive parallel process and initiating a more constructive one.

Triangulation Processes in the Supervisory Situation

Triangulation processes occur rather often in the supervisory situation. In such a process, the therapist does not reflect or engage in parallel interactions in his two sets of *dyadic* relationships (therapist–supervisor and therapist–patient); rather, in his manner of relating to the patient and supervisor, he choreographs a three-party, or *triadic*, system. For example, it is not uncommon for a therapist to (unconsciously) perceive and set about enacting some aspect of his oedipal conflict, with patient and supervisor assigned specific roles (Meerloo 1952); in such situations, the gender of the participants is usually crucial. But although the triangular relationship lends itself obviously to oedipal-like scenarios, it may also be used for the enactment of a preoedipal theme, especially the theme of therapist and patient engaged in blissful symbiosis, with the supervisor (regardless of gender) construed as an outsider, or more perniciously, as a third-party interloper (Searles 1962).

    In all these situations, as the therapist goes about his choreographic work, the supervisor is bound to feel, in some measure, pushed and prodded into a specific role or imago. Thus, by attending to the feelings and fantasies aroused within himself, the supervisor is often able to gain valuable information about what is transpiring between the therapist and patient, and also about where he may fit into the triangulation process. With this awareness, the supervisor is better able to make appropriate observations and, if necessary, adjustments in his supervision of the therapist. Following are two examples of triangulation processes that occurred during my own supervisory experience.

The first example took place shortly after I began working as a supervisor. Although I have since found that what ensued in this case is quite common, at the time I was not familiar with such triangulation processes. E., the therapist I was supervising, was in the second year of his psychology internship, a bright and serious man who seemed on first impression more mature than his age (25) would lead one to expect. In the first two months of supervision, we had begun work on three cases—all males—and I was already comfortably content with the work he was doing. I could also feel that E. was content with the supervision. The emotional nature of our relationship was something on the order of a warm, respectful older brother to younger brother.

As we began work on the fourth patient he brought for supervision, however, I started to experience, during the ever-increasing time we discussed this patient, a distinct shift in our emotional relatedness. The patient was someone E. had already been treating for a year, and as best I could tell from his initial presentation, he had done solid work with her. She was a 30-year-old woman, recently and tragically widowed, and in the year of therapy she had seemed to emerge from her deep depression. She had returned to work and had begun again to take pleasure in people and activities. One could sense her involve-

ment with the therapy and the therapist, and furthermore, that with the abatement of the crisis she had
begun to explore more long-standing issues. It was
thus surprising to me when, shortly after beginning
supervision on this patient, E. questioned whether
the time had come for him to reduce this patient's
sessions from twice to once a week: Her crisis had
abated, he said, and he felt the patient could do just
as well now with less therapeutic contact. When I
answered matter-of-factly that I thought it better to
postpone this decision, he gave me an abrupt look of
disappointment such that I felt I had failed him in
some way.

In the next few weeks he did not again raise the
question, and I neglected to bring it up with him. I
did raise with him, though, the question of whether
the patient's obvious fondness of him—as reflected
in a recent dream—was not anxiety-provoking for
him. He acknowledged that it might be and then, in a
boy scout–like manner, promised to work on it. Because I knew he had just begun his personal treatment, I pressed him no further. Instead, we continued to focus on the patient, and as we did so he
began to ply me with more and more questions—so
much so that I had the distinct sensation that E.
wished this case to be *mine*, not *his*. As I tried to
refrain from answering his questions, and instead to
support him as a competent therapist who had already shown he could find his own way, he reacted as
if I were distancing myself from him, even abandoning him. Also, when I suggested at one point that he
not be quite so quick to interpret the patient's positive transference, but rather allow it to gain intensity,
he responded with such anxiety and hesitation that I

was sure he felt I was throwing him to the wolves. Indeed in my internal experience, I did begin to feel like I was abandoning him and almost sadistically neglecting him.

It was then that I began to silently analyze the triangulation process in which we had become enmeshed. I could see that I had entered into this therapist's oedipal conflict as a participant. It had been apparent from the start that he was frightened of his oedipal wishes toward this older female patient who, as a necessary part of her treatment, had begun to regard him with increasingly obvious warmth. What had taken me more time to understand was that in our supervisory work on this case, E. had choreographed for me the role of inattentive and neglectful father, one who would not protect him from this frightening woman. In his manner of interacting with me, he had managed to induce in me the feeling that I was just such a father; further, for subjective reasons of my own, I had begun to enact this role, most especially by being somewhat patronizingly and hollowly "supportive" of him.

Sensing this to be the case, I set about addressing our enmeshment, not initially in terms of the therapist's oedipal fears toward the patient, but rather in terms of his sense of my neglect of him. It was this emphasis on our supervisory relationship that finally struck home. He responded that, unlike in our other work, he felt me to be "distant" in the supervision of this case. He said, "I feel you're telling me I can handle her, and I feel I can't." His choice of phrasing gave us the chance to explore the double meaning of *handle*, and it soon became poignantly obvious to him that his own oedipal fears were getting in the way, and that he sought me as a father-protector, which, he added sadly, "my old man never was." We did not explore further the details of his background, nor did I encourage him to take up this matter in his personal treatment. I felt that such a suggestion, coming from me at that time, would be experienced as a further rejection. We both sensed with great relief, however—and in time this impression was validated—that we had begun to unravel the triangulation process in which we were both so uncomfortably enmeshed.

The second example of triangulation processes is a supervisory experience in which both preoedipal and oedipal elements were predominant, albeit at different stages of the supervision.

The therapist, G., was a woman psychologist with whom I was working on several cases. We had a good rapport right from the outset; in fact, she was the kind of person who is a pleasure to supervise—sensitive, warm, and open to self-exploration. She was able to articulately describe her work with patients, usually welcoming whatever comments I had to offer.
There was only one exception to this pattern. This was the case of a teenage girl whose symptomatology was vaguely hysteric, or possibly masochistic; I could not be sure. The principal reason for my uncertainty was that G. lost almost all her articulateness in reporting this case. Actually, "reporting" is too elaborate a description of what took place. Rather, she provided me with just enough detail to let me know that the girl was not in serious trouble and was actually responding well to treatment, but never

enough detail for me to feel either that I was part of the treatment or that I had anything to contribute to it. Not once over the first year or so of treatment did the therapist ever pose a question or solicit any observation from me regarding this case.

A curious process began to evolve within me. For some months, I felt quite frozen out and not a little annoyed at the situation. Two or three times I attempted to probe further as to what might be happening in the case, and once I made some snide remark about their "mutual admiration society." It was apparent that these probings disturbed G., but to her credit (I later realized), she gently tried to reassure me that all was well in the therapy and asked, in a sense, that I let her go about her business. So I did.

Before continuing to describe the evolution of this case, I want to make a slight detour to introduce some theoretical considerations. When a supervisee refuses to talk about or otherwise avoids discussing a case with the supervisor, it is apparent that some type of resistance may be taking place. The supervisee may be enacting some destructive process with the patient that he consciously or unconsciously wishes to hide. Alternatively, he may have arrived at a stalemate with the supervisor, whom he has ceased to trust and whom he therefore tries to fend off from interfering in his work. In both these circumstances, the supervisor is apt to experience at least a modicum of resentment, as if his side of the "triangle" had been hostilely erased. I believe, however, that my initial resentment in the supervisory case I am describing was due more to subjective issues of my own than to anything this therapist was doing to me. I eventually began to realize this when a certain untroubled acceptance and warmth entered into my countertransference vis-à-vis this particular therapist–patient dyad. I sensed that I had been gently placed to the side, but not hostilely erased.

It is this kind of countertransferential experience that Searles seems to describe in his discussion of the supervisor's reactions to working with a therapist who is engaged in a "preambivalent symbiosis" with the patient (1962, pp. 593–595). Searles considers this phase to be a normal and necessary part of the treatment of all patients, neurotics as well as psychotics. I am not prepared to argue this point. What I do want to affirm is that in my experience as a supervisor, there are sometimes periods of quite long duration when the supervisee and patient (no matter what the diagnosis) do seem to be engaged in a highly beneficial "mutual admiration society." In these instances, the supervisor's being held at some distance from the treatment by the supervisee may *not* be a supervisory resistance; it may be in the service of the treatment. Ultimately, then, as Searles suggests, the supervisor's ability to allow this process to go on is most constructive and beneficial. What I have learned to do is trust my countertransferential reaction of untroubledness and somewhat distant warmth as an indicator that the "preambivalent symbiosis" is occurring and that, for the time being, my role is simply to let the therapist go about his business.

What happened in this case (though this does not always happen) is that after a period of more than a year of my remaining on the sidelines, G. gradually began to introduce more revealing details of her work with the patient. For the first time I began to have a solid sense of who this teenage girl was; the diagnostic picture of her as a "good hysteric" who had historically been cocooned with her mother, and now for the past year or so with her therapist, became sharply evident. It also became evident that the cozy relationship between therapist and patient was no longer quite so cozy.

Interestingly, my initial awareness that there was a new pattern emerging in the patient–therapist relationship came not so much from what was told to me, but more from the sense that I was finally being drawn into the case by G. She seemed to need something from me: observations, advice, and above all, participation. She and I became active partners in working on this teenage girl, and I had the vague fantasy that my wife was at last consulting and commiserating with me about our slightly troublesome daughter. It became clear that our "daughter," too, had begun to express her first feelings of disenchantment with her therapist/mother, and in a manner that seemed quite healthy, she too had begun to show renewed interest in her outside contacts, especially a new boyfriend. This pattern, once begun, continued to take root.

The patient and therapist did not renew their exclusive, mutual admiration society for the following year and a half—the period during which I continued as supervisor. During that time, G. continued to involve me as a valuable consultant and participant—a part of the triangle, so to speak. Eventually, at the end of our supervisory collaboration, I decided to inform her of the triangulation processes that, in my estimation, had occurred. I did this more for her intellectual appraisal than as a necessary part of the supervisory process. G.'s confirmatory remarks and

acceptance of this data might not qualify as "significant" among our more statistically oriented colleagues, but I found her agreement to be happily
meaningful.

Subjective Countertransferences in the Supervisor

It is well known that supervisors sometimes bring to the
supervisory process their own quirks and conflicts that, in
one way or another, interfere with the treatment that the
therapist is attempting to conduct. We all know this in
principle, and yet it seems that we are more apt to over-
look our "subjective" countertransferences in our role as
supervisors than in our role as therapists; that is, we are
not quite so vigilant and self-scrutinizing in our supervisory work as we are in our therapeutic work. Indeed I
suspect that one of the appeals of becoming a supervisor is
that one feels free to be more spontaneous with a colleague than with a patient; one can relax and be more
oneself. Moreover, it is quite easy for a supervisor to
incorporate into his teaching style or position a variety of
subjective countertransference attitudes and dispositions—confrontiveness, pervasive advice-giving, nonstop
chattiness—that would be far more evident to him in his
role as therapist. These countertransferential intrusions
may be neutralized and managed by the supervisee and
therefore may not interfere in the treatment of the patient. Alternatively, they may unsettle the supervisee, and
in various ways—including the mechanism of parallel process—they may be deflected into the arena of the therapy.
In these circumstances, it can be said that the supervisor
becomes a major source, if not *the* major source, of the

treatment difficulty between the supervisee and the patient. The sections that follow will outline some of the more common and troublesome difficulties brought by supervisors to the supervisory process.

Issues Involving the Supervisor's Position in an Institutional Setting

Among the countertransferential impingements that commonly enter the supervisory process are those that issue from the fact that supervision is generally carried out in an institutional setting—a training institute, graduate school, clinic, or hospital. In these settings, the supervisor is frequently in a position of "authority" in relation to the supervisee, and he may actually exercise a good deal of power over the latter's chances of advancement. Just how he chooses to wield—or not wield—this power is likely to influence, and may intrude on, his work with the supervisee. In addition, the supervisor has a particular status and position within the institution. He may be a senior or junior supervisor, well or poorly regarded, and staunchly or loosely identified with the institution. In one manner or another, these "indirect" influences (Racker 1953) may also be brought to bear on the supervisor's relationship to the supervisee and may ultimately impinge upon the supervisory process.

The issue of the supervisor's authority in relation to the supervisee has been discussed rather frequently in the literature (DeBell 1963, Doehrman 1976, Emch 1955, Lesser 1983, Lower 1972, Searles 1962). It has long been recognized that there are inherent difficulties in the supervisory situation arising out of the supervisor's role as one who must evaluate and judge the supervisee's progress, and as one who is called upon to implement institutional policies. In performing these roles, the supervisor is not in an equal colleagueal relationship to the supervisee. Rather, he must super-vise—literally, over-see. Most supervisors manage this aspect of their work with a good deal of tact and conscientiousness. But as we all know (if not from our own work, then certainly from our experience as trainees!), supervisors do occasionally mismanage their authority.

Most obvious, and perhaps most immediately anxiety-provoking for the supervisee, is when the supervisor exercises his authority and power with a certain sadistic touch, if not with outright glee. Such a supervisor may have endured a similar abuse of power during his own traineeship, and now at last he is in the position to do unto others as was done unto him: He can enact his identification with the aggressor.

A less obvious mismanagement of authority is when the supervisor hesitates to exercise power at all and instead insists on remaining a coequal with the supervisee. Perhaps because of his own hatred of authority, such a supervisor avoids assuming the role of evaluator or standard-bearer with the supervisee. He may fear the supervisee's negative response, so instead he enacts his identification with the "oppressed." As a speculation, I imagine that this latter type of supervisory mismanagement is more likely to occur in a cultural milieu in which antiauthority attitudes are widely accepted (the United States of the 1980s, for example); similarly, the problem of excessive flexing of supervisory authority is no doubt more endemic to a cultural milieu in which authority is admired for itself (such as Vienna in the 1920s).

Both types of mismanagement of supervisory authority can adversely affect the supervisee's work with the patient. The supervisee who feels harshly treated by the supervisor may unconsciously enact these attitudes by behaving critically and judgmentally with the patient. Likewise, the supervisee who is managed with "kid gloves" may find himself quite unable to confront his patients when such confrontation is needed. For instance, some supervisors are quite unwilling to insist upon conformity to certain institutional policies; fee collection is a prime example. In an enactment of his own antiauthority attitudes, the supervisor does not insist that the supervisee collect fees on time and in the expected amounts. He refuses to assert himself with the supervisee and instead forms a rebellious alliance with him against the institution. The supervisee in turn reflects this laxness and rebelliousness with the patient and forms a similar unholy alliance with him. A destructive parallel process is thus given impetus by the supervisor's countertransferential inability to assert authority.

In addition to issues of authority, there are other problems that may impede the supervisory process in an institutional setting. The supervisor's relationship to others in the institution—that is, his indirect, or third-party, countertransferences—may come into play, sometimes negatively, in his work with a supervisee. For instance, it is not at all unusual for a measure of competition to exist among supervisors in a training institute or clinic, and some supervisors will naturally be more popular than others (Lesser 1983, Lower 1972). This alone need not cause problems in the supervisory situation. But what can be problematic are the methods by which some supervisors consciously or unconsciously seek to establish popularity. Some supervisors create a following by being excessively "supportive," while others woo supervisees by bestowing a protectiveness over their "own" people. Quite obviously, these manipulations can have an adverse effect on the supervisee. They may lead to parallel enactments—excessive "supportiveness" or narcissistic overinvolvement—in the supervisee's work with his patients, or they may lead to quite opposite maneuvers, whereby the supervisee attempts to deal with the patient in the way he wishes the supervisor would deal with him. In either case, the treatment may be adversely affected.

In addition, in some institutional settings (for example, graduate schools or post-graduate training institutes), the supervisor may be only one of several working with a particular student. The supervisor may respect his student's other supervisors, or, not atypically, he may dislike them on personal or ideological grounds. In the latter circumstance, it will often require a good deal of control over one's countertransferential feelings of competitiveness (as well as hatred and disdain) not to subtly disparage a fellow supervisor, especially if the supervisee attempts to play off one supervisor against the other. In analytic training institutes, the possibility of the supervisor's enacting his "sibling rivalry" or hatred and disdain may also occur vis-à-vis the supervisee-candidate's training analyst (Ackerman 1953, Lesser 1983); and again, the supervisee's participation in these enactments may not be passive. In this way, splitting processes can be encouraged such that one supervisor is idealized while another supervisor, or training analyst, is demeaned, often with the result that similar splitting is encouraged by the supervisee in his work with the patient.

In sum, then, the supervisor who is conducting supervision in an institutional setting may find himself tempted to enact various subjective countertransferences. These enactments are sometimes so thoroughly interwoven with the supervisor's teaching style or ideological orientation that the supervisor becomes quite blind to them and is thus unlikely to alter them. While the precise impact of these enactments is often difficult to gauge, there is little doubt that at times they unsettle the supervisee and, in turn, impinge on his work with the patient.

Envy of the Supervisee

Years ago, in making some brief observations about the supervisory process, Meerloo acknowledged what *he* had gained from his experience as a supervisor: "The intimate cooperation between the supervisor and the candidate often rendered as much insight to me as it did to those who came to be introduced to the secrets of the profession. They brought to life questions which everyday routine is inclined to bypass or to neglect. They kept my own wish to know and to understand young and alert" (1952, p. 467).

Most supervisors would probably agree with Meerloo's warmly expressed remarks. When the supervisory relationship is at its best, there is no doubt that the supervisor is gaining a good deal from the supervisory experience. He learns from the supervisee just as the supervisee learns from him. He has every reason to feel grateful to the supervisee for affording him this opportunity—and he usually does.

It is also true, however, that many supervisors occasionally experience, consciously or unconsciously, quite the opposite feeling—namely, envy of the supervisee. Out of a narcissistic wish for perfection (which nobody ever fully renounces), the supervisor may find himself envying the superior qualities or capabilities of a particular supervisee. Among the more obvious qualities that might be envied are those natural gifts that training can never create, but can only hone—intelligence, creativity, personal warmth. If a supervisor feels himself to be painfully deficient in any of these areas—that is, if he has failed to come to terms with his own limitations—he will be likely to envy a supervisee whom he senses as having the quality in abundance. Instead of appropriately admiring and praising this quality of the supervisee's work, he may attempt in one way or another to take it away from him.

What makes this countertransferential problem all the more insidious is that it usually occurs in a camouflaged manner. For instance, several writers have commented on the tendency of some supervisors to compete with their supervisees (Blitzsten and Fleming 1953, Gediman and Wolkenfeld 1980, Goin and Kline 1976). My impression is that when this happens, it is often motivated in part by the supervisor's wish to prove that he has more of some quality—intelligence or sensitivity, for example— than the supervisee, and that he therefore has no reason to envy him. Or, a supervisor may camouflage his envy by subtly minimizing his supervisee's unusual ability in a given area—a talent for rapidly creating a working alliance with patients, for example—and instead stress the importance of abilities that he himself possesses, or believes he possesses, in greater abundance. Needless to say, these countertransferential impingements can create serious difficulties for the supervisee in his work with patients.

I have mentioned some of the more obvious gifts or talents that tend to be the target of supervisors' envy. There is another manifestation of supervisory envy that is not at all uncommon, and yet to my knowledge it has not been noted in the literature. I have in mind the kind of experience one can have when supervising a trainee or relatively new therapist who brings to his work, as beginning therapists often do, an abundance of enthusiasm, hopefulness, and willingness to put himself on the line—

in short, the joy of being "in love" with his new profession. As in all love affairs, there is likely to be an element of unreality and idealization, or even omnipotence, in the new therapist's enthusiastic approach to his work. But there is also something undeniably fresh and healthy about it, something that those who have been working for many years frequently lose or—perhaps more accurately—relinquish with a mixture of relief *and* regret. It is this regret over the loss or diminution of a joyful approach to one's work that leads some supervisors to a (usually unconscious) envy of the new therapist's unequivocally experienced joy and may impel the supervisor, subtly and unwittingly, to try to dampen the supervisee's enthusiasm.

I have experienced this phenomenon from both sides: as a supervisee and later, to my dismay, as a supervisor. As a psychology intern, I can recall working with at least one supervisor who, in retrospect, was probably experiencing something of this type of envy. I might add that as a student I, too, went through a "love affair" with my new profession. It is difficult to imagine now, but in those beginning years I used to regret when I had days off and therefore could not work with patients; and at the end of the month, when a paycheck showed up in my clinic mailbox, I would find myself thinking how wonderful it was to actually be paid for doing what I loved. This enthusiasm came through, of course, to my supervisors, a couple of whom seemed to welcome it. But there was one senior supervisor, a highly respected senior member of the staff, who I sometimes felt was subtly trying to dampen my joy in the work. What he said was reasonable enough—in sum, that it took a very long time to accomplish sometimes only very little, and sometimes with only a few patients. Yet more important than what he said was how he said it. There was a certain weary paternalism in his style, and sometimes a bit of irony or barely disguised cynicism. I sensed, without his ever saying so, that my enthusiasm somehow put him off. At the time I felt quite baffled by all this. Today, however, I am inclined to believe that this highly talented man, whom I later came to know as a colleague, was experiencing, knowingly or not, a measure of envy toward one who was youthfully in love with his chosen profession.

Part of what led me to this conclusion was an empathic awareness, occurring many years later, of just what it can be like to supervise enthusiastic, fresh trainees. Without going into elaborate detail, I can state that more than once in recent years, I have had the conscious sense of envying one or another supervisee's energy and enthusiasm in taking on the most god-awful case, doing it with an unflinching hopefulness, and alas, doing it for so little pay. More than once, I have had to bite my tongue to avoid spewing out some piece of wisdom about the limitations of our trade, which wisdom, if truly learned, can only be learned on one's own; and besides, coming from me *at that time* would have been primarily a manifestation of my own nostalgia-based envy. Also, more than once, I have had to refrain from offering some sagacious remarks on the dangers of "burn out" to a supervisee who was devotedly giving his all to a patient; again, observations which *at that time* were issuing at least as much from my envy of the supervisee's unflagging devotion as from my desire to protect him. In short, I have learned that in supervising trainees, especially those who joyfully embrace their new profession, there is the danger of subtly attempting to dampen their joy because, at bottom, one envies it. As Meerloo contends, the supervisor can, and must, learn to drink gratefully from the waters of the trainee's enthusiasm and vitality. But I think it is too much to expect, at least for many of us, that such refreshment will always arrive purified of envy.

The Attitude of Omniscience

Of the various supervisory attitudes and dispositions that can intrude on the supervisory process, none has been more thoroughly discussed than that of supervisory omniscience. Warnings have repeatedly been issued against the supervisor's assumption of an all-knowing stance with the supervisee, who—it is stressed—must be allowed room to develop his own therapeutic convictions and style (Ackerman 1953, DeBell 1963, Lesser 1983, Levenson 1982, Lower 1972, Meerloo 1952, Searles 1962). It is probably safe to assume that one of the reasons for such repeated and stern advisories (including the one about to be issued here) is quite simply that there is a strong temptation at times to assume an omniscient pose. Indeed it would seem that there are factors inherent in the supervisory situation that provide such temptation.

One of these is the obvious fact that, as a relative outsider to the treatment, the supervisor is not subject to the same countertransferential pulls toward the patient as is the therapist. Generally, then, he is able to hear and sense things that have escaped the notice of the therapist and, in particular, he can sense things that are giving the therapist trouble with the patient. Thus, modest though the supervisor may be, it is nonetheless tempting at times to assume that he does have a superior, if not definite, grasp of what is happening in the treatment.

Another factor that encourages omniscience is the seductive quality of supervisory knowledge itself, which tempts one to assume a far greater knowledge about a supervisee's cases than one usually feels about one's own. As Levenson (1982) points out, the supervisor's "apparent clarity" and "infallibility" stem from the fact that "we are never really discussing, in supervision, a specific patient; but a class of transactions applicable to *all* patients and illustrated by a specific patient." In addition, "supervision is of an entirely different level of abstraction than therapy" (p. 2). To put this point another way, in our work as supervisors—as compared with our work as therapists—we tend to be less focused on and aware of the *unique* qualities and quirks of the patient and more focused on the *general* characteristics (like transference paradigms) that the patient is displaying. As supervisors, we see the forest more than the trees. Hence, at this higher (and sometimes Olympian) level of abstraction, we are tempted to feel as supervisors a measure of omniscience that in our groping as therapists simply eludes us.

Finally, it is worth mentioning still another factor in the supervisory situation that may contribute to the supervisor's sense of omniscience: the supervisee himself. Not uncommonly, a trainee or new therapist, overwhelmed by a caseload of difficult patients, will turn to the supervisor in expectation of the magic words that will bail him out. As DeBell states: "Early in their training, candidates may be quite uncertain and be seductive in their attempts to get help and reassurance from the supervisor. The supervisor who is susceptible may discover (and perhaps some never do!) that he has been conducting a monologue about the case which he had been led to think all along was a dialogue. . . . Sometimes the candidate is less subtle but no less effective when he presents the case in such a way as to alarm the supervisor and thereby move him to overly directive 'rescue' operations" (1981, p. 49). The supervisee may thus seek to alleviate his anxiety

about his work by projecting onto the supervisor an idealized imago of all-knowing seer, and he may, in one manner
or another, exert pressure upon him to enact this role.

Precisely how the supervisor reacts to all these temptations will depend, in large measure, on his own inclinations to play out the omniscient role. As is evident, some
supervisors are more inclined than others toward omniscience, and they thus find themselves overreacting or
succumbing to these inherent temptations. Some supervisors, for example, may defend against the temptation to
play out an omniscient role by assuming a supervisory
stance of exaggerated modesty. They say as little as possible, ask questions and avoid giving answers, and *never*
allow that they may have a superior knowledge of what is
happening in the treatment. Such supervisors become
aficionados of the Socratic method, or devotees of the
shrug-the-shoulder approach. Personally, as a supervisee,
I used to find this supervisory stance absolutely exasperating. In retrospect, I suspect that with at least one or two
supervisors of this type, their exaggeratedly *un*-knowing
stance was a defensive reaction against unresolved wishes
to exhibit an *all*-knowing pose.

On the opposite end of the spectrum is the supervisor
whose omniscience is egosyntonic. This type of supervisor—familiar, no doubt, to everyone who has had an
extensive training period—brings to the supervisory situation the fervor of a true believer. The supervisee, in his
newness and uncertainty, is viewed as a potential convert;
and the supervisory situation, with its inherent potential
for Olympian overviews, is just the right forum for a
conversion process. Meerloo (1952) refers to this type of
supervisory stance as "adeptomania," and DeBell (1963)
calls it "disciple hunting." Depending on the personality
of the supervisor, this stance can be obnoxious and ludi-

crous, or more perniciously, it can be seductively appealing. Unfortunately, as it turns out, some of the most perspicacious supervisors are individuals who have an excessive, narcissistic disposition toward assuming an omniscient stance. If charismatic and powerful enough, they sometimes create around themselves, in the clinics and schools where they supervise and teach, a bevy of like-minded true believers. When this happens, the ultimate sufferer is apt to be the patient, for in the manner of a parallel process, he is likely to be subjected to this dogmatism. Thus, instead of finding himself in treatment with a therapist who is willing to grope along with him for his own elusive truth, he finds someone who has "the answers"—which, in the end, are likely to prove no more enlightening to him than they were to the therapist who passed them on to him.

The Supervisor's Disclosure of Countertransference

As indicated in some of the foregoing vignettes, I do selectively disclose my countertransferences, both subjective and objective, in the course of my work with supervisees. It would seem to me that those of us who advocate the selective disclosure of the supervisor's countertransferences do so with a basic set of premises in mind. Put rather simply, these premises are as follows: In order to carry out one's teaching function as a supervisor, one is called upon at times to provide a therapeutic function. Further, this therapeutic function can involve the supervisor's addressing the therapist's emotional responses (including his conflicts) not only in the treatment arena, but also in the supervisory situation. Finally, sometimes the

most helpful way of working with the supervisee's emotional responses and conflicts in the supervisory situation
is for the supervisor to openly discuss some of his own
countertransferences toward the supervisee. These three
premises are explicit or implicit in the work of all those
who advocate the supervisor's selective disclosure of countertransferences (Caligor 1981, Doehrman 1976, Issacharoff 1982, Lesser 1983, Searles 1962, Tauber 1952, Winokur 1982, Wolstein 1972).

One additional premise underlies the reasoning of
some supervisors—including this one—who disclose countertransferences to supervisees. Specifically, it is thought
that if one is to teach and encourage the supervisee to use
selectively his own countertransferences in his work with
patients, one needs to provide something in the way of
"teaching by example." This premise is predominantly
found in some of the writings of those representing the
Sullivanian interpersonal school (Issacharoff 1982,
Tauber 1952, Wolstein 1972).

The questions of when and with whom it might prove
useful to disclose countertransferences are best answered
by reference to specific examples. However, it would require a lengthy monograph to depict at all adequately the
varied circumstances in which disclosure is of value. Here,
I can only discuss some of the factors that I consider in
deciding whether a particular disclosure will be useful to a
supervisee.

Of paramount importance is the matter of who the
supervisee is and what he can work with at the time.
Especially important are his level of self-awareness, his
personal integration, his analytic sophistication, and, perhaps above all, the nature of the learning alliance. The
more these facets and qualities are solid and well developed, the more I feel free to disclose my countertransfer-

ence. My decision is also influenced by whether I have
enacted the countertransference, or whether I have been
able to contain and manage it internally. If I realize that
an enactment has taken place (especially over some time
and with some destructive result), then I feel a greater
necessity to discuss openly my countertransferential experience. Finally, there is the question of how much I have
been able to understand the nature of my countertransference, quite apart from whether I have enacted it or not.
When possible, I generally prefer to wait until I have
substantially fathomed the nature of the countertransference, rather than spontaneously bringing it to the supervisee's attention as soon as I become aware of it.

Having articulated these considerations, I am left
with a somewhat uncomfortable awareness of how little
can be captured by a set of general "rules." So much
depends on the unique equation that occurs from session
to session with a supervisee. The previously cited case of
group supervision with "V." is an example. In this instance, I had been able to contain my internally experienced wishes to enact the role of "revivifier." Yet, inasmuch as the group had become stuck in such an
enactment, and inasmuch as I had reason to believe that
V. was personally and psychologically sophisticated
enough to use the open discussion of countertransferential material, I chose to bring these matters forward. Had I
been working one to one with V., and had she similarly
induced within me the experience of "revivifier," I might
have revealed my countertransference even though I had
not enacted it; and in light of my solid learning alliance
with her, I might also have done so spontaneously, before
I had fully evaluated these feelings.

With a supervisee who was not as psychologically
sophisticated as V. and with whom the learning alliance

was less well established, I might not have disclosed my induced feelings and might instead have focused only on what was occurring between the therapist and the patient—unless perhaps I had become caught up in these countertransferential feelings, enacted them over a period of time, and then come to understand what had been transpiring. And so on. The possibilities are clearly quite endless and escape quantification. One must ultimately rely on a rather inexact calculation—a hunch really— when disclosing countertransferences to a supervisee, and it is only in the aftermath that one can know whether the disclosure was worthwhile—that is, whether it contributed to greater understanding and well-being within the supervisory situation and/or within the treatment situation.

While I am convinced that disclosures of countertransference can, and do, work, it is important not to overdo it. Disclosures of the supervisor's countertransferences are best made occasionally, and not as the central, ongoing focus of supervision. This is so because whenever the focus of supervision shifts to the supervisor–therapist relationship, there is the danger of losing sight of the patient. There is also the danger that the supervisor will cease to be therapeutic only as needed, but rather will lapse into the role of ongoing therapist to the supervisee— a role best left to the supervisee's personal therapist.

In sum, just as there is a place for the therapist's occasional disclosure of countertransferences to patients, so also is there a place for selective and occasional disclosure of the supervisor's countertransferences to the supervisee. And indeed, as with other good things in therapy (and in life), sometimes less turns out to be more.

10

Countertransference in Termination

One of the most difficult technical tasks for the therapist, regardless of experience, is to manage the end -phase of treatment. The therapist must cope not only with the patient's struggles over the termination of treatment, but also with his own feelings. This chapter will focus on some of the more familiar and poignant countertransferential reactions that arise during this period, specifically (1) the tendency to seek perfect results, (2) mourning reactions, (3) feelings of delight in the termination, (4) the wish for gratitude, and (5) the wish to be known by the patient as a "real" person. The chapter will conclude with some observations on the infrequently mentioned topic of the "last session," with particular reference to the countertransferential difficulties in managing this final meeting.

Before proceeding, it is necessary to define the term *end phase*, or *termination phase*, of treatment. These terms denote the period in long-term psychoanalytic therapy, prior to the closing date, when issues of termination are a principal, or *the* principal, focus of the therapy. The justification for distinguishing such a period is not that the issues involving separation and termination are unique to this period, but rather that the conscious or unconscious importance of these issues during this time—with the relative lessening of significance of other matters—seems to warrant identifying this phase with its own nomenclature (Firestein 1978, Hurt 1971).

The Therapist's Struggle with Perfectionism

The question of how complete a result can be expected from psychoanalytic treatment has intrigued and troubled investigators from the beginning. From the early statements of Ferenczi (1927) and Freud (1937) to some of the more recent panel discussions on termination (Firestein 1969, Hurn 1971, Pfeffer 1963, Robbins 1975), psychoanalysts in particular have sought to elaborate just what treatment can and cannot do for a patient. Ferenczi's and Freud's conflicting perspectives early on set the terms of the discussion. Ferenczi, in his bright and ebullient optimism, suggested that it was already possible (in 1927) to completely cure *some* patients of their transference neuroses, and said that in time he expected even more widespread therapeutic successes for the new science. Freud, on the other hand, writing toward the end of his life (1937) was far more skeptical and pessimistic about the possibility of psychoanalytic treatment ever offering a complete cure: Conflicts that were once resolved could reemerge, and conflicts left unresolved like sleeping dogs (Freud's metaphor) might arise at any time after treat-

ment; such was the nature of human beings, and psycho-
analysis could not change that.

Over the years, with the weight of much accumulated
experience, analysts have tended to lean intellectually
toward Freud's more skeptical perspective. Although most
are somewhat more enthusiastic than Freud about what
can be accomplished therapeutically, few analysts today
would claim to bring about "complete" cures—that is,
transference neuroses cured in all aspects for all time.
There is a certain modesty in what analysts claim to
achieve even in the most thoroughgoing treatments. Experience, if not theoretical understanding alone, has tended
to bring about a proclaimed cautiousness.

Nevertheless, intellectual convictions notwithstanding, there still seems to live on within many analysts, as
well as psychoanalytically oriented therapists, the ghost of
Ferenczi. We still seem to wish for the perfectability of
our technique. We strive to completely cure the patient,
and when the end of treatment arrives with work left
undone, many of us find ourselves struggling with feelings
of disappointment. This underlying "perfectionistic"
wish or aspiration has been noted by a number of investigators. Firestein (1978), in discussing his research on the
termination process, notes how, at the end of treatment,
analysts commonly find themselves anxious over the results of their work and skeptical as to whether the treatment has been comprehensive enough. Similarly, Ticho
(1972), a member of the Psychotherapy Research Project
of the Menninger Foundation, has observed a trend of
what he calls "unjustified skepticism" among analysts,
often even when the patient is satisfied with the results of
the treatment. As Schafer (1973) succinctly puts it:
"Many therapists, and in my view many analysts too, do
not like to face the prospect—I would call it the fact—that

irrationally based or neurotic problems are not entirely eradicable by the best of therapies" (p. 142).

From whence comes this wish to perfectly cure the patient, which seems so prevalent among therapists? Schafer eloquently suggests at least a partial answer to this question:

> The roots of these ideas and ideals lie in infantile fantasies of omnipotence, which no one ever renounces completely. These are ideas and ideals that most likely played an important part in his having chosen to become a therapist. These ideas and ideals concern valuing activity over passivity (at least with regard to other people's problems!) and, in the extreme, "choosing" to be omnipotent rather than helpless, a savior rather than a destructive force and/or a breast of infinite capacity rather than a ravenously hungry parasite [p. 141].

Ideally, of course, the therapist becomes aware of his own omnipotent strivings and substantially relinquishes them during his own therapy or training analysis. But Schafer's point, if I read him correctly, is this: We are never fully free from perfectionistic strivings, and in the final tallying of therapeutic results that occurs in the termination phase of treatment, we are especially susceptible to the rearousal of these omnipotence-based standards.

This countertransferential impingement can obviously interfere with the therapist's ability to help the patient through the termination process. It is likely that at this time the patient is having to face, among other things, the fact that not everything he hoped to gain from treatment has come to pass. He therefore requires from the therapist a steady and confident belief in the value of what *was* accomplished during the months and years of collaborative work. Should the patient go through a period of regression during the termination phase, as so often happens, he needs to find that the therapist can bear this stress, much as the mother of a toddler in the "rapprochement phase" of separation and individuation (Mahler et al. 1975) must be able to bear, with that subtle mix of confidence and concern, her child's regressive swings as he prepares to sally forth in the world.

The therapist who has been unable to work through or manage his own perfectionistic strivings is almost certain to inject this countertransferential material into the end phase of treatment, sometimes in rather well-disguised ways. For instance, it is possible to camouflage one's irrational and omnipotent ideals under the banner of a commitment to "truth," such that one just does not feel honest enough with the patient unless one mulls over with him what was *not* accomplished in the treatment. This is not to suggest that these lacunae should be avoided, painful though it may be to discuss them. But the therapist who himself is unduly disappointed that such gaps remain is likely to inject this disappointment into his "truthful" discussion with the patient. In addition, what sometimes passes for a kind of wisdom or philosophical acceptance of the limitations of therapy, is in some therapists not a true emotional acceptance of these facts but more a detached intellectual awareness of the way things are; that is to say, the therapist has not succeeded in relinquishing his perfectionism, but instead defends against it by an ironic or depressed philosophical stance. The termination phase is then likely to be colored by the subtly depressive mood injected by the therapist, who, at the deepest level, experiences the patient's leaving as one more withering piece of proof of his own limitations and the limitations of his craft.

An additional manifestation of the therapist's perfectionism, and one that occurs perhaps most commonly in the work of new therapists, is the attempt to salvage an "incomplete" treatment by a perfect or near-perfect ending. Out of his own perfectionistic needs, the therapist attempts to get the patient to deal with all of his underlying feelings about termination—sadness, anger, remorse, disappointment, gratitude—quite apart from the patient's ability to face up to all or any of these feelings at that time. Overlooking the well-known evidence that the termination process most often continues after the actual closing date, the therapist aims to "get it all in" before the patient and he part. Or, failing to achieve that, he attempts to prepare the patient for the emergence of these feelings at a later date; the patient is warned, for example, of possible later feelings of sadness or anger toward the therapist. Needless to say, these technical errors, issuing from the therapist's perfectionistic strivings, are likely to hamper the patient's ability to work through in his own best way the separation from treatment and from the therapist—before and after the closing date.

The Therapist's Capacity to Tolerate Mourning Reactions

One of the most essential tasks for the therapist in the termination phase of treatment is to facilitate the patient's mourning of the loss of treatment and of the therapist. To do this the therapist needs to be able to (1) make "trial identifications" (Fliess 1942) with the patient as a mourner, and (2) manage his own "mourning reactions" (sadness, disappointment, anger, and guilt) at losing the patient. Unquestionably, the therapist who himself has been a patient in long-term treatment and has known what it is to mourn the loss of his own therapist is in a far better position to help his patient than one who has not had such an experience. But even with this awareness, any therapist can find himself at a given time, with a given patient, subtly or obviously interfering with the patient's attempts to mourn. In his countertransferential reluctance to accept the end of treatment and the loss of that patient, he may actually become the chief obstacle to the patient's mourning process. Let me give an example from my own work, illustrating a countertransferential intrusion into the patient's work of mourning.

A few years ago I was in the uncomfortable position of having to dissolve my practice because I was moving out of the country. It was difficult to make the announcement of my impending departure to all my patients, but it was especially difficult with one particular patient. This patient, R., was a social work student who had been with me a relatively short time (two years). She was a person whose obvious talents were matched by an equally obvious narcissistic deficit. An only child, R. had been very close to her mother, also a social worker, who suffered from diabetes, a heart ailment, and a history of depression. The mother, out of her own narcissistic needs, had sought throughout R.'s life to protect her from the disappointments of daily life. So determined was she to accomplish this that she had managed to discourage R. from ever giving voice to her own experiences of disappointment and discouragement. Not until she entered treatment was R. able to look at this pattern, and then only after a good deal of trepidation. But she had finally begun to explore her relationship to her mother in great detail, and it was precisely as we were in the midst of this material that I had to announce my upcoming departure.

As can readily be imagined, I was most reluctant to make this announcement to her. I felt sad and guilty. In my guilt I found myself quickly—much too quickly—wondering to whom I could send this "good" patient. For her part, R. initially took the announcement with measured calmness. She wanted to know where I was going and what had prompted me to leave, and (as I provided her with more than the usual number of details about my departure and plans) she ruminated about how hard it was for *me* to make such a move. Within a few sessions, however, her calm shifted to disappointment, anger, and sadness. She wept profusely, scolded me, and wept again. Having begun to mourn me, she could not stop. This went on for weeks, and I soon found myself becoming detached and tuning her out for most of the session. Then, unwittingly, in reaction formation to my own underlying anger and guilt, I began hollowly "supporting" her, encouraging her to look at what we had accomplished and suggesting that she consider resuming treatment elsewhere.

It was at this point, with about a month to go before I left, that she brought me an article that she had just been assigned in class. The article was Miller's "The Drama of the Gifted Child and the Psychoanalyst's Narcissistic Disturbance" (1979). I was not then familiar with this article, but I soon realized that she had given me the right "assignment." As the article so clearly elaborated, like her mother I also had been unable to tolerate her depression and anger. In my own overwhelming guilt about leaving, I had attempted to stifle R.'s feelings and encourage her to look at the "bright side" or, even more perniciously, to comfort me in my leaving. I had been unable to tolerate her mourning. Fortunately, in this instance, the patient was aware enough and brave enough to bring it directly to my attention, and I was able to do something about my countertransferential intrusion. And I will say, I hope without sounding too pollyannaish, that those final weeks of treatment turned out to be highly meaningful for R., and in no small measure, for me too.

This kind of situational pressure on the therapist probably occurs more often than we care to imagine. Any situation in the therapist's life that confronts him with loss can make it especially difficult for him to manage his patients' mourning reactions. Included here are such inescapable life circumstances as the death, illness, or long-term departure of loved ones, as well as serious illness or the trials of old age in oneself. In addition, new therapists and trainees frequently confront situational pressures of this sort as they find themselves having to terminate with many patients at one time.

In all of these circumstances, the therapist may be so preoccupied with his own losses that he is unable to help the patient. He may be unable to tolerate the patient's mourning and may in some manner discourage it. Alternatively, he may unconsciously use the patient as a vehicle for his own mourning processes. By means of projective identification, he may attempt to goad the patient prematurely or prolongedly into expressing a particular mourning reaction (such as sadness) and then interpret it to or succor the patient, who is a stand-in for himself. In short, the therapist may fail to maintain sufficient distance from the patient, and may instead become overidentified with him as a mourner because he is overburdened with loss in his own life.

A further source of potential countertransference difficulty for the therapist is that the patient's departure is often a loss in itself. This is especially so in long-term, successful treatments in which a good deal of mutual intimacy has evolved. The therapist in this situation becomes a comourner; thus, if he is to help the patient work through his mourning reactions, he must become aware of and manage his own reluctance to see the patient go.

Several writers have commented on the mourning process in the therapist (Firestein 1978, Hurn 1971, Searles 1979, Weigert 1952). Hurn suggests that for the therapist, the loss of the patient may involve the loss of someone who over time has served as: "(1) a figure who functions primarily as a stimulus for the analyst's self-analysis; (2) a figure who enables the analyst to further his professional development by the exercise of his unique skill and who collaborates with the analyst in that endeavor; (3) a figure who provides a conflict-free experience for psychic enrichment." And he adds, "It goes without saying that all three of these aspects of the patient blend with and overlap one another" (p. 344).

In far more emotional and experience-near language, Searles discusses the painful aspects of terminating with patients who, in part because of the success of the treatment, have become more "likeable, admirable and basically speaking lovable"—people with whom the therapist might very well wish he could go on knowing (1979,

p. 300). More than any other writer, Searles makes clear the grieving process in the therapist, a process that he assumes to be largely unavoidable in any thoroughgoing treatment.

The danger as I see it—and here I am much in agreement with Searles—is not that the patient comes to have such meaning for the therapist, but rather that the therapist remains unaware of this development; in other words, that the therapist fails to realize how much he mourns the loss of the patient. If the therapist is not in touch with his sense of loss, he is almost certain to intrude on the patient's termination process. For instance, in order to escape his own sense of loss, the therapist might be inclined to go along with or encourage a certain watering down of the termination phase; he may, for example, not allow a long enough termination phase, or he may reduce the number of sessions as the end nears. Alternatively, in his unwillingness to face the loss of the patient, the therapist might hold onto him, continually looking for and discovering lacunae that require further exploration. In this connection, I suspect that rather long treatments with neurotic patients often involve an element of the therapist's—not just the patient's—refusal to let go and mourn.

If we assume that the therapist's sense of loss is a part of the termination of long-term treatment, the question again arises of what might be usefully disclosed about this loss to the patient. It can be reasonably argued—and most "classical" analysts would probably so contend—that direct communication of this sort to the patient runs the risk of providing gratification to the patient; thus, by disclosing his sense of loss, the therapist may succeed in binding the patient to him even after they have parted.

This important argument should not be dismissed lightly. Above all, it would seem to apply in those cases in which less-than-satisfactory results have been achieved, or in which termination occurs after some years in serious deadlock. Here, statements of sadness or mourning on the therapist's part are likely to hinder the patient's ability to relinquish his tie to the therapist and may interfere with his eventually turning elsewhere for treatment.

In cases in which satisfactory results have been achieved, however, and the patient has been able substantially to work through his transference neurosis or psychosis and turn to other people in his environment for the richer satisfactions of day-to-day living, I would view it as a useful part of termination for the therapist to disclose some of his feelings of loss. At that point in the progression of the therapeutic relationship, the patient has generally become at least preconsciously aware of some of these feelings in his therapist, though in the regression which often occurs in the final phase, he may temporarily disregard this knowledge. It would seem to me that as part of the "mature" and far more equal relationship that obtains in the termination of satisfactory treatment, the therapist can feel free to let the patient openly know these things about himself. More to the point, the therapist's refusal to let the patient know of his sadness (as well as other feelings) may serve as a way of *not* acknowledging and validating the patient's independence and hard-won autonomy—not acknowledging, that is, the fact that the patient now can receive such gratification from the therapist without being unduly stimulated by it. Many therapists, including analysts, apparently do communicate their sense of loss in these circumstances, perhaps sensing that it is a "human" thing to do. My point is that it is also a "therapeutic" thing to do.

The Therapist's Sense of Delight in the Termination Phase

The patient approaching the end of a successful, long-term treatment usually experiences not only a feeling of loss, but also a feeling of "joy, relief and a hunger for new experience" (Robbins 1975, p. 172, quoting Kanzer). The patient "feels truly liberated and is aware of a considerable amount of energy that he could never before muster"; and, "he often experiences this phase as a new beginning" (Ticho 1972, p. 325). For the therapist who is empathically in touch with his patient, there is apt to be a corresponding sense of delight in this "new beginning." From his own experience as a former and more or less successfully treated patient, the therapist is able to identify with the patient. Moreover, in his "generative" (Erikson 1950, pp. 266–268) relationship to the patient, the therapist experiences a sense of fulfillment: He has helped another to flourish and grow.

This, in a sense, is the ideal case; it is the result one hopes for. But obviously, this does not always happen. The therapist may not be able to experience an *appropriate* sense of delight in the patient's new beginning. Because of difficulties of his own, the therapist may fail to empathize with the patient's feeling of joy, or he may coopt the patient's joy in a narcissistic manner, such that the patient's success in leaving is excessively experienced by the therapist as his own success. Either of these countertransferential impingements can interfere with the patient's ability to delight in his new beginning and to experience it sufficiently as his own.

A number of factors can contribute to the therapist's inability to experience delight along with his patient. Some of these have already been mentioned—namely, the therapist's perfectionism, which causes him to downplay the satisfactory results, and the therapist's mourning reaction, which makes him reluctant to see the patient leave. To these factors I would add a third: the therapist's unconscious envy of the patient's delight in a "new beginning." The therapist himself may never, or not yet, have arrived at this stage in his own treatment, and he may consequently resent the patient for arriving there first, or at all. In one manner or another, then, he may seek to dampen the patient's sense of liberation, perhaps by withdrawing from the patient as he expresses his relief and joy in separation, or by misconstruing and misinterpreting these feelings as resistance.

At the other extreme, the therapist may impinge upon the patient's joyful sense of success and delight in a new beginning by taking over this experience as his own. In this instance, the therapist feels no lack of delight. On the contrary, he is full of delight. But it is a delight in the patient's achievement primarily, or excessively, because of what the patient's achievement reflects about him, the therapist. A measure of narcissistic investment in the patient's success is to be expected; the patient's success *is*, up to a point, the therapist's success. Yet, in those cases in which the therapist has an excessive narcissistic investment in the patient or in the outcome of treatment, he may coopt the patient's experience of success. In Searles's apt metaphor (1979), just as Pygmalion fell in love with the statue of Galatea he had sculpted, so the therapist enthuses over the successful patient as his own creation. When this happens, the patient is likely to feel, consciously or unconsciously, that the new beginning is not sufficiently his own. As a result, posttermination "negative therapeutic reactions" may occur as the patient self-destructively damages his therapist's fine sculpture.

Generally, though, I think that in the end phase of treatment, most therapists do find themselves sharing appropriately in the patient's joy and relief at a new beginning. Again the question arises of what might be usefully disclosed to the patient of these shared feelings. My impression is that in brief but meaningful ways, most therapists do let their patients know of their shared feelings of delight, and even relief, at termination. For instance, in the end phase, as a patient flexes his new freedom, he will often revel in his ability to accomplish something he was not able to before: A formerly inhibited woman manages for the first time to throw a dinner party, for example, or a depressed middle-aged man finally decides to quit a job he never liked and open his own business. When this kind of development occurs—as it did with these two patients of mine—the therapist who is empathically with his patient is almost certain to feel the patient's joy along with him. I do not remember exactly how I expressed my delight in these acts that symbolized the patient's "new beginning," but I am sure I said something, and/or that my tone of voice reflected my delight. In another instance, I can remember a patient whom I saw for several years at an early morning hour, a young man who had been unusually rewarding inasmuch as he had successfully worked through a painful and severe character disorder. Among the many feelings he expressed during termination was the sense of relief at not having to come to the office any more. "How good it will be," he said at one point, "to no longer have to get up at 5:30 in the morning, twice a week, and get myself over to you." And then he added: "For you too, I bet. Now you don't have to get up to see me either!" Together, we laughed unabashedly at this statement, which was so true for both of us.

Some therapists might not characterize my reactions

as disclosure of countertransference. In my lexicon, though, that is what they are. Furthermore, it is my impression that many therapists reveal their delight at least in these small ways, no matter what they choose to call these reactions. When the therapist is not narcissistically overinvested in the patient or in the outcome of the treatment, his expressions of shared delight will cause no harm. Quite the opposite, they will provide the patient with a sense of being understood and appropriately cared for and valued. At the end of a successful treatment, to withhold such feelings out of a conviction that by so doing one continues to respect the patient's autonomy is to render autonomy a more lonely and isolated state than it rightfully ought to be.

The Therapist's Wish for Gratitude

For years I had noticed an uncomfortable countertransferential reaction that I often seemed to experience at the end of treatments, even when (or more accurately, *especially* when) they were successful. Roughly speaking, it was a wish for gratitude from my patients—a gratitude, however, that they in no way could ever fully extend to me, but which an occasional fantasy or a stray remark would make me aware of. With one patient who had entered treatment in difficult financial straits, but who left treatment—in part as a result of it—with an extremely well-paying job, I fantasized that when he earned what he called his "first million," he might send some of it, under some pretext, to me. I would regretfully refuse the money, even if I could not refuse the fantasy. In another instance, a terminating patient stated that she very much wanted to buy me a gift and hoped I would feel free to take it. She was rather open in her gratitude toward me, feeling—as I did—that she had benefited enormously from treatment. After discussing the meanings of the gift, she finally summoned the courage to ask whether I would in fact be willing to accept "some token" from her; to which I replied, "Yes, as long as it's something smaller than a Mercedes Benz!" We both laughed, though later, as I thought about my spontaneous remark, I was aware that it partly reflected my wish for at least a Mercedes Benz.

Having noticed in myself a wish for special tribute, and having observed it also in supervisees (even those who seemed relatively free of neurosis), I was very interested, and to some degree relieved, when I came across Feiner's statement (1979) about this need for a special kind of gratitude: "This expected undying gratitude goes far beyond rational gratitude and objective remuneration, the success of the analysis, even the joy of exultation in the intimacy achieved. Despite the reasonableness of the patient's actual gratefulness, no amount can satisfy our innermost need for it, a need in all of us (I mean this literally—and see it deriving from our own 'primal' transference) since no one outside of us knows the painful, sacrificial, hazardous side of our analytic efforts" (p. 118).

I think Feiner is absolutely right in his observation that the need for "undying gratitude" is present in some measure in all of us. I also think he is correct, in general, in tracing this need to the therapist's "primal" transference—that is, the wish to be completely satiated by another. More specifically, however, I believe that there are often also environmental factors in the early lives of therapists-to-be that contribute to a heightened wish for gratitude. (Some of these factors are discussed in Chapter 3.) As children, many therapists were drawn by their own sensitivity, and by the needs of a parent (or sibling) for this sensitivity, into an early therapeutic relationship with the other. This relationship often went unrecognized; or if it was recognized, it felt to the child-cum-therapist, at least unconsciously, as if it was not adequately recognized. In short, he never felt he received enough gratitude. And, I would argue, it is this background that often contributes to the therapist's need to receive, from someone who has benefited from the "painful, sacrificial, hazardous side of our analytic efforts," an overdue expression of "undying gratitude."

Whether the therapist's need for undying gratitude impinges upon the treatment will depend on just how prominent the need is, as well as on the therapist's aware-ness of it. In moderation, and if understood and managed by the therapist, it need not interfere. But if prominent or unconscious, or both, it obviously can impinge upon the treatment. The therapist, then, may be inclined to coax the patient into expressing gratitude. (In one extreme example with which I am familiar, the therapist's office had become a veritable trophy room of gifts from departed patients.) Alternatively, in defense against the desire for expression of such gratitude, the therapist may subtly steer the patient away from even appropriate expressions of gratitude, as happened in the following case.

H. was a psychologist whose work I supervised for two years. She was a relatively new therapist, but a person of remarkable abilities. At one juncture of the supervision, she happened to be terminating with two patients at approximately the same time; thus, a coun-tertransference maneuver of hers that might have escaped my attention in any single instance became more obvious when it took place in two separate instances.

With both patients—a narcissistic man in his mid-fifties and a teenage girl—she had achieved excellent results. She knew it and the patients knew it. Nevertheless, both patients struggled during the end phase of treatment to give voice to their feelings of gratitude, and what became apparent to me was that H. herself stumbled in helping them clarify this difficulty. From her presentation of process material, it seemed that with the narcissistic man she at one point had mistakenly avoided commenting on his slightly mocking tone in delivering a tribute to her. And when the teenage girl had shyly tried to express gratitude, this otherwise extraordinarily sensitive therapist had abruptly changed the subject.

I commented on this to H. and then suggested that perhaps she was uncomfortable with expressions of gratitude. My comment seemed to strike an immediate chord; she said she was sure there was something to it, but she was not sure what. I knew she was in her own treatment, and so decided not to press her. A week or so later, however, she (gratefully) mentioned that she had begun to uncover some of the issues behind her difficulty with receiving gratitude from patients, and from others as well. It had apparently been a life-long problem of hers. Parenthetically, a salient feature in her background—which I had not known about until then—was that an older brother of hers had been a schizophrenic from childhood, and H. had ministered to him from the time she was quite young, as both her parents had to work in the family grocery store. I do not suppose this factor

alone accounted for all of her difficulty in the matter
of receiving gratitude, but I suspect it was part of it,
just as her early "training" had had a part in making
her the talented therapist she was.

The Therapist's Wish to Be Known as a "Real" Person

A number of investigators, particularly analysts, have
noted that as the end phase of treatment approaches, the
patient increasingly perceives the therapist as a "real"
person (Hurn 1971, Ticho 1972, Weigert 1952). This
development is part and parcel of the patient's successful
resolution of his transference neurosis. And while a resi-
due of idealization is almost certain to remain (Reich
1950), the patient is nonetheless more aware of, and accepting of, the therapist as a human being, with the foibles
and quirks that flesh is heir to.

A question that arises is whether the therapist need
contribute to this development by becoming more himself,
more "real," during the end phase. Some investigators
have suggested that it is indeed necessary for the therapist
to allow himself to be, as Weigert put it, "more spontaneous, a real human being, whatever vulnerabilities may be
revealed in spontaneous, emotional responses" (1952,
p. 475). Others, however, have eschewed any such "ma-
nipulative moves" (Hurn 1971, p. 340), arguing that the
patient will naturally be inclined to perceive and react to
the therapist as a more real person, without his shifting
his therapeutic stance in any way.

This question of the therapist's technical stance in
the end phase of treatment can be approached by introduc-
ing a premise about the countertransference and, specifi-

cally, about the countertransferential wish to be known as a real person. The premise is this: As the patient increasingly comes to perceive and appreciate the therapist as a real person, there is activated within the therapist a wish to be so known by the patient. To put this another way, just as the patient's transference tends to evoke a corresponding "role-responsiveness" (Sandler 1976) in the therapist, so his increasing whole-object relatedness tends to evoke in the therapist a wish to relate as his real self to the patient. I assume this trend to be present in some degree throughout the treatment, but that it is especially prominent in the end phase of a successful treatment. Weigert seemed to be saying something quite similar, though she was calling attention to the therapist's growing *willingness* to relate spontaneously as his real self, whereas I am defining the issue in terms of the therapist's *wish* to so relate.

If this premise is correct, the important technical question becomes one of what the therapist does with his wish to be known as a real person by the patient (and the patient's desire to so know him). My answer is that up to a point it is useful to indulge (i.e., act upon) this wish. In substantial agreement with Weigert, I think that it is technically correct for the therapist to reveal his real self by reacting in a less measured and more emotional manner, allowing a greater degree of spontaneity which may reflect personal views and vulnerabilities, and permitting more of the feeling tone of his relatedness to the patient to become evident. This reactivity on the therapist's part is useful inasmuch as it acknowledges and supports the growing maturity of the patient and the patient's more real awareness and acceptance of the therapist.

The principal danger occurs when the therapist's

wish to be known is excessive, and is not motivated so much by the specific, evolving real-relatedness of the patient, but rather by the therapist's own unfulfilled needs (in his private life) for a relationship with another. If, for example, the therapist is experiencing a stressful personal situation in which there is a loss of meaningful relationships with others, and/or if the therapist has an excessive narcissistic investment in the patient, then he may be inclined to seek a real-relatedness with the patient, irrespective of the patient's readiness for it. There are many therapies in which the therapist can never emerge as his real self, and in these cases the therapist's excessive need to be so known can obviously be detrimental. I am thinking here of the many cases in which treatment is interrupted for external reasons, or in which there is an impasse. The therapist, sensing that the end has come, may attempt to get the patient to see him as he is in the name of fortifying, in those closing hours, the patient's awareness of reality. When this happens, the therapist is often acting out of his own excessive need to be known (as well as his perfectionistic need to achieve greater results), and *not* out of any evolving intimacy.

As an example of this kind of countertransferential impingement, I recall treating Z., a borderline woman in her mid-twenties, who had made good progress over the three years of our work together. She had entered treatment in a state of collapse, unable to continue her work as a fashion designer or, for that matter, to maintain any social contacts at all; she had recently slashed her wrists, and further self-destructive acts seemed quite possible. From this abyss, she slowly emerged, struggling with great courage to go on. I cannot possibly detail the course of our work together, but suffice it to say that during those three years I developed a deep admiration for her. She was unquestionably one of my favorite patients, and I felt proud of what we had accomplished so far. I knew, however, that there was still much work to do, and so it was with a sense of disappointment and sadness that I received the first news—and later the final decision—that she would be leaving to take what was admittedly an excellent career opportunity in another city.

The termination of the treatment, lasting some four months, turned out to be the least successful part of the treatment. In retrospect, I am sure this is so because of the excessive narcissistic investment I had developed in Z. During the termination, I found myself making a number of spontaneous and personal remarks, after which I felt a certain awkwardness, even embarrassment. (Incidentally, I do not feel awkward when reacting spontaneously at the end of a more fully completed treatment.) At one point, I went so far as to ask her if she ever wondered how *I* felt about her leaving, what *my* personal reaction was. Her response, blunt as it was, snapped me into an awareness of what I was doing. "This may seem strange, Dr. Gorkin," she said, "but right now I don't want to know anything about you. I only want to think about me!"

I realized then that it was my narcissistic wish to be known by her that had prompted my personal and spontaneous remarks during the closing weeks of treatment. My spontaneity here did not evolve from a mutual sense of growing real-relatedness, but rather from this narcissistic wish. In short, my spontaneity and personal remarks were an impingement, one which unfortunately left the patient and me feeling somewhat uncomfortable with each other as we parted.

The Last Session

While there have been a number of articles and even books on the subject of termination, there has been almost nothing written on the specific topic of the final session. This is unusual because, quite obviously, the final meeting between therapist and patient is an occasion of some significance. It is the last time, most likely, that the two parties will ever see each other. As a result, there is generally a heightening of anxiety in both, accompanied by mutual wishes to end on a "right note." Moreover, in my experience, there are frequently distinct events that occur during this final meeting—events which at best can only be partially analyzed at the time. In short, the last session often enough does not fall easily into one's hand like a ripe fruit plucked from the tree. It has, rather, its own special difficulties and its own distinct character.

The principal point I wish to make here is that the distinct character of this last session requires of the therapist a certain flexibility and tact. He must be prepared for surprises. He must be as open to the spontaneous gesture from the patient as he is for a last-minute piece of hard analytic work. And he must be ready, if necessary, to forego ending on a "right note," secure in the knowledge that for the patient (and himself) the termination process will continue after the session ends. Should the therapist be hindered by a need to end on a right note, or should he be perfectionistically determined to analyze every last piece of data, or should he be blocked in his ability to respond to (or with) the spontaneous gesture, he will not be able to bring to the last session the kind of flexibility that it requires. He will instead be liable to substitute therapeutic ritual for therapeutic meaning, to the detriment of the patient and himself.

In an article entitled "The Last Hour"—the only article of which I am aware that specifically addresses this topic—Lipton (1961) makes the observation that significant analytic material can, and sometimes does, emerge in the last meeting. As evidence, he offers the case of a compulsive man with a sexual disorder who, in the last two minutes of the last session, finally recovered an important memory involving incestuous fantasies toward his sister and mother. Such last-minute fireworks, while not usual, nonetheless do happen. Every therapist who has engaged in long-term analytic treatment can, I suspect, recall a similar event—an important dream, secret, or insight that springs forth at the final session. As in Lipton's case, there is seldom enough time to work on this material, and the therapist needs to accept that the treatment ends on such a note.

My difference with Lipton—and it is a fundamental one—is that he believes that because this kind of analytic material can still appear up to the last moment, the therapist must retain a "neutral" stance, by which I understand him to mean that the therapist must refrain from any spontaneous or emotional interchange with the patient, inasmuch as real-relatedness on the therapist's part would block the emergence of this material. In my view, he is empirically incorrect in this assumption. Furthermore, for reasons already stated, I think it is a technical error if at the end of a relatively successful treatment, the therapist refuses to allow a greater spontaneity and emotionality to enter into his relatedness with the patient.

In the last session, the patient will sometimes attempt to enact a wish for closer contact with the therapist. Although it is at times advisable to assume a neutral analytic stance vis-à-vis these enactments (as Lipton claims), at other times it may be tactless and unnecessarily hurtful to do so. For example, patients will sometimes ask the therapist to impart some piece of personal information that they long wanted to know; or they may request to change chairs, or move from the couch to a chair, in order to have a final look at the therapist; or they may bring some food they want to share, or a gift they want the therapist to open right away. Although the therapist can at times usefully analyze an enactment of the wish for closeness (or the fear of being forgotten, or that they themselves will forget), at other times it is hurtful and inadvisable to do so. On the altar of so-called analytic responsibility and consistency, one may tactlessly pursue the meaning behind a proffered gift or hurtfully insist upon articulating the motive behind a personal question or the offer to share a piece of homemade cake. What the therapist says and does on these occasions should depend on who the particular patient is and on the therapist's empathic understanding of the patient's need at that time. Adherence to a formalized analytic stance, and a perfectionistic determination to analyze every last piece of data, can intrude on the kind of flexibility and emotional responsiveness that is needed on these occasions.

The final session will sometimes have a special poignancy because mourning reactions, heretofore unexpressed, will finally erupt. Ideally, one hopes that the patient has been able to work substantially on this material during the entire period of the termination. Yet sometimes, even in relatively successful treatments, the patient is simply unable to do so. The expression of grief and sadness, in particular, may be quite delayed. On occasion, it is only in the last session, as the patient is about to depart, that these feelings rise to the surface, sometimes with enormous intensity and suddenness. What is required from the therapist at these moments is an intuitive emotional responsiveness that enables him to permit one patient to leave without a final word said, and yet another to stay on in the consultation room with him past the allotted time if need be.

The patient, of course, may not be the only one who is suddenly overcome with sadness in the closing hour. For the therapist who allows himself spontaneity and emotional responsiveness during the end phase of a relatively successful long-term treatment, there also may arise an intense, and surprisingly sudden, rush of grief during those last moments with the patient. I am reminded of the description of the austere analyst, Fairbairn, who stood beside his patient of many years, Guntrip, weeping visibly as he bid the latter farewell (Guntrip 1975). Many of us have no doubt had this same experience. And as embarrassing as it may have been at the time, when it has happened to me I have not felt upon reflection that anything harmful came of it, but rather that it was an acceptable part of my overall relationship to a long-term patient whom I came to know and cherish.

A further "surprise" that may take place during the last meeting is that almost nothing happens; that is, the final session is surprisingly devoid of any mention of finality. The patient fills the hour with a topic of little import, as if he were merely passing time in the train station before a long voyage. This can happen both in treatments that have come to an impasse and in those which have been overwhelmingly successful and in which separation reactions have been rather thoroughly explored. When it does happen, there is usually an element of resistance against the pain of separation. But I also sometimes have the impression that the patient, aware that he is about to embark on a "new beginning" in which he will be alone, in a sense enacts this aloneness while still in the presence of the therapist. For his part, the therapist may be taken by surprise at this early departure and may even experience a sense of abandonment or annoyance at the patient for disappearing in the last session. Should the therapist also have some hidden agenda for the last meeting, he will be liable to intrude upon the patient's way of leaving, perhaps by pressing him for some expression of feeling about separation which the patient in no way feels inclined to express at the moment. In short, the therapist must be quite willing, if need be, to allow the patient his own unemotional, and even detached, way of bidding farewell.

There is one other small but meaningful aspect of the last session that is often anxiety-provoking for patients, and sometimes for therapists too: the manner in which the two parties physically part. I think many therapists attempt to manage this anxiety—the patient's and their own—by demonstrating a certain ritualized form of physical leave-taking, like a firm handshake. For several years that is what I did. More recently, though, I have found myself allowing a more spontaneous and personal response to the patient. I no longer assume the lead, but instead share the lead with the patient. What evolves, then, is a moment of groping in which both the patient and I seem to reach for what is most comfortable between us. This may result in no physical contact being made at all, or a shaking of hands, one or both, or a firm hug. I have seldom been uncomfortable with this more flexible approach and have not felt that any harmful enactment has ever taken place. Rather, it was when I used to approach this physical parting with a ritualized handshake that I sometimes wound up feeling that a forced quality or stiffness, had unfortunately crept in during my last moment with the patient.

To summarize, then, the last session quite often presents its own particular set of tasks and challenges for the therapist. The principal point I have attempted to stress is the importance of the therapist's bringing to this session the kind of flexibility, as well as analytic readiness, that it may require. I do not find a so-called neutral stance to be always the most useful or therapeutic approach. And while the therapist's greater spontaneity and emotional responsiveness can open the door to all sorts of acting out, it also—if applied sparingly and wisely—can admit just the right amount of fresh air between the therapist and his terminating patient.

References

Abel, T., and Métraux, R. (1974). *Culture and Psychotherapy.* New Haven: New Haven College and University Press.

Ackerman, N. W. (1953). Selected problems in supervised analysis. *Psychiatry* 16:283-296.

Alexander, P. (1977). A psychotherapist's reaction to his patient's death. *Suicide and Life-Threatening Behavior* 7:203-210.

Anzieu, D. (1959). *L'Auto-analyse.* Paris: Presses Universitaires de France.

Arlow, J. A. (1963). The supervisory situation. *Journal of the American Psychoanalytic Association* 9:576-594.

Asch, S. S. (1980). Suicide and the hidden executioner. *International Review of Psycho-Analysis* 7:51-60.

Balint, A., and Balint, M. (1939). On transference and countertransference. *International Journal of Psycho-Analysis* 20:223-230.

Balint, M. (1968). *The Basic Fault.* London: Tavistock.

Basch-Kahre, E. (1984). On difficulties arising in transference and countertransference when analyst and analysand have different sociocultural backgrounds. *International Review of Psycho-Analysis* 11:61-67.

Berman, L. (1949). Countertransferences and attitudes of the analyst in the therapeutic process. *Psychiatry* 12:159–166.

Bernard, V. W. (1953). Psychoanalysis and members of minority groups. *Journal of the American Psychoanalytic Association* 1:256–267.

Bettelheim, B. (1950). *Love Is not Enough.* Glencoe, Ill.: Free Press.

Binswanger, L. (1967). The case of Ellen West: an anthropological–clinical study. In *Existence: A New Dimension in Psychiatry and Psychology*, eds. R. May, E. Angel, and H. F. Ellenberger, pp. 237–364. New York: Simon & Schuster. Original work published 1944.

Bion, W. R. (1955). Language and the schizophrenic. In *New Directions in Psychoanalysis*, eds. M. Klein, P. Heimann, and R. E. Money-Kyrle, pp. 220–239. London: Tavistock.

—— (1963). *Elements of Psychoanalysis.* New York: Basic Books.

—— (1965). *Transformations.* New York: Basic Books.

—— (1970). *Attention and Interpretation.* London: Tavistock.

Blitzsten, N. L. and Fleming, J. (1953). What is a supervisory analysis? *Bulletin of the Menninger Clinic* 17:117–129.

Bloom, V. (1967). An analysis of suicide at a training center. *American Journal of Psychiatry* 123:918–925.

Blum, H. (1973). The concept of erotized transference. *Journal of the American Psychoanalytic Association* 21:61–76.

Bollas, C. (1983). Expressive uses of the countertransference. *Contemporary Psychoanalysis* 19:1–34.

Breuer, J., and Freud, S. (1893–1895). Studies on hysteria. *Standard Edition* 2.

Bromberg, P. M. (1982). The supervisory process and parallel process in psychoanalysis. *Contemporary Psychoanalysis* 18:92–111.

Caligor, L. (1981). Parallel and reciprocal processes in psychoanalytic supervision. *Contemporary Psychoanalysis* 17:1–27.

Cohen, M. B. (1952). Countertransference and anxiety. *Psychiatry* 15:231–243.

Colm, H. (1955). A field-theory approach to transference and its particular application to children. *Psychiatry* 18:339–352.

Crowley, R. (1952). Human reactions of analysts to patients. *Samiksa* 6:212–219.

Davis, H. (1978). The use of countertransference feelings in resolving resistance. *Psychoanalytic Review* 65:557–568.

DeBell, D. E. (1963). A critical digest of the literature on psychoanalytic supervision. *Journal of the American Psychoanalytic Association* 11:546–575.

——— (1981). Supervisory styles and positions. In *Becoming a Psychoanalyst*, ed. R. S. Wallerstein, pp. 39–60. New York: International Universities Press.

DeForest, I. (1942). The therapeutic technique of Sandor Ferenczi. *International Journal of Psycho-Analysis* 23:120–139.

Deutsch, H. (1926). Occult processes occurring during psychoanalysis. In *Psychoanalysis and the Occult*, ed. G. Devereux, pp. 133–146. New York: International Universities Press, 1953.

——— (1942). Some forms of emotional disturbance and their relationship to schizophrenia. *Psychoanalytic Quarterly* 11:301–321.

Devereux, G., ed. (1953). *Psychoanalysis and the Occult*. New York: International Universities Press.

Doehrman, M. J. G. (1976). Parallel processes in supervision and psychotherapy. *Bulletin of the Menninger Clinic* 40:9–104.

Eber, M. (1981). Don Juanism: a disorder of the self. *Bulletin of the Menninger Clinic* 45:307–316.

Eissler, K. R. (1953). The effect of the structure of the ego on psychoanalytic technique. *Journal of the American Psychoanalytic Association* 1:104–143.

Ekstein, R., and Wallerstein, R. S. (1958). *The Teaching and Learning of Psychotherapy.* New York: International Universities Press.

Elms, A. C. (1980). Freud, Irma, Martha: sex and marriage in the "dream of Irma's injection." *Psychoanalytic Review* 67:83–109.

Emch, M. (1955). The social context of supervision. *International Journal of Psycho-Analysis* 36:298–306.

Epstein, L. (1977). The therapeutic function of hate in the countertransference. *Contemporary Psychoanalysis* 13:442–461.

—— (1979). On the therapeutic use of countertransference data with borderline patients. *Contemporary Psychoanalysis* 15:248–275.

—— (1981). Countertransference and judgments of fitness for analysis. *Contemporary Psychoanalysis* 17:55–68.

Epstein, L., and Feiner, A. H., eds. (1979). *Countertransference.* New York: Jason Aronson.

Erikson, E. H. (1950). *Childhood and Society.* New York: W. W. Norton.

—— (1954). The dream specimen of psychoanalysis. *Journal of the American Psychoanalytic Association* 2:5–56.

Ernsberger, C. (1979). The concept of countertransference as therapeutic instrument: its early history. *Modern Psychoanalysis* 4:141–164.

Fairbairn, W. R. D. (1940). Schizoid factors in the personality. In *Psychoanalytic Studies of the Personality*, pp. 3–27. London: Tavistock.

Farberow, N. L. (1970). The suicidal crisis in psychotherapy. In *The Psychology of Suicide*, eds. E. S. Shneidman, N. L. Farberow, and R. Litman, pp. 415–428. New York: Science House.

Feiner, A. H. (1979). Countertransference and the anxiety of influence. In *Countertransference*, eds. L. Epstein, and A. H. Feiner, pp. 105–128. New York: Jason Aronson.

Fenichel, O. (1945). *The Psychoanalytic Theory of Neurosis.* New York: W. W. Norton.

Ferenczi, S. (1920). The further development of an active therapy in psycho-analysis. In *Further Contributions to the Theory and Technique of Psycho-Analysis*, pp. 198–217. London: Hogarth Press, 1926.

———— (1925). Contra-indications to the "active" psycho-analytical technique. In *Further Contributions to the Theory and Technique of Psycho-Analysis*, pp. 217–230. London: Hogarth Press, 1926.

———— (1927). The problem of the termination of the analysis. In *Final Contributions to the Problems and Methods of Psycho-Analysis*, pp. 77–86. London: Hogarth Press, 1955.

———— (1930). The principle of relaxation and neocatharsis. In *Final Contributions to the Problems and Methods of Psycho-Analysis*, pp. 108–125. London: Hogarth Press, 1955.

———— (1931). Child-analysis in the analysis of adults. In *Final Contributions to the Problems and Methods of Psycho-Analysis*, pp. 126–142. London: Hogarth Press, 1955.

———— (1933). Confusion of tongues between adults and the child. In *Final Contributions to the Problems and Methods of Psycho-Analysis*, pp. 156–167. London: Hogarth Press, 1955.

Firestein, S. K. (1969). Termination of psychoanalysis of adults: a review of the literature. *Journal of the American Psychoanalytic Association* 22:873–894.

———— (1978). *Termination in Psychoanalysis.* New York: International Universities Press.

Fleming, J., and Benedek, T. (1964). Supervision: a method of teaching psychoanalysis. *Psychoanalytic Quarterly* 33:71–96.

Fliess, R. (1942). The metapsychology of the analyst. *Psychoanalytic Quarterly* 11:211–227.

Freud, S. (1900). The interpretation of dreams. *Standard Edition* 4.

———— (1910). The future prospects of psycho-analytic therapy. *Standard Edition* 11:141–151.

———— (1912). Recommendations to physicians practising psycho-analysis. *Standard Edition* 12:109–120.

———— (1915). Observations on transference-love. *Standard Edition* 12:159–171.

———— (1917). Mourning and melancholia. *Standard Edition* 14:243–258.

———— (1919). "A child is being beaten": a contribution to the study of the origin of sexual perversions. *Standard Edition* 17:179–204.

———— (1937). Analysis terminable and interminable. *Standard Edition* 23:209–253.

———— (1954). *The Origins of Psycho-Analysis: Letters to Wilhelm Fliess, Drafts and Notes: 1887–1902*, eds. M. Bonaparte, A. Freud, and E. Kris. New York: Basic Books.

Fromm-Reichmann, F. (1950). *Principles of Intensive Psychotherapy*. Chicago: University of Chicago Press.

———— (1955). Clinical significance of intuitive processes of the psychoanalyst. *Journal of the American Psychoanalytic Association* 3:82–88.

Gediman, H. K., and Wolkenfeld, F. (1980). The parallelism phenomenon in psychoanalysis and supervision: its reconsideration as a triadic system. *Psychoanalytic Quarterly* 49:234–255.

Gill, M. M. (1982). *Analysis of Transference*: Vol. I: *Theory and Technique*. New York: International Universities Press.

———— (1983). The interpersonal paradigm and the degree of the therapist's involvement. *Contemporary Psychoanalysis* 19:200–237.

Giovacchini, P. L. (1981). Countertransference and therapeutic turmoil. *Contemporary Psychoanalysis* 17:565–594.

Gitelson, M. (1952). The emotional position of the analyst in the psycho-analytic situation. *International Journal of Psycho-Analysis* 33:1–10.

Goin, M. K., and Kline, F. (1976). Countertransference: a neglected subject in clinical supervision. *American Journal of Psychiatry* 133:41–44.

Gorkin, M. (1984). Narcissistic personality disorder and pathological mourning. *Contemporary Psychoanalysis* 20:400–420.

Greenson R. R. (1967). *The Technique and Practice of Psychoanalysis*. New York: International Universities Press.

Griffith, M. (1977). The influence of race on the psychotherapeutic relationship. *Psychiatry* 40:27–40.

Grinberg, L. (1979). Countertransference and projective counteridentification. *Contemporary Psychoanalysis* 15:226–247.

Grinstein, A. (1968). *On Sigmund Freud's Dreams*. Detroit: Wayne State University Press.

Guntrip, H. (1975). My experience of analysis with Fairbairn and Winnicott. *International Review of Psycho-Analysis* 2:145–156.

Hartman, F. R. (1983). A reappraisal of the Emma episode and the specimen dream. *Journal of the American Psychoanalytic Association* 31:555–585.

Heimann, P. (1950). On counter-transference. *International Journal of Psycho-Analysis* 31:81–84.

Hendin, H. (1961). Suicide: psychoanalytic point of view. In *The Cry for Help*, eds. N. L. Farberow, and E. S. Shneidman, pp. 181–192. New York: McGraw-Hill.

Hurn, H. T. (1971). Toward a paradigm of the terminal phase: the current status of the terminal phase. *Journal of the American Psychoanalytic Association* 19:332–348.

Hyland, J. (1978). Death by giving up. *Bulletin of the Menninger Clinic* 42:339–349.

Issacharoff, A. (1982). Countertransference in supervision. *Contemporary Psychoanalysis* 18:455–472.

Jackson, A. (1983). Treatment issues for black patients. *Psychotherapy: Theory, Research, Practice* 20:143–151.

Jensen, V. W., and Petty, T. A. (1958). The fantasy of being rescued in suicide. *Psychoanalytic Quarterly* 27:327–339.

Jones, E. (1953–1957). *The Life and Work of Sigmund Freud.* Vols. 1–3. New York: Basic Books.

Kernberg, O. (1965). Notes on countertransference. *Journal of the American Psychoanalytic Association* 13:38–56.

—— (1975). *Borderline Conditions and Pathological Narcissism.* New York: Jason Aronson.

—— (1976). *Object Relations Theory and Clinical Psychoanalysis.* New York: Jason Aronson.

—— (1984). The influence of projective identification on countertransference. Paper presented at the First Conference of the Sigmund Freud Center, Hebrew University, Jerusalem, May 27.

Khan, M. M. R. (1963). Silence as communication. In *Privacy of the Self*, pp. 168–180. London: Hogarth Press, 1974.

King, C. H. (1976). Countertransference and counter-experience in the treatment of violence-prone youth. *American Journal of Orthopsychiatry* 46:41–52.

Klein, M. (1946). Notes on some schizoid mechanisms. *International Journal of Psycho-Analysis* 27:99–110.

—— (1955). On identification. In *New Directions in Psycho-Analysis*, eds. M. Klein, P. Heimann, and R. E. Money-Kyrle, pp. 309–345. London: Tavistock.

Knight, R. F. (1953). Borderline states. *Bulletin of the Menninger Clinic* 17:1–12.

Kobler, A. L., and Stotland, E. (1964). *The End of Hope.* New York: Free Press of Glencoe.

Kohrman, R., Fineberg, H. H., Gelman, R. L., and Weiss, S. (1971). Technique of child analysis: problems of countertransference. *International Journal of Psycho-Analysis* 52:487–497.

Kohut, H. (1971). *The Analysis of the Self.* New York: International Universities Press.

————— (1977). *The Restoration of the Self.* New York: International Universities Press.

Kolodny, S., Binder, R. L., Bronstein, A. A., and Friend, R. L. (1979). The working through of patients' suicides by four therapists. *Suicide and Life-Threatening Behavior* 9:33–46.

Kraemer, W. P. (1957). Transference and countertransference. *British Journal of Medical Psychology* 30:63–74.

Langs, R. (1974). *The Technique of Psychoanalytic Psychotherapy.* Vol. 2. New York: Jason Aronson.

————— (1975). Therapeutic misalliances. *International Journal of Psychoanalytic Psychotherapy* 4:77–105.

————— (1976a). *The Therapeutic Interaction.* Vol. 2. New York: Jason Aronson.

————— (1976b). *The Bipersonal Field.* New York: Jason Aronson.

————— (1979). *The Supervisory Experience.* New York: Jason Aronson.

————— (1980). *The Therapeutic Environment.* New York: Jason Aronson.

Lesser, R. M. (1983). Supervision: illusions, anxieties and questions. *Contemporary Psychoanalysis* 19:120–129.

Levenson, E. A. (1972). *The Fallacy of Understanding.* New York: Basic Books.

————— (1982). Follow the fox. *Contemporary Psychoanalysis* 18:1–15.

Levinson, P. (1972). On sudden death. *Psychiatry* 35:160–173.

Lipton, S. D. (1961). The last hour. *Journal of the American Psychoanalytic Association* 9:325–330.

Litman, R. E. (1965). When patients commit suicide. *American Journal of Psychotherapy* 19:570–576.

————— (1967). Sigmund Freud on suicide. In *Essays in Self-Destruction*, ed. E. S. Shneidman, pp. 324–344. New York: Science House.

————— (1970). Treatment of the potentially suicidal patient. In *The Psychology of Suicide*, eds. E. S. Shneidman, N. L.

Farberow, and R. E. Litman, pp. 405–413. New York: Science House.

——— (1980). The dream in the suicidal situation. In *The Dream in Clinical Practice*, ed. J. M. Natterson, pp. 283–299. New York: Jason Aronson.

Little, M. (1951). Counter-transference and the patient's response to it. *International Journal of Psycho-Analysis* 33:32–40.

——— (1957). "R"—the analyst's total response to his patient's needs. *International Journal of Psycho-Analysis* 38:240–254.

Lower, R. B. (1972). Countertransference resistances in the supervisory situation. *American Journal of Psychiatry* 129:156–160.

Mahler, M. S., Pine, F., and Bergman, A. (1975). *The Psychological Birth of the Human Infant*. New York: Basic Books.

Malin, A., and Grotstein, J. (1966). Projective identification in the therapeutic process. *International Journal of Psycho-Analysis* 47:26–31.

Maltsberger, J. T., and Buie, D. H. (1974). Countertransference hate in the treatment of suicidal patients. *Archives of General Psychiatry* 30:625–633.

Marshall, R. J. (1979). Countertransference with children and adolescents. In *Countertransference*, eds. L. Epstein, and A. H. Feiner, pp. 407–444. New York: Jason Aronson.

Masterson, J. F. (1981). *The Narcissistic and Borderline Conditions*. New York: Brunner/Mazel.

Masterson, J. F., and Rinsley, D. B. (1975). The borderline syndrome: the role of the mother in the genesis and psychic structure of the borderline personality. *International Journal of Psycho-Analysis* 56:163–178.

McLaughlin, J. T. (1975). The sleepy analyst: some observations on states of consciousness in the analyst at work. *Journal of the American Psychoanalytic Association* 23:363–382.

Meerloo, J. A. M. (1952). Some psychological processes in supervision of therapists. *American Journal of Psychotherapy* 6:467–470.

—— (1959). Suicide, menticide, and psychic homicide. *Archives of Neurology and Psychiatry* 81:360–362.

Meissner, W. W. (1977). Psychoanalytic notes on suicide. *International Journal of Psychoanalytic Psychotherapy* 6:415–447.

Menninger, K. (1938). *Man Against Himself.* New York: Harcourt, Brace.

Miller, A. (1979). The drama of the gifted child and the psychoanalyst's narcissistic disturbance. *International Journal of Psycho-Analysis* 60:47–58.

Money-Kyrle, R. E. (1956). Normal counter-transference and some of its deviations. *International Journal of Psycho-Analysis* 37:360–366.

Nadelson, T. (1977). Borderline rage and the therapist's response. *American Journal of Psychiatry* 134:748–751.

Nagera, H. (1975). *Female Sexuality and the Oedipus Complex.* New York: Jason Aronson.

Nydes, J. (1963). The paranoid-masochistic character. *Psychoanalytic Review* 50:215–251.

Ogden, T. H. (1979). On projective identification. *International Journal of Psycho-Analysis* 60:357–373.

Orr, D. W. (1954). Transference and countertransference: a historical survey. *Journal of the American Psychoanalytic Association* 2:621–670.

Pfeffer, A. Z. (1963). The meaning of the analyst after analysis. *Journal of the American Psychoanalytic Association* 11:229–244.

Poggi, R. G., and Ganzarian, R. (1983). Countertransference hate. *Bulletin of the Menninger Clinic* 47:15–35.

Racker, H. (1953). A contribution to the problem of countertransference. *International Journal of Psycho-Analysis*
34:313–324.
—— (1957). The meanings and uses of countertransference.
Psychoanalytic Quarterly 26:303–357.
Rappaport, E. (1956). The management of an erotized transference. *Psychoanalytic Quarterly* 25:515–529.
Reich, A. (1950). On the termination of analysis. *International
Journal of Psycho-Analysis* 31:179–183.
—— (1951). On countertransference. *International Journal of
Psycho-Analysis* 32:25–31.
—— (1960). Further remarks on countertransference. *International Journal of Psycho-Analysis* 41:389–395.
Reik, T. (1937). *Surprise and the psycho-analyst: on the conjecture
and comprehension of unconscious processes.* New York: Dut-
ton.
Richman, J., and Rosenbaum, M. (1970). A clinical study of the
role of hostility and death wishes by the family and society
in suicidal attempts. *Israel Annals of Psychiatry and Related
Disciplines* 8:213–231.
Rinsley, D. B. (1980). The developmental etiology of borderline
and narcissistic disorders. *Bulletin of the Menninger Clinic*
44:127–134.
Roazen, P. (1975). *Freud and His Followers.* New York: Knopf.
Robbins, W. S. (1975). Termination: problems and techniques.
Journal of the American Psychoanalytic Association 23:166–
176.
Rosenfeld, H. A. (1952). Transference-phenomena and trans-
ference-analysis in an acute catatonic schizophrenic patient. *International Journal of Psycho-Analysis* 33:457–464.
—— (1954). Considerations regarding the psychoanalytic approach to acute and chronic schizophrenia. *International
Journal of Psycho-Analysis* 35:135–140.

Sandler, J. (1976). Countertransference and role-responsiveness. *International Review of Psycho-Analysis* 3:43–47.
Sandler, J., Dare, C., and Holder, A. (1973). *The Patient and the*

Analyst: the Basis of the Psychoanalytic Process. New York: International Universities Press.

Saretsky, T. (1977). The resolution of impasses in borderline states. *Contemporary Psychoanalysis* 13:519–532.

Schacter, J. S., and Butts, H. F. (1968). Transference and countertransference in interracial analyses. *Journal of the American Psychoanalytic Association* 16:792–808.

Schafer, R. (1973). The termination of brief psychoanalytic psychotherapy. *International Journal of Psychoanalytic Psychotherapy* 2:135–148.

Searles, H. F. (1955). The informational value of the supervisor's emotional experiences. In *Collected Papers on Schizophrenia and Related Subjects*, pp. 157–176. New York: International Universities Press, 1965.

—— (1962). Problems of psycho-analytic supervision. In *Collected Papers on Schizophrenia and Related Subjects*, pp. 584–604. New York: International Universities Press, 1965.

—— (1965). *Collected Papers on Schizophrenia and Related Subjects.* New York: International Universities Press.

—— (1975). The patient as therapist to his analyst. In *Countertransference and Related Subjects*, pp. 380–459. New York: International Universities Press, 1979.

—— (1979). *Countertransference and Related Subjects.* New York: International Universities Press.

Shneidman, E. S. (1973). *Deaths of Man.* New York: Quadrangle.

Spotnitz, H. (1963). The toxoid response. *Psychoanalytic Review* 50:81–94.

—— (1976). *Psychotherapy of Preoedipal Conditions.* New York: Jason Aronson.

—— (1979). Narcissistic countertransference. In *Countertransference*, eds. L. Epstein, and A. H. Feiner, pp. 329–343. New York: Jason Aronson.

Stern, A. (1938). Psychoanalytic investigation of and therapy in the border line group of neuroses. *Psychoanalytic Quarterly* 7:467–489.

Stolorow, R. D., and Lachmann, F. M. (1980). *Psychoanalysis of Developmental Arrests.* New York: International Universities Press.

Sullivan, H. S. (1953). *The Interpersonal Theory of Psychiatry.* New York: W. W. Norton.

Szasz, T. (1956). On the experiences of the analyst in the psychoanalytic situation. *Journal of the American Psychoanalytic Association* 4:197–223.

Tabachnick, N. (1961). Countertransference crisis in suicide attempts. *AMA Archives of General Psychiatry* 4:572–578.

Tähkä, V. (1977). Presentation at the Sixth World Congress of Psychiatry, Honolulu, Hawaii.

Tauber, E. S. (1952). Observations on counter-transference phenomena: the supervisor–therapist relationship. *Samiksa* 6:220–228.

—— (1954). Exploring the therapeutic use of counter-transference data. *Psychiatry* 17:331–336.

Thomas, A. (1962). Pseudo-transference reactions due to cultural stereotyping. *American Journal of Orthopsychiatry* 32:894–900.

Thompson, C. (1943). The therapeutic technique of Sandor Ferenczi: a comment. *International Journal of Psycho-Analysis* 24:64–66.

Ticho, E. (1972). Termination of psychoanalysis: treatment goals, life goals. *Psychoanalytic Quarterly* 41:315–333.

Ticho, G. (1971). Cultural aspects of transference and countertransference. *Bulletin of the Menninger Clinic* 35:313–334.

Tower, L. E. (1956). Countertransference. *Journal of the American Psychoanalytic Association* 4:224–255.

Tseng, W., and McDermott, J. (1972). *Culture, Mind and Therapy: An Introduction to Cultural Psychiatry.* New York: Brunner/Mazel.

Van Del, R. A. (1977). The role of death romanticization in the dynamics of suicide. *Suicide and Life-Threatening Behavior* 7:45–56.

Weigert, E. (1952). Contribution to the problem of terminating psychoanalyses. *Psychoanalytic Quarterly* 21:465–480.

—— (1954a). Counter-transference and self-analysis of the psycho-analyst. *International Journal of Psycho-Analysis* 35:242–246.

—— (1954b). The importance of flexibility in psychoanalytic technique. *Journal of the American Psychoanalytic Association* 2:702–710.

Whitman, R., Kramer, M., and Baldridge, B. (1969). Dreams about the patient: an approach to the problem of counter-transference. *Journal of the American Psychoanalytic Association* 17:702–727.

Winnicott, D. W. (1949). Hate in the countertransference. *International Journal of Psycho-Analysis* 30:69–75.

—— (1960). Countertransference. *British Journal of Medical Psychology* 33:17–21. Reprinted in *The Maturational Processes and the Facilitating Environment*, pp. 158–165. London: Hogarth Press, 1965.

—— (1974). Fear of breakdown. *International Review of Psycho-Analysis* 1:103–107.

Winokur, M. (1982). A family systems model for supervision of psychotherapy. *Bulletin of the Menninger Clinic* 46:125–138.

Wohlberg, G. (1975). A black patient with a white therapist. *International Journal of Psychoanalytic Psychotherapy* 4:540–562.

Wolstein, B. (1972). Supervision as experience. *Contemporary Psychoanalysis* 8:165–172.

Zee, H. J. (1972). Blindspots in recognizing serious suicidal intentions. *Bulletin of the Menninger Clinic* 36:551–555.

Zwiebel, R. (1985). The dynamics of the countertransference dream. *International Review of Psycho-Analysis* 12:87–99.

Index